ANDRE DUBUS III

BLUESMAN

Andre Dubus III is the author of two other books, *House of Sand and Fog,* a novel, and *The Cage Keeper,* a collection of stories. *House of Sand and Fog* was a finalist for the 1999 National Book Award for Fiction, the *Los Angeles Times* Book Prize, and the L. L. Winship/PEN New England Award and was an American Library Association Notable Book for 1999. Dubus was awarded the 1985 National Magazine Award for Fiction for his story "Forky" and a Pushcart Prize for his essay "Tracks and Ties." His work has appeared in *The Best Spiritual Writing 1999* and *The Best American Essays 1994.* In 1994 Dubus was one of three finalists for the Prix de Rome given by the American Academy of Arts and Letters. He lives in Newburyport, Massachusetts, with his wife and three children.

ALSO BY ANDRE DUBUS III

The Cage Keeper and Other Stories

House of Sand and Fog

BLUESMAN

BLUESMAN

ANDRE DUBUS III

VINTAGE CONTEMPORARIES

Vintage Books

A Division of Random House, Inc.

New York

FIRST VINTAGE CONTEMPORARIES EDITION, FEBRUARY 2001

The Library of Congress Cataloging-in-Publication Data
Dubus, Andre. 1959–
Bluesman / by Andre Dubus III.
p. cm.
ISBN 0-375-72516-4
1. Vietnamese Conflict, 1961–1975—Fiction.
2. Blues musicians—Fiction. 3. Young men—Fiction.
I. Title.
PS3554.U265 B58   2001
813'.54—dc21
00-063411
CIP

Printed in the United States of America
10   9   8   7   6   5   4   3   2   1

For my wife, Fontaine,
and for my son Austin.

BLUESMAN

HEYWOOD, MASSACHUSETTS

The Connecticut River sounded different every season; it was a gushing stone roller during the spring runoffs, a narrow and quiet flow in the summer that in the fall receded to a thin clear wash leaving banks of leaf-covered mud and sunken tree root until winter, when the Berkshire snows came, and the ice formed over the rocks, and the water gurgled beneath it all as though behind a mask.

On its west bank, halfway through the trees up Saunders Hill, Jim Suther picked the guitar most every night. Though he was a white man he only sang blues songs, songs by men like Big Bill Broonzy, Mississippi John Hurt, Son House, and Champion Jack Dupree. After a supper he would cook for both himself and his seventeen-year-old son, Leo, Jim sat in the parlor on a stool in front of the window overlooking the woods and he'd start to play. He sang all kinds of songs, some fast that Leo could hear in the kitchen while he was cleaning up or doing his homework and he would tap his feet, or else slow ones like "Lonesome Road," "Up, Sometimes Down," and "Motherless Child." Most times they were slow like that, and Leo would sit in the parlor and listen for a while.

He liked to watch his father's face. That was easy to do because most times Jim kept his eyes closed while he picked and sang. Leo liked how soft it got around the mouth under his mustache, how tender-looking. And Jim was a big man. Not tall and lean like Leo, but wide with thick legs, rounded shoulders, and upper arms that always needed more room than his shirtsleeves gave them.

Wednesday nights, four or five men from Jim's union at Heywood Paper Products would drive up in their Ramblers and station wagons to play poker at the kitchen table and drink cold Narragansetts out of cans. Leo was already taller than some of the men and they rarely talked to him like he was a junior at Heywood High School, graduating class of 1968.

One man, Lars, who was bald and had a clean-shaven pink face, he was always telling jokes about men screwing women who weren't their wives. Sometimes he'd tease a punch as Leo passed the table on his way to the fridge and he'd say: "Hey Einstein, tell your pop to play some white music for a change." Leo would smile and raise his Coke in a mock toast, then go out to the parlor where Jim was bluesing it with Leo's Uncle Ryder. That's what he liked Leo to call him, though he wasn't really his uncle. One night Lars said to Ryder: "You're so skinny I can smell the shit in you, Stillwell." And Ryder was skinny. He also favored his left leg a little bit when he walked, and every day he wore his fake lizard-skin cowboy boots, even to the mill. But Wednesday nights he played the most wonderful instrument Leo could imagine on this earth: a German-made, M. Hohner Marine Band harmonica; The Harp of the Blues, Ryder called it.

He owned nine of them he kept in a wide leather harness around his waist. Most of these were in different keys though Leo knew four were in C, a bluesman's standard. When Ryder played he liked to stand and he never opened his eyes at all, just cupped that silver mouth harp in his two hands, the left never moving, the right opening and closing, or staying still depending on the effect he was trying for. When Leo's dad sang a train song, Ryder's harp sounded like a freight liner chugging down the rails. He'd suck out a long wah-wah whistle like you imagine hearing after midnight when a diesel's pulling through town with no one to appreciate it unless it makes some noise. Then when Jim picked and sang a Saturday night special like "Whoopin' the Blues" or "Sittin' on Top of the World," Ryder would rock back and forth on his feet and put both lungs to work with trills and flutters, throat pops and hand smacks, all the while staying in perfect time with Jim's guitar.

On songs like that, loud Lars and the other men would come in from the kitchen with their beers and smoking cigars. They'd tap their feet and let out a holler or two, and Jim and Ryder showed their appreciation by quickly sliding into two or three more room-movers. But with the blues, Leo noticed, you couldn't go too long without coming back to a slow one that either made you sweetly down-hearted, or else reminded you of when you were. After one or two of those, Don't-Mistreat-Me or All-Alone-Blues, Lars and the others would either go back into the bright smokey kitchen to finish their game, or else stub out their cigars, drain their beers, and call it a night.

But the best part of Wednesday nights was right before all that happened, when the parlor was full of people with their eyes on Ryder and Leo's dad, when Jim Suther's guitar and wavering alto voice didn't just match Ryder's harmonica, but rose above it so that Ryder was huffing to keep up and the more he did that the more Jim seemed to sit back because now it was the number itself that had come alive, the walling woowahing Oh-She-Up-and-Left-Me beauty of it, as if the song was now gentle flesh and blood that Ryder and Jim had no more hold on than moist-eyed smiling Lars or the foot-stomping, hand-clapping rest of them.

And while Leo clapped his hands in time, he would sometimes watch those faces that were soft with beer and wonder, even grati-tude, in his father's house. Leo thought about girls and women then and how content they'd be in this room too, how sad it was that there never were any. And children, six or seven of them jumping up and down or curled up under blankets on the floor asleep.

1

Tonight, after the paper mill men had all gone home and Jim was placing his guitar in its case, Ryder sat on the couch and sipped a fresh Narragansett. He glanced over at Leo still watching him from the corner chair near the window. The only light in the parlor came from the kitchen and when their eyes met, Leo looked away and swigged his warm Coke.

"Heads up."

Leo caught it just as he saw it, a cool metal-worn Marine Band.

"It's a C. Next week I'll come over early if you want, show you a few tricks."

Which he did. His Impala pulled into the yard just as Leo was in the kitchen sopping up the last drippings of clam chowder from his bowl with a slice of Wonder Bread. It was mid June. The sun had just slipped behind Saunders Hill so the bark on the pines was gold and orange like there was a big fire nearby. Leo got up and rinsed his dish. He could smell the coffee his father had brewed before pouring it over ice and going outside for his after-supper stroll down to the river. Ryder walked in with his harmonica harness hanging over one bony shoulder, a six-pack of Pabst Blue Ribbon bottles in his hand.

"I've been thinking about you on the way over here, Leo. Thinking about how to start you out on the harp of the blues, you, a very smart kid. And it came to me the big thing you should know up front." Ryder opened the fridge and put the beer inside. He walked to the stove and poured himself some coffee.

"Yeah?"

"You see, Young Buddy, the way I see it, there are thinkers in this world, and there are feelers. Sometimes there's a little bit of both in one but those fellas don't do much." Ryder sipped his coffee and looked at Leo. "You understand?"

"Yep."

"I was afraid of that."

"*What?*"

"That you'd get that concept right out of the chute. Thinkers are like that. Feelers take longer, but then they come up with a painting or a poem or a blues riff to show you what they see and hear."

Leo shrugged. "But you play the blues like no tomorrow and you just thought that all up."

Ryder sipped his coffee. He looked at Leo over the cup. "All right then, shitcan my theory. But look, you have to start from scratch. When you play you gotta *feel* something, not think it. That's all I'm saying. Now go get your harp before Larsmouth and the others show up with their piggy banks."

In the parlor Ryder cinched the harness in around his waist and pulled an A harp from its sheath. "First thing you want to start doing, Young Buddy, is to listen very closely to everything you hear. Concentrate on this song; it's gonna be your cherry-breaker." He put a foot up on the windowsill and began to suck and blow the first few notes of a tune Leo had heard many times before. After Ryder played the intro, he sang the first verse,

"My baby says she's leavin' me, and I ain't done nothin' wrong,
  My eyes on you baby, you can't do me no harm,
  I got my eyes on you, I got my eyes on you,
  I got my eyes on you woman, there ain't nothin' in this world
    you can do—"

Ryder cupped the harp back to his mouth and played a popwailing riff that was so pure and heartfelt Leo's eyes got wet and he had to look down at the floorboards. Ryder's playing was a lot better than his singing, and when he finished the song, Leo said, "Teach me a number I don't have to sing in."

"What have you got against croonin'?"

"Nothing. Jim does it good. But I want to play, not croon. Show me some tricks."

Ryder shook his head. His red chin stubble caught the dusklight and looked gold. Leo couldn't tell if he was smiling or not.

"Go look up *trick* in the dictionary and I'll bet you'll find the word deception in there somewhere. Hear me, Leo: when you enter the world of music, *real* music, like from Beethoven on up to Big Bill Broonzy, you're stepping into Truth City. That's what it's all about, so no tricks, all right? Technique, yes. Tricks, no."

"*You* said tricks last week. You said you'll come over and show me some tricks."

"Forget last week and forget technique for now too. When you hear a song you want to play, I want you to crawl inside it like it was a sleeping bag that maybe has a snake in it. What kind is it? How'd it get in there? What's it gonna do now? You want to learn to play from the inside out. If you do it the other way then you'll be pretending and even somebody as thick as Lars will see that."

Ryder smiled and tilted his head to better see Leo's face. "See, musical people are important. If we can take what's in the air—pleasure or pain—and push it back out in a sound that lets people touch what they themselves are putting out, then you can call us bridges to Truth City. I like that: 'Bridges to Truth City.' And that's hands down better than being a party to lying, don't you think?"

Leo nodded.

"Okay then." Ryder pushed his harmonica back into its harness. "Put yours away too. First lesson's over. I want you to walk around all week trying to *feel* the meaning of things."

"We're not gonna play anything?"

"And when you find something that you're feeling strong about, Young Buddy, throw together a couple verses on it. Forget 'I Got My Eyes on You,' you tell me what *you* got *your* eyes on, then we'll present that to Mr. Harp of the Blues. Next week, not tonight. First things first."

2

This was easy. This was a thing that didn't have to be thought about: Allie Donovan. Also a junior at Heywood High School, she was the only one who wore those bell-bottom jeans that were all floppy from the feet to the knees but from there they straightened up and got very tight, hugging her thighs and round soft-looking butt, even cleaving in a little at her crotch.

She had green eyes, a tiny nose, and a wider-than-average mouth that was always either talking, laughing, or else being very quiet and still when no one else's was. She wore baggy white T-shirts that she tucked into her jeans, and even though she dressed like a boy, she was prettier than Nancy Titcomb and AnnaMaria Slavitt combined.

Nancy's old man ran the bank or Heywood Electric or something. And AnnaMaria, who wore imitation pearls to school a lot, was one of Tony Slavitt's Chevrolet kids. Girls like that always dressed in skirts and blouses and dresses, period. They were still girls, hardly women, but they wore their hair like Lady Bird Johnson, who wore hers like Jackie Kennedy, who Leo figured wore hers like Ann-Margret or Liz Taylor. And in a strictly untouchable sort of way, these were good girls to look at; but it was the kind of good you feel when you see something new, Leo thought, like a gleaming red Schwinn bike, or even better, one of Slavitt's sparkling white-walled four-on-the-floor supremes: the exact moment you pause to appreciate its clean, beautiful newness is also the precise second you feel it pull away from you.

It was Thursday, late June, and Leo sat three desks back from Allie, watching her. The air was hot, and even with the windows open the room smelled like desk wood and B.O. sweat. The trees were leafed out green outside and Leo heard a squirrel scampering up a trunk, down a limb, and off it to another. Most of the kids were asleep with their foreheads resting on their folded arms, but Allie was drawing something with three colored pencils. Her blond hair was pulled back in a single braid. Her neck was long and already tanned too. Whenever she dropped one color for the other, she'd turn her head sideways and look at her picture before she started up again. Leo lifted his chair when he scooted back so he wouldn't make any noise, then he walked up the aisle, stood a desk's length behind Allie, and looked over her shoulder.

With a blue pencil she was sketching in a smoke trail that curled up from the chimney of a three-story house. It had four white porch columns on the front like those mansions in the Civil War chapters of the U.S. history book, and to the right of the house was a huge tree with a noose hanging off one branch.

"Is Allison's work more intriguing than yours, Mr. Suther?"

At first Leo didn't match "Mr. Suther" up with himself, but when

Allie looked at Mr. Jewett, then up and back into Leo's face, Leo stared into her slightly startled green eyes and said, "Yes. It is," and he walked back to his desk and sat down.

A few kids lifted their heads to see what was up. One of them was Leo's flat-topped buddy, Gerry Poitras. He glanced at Leo and Mr. Jewett, before going back to his nap. Allie Donovan turned around quickly but quietly. She smiled at Leo a good four seconds.

That afternoon, while his father was still at the Elks, Leo sat at the kitchen table with his notebook and pen:

That Allie's got a neck,
a neck so fine,
I want to kiss it,
Kiss it all the time.
We got a house,
Me and her on the hill,
It's got a porch
bigger than the paper mill.
Sometimes when we hug
I feel like I'm gonna explode,
But then we do what we have to
Up there in our Love Abode.

He signed it and called it "The Love Abode." The following Wednesday he handed it to Ryder who held it up in the afternoon kitchen light and read it out loud. When he got to the part about exploding and doing what we have to, he laughed and shook his head, then laughed some more.

"Now it's my turn." He showed Leo first how to hold his harmonica, how he should wedge the bass-notes end of it between the thumb and forefinger of his left hand so his right would be free to cup in around the harp, making an echo chamber in there he'll want to use later. Leo had long thin fingers. Ryder's were long too, but meaty. He said short fat fingers were best for the blues harp, the kind you get working with your hands your whole life like cotton pickers or mill workers, something like that. But Leo being only seventeen,

10

he shouldn't worry about that because he was his father's son and was bound to flesh out more soon anyway.

Right about then Jim showed up in the kitchen doorway. He held a tall iced coffee with milk and between his fingers was a smoking Lucky Strike. The sun was getting low behind Saunders Hill so Leo couldn't see much of his face too well. Jim watched while Ryder showed his son how to find do re mi, then how to choke the mi note into a maw sound by constricting the air flow in the throat. All of this Leo picked up on by the second or third try, which surprised Ryder until Leo reminded him he'd been watching and listening to Ryder play since he could remember.

"Your boy's a songwriter too, Jimmy. Did you know that?" Ryder started to unfold "The Love Abode," but Leo touched his hand. Jim let smoke out his nose and walked over to the two of them near the window. He looked up at Leo. "I'll take a little credit for the music you might have in you but whatever wordsway you conjure, you're getting from your mother. She was a poetess. I never told you that." Jim turned his back on them, then he took his guitar out of its case and started to tune it up on his stool. Ryder winked at Leo and put the song back in his front shirt pocket behind three Heywood Paper Products ballpoint pens.

Without glancing at his old man, Leo left the parlor and the house and walked down Saunders Hill Road. In the early evening light, the river was a slow-moving brown and blue. Its pebbled bank was pink in some places, gold in others, and Leo picked up three stones. He threw one in a high arc into the trees. He threw the other two downstream. One hit a boulder and bounced off it into the water. Leo didn't see where the other went and he couldn't see why his father didn't have another woman yet either. Jim wasn't the only man to ever lose his wife. Gerry Poitras's mother left his dad to go live with a phone lineman in Springfield. That was when GP was nine or ten. But he had a new mom now, a blonde woman with big breasts whose name was Betty. Gerry's old man had met her on a train to Boston on business. She had no kids of her own and she seemed to like Gerry and his little sister Ruth as if she had invented them herself.

And Mr. Poitras wasn't nearly as handsome as Jim Suther; he didn't have the muscle, he didn't have the thick black mustache, he probably couldn't pick a tune or sing a note. He just had a flattop haircut like his son, a fat close-shaved face like Lars, and a big round gut that always made his neckties look short and his pants too low. But still, he had Betty, and Jim had nothing but this piece of the Connecticut River every day at sundown.

Leo wedged his sneaker under a softball-sized rock, picked up the stone, then threw it as far upstream as he could. It made hardly a splash, just got gulped into the current. A family of birds was making all sorts of sound above and behind him and Leo thought he should get around to learning their names and migrating habits and stuff like that. Then he saw one up in an alder branch. The bird was all black except for the tips of its wings which were bright red. Leo heard cars parking behind the house up the hill, the slamming of the screen door, Lars's laugh. When the door slammed again, the bird flew off the branch, out over the river, and into the trees on the other side.

Ryder and Jim were playing already. The parlor windows had to be open because it sounded like the two men were standing right there behind Leo. It was a slow song too, one he hadn't heard before about a man who loses his family in a fire and keeps asking God how come hell came calling, Lord? How come? Jim was singing clear and to the point, like he wanted an answer tonight. When Ryder's harmonica came sweeping in behind Jim's voice, it sounded like a chorus of Yeah, tell us, Lord, why don't you tell us, tell us right now?

Leo began walking up the road, though he didn't want to get any closer to the poor-me chorus. He kept on until he reached the top of the hill where the gravel ended at Paper Boulevard and he went right because a quarter mile later was downtown where on this side of the road was an Esso Station with two red pumps, then the Hungry Pioneer Inn and the red brick courthouse with the police station in the basement. Across the street, all on a raised concrete walkway with the same long slanted roof over their doors was the hardware store, B&G Grocery, and Shorty's Billiards. Down the steps and farther down the sidewalk was the Fremont Theater where *The Cincin-*

nati Kid with Steve McQueen had been playing all week. Then came Thompson Green, a square park surrounded by white wood rails in granite posts, named after the town's only family to lose all five sons to Confederate cannonballs. This time of year the grass was thick and soft to sit on. There were a few trees but not so many Leo and Gerry couldn't throw a football around if they wanted to. And in the middle of the park was a wooden gazebo that later in the summer would hold a string quartet from the Ladies Auxiliary League, or a six-piece brass section of fat guys who practiced in the American Legion building next to the Elks Club on the other side of town. They'd play songs like "Greensleeves," then "The Battle Hymn of the Republic" followed by "Home on the Range." But past the Green and the goofy gazebo was where Leo was hiking to: Beatrice's UFO Show. That's what it was called, though the only thing UFO-ish about it was that it was silver and metal and on top of the cash register was glued a plastic model of a flying saucer.

By the time Leo got through town and to Thompson Green, the sun was down and he was sweating. When he saw all the Buick Wildcats and Ramblers, even a motorcycle in Beatrice's lot, he wished he'd gone back into his house to change into a fresh shirt and comb his hair, which lately he'd been letting grow out at the top. Gerry's after-school shift got over at seven and Leo was going to meet him at the back door so they could pal around awhile, maybe go to Gerry's house which was only a half mile back through Heywood and down the same road the school was on. He hoped that's what they were going to do. It was a weeknight so he would only be able to stay an hour or so, but that would be sixty minutes in a living room where the whole Poitras family was gathered together until bedtime.

GP's father would be in the big chair under the standup lamp. His shoes and tie would be off, his white shirt unbuttoned past his T-shirt collar. Sometimes he'd have a bunch of papers laid out on his briefcase in his lap. Gerry's sister Ruth, who was twelve and pudgy but cute in the face, she'd be in her pajamas already, laying belly down on the rug watching Danny Kaye or "The Patty Duke Show." Betty always sat on the side of the couch closest to the kitchen in case anybody needed anything. Most times when Leo was there with Gerry,

---

13

she'd bring them tall glasses of cold chocolate milk and a plate of warm oatmeal cookies. Once Betty patted Leo's arm and remarked how nice it was having him over. She went back to her knitting and Gerry whispered in Leo's ear how she just found out he didn't have a mother—who knows, maybe she'll let you touch her boobs.

From the parking lot, Leo could hear the jukebox playing inside Beatrice's. The Box Tops, it sounded like, though with all that laughing and talking going on in there he couldn't be sure. He walked around to the kitchen door out back. Somebody had stuck a mop handle under the knob to hold it wide open, and Leo smelled fry grease and dish soap, heard meat sizzling, something else getting water-sprayed. He poked his head inside and looked left down at the pots-and-pans sink because where else would a night manager who thinks he's funny put a kid named Poitras. But it wasn't flat-topped tubby Gerry Leo saw there. Instead he found himself looking at a girl's back. Her blond hair was tied off in a braid, her apron strings dangled right along her round and soft-looking butt.

"Hey Suther, look." Gerry stood to the right of the door in an all-white fry cook uniform. On his blocky head was a white cap with "UFO" printed above the visor. He held both arms out and turned around in a circle. "Promotion of the summer, man. More money, more grease, *no* pots. I'm in training so I'll see you later, my old man's picking me up at eight." Gerry went back to the fryolator next to the grill and Beatrice's huge thirty-year-old brother Sidney who always sweated and never smiled.

At the wash sink, Allie Donovan was untying her apron, smiling at Leo as she did.

"Since when do you work here?"

"About an hour. My real shift starts next week, you know, when summer starts."

"Oh."

She dropped her apron in a canvas hamper and smiled at him. "Come to walk me home?"

"Where's that?"

"Spoon Hill."

Spoon Hill was a mile north of Beatrice's on the other side of the river. The closest way across was back through town to the covered bridge built out behind the Hungry Pioneer Inn and the courthouse building. Leo and Allie walked through the parking lot to Thompson Green. She jumped over the white rails onto the grass, and when Leo did the same she called him a copy cat, walking backwards, smiling.

"Who, me?"

"Is Allison's work more intriguing than yours, Mr. Suther?"

"Maybe."

Allie turned and ran to the gazebo, her braid bouncing and swaying against her neck. Leo couldn't believe his good luck and he wasn't going to jinx it by running after her either. The night air smelled like pine sap and the fryolators from Beatrice's. He walked slow and straight as Big Bill Broonzy.

When he got to the gazebo steps he stopped and watched Allie up on the floor swinging her arms in little semicircles like a conductor. She stopped almost as soon as she started, though. They were both quiet a second.

Leo put his foot up on a stair. "You want to live in that mansion you were drawing?"

"Want? Do I *want*? That's immaterial, Mr. Suther. You like that word? I just learned it, I love it. I'll probably have to use it down in Mississippi. Jackson, to be precise."

"Jackson?"

"Oh yes, didn't I tell you?" Allie jumped again, this time over the steps onto the grass. "My dad fixes up old houses. Everybody talks about having a new home but, you know, Leo, a lot of people out there like old houses more. They don't admit it, though." Allie put her hand loosely inside his and they began walking across the grass to Paper Boulevard. Leo wondered when she thought she would have told him anything, being this was the first time they'd ever said two words to each other. Once or twice her hip rubbed his and Leo felt the beginnings of an erection that he hoped wouldn't point in any sort of way noticeable.

"You're *moving* moving?"

"Yep. My mom and dad and three-year-old brother and me. All four of us, and we're going to be living in a trailer home on this grand plantation while my dad rebuilds a real Southern mansion with a bunch of other men."

"Then you'll come back."

"Come back? *Why?* What in the world is going on in Heywood, Massachusetts? Do you know I'll probably meet some disgusting Ku Klux Klan men face to face? And with all that waterhosing and dogging going on down there with the Negroes, why, I'll be in a very exciting place, Leo. Very exciting."

"Waterhosing and dogging?"

"Don't tell me you don't watch the news, Leo Suther. You're one of the smartest kids around."

"We don't have a television set."

"Us either, but I bet you read the whole newspaper every day."

"Sometimes." Which was true. If he was finished with his homework and if Jim was done with the *Globe,* had maybe gone to bed already, Leo would sit at the kitchen table with a Coke and glance through the pages about this and that; what Governor Volpe was doing at the State House, what movies were coming out, and he had seen things in the national news section about trouble in the South and lately Michigan and New Jersey, even Boston—but he found himself most interested in U.S. soldier stories over in Asia, stories With headlines like U.S. PLANES POUND CONG, RIOTS RIP SAIGON, YANKS HURL BACK BIG RED FORCE. And there were lean-and-mean sounding army maneuvers with names like Operation Nathan Hale, Operation Paul Revere, and Operation Junction City. "I read about the Asian conflict a lot."

"You mean war. I know we haven't declared one but my dad says when we bomb people and send in the army to shoot who's left, that's war. You burn your card yet?"

"Don't have one. My birthday's in August. How come you drew a hangman's noose in your picture?"

"Because I did."

They walked quietly now past the Fremont Theater. In glassed-in windows were posters showing next week's movie, *That Darn Cat.* At the ticket booth a man licking an ice cream cone bought himself and his wife tickets to the seven o'clock show of *The Cincinnati Kid.*

Leo stopped. "You like Steve McQueen?"

"In an immaterial sort of way, yes."

"Would you like me to take you to this immaterial movie, then? Immaterially speaking?"

Allie held her chin up. "I don't see why not."

There were only a dozen people or so in the theater. Leo and Allie sat off on the right side and shared a bucket of popcorn through the show. It was a good movie, Leo thought. And McQueen was real slick with a rifle. A couple times, when the action scenes were going on, Leo turned his head just a little in Allie's direction and watched her watch the movie. She ate her popcorn one piece at a time, real slow. Her hair looked yellow. When the lights came up she smiled over at him with a sleepy face.

They crossed Paper Boulevard and walked down the short darkened street between the courthouse building and the Hungry Pioneer Inn to the river. There was a single lamp hanging over the center of the covered bridge entrance and there was another light as you came out on the other side, but inside was black as a cave. When they stepped into it, walking over the wide heavy planks that felt as solid as the earth, Allie stopped.

"You like me, huh?"

Leo could tell by her voice that she was looking straight up at his face. The bridge smelled like wet wood and dust, and with Allie standing so close, he could still smell Beatrice's too. "Sure thing."

Allie placed her hands on his hips, and Leo held her shoulders to keep her from rubbing right up against the full-blown erection that until this moment no other human being had ever been so close to.

"Do you just like me, or do you really *like* me?"

"I really like you." His mouth had gone dry and it was a good thing the river was gurgling beneath them or else she'd hear his heart bucking for sure.

She pulled herself in until Leo felt his erection press high on her flat stomach. She didn't budge. She kissed his neck and chin. He lowered his face. His first kiss landed half on her nose, half on her cheek. The second touched the corner of her mouth. But the third met soft lips that parted for the sweet-tasting tongue she slid along his.

On the river road they stopped every few feet to kiss some more and they hardly spoke. From the mailbox at the foot of Spoon Hill, Leo could see lights on in the house up on the ridge. There was a line of trees there, black against the stars. "That's yours?"

"Yep, you can see the whole town from there."

It was a steep climb, and Leo knew he'd walk up better if he had both arms free to swing but he didn't want to let go of Allie. Somehow that would be a mistake, to let go of each other just before they said good night; it would mean all this kissing was just something to do on the way home, not anything they were both building up to they could keep for later.

Up near the Donovans' house there was a night breeze that cooled the sweat under Leo's T-shirt and blue jeans. He was breathing hard. He turned around with Allie and looked out at Heywood below. Beatrice's seemed to be the only light down there, that and the top of the Fremont Theater marquee. She put her arm around his waist and he turned and kissed her on that long tanned sweaty neck.

She whispered that her daddio was sitting on the porch behind them. "See him?"

Leo did. He sure did, and as soon as he straightened up he heard him too.

"How'd it go, Allie Cat?"

"Super cool." Allie led Leo to the porch steps. He wanted to slip his hand out of hers but their fingers were intertwined and she wasn't letting go. When her father stood up it was too dark for Leo to make out his face, but he could see that he had wide shoulders and he wore glasses that were catching the window light behind them.

"Want to meet my new beau?"

"If he rates."

"'Course he rates. This boy just published an essay in the *Monthly Writer*, can you believe it?"

"What about?"

"His name's Leo Suther, Dad. Leo, this is my dubious father."

Mr. Donovan offered his hand. Its skin was dry and so callused it reminded Leo of a dog's padded paw. "Chick Donovan. What are your writings about?"

"We all wrote some, sir. But our teacher, Mr. Jewett, sent mine in."

"It was real good, Dad. About blues music."

"Blues music." Allie's father said it slowly, nodding his head like he either just understood something he hadn't before, or else wasn't listening at all. "Good, good. Come on in a minute, meet Allison's mother."

The inside of the house was one big room and Leo noticed the walls were made of blond logs with beige chinks in between.

"Dad built this himself. I can't believe he wants to sell it out of our lives."

Her father smiled and walked up wooden stairs with no railings to the second floor. Allie led Leo to the couch which faced a huge knit rug in front of a coal-black fireplace. Above the mantel was the painted portrait of a man with a squared-off bushy beard. He was dressed in a brown jacket and vest. His shirt was buttoned up under his chin and he was looking off towards his left like someone in that direction had just insulted him. At Leo's right, on a wood plank floor, was a picnic table and two benches. In the middle of the table was a brass candle holder for eight candles, but there weren't any in it, or even any melted wax. Beyond that, the wood floor ended and the red brick floor of the kitchen began. Scattered in a corner were red, yellow, and blue building blocks, and a bright red ball. Leo could see a radio on the counter near the gas stove. All along the walls between the windows were unframed paintings of lakes, trees, sunrises, and sunsets. Beneath those were three-foot-high shelves full of hardcover books.

"You like it?"

Leo nodded at the portrait over the fireplace. "Is that your grandfather?"

"That's one of the great minds of the nineteenth century," Allie's father said from behind. Leo stood as Mr. Donovan walked down the last few stairs with Mrs. Donovan following him. Leo had seen her before; on mornings she drove Allie to school when Allie missed the bus. She kept her long brown hair tied back in a single braid. She was wearing a red-, orange-, and yellow-flowered robe that she held up over her bare ankles as she walked down the stairs.

"And this is one of the great hearts of the twentieth century: Tess Donovan, Cleo. Cleo—"

"*Leo, Dad*, not Cleo."

"Oops. Sorry, amigo." Mr. Donovan turned and walked back to the kitchen. Mrs. Donovan smiled and said he looked much more like a Leo than a Cleo. She sat on the other side of Allie. Leo sat down too.

"So was it awful in that kitchen, hon?"

"Whether it was awful or not is immaterial, don't you think? Dad wanted me to know what working is like so now I'm learning. Isn't he alluring, Mother?"

Mrs. Donovan looked past Allie at Leo and smiled again. She asked Allie more questions about her new job which Allie answered in one or two words, all the while smiling at Leo. Then Mr. Donovan walked across the knit rug carrying a pine wood tray that held a full pitcher and four glasses. He set it on the coffee table, poured each glass full of something that looked like iced tea with no ice, and sat down in a rocking chair near the fireplace.

"You graduating this month, Leo?"

"No sir, I should be but I started kindergarten a year late, after my mom died." Leo reached for a glass and sipped what he thought would be tea but was instead apple cider and his mouth was so surprised he didn't swallow at first and now his cheeks were flushed and he had no idea why he just offered such a personal piece of history to Allie Donovan's parents.

"Wow, Leo, I didn't know that." Allie's fingertips touched his knee.

He swallowed the cider and shook his head. "No, I was a little kid, I hardly remember her."

"How did you get hooked into blues music?" Mr. Donovan was looking at him like he was surprised he was truly interested in what sat on his couch next to his daughter and wife.

"My dad plays it, sir."

"Call me Chick."

"Yes sir, I mean Chick."

Allie's mother laughed. Leo let himself smile, then, to somehow balance what he just said, he added: "He plays the guitar, but I play the harmonica myself."

"So you appreciate Negro culture."

Leo nodded and sipped more cider.

"This civil rights struggle is just the beginning of things as I see it, as *he* sees it." Chick nodded up at the portrait of the bearded man above the mantel. Leo glanced at Allie. She was staring at the empty glass she held in her lap.

"Have you got summer work yet?"

"I'll probably get something at the mill, where my father works. You know, cleaning the trucks."

"Full time?"

Leo shook his head. Chick Donovan drained his glass and stood up. "Well look, I need one strong kid for the summer to be an all-around laborer and helper. I was going to give Allison a 'help wanted' sheet to post at the high school, but if you think you're the man, why then we'll cut a deal tonight."

"I can do it," Leo heard himself say, though getting a job had occurred to him only vaguely and that was because Gerry had one.

"Super fine. I'll pay you the minimum, a dollar and a quarter an hour, but you can count on cash; we don't pay war taxes in this family. When does your vacation start?"

"This coming Monday."

"Meet me here next Monday morning at seven."

Leo took this as a sign for him to drink up and go. He stood and reached down past Allie to shake her mother's hand. "It was a pleasure meeting you, Mrs. Donovan."

"Likewise, Leo."

Allie stood and walked with Leo to the door where her father put his arm around her shoulders and squeezed. "Thanks for walking Allie Cat home. See you then."

3

Leo didn't know which he was more excited about, being called Allie's new beau, or getting the chance to work under the sun with iron tools and wood until he had the kind of hands Ryder said were best for a harp player. As he walked down the river road, lit only by an occasional floodlight reflecting off the water from the other side, he pulled his C harmonica from his pants pocket and blew and sucked out do re mi, then do re maw, then do re mi again. He walked fast and put as much air into the harp as he could without bending the little metal reeds inside it. When he got to the covered bridge he thought of Allie all over again, the way she put her hands on his hips and slipped her tongue inside his mouth.

He walked through town, and at the gravel road of Saunders Hill he put his harmonica back into his pocket. Soon he could hear the men in his house. There was no music and at first Leo thought some-body was telling a game-buster of a joke because the voice was loud and nobody else was talking. When he got closer he could see into the lighted windows of the kitchen from the road. It was Lars's brother-in-law, Dwight. He was one of the only poker men who didn't work at Heywood Paper. He painted houses and he had a brand new Ford van which said so on both doors: "Call Dwight—He Paints It Right." He was tall with no muscles to speak of, but not skinny either. Standing at the kitchen table, Dwight had a face the color of a cooked lobster, and Leo didn't know if that was because he was sunburned or drunk or maybe both. He sure sounded drunk and he wasn't telling a joke.

"That's all I'm saying. We burned witches in this very state, den we? Den we? And those girls weren't doin' no treason either—a little hookey-poo maybe."

One man laughed. So did Lars. He was sitting next to Dwight. He put his arm on the back of Dwight's chair. "Good enough, Dewey. Let's get back to the game."

"No it is *not* good enough. Next time those pink-ass shitheads hold a match, I say we spray 'em down with gasoline. They wanta burn their citizen 'sponsibility, they burn the right to live far's I'm concerned. I'm telling ya, we're starting to look like weak little shits." Dwight picked up his beer and drained it. He sat, but didn't pull his chair up to the table. He was looking down at the floor like he had dropped something there and couldn't reach it and nobody would get it for him. A man's hands were shuffling the cards. It was Jim.

Leo walked back down the road to the river where there was no moon, just stars above the trees. Water trickled over a rock in a small eddy somewhere ahead of him. He remembered that cartoon sketch he'd seen in the paper of an army sergeant at a shooting range. The sergeant had his cap pulled low over his eyes and was chewing on a half-smoked cigar with his hands on his hips. At his feet was a young soldier aiming a rifle over sandbags at a target, and underneath this were the sergeant's words: "Make like every target's a stinking flag burner."

Leo thought of the covered bridge and Allie pressing herself against him like his penis belonged to them both. He was hard in no time. He unzipped his jeans and let it out, though he wasn't sure what he was going to do next. He could kneel and splash river water on it, or he could do the other. The air felt warmer down here and somebody must've closed the parlor window up the hill because Leo could barely hear the muffled poker talk of the men. It was getting towards the end of playing time, when they were either giddy and reckless about the money left on the table, or else hushed and focused on their last lap, almost respectful. Tonight they were the latter, and Leo took that as a sign for him to go ahead and do what he had to while the night was quiet and he was alone here to pull back and forth with his eyes closed, thinking of his hand being Allie's instead, of the June air getting ready to receive what Allie would surely not shy from once it came gushing, once it did.

4

Heywood High School's colors were black and blue, a combination that made its football uniforms seem a Civil War triumphant if the Woodies won, pathetic if they lost, especially if they got really bruised. From the top bleacher of Heywood Memorial Stadium, the band in front of the graduation platform looked like a square of blueberry cobbler. When Leo leaned over and told his date and new girlfriend this, Allie, dressed in her usual white T-shirt and bell-bottoms, rested her hand on his knee and squeezed.

The bleachers were full of families waiting for the big moment. Down in the first bench Mr. Poitras had his box camera positioned on the concrete knee wall in front of him, aiming the lens at the platform where diplomas would be handed out as soon as the last speech finished. On the freshly cut grass in front of the band stood the black-robed graduating class which Gerry Poitras belonged to. Leo wasn't sure, but he thought his friend was the one standing between two kids who had "'67" taped to the top of their mortar boards.

Nancy Titcomb was the student speaker. Behind the lectern, in straight rows of folding chairs, sat the faculty of the high school. She read her speech without once looking up, and the sun glinted so bright off the microphone it was hard to see her face. She spoke in her trademark sustained squeak, as if the whole world needed cheering up, and that's just what she got up this morning to do. She finished by summarizing the major points of her talk: Team Spirit, Sacrifice, and the Pursuit of Happiness—"On your mark, get set, *go!*" The whole stadium welled up into clapping and whistling, and Allie rolled her eyes at Leo. When he smiled and nodded back, she leaned over and kissed him on the neck. They stayed and watched the seniors march one at a time up onto the platform to get their diplomas until the P's, when Gerry Poitras clomped up the wood steps smiling out at the crowd like they had come just for him and, "Geez, how white of you all to come!"

On the way out of the stadium, Leo let go of Allie's hand long enough to tell Ruth they'd be over in a while. He would've told Mr. Poitras himself, but GP's old man was still taking pictures even though Gerry was somewhere back in the black mass of giddy seniors.

Out in the dirt parking lot, Allie wrapped her arms around Leo's neck and kissed him soft on the mouth. "You know, Gerry's sweet, Leo, but I don't see you as the football type."

"Neither is Gerry, he was second string."

"But he's a *square*. He probably ate up all that candied crap

Nancy Titcomb was spewing out. Can you believe she didn't mention the war or the riots *once?* Not once."

"Yeah, I can."

Without talking about it, they headed quietly up the road past the stadium into the woods of the National Park Service. They walked along a narrow paved path until there was nothing but spruce around them. A bed of brown pine needles covered the ground. The band was playing a marching tune and sounded closer than it was.

"You want to hike up to the top, see if we can see your place from there?"

"Nope." Allie took his hand and stepped onto the pine needles. "I want to get lost."

"We'll miss Gerry's party."

"So? Probably a bunch of talky kids sitting around some clean garage, drinking Cokes, eating a frightening amount of potato chips while they groove to some bad forty-fives. What on earth are we going to miss?"

Leo followed a few feet, but then he pulled his hand free and walked faster so he was leading. Soon the ground dipped into a small flat crater with green brush growing up two sides. Allie sat down.

"I thought you wanted to get *lost* lost." He squatted next to her and ran his finger through the pine needles. She looked off into the blue spruce, then lay back and stared up at the treetops. Her blond hair was spread out on the ground. Today she wore sandals and Leo noticed her toenails were clipped and clean.

"I'm glad you'll be working for my dad. Now I know I'll see you every day."

"What about night?" Leo leaned over and kissed her on the mouth. He could hear the roar of the seniors in the stadium, and he pictured their mortar boards rocketing above them, spinning out and away to the bleachers behind. Allie pulled him on top of her and they kissed a long while, until there was blue twilight all around and Leo didn't even think anymore about the erection behind his jeans, or that his hips were humping against Allie's, and she was gently humping back.

––––––

5

Chick Donovan was a communist.

It was the second thing he said Monday morning after Leo walked up Spoon Hill with his bag lunch at just before seven. The sun was still low behind the trees at the ridge. The blond logs of the cabin were bark-shaved, the lower ones wet with dew. Off to the side, a flatbed truck was parked behind the ten-year-old black Star Chief Leo had seen Allie's mother drive. On the flatbed's doors was "DONO-VAN'S RENOVATORS," and Leo looked for Allie. Last night, Sunday, as they lay on the grass of Thompson Green, she hugged him and whispered she'd have a nice cup of hot coffee waiting for him in the morning on the porch, but he didn't see her now.

He turned and looked over the ground he'd covered. Down in Heywood the roofs of the store buildings were sunlit but the river behind them still moved through shadow. On the other side of town rose the wooded hills of the national park. The screen door slammed and Chick Donovan walked off the porch without touching a step. He was dressed in a work shirt, jeans, and boondocker boots. A square tape measure was stuck on his belt, and there was a pencil behind his ear pinched between his glasses frame and his head. He tossed Leo a set of keys and told him to light her up.

That was all he said at first. He sat on the passenger side and was quiet while Leo meshed the gears looking for reverse. When they got to the bottom of the drive, Chick pointed his thumb right and Leo steered the flatbed in that direction. They drove along the river a mile, maybe more, and still Allie's father hadn't spoken a word since the cabin. Leo wondered if he'd gotten the time wrong and was late. Both windows were down and he could smell flowering blue dog-wood, a hint of cow manure, though he didn't see a pasture anywhere. He held the steering wheel at nine and three o'clock. It was smooth and hard and big as a tractor's. He was relieved at how well he was handling it, wishing Chick Donovan would say something, and he did.

"Since I'm a dyed-in-the-wool communist, you can count on some profit sharing on this job. I assume you're saving for college."

"Who do you write for?"

"Write?"

"Your column?"

Chick laughed. "I said *communist,* Leo. You know? The red flag and all that?"

Leo did know. And he wasn't sure he wanted to know much more. They were passing through a poplar grove where the road split off. Chick was shaking his head and smiling. He pointed his thumb out the window and Leo downshifted with more noise than he wanted, accelerating past the trees up a long hill. At the top of the rise the road cut left, and on both sides were fields of tall grass. To the right was a barn. In front of that was the burned out basement of a long-gone house. A lone sapling grew out one corner. Chick had Leo pull the truck up beside it.

"New owner wants that turned into a home. It'll take the four of us all summer. Good job for you though, Leo. You'll see all the steps from appetizer to dessert."

The day was hot and dry with no wind and the whole gang, even Chick, had their shirts off before coffee break. Chick had some build for a family man. He was short all right, and small-boned, but he had biceps that became hard little balls everytime he moved his arms, his back was wide and lumpy at the shoulders and narrow at the hips, and his chest muscles weren't big, just easy to see, two lean squared plates under his collar bone with a few tufts of hair in between. The rest of Donovan's Renovators were two men named Tom Burrell and Floyd Starrett. Tom was quiet and naturally big. Leo knew his son Billy from the high school. Floyd was probably twenty-five or -six. He was shorter than Leo but there were thick veins running down each tanned arm. His blond hair was almost shaved off and he had a USMC tattoo on the back of his neck right between his hairline and his backbone. Chick had introduced Tom as his foreman and Floyd as his crack carpenter. Tom shook Leo's hand and Floyd offered him a stick of Wrigleys, smiling, his strangely bright gray eyes staring into Leo's, Leo thinking *cracked* carpenter, that's what Chick must've meant.

But all morning Leo didn't see Floyd be anything but a coal miner

27

like him. That's what it seemed like working down in the old basement among charred posts, broken panes of glass, two sets of bedsprings, a rusted radiator, weeds, a few empty pots and pans, and mountains of damp ash over more stuff. The hole was deep, but with all that ash to walk over, Leo had to stoop under the sooty boards that ran the width of the foundation. Floor joists, Chick said they were called, and he set up a winch and pulley off one of them, tied a rope to an empty bucket, and lowered it down to Floyd and Leo to fill again and again. They took turns, Leo shoveling ash into the bucket for a few loads and Floyd hoisting it up, then they would switch. Floyd chewed his gum quick and shoveled even quicker. But he was sloppy and spilled some ash around the bucket. When it was full, Leo pulled on the rope and watched their load rise, turning up between the joist boards into the sun. In those rare seconds when it seemed like there was nothing to do, like when Tom was unhooking the ash bucket to dump into the wheelbarrow that he'd later dump out behind the barn, Floyd never stopped moving. If there wasn't a big enough mound to sink his shovel blade into, he'd make one. If that wasn't a problem, he'd pick through the debris for solid stuff—a dining chair leg, half a plate, a whole medicine cabinet, a doorknob with a hunk of door still attached to it—and he'd chuck them up between the joists and out of the hole. As soon as Leo lowered the empty bucket down, Floyd would be back shoveling, the rivulets of sweat running down the muscular groove of his spine.

He worked at this pace right up to coffee break—Leo's job, Chick called down to him, one Leo instantly liked because it meant climbing out of the basement, pulling on his shirt, taking a five from Chick, then driving the flatbed down the river road through the shady cool of the covered bridge up onto Paper Boulevard and into Beatrice's almost vacant lot. And man, there Allie was, not out back out of sight in the kitchen, but up front, behind the counter in a snug-fitting white diner dress. Her blond hair was pulled back in a pony tail. Around her waist was a black apron with a white flying saucer etched in at the middle.

"Welcome to the UFO Show, will you be dining here or order to go?"

Leo laughed. There wasn't anyone sitting at the counter and only five or six men were scattered in the booths. They all wore suits and ties like GP's old man. Sipping coffee and smoking cigarettes, they talked in low earnest voices about money. Leo could see Sidney through the food tray window in the wall scraping the grill with a wire brush. Allie leaned over the counter and kissed Leo on the chin. She jerked back smiling, glanced at the booths, then kissed him on the lips.

"I didn't see you this morning, Miss Donovan," he whispered.

"I needed my beauty rest, can't you tell?" She held out her hands and turned from side to side. "Beatrice saw me doing dishes this morning. She whacked Sid on the arm and told him he didn't have a single hair of hiring sense, *even on his ass.*" She whispered the last part, then laughed so loud Leo wondered why she'd whispered at all.

Sidney peeked through the window. Leo stepped back and put in his order: two blueberry muffins, two corn, three regular coffees, and a Coke for himself. He watched her bag the muffins, pour the coffees, and put the full cardboard cups in a carrier. Allie bit her lower lip as she slid his Coke into place. If he had ever seen a finer looking girl in his life, he didn't know where.

"Do you need a hand to your truck, sir?"

They had to walk around the back of the flatbed to get out of Sidney's view, but still anybody driving by on Paper Boulevard could see the two of them French kissing, the blonde girl reaching into the tall boy's back pockets, pulling him in as close to her as she could. Leo took a breath. "Meet me here at six?"

Allie nodded and smiled, licking her tongue along his front teeth. When she got back behind the counter, Sidney was at the register ringing up a man's check. He stopped to look at Allie, then out the window at Leo. Allie waved and blew Leo a kiss.

Just before lunch Leo and Floyd hoisted up the last bucket of ash and climbed out of the hole to help Chick and Tom unload from the truck a generator and a load of new two-by-fours and two-by-sixes. Noontime the three men and Leo sat on a grass slope in the shade of a willow a few yards behind the barn. Floyd finished his lunch pretty quick, two chocolate Devil Dogs that he washed down with a warm Fresca. He leaned back on one elbow and smoked an L&M, looking off in the distance between where Tom and Chick ate, and he was either smiling at something or squinting, maybe both, Leo couldn't tell. Floyd spat and asked Chick if they were going to hack off the old joists and start from scratch. Chick nodded yes while he chewed, not looking at him. Floyd asked if the foundation was still level, and if it wasn't, were they going to use things called shims under things called base plates. Chick nodded twice again, but when Floyd started up with a third question Chick looked into his face and that made Floyd look away and wink at Leo, who glanced down at his half-eaten blackberry jelly sandwich. Tom held up a cold chicken drumstick and asked if anybody wanted it.

"Your dad in the union over to Heywood Paper?" Chick said.

"Yes, he is."

"An official?"

"Some of his friends are. They wanted him to run for treasurer or something once, but my pop's the quiet type. He sticks to himself."

"What's he think of you working for me?"

Leo shrugged. "It's fine with him."

Floyd lay on his side and propped his head on his elbow. "What Chick's asking you is what are your old man's feelings about reds? Seeing we're at war with them and all."

"Ease off, Floyd," Tom said.

"Just a statement of fact, TB. Nothin' more, nothin' less."

Leo glanced at Chick to see if that was it, but Chick was smiling and shaking his head at Floyd. "Floyd was a marine before all the fun started, Leo. He tells Tommy and me he's going to re-enlist so he can ship out to kick some ass but I notice he's here every morning ready to work. It's my commie generosity, isn't that it, Floyd?"

"Go tell it to the Viet Cong, boss." Floyd was sitting back up smoking another cigarette. "Look out, Tommy, he's getting that look." Floyd let the smoke out his nose and glanced at Leo. "Somebody should've warned you: now and again we here at Donovan's Renovators get an hour lunch instead of thirty minutes. The second half is pure propaganda but we get paid to sit on our rump. Want a cig?"

Leo said no thank you, he didn't smoke.

"I prefer to call it the truth, Floyd." Chick stood, wiped his palms on his pant legs, and began to pace back and forth. Tom rolled up his lunch bag and walked over to sit next to Leo. Tom smiled at him and nodded at Chick like Chick was about to tell a good joke.

"Story time," Floyd whispered. "Fire and brimstone."

"Ever hear of the Ludlow Massacre?" Chick said.

Leo shook his head. Tom too.

"You've heard of the Rockefellers though."

"They took the pennant in '63."

Chick stopped to give Floyd his full attention. Floyd smiled down at the grass.

Chick walked three feet to the east. "Okay. It's September of 1913. The Rockefeller clan owns the Colorado Fuel and Iron Corporation, which happens to employ about 11,000 workers in the southern part of that state. Foreign-born Americans mainly—Greeks and Italians, a few Serbs—and their whole families worked in the mines right down to the five-year-olds." Chick held his hand down around his knee. "They worked long-ass days for nine-tenths of a paycheck they never saw. You've heard of this devilish old company arrangement, I'm sure." Chick glanced at Leo. Leo nodded, though he didn't know what kind of arrangement Chick could be talking about. "The miners understandably go on strike and the *corporation* evicts them from their shacks, so in steps the United Mine Workers Union. They go and set up tents in the local hills, they organize food banks, they get blankets and help cut wood, they give all-around moral support so the miners can carry on their picketing for some kind of a life. 'Course the Rockefellers can't have *this*—profit margins might lose a little weight—so they hire a gang of thugs from a detective agency to go raid the tents with gatling guns and long rifles. You're all ears now, aren't you Floyd?"

"Don't bet your house on it."

"A few families get slaughtered. The miners dig in for a cold winter. By April, without ever sending in a negotiating team, these Rockefellers get the governor of Colorado to send in the National Guard. You heard me, The *National* Guard. Against *American citizens.* That first sunup all unholy hell breaks loose. The Guard sets up their machine guns and go at it. The miners return fire. Women and children dig pits under their tents." Chick put his hands on his hips. He

———

31

shook his head and looked out at a stand of spruce down at the edge of the back field. "When the sun went down, the Guard moved in with torches, more shooting. The next day a telephone lineman is picking through the rubble. He goes to where a family tent once stood. He lifts up this scorched iron cot frame and underneath, in a shallow pit, are the burnt bodies of eleven children and two women." Chick looked at Floyd. "Sixty-six men, women, and kids killed in that strike. The union wasn't recognized there and not one hired dick or guardsman got charged with a crime. My question to you is why not?"

Nobody said anything for a second or two, then Floyd looked off to the south and said, "'Cause them guys were just following their orders, that's why."

"Then why," Chick said, "wasn't the governor of Colorado or the Rockefellers indicted?"

Floyd chuckled to himself.

Chick glanced at Leo. Leo shrugged. "No proof?"

"Uh-uh, no power. No clout. This handful of doomed families had no clout. And why didn't they? Floyd?"

"Because they was outgunned."

"*Exactly.* Outgunned. Every laboring man, woman, and child from coast to coast should have dropped everything they were doing in a show of solidarity, like the Wobblies, the International Workers of the World. But the majority of them never heard about it. And why is that? Tom? Any ideas?"

Chick looked next at Leo but spared him the question.

"I'll tell you why: because the media machine in this fair land is controlled by rich Wonder Bread boys, that's why. The Hearsts, all those fat cats, they feed at the same silver-lined trough, comprendo?" Chick paused to catch any rebuttals, but Leo didn't see any coming. Floyd was smiling at nothing in particular. Tom was looking out at the field like he forgot to do something.

"The sad fact of the matter is Karl Marx was right when he said that all human history is the history of class struggle." Chick put his finger up in the air. "But he also said something even more germane—"

"I put it in a colored jelly roll who called herself Jermaine." Floyd laughed and winked at Leo.

_____

Chick yelled at Floyd to shut up.

Floyd looked like he was about to say something but then he stared at the grass, not smiling either.

"What Marx said is, 'The point is not to understand the world, but to *change* it.' So remember, a crime against one is a crime against us all."

"Sounds good to me," Tom stood and wiped off the back of his pants. Floyd stayed where he was. Leo didn't know what to do next.

"Okay then, enough said. Let's get back to work, lads. Thank you for your attention." Chick walked fast up the slope and around the barn. Floyd followed him but went slower, lighting up an L&M as he went.

"Chick missed his calling as a minister, that's all," Tom said. "Don't worry about that red talk, he'll trip over The New Testament one of these days."

But Leo did worry about that talk. For the rest of the afternoon as he worked alongside Floyd sweeping the basement, then hauling the black joist boards that Chick and Tom sheared off with power saws they'd plugged into the gas-powered generator, as he carried alone all the new lumber into the barn while the others marked with pencils where the brand new floor joists would be nailed, Leo had to know: what about Chick Donovan's daughter? Leo's first real girlfriend, the only one to ever stick her tongue in his mouth while she held herself against an erection she couldn't possibly not be knowing about—was she one too? Didn't she know that's who the Americans were fighting over in Asia? Didn't she read how these Viet Cong went around stabbing bayonets into our soldiers after they were dead just to make sure they were? And around four, when Chick dropped him off at the bridge and Leo crossed it and walked through town towards Saunders Hill Road, he knew he had to talk to somebody, somebody who wouldn't tell anyone else.

GP wasn't the one to spill it to. One weeknight in May, Leo had been over at his house watching the five o'clock news on the couch with Gerry. Mr. Poitras was in his recliner. On the TV the news camera showed pictures of American soldiers climbing out of a helicopter and running through blowing grass with their packs and machine guns and helmets. Gerry backhanded Leo's knee and smiled at him. Leo smiled back and watched more news.

Truth is, he didn't know what to think. Not then and not now. It's not that he wasn't going to do his fair share, nothing like that. And it wasn't that he was really scared of going, either, though when he let himself think about what could happen—about getting shot at, or bayoneted after he was shot, or else to have hot shards from an exploded hand grenade flying at his stomach or chest or head or (the worst) his penis and balls—then he felt for a second like he had to go to the toilet. But there was another picture in his head too, more good than bad, a picture of Leo Suther coming home to Heywood from the war in a spiffy uniform with three rows of silver and gold medals pinned over his heart. His face would be tanned, his hair military-short, almost shaved. His arm would be in a clean white sling, from a single bullet wound he suffered on his last day when he saved a dozen American GI's pinned down in a foxhole by three of the enemy. They were in a machine gun nest and he was the one behind them, making his way through a minefield on his belly, then finally getting there to pull his .45 and shoot each Cong once in the chest, the deed done just like that, a far-off sniper putting one in his arm just as his rescued comrades rushed to his aid.

So everything was basically all right, except Leo didn't know what a Viet Cong was. And who was their leader? Was there a King Cong? An Oriental Hitler? Because if there was, he could get a picture of him to put on his bedroom wall and stare at it every night. He'd gather all the information he could on how hateful this guy was, on all the shitty things he must be doing over there to have us get mad enough to travel so far to put up a fight. Then Leo would feel more than ready. But what did Chick think? If he's a communist he must be on their side. And if he's on their side, then he must think it's okay to do terrible things. But that didn't make sense either because today, at his lunch story, when he told about terrible things happening to people, he looked unhappy and mad about it, and he said somebody should have done something. So what gives? And when? And who with?

Leo wished it was a Wednesday so he could talk to Ryder before his harp lesson. Ryder would have an opinion on all this. But would he keep it to himself? Sometimes Ryder drank a lot of beer and he would talk about nothing really, but loud and to the point like it was very profound: "Hey," he'd say. "Big mosquitoes should just go, shouldn't they? Shouldn't they just get up and *go*?"

Leo walked down the gravel two-track of Saunders Hill, getting close to his house, and he thought of asking his dad. Jim didn't offer much, but if he was asked a direct question, eye to eye, he would listen, give it some thought, and come out with an answer. Heading under the canopy of branches and leaves for the cabin, Leo thought he'd ask him about communism, period. He wouldn't mention Chick Donovan, his boss and the father of his new girlfriend whom Jim had yet to meet. He would just ask him about commies and how come we're fighting them on the other side of the world, that's all.

But Jim's Valiant wasn't pulled up to the kitchen door and no dinner smells came through the screened windows, even though it was past 4:30. Then he remembered it was a Monday, Numbers Night down at the Elks, the only time in the week Jim left him to cook for himself. Leo went inside and lay down on his bed with his work boots still on. He could feel the sunburn on his back. He took his harmonica from the bedside table, but instead of playing do re mi he went right in with a long throat-constricted maw wah wah. When his lungs were full, he blew air out into the next hole up, this time opening and closing his free hand until he heard a Ryder sound, but it was him, Leo, making fo wah, fo wah, fo wah. He did it again. *For what, for what*, it sounded like. He did it three times. On the fourth, when his lungs were empty, he moved his pursed lips over to the next higher note, sucking in this time, moving his hand and closing up his throat. He heard *See you, you, you, you.* He slid back and forth between the two notes, going long on one, short on the other, then switching. *See you, see you, see you* . . .

Fo wah, fo wah, fo wah . . .

The "see you" note was higher, and when Leo felt its air vibrate against his tongue, he thought girl, woman. The "for what" note was low, a man's no matter how you look at it, his low persistent question asking what for to the woman's see you, see you, see you later.

Leo kept playing, staring at a small crater in the plaster ceiling. He found more notes. When he relaxed his lips and covered three or four holes, working his free hand back and forth, he heard a whole family of voices, a neighborhood of "Oh she's leavin', she sure is. Oh she's leavin', she sure is." He moved back down to the first note, pursing his lips again, using his hands and blowing out *For what? For what? For what?* Then he slid his lips right up to *See you, see you, bye bye.* The "bye bye" note was the highest and it sounded more like *why* than *bye,* but it was a nice cap to everything and Leo thought *bye* was a cleaner way to end it.

6

It didn't hit him until he had taken a shower and dressed in a clean pair of jeans and a white button-down shirt that he had just played an original harp tune for the first time, not the harmonica anymore and not yet The Harp of the Blues, but he had definitely touched harpness. And he felt different. He felt okay, which meant he was either feeling truly wonderful, or else had been feeling bad and wasn't anymore so he felt good, which was really just normal but better than before.

Then Allie pulled up in her mother's black Star Chief. Leo glanced at the wall clock. It was still a half an hour before six. He watched her through the kitchen window as she looked out at the house, then checked her face in the rearview mirror. She opened the door and slid off the seat, her cotton skirt catching itself halfway up her long thighs. She had sandals on and instead of a T-shirt she wore a white blouse with a low neckline and puff sleeves. The sun was down behind the hill. Her hair hung thick and loose around her shoulders and in that light looked like it almost gave off its own. Leo pushed open the screen door with his foot. "Your mom lets you take her wheels?"

Allie smiled and whispered, "Is your father home?"

"Nope."

"*Shucks,* I dressed up to meet him."

36

"How'd you find my house?"

She stepped closer, slid her arms around his neck, and touched her nose to his. "Gerry told me down at the UFO. I couldn't wait." She flicked her tongue inside his mouth. Leo's hand fell and grazed her bottom. It was round and firm, but soft too. When they pulled away Allie kissed his chin. "Show me your room."

He held her fingers as they walked through the kitchen and past the parlor down the hall to his bedroom. She went straight to the window. The woods were getting dark, but Leo could still see some of the river down between the trees. Allie stood there real quiet, not even glancing around like he figured she would. He could feel his pulse beating between his ears. He stood beside her and kissed her forehead and temple. Her eyes were shiny, the green in them almost blue. He moved to kiss her lips but she stepped away and closed the door. She leaned against it and slid out of her sandals, looking right into his face. Leo thought he should say something. He wanted to look away, so he went to the bed and sat down instead. When she joined him there things went really fast, and Leo knew later, when she'd been gone for hours and Jim was back from the Elks asleep in his room across the hall, that that was the only way tonight could have gone, that the way to have changed things was to talk when he had the chance—for him and Allie both to talk—but when neither of them did, when they just looked across the room at each other, then lay on the bed side by side, not kissing, just looking, their breathing short and shallow and quick, when Allie reached over, unzipped his pants and held his erection, her hand warmer than his warmth, Leo knew this was the conversation they were having.

He ran his fingers under her skirt along her smooth thigh to her hip and underpants. With her other hand Allie unsnapped his jeans, tugged at them, then she turned on her back and lifted up enough for Leo to pull her panties down over her knees, past her shins and off her feet. At the foot of the bed Leo got rid of his pants. While he unbuttoned his shirt and dropped it to the floor, Allie pulled the hem of her skirt up to her blouse and lay there with her blond hair spread out on the pillow. The hair between her legs was some shade of brown, maybe honey, but Leo couldn't tell for sure because he didn't look at it, just felt its dark tug as he moved himself up between the thighs she spread for him, as she raised up her knees, squeezed his butt with both hands and pulled him into that soft opening of something so clutchingly warm and damp it was over very quickly.

After a while Leo put on his underwear and sat on the edge of the bed. Allie leaned up on one elbow and ran her fingers along his sunburned back. It stung his skin, but he didn't move. The room had gotten darker, the corners the darkest. She pointed to the black and white poster above his chest of drawers. "Who's that?"

"Big Bill Broonzy." Leo glanced at her, then looked off towards the window. "He's a bluesman, one of the kings."

"My dad says the Negroes are the only ones ready to hear about the Revolution. That's the main reason he wants us to go to Mississippi, you know."

"What does your mom think?"

"She thinks he's God. She must, because she never sees him. He works all day and goes to meetings almost every night at that campus in Amherst, but whatever he says goes. Sometimes I hear them making love and it sounds like she's crying, but I know she's not. It sounds like it, though." Allie rested her chin on his shoulder and whispered, "Was that your first time?"

Leo nodded. "Sort of. You?"

"What do you think?"

"I think it wasn't."

"Is that okay?"

Leo nodded again, though he wasn't thinking or feeling anything and so it probably *was* okay. Everything was probably okay.

Though now, lying in bed awake close to midnight, things didn't seem so smooth and wonderful. And he wasn't sure why, except he was more worried than before about Chick being a communist. The moon was bright outside. A river breeze moved through the woods and made the shadows in Leo's room tremble.

7

But the notes don't get bent too much in the daytime and from seven to four all week Leo knew he was working for Chick the builder because that's all Chick talked to him about. Every time he sent Leo to a toolbox or the truck for something, he'd explain what it was Leo was holding in his hands. Those first few days, working shirtless in the sun with big quiet Tom and lightning-eyes Floyd, helping those two and Chick do whatever they asked him—mark this board here, pull this tape there, cut this two-by-four along this line here—Leo learned the names of things he's never even heard of before: stud, plumb bob, ripsaw, level, framing hammer, galvy, square, chalk line, toe plate, top plate, shim, fir, sheathing, return, joint, hammer moon, nail punch, seven-sixteenths, an eighth, three-sixteenths, five-eighths, move that stud over a black cunt hair which is wider than a brown CH which is wider than a blond one which is wider than the thinnest of them all, a red CH.

Beginning of the week they had laid a solid plywood floor on new joists over the cleaned out basement. By late Wednesday afternoon the first floor's walls were framed out plumb, square, and level. After cleanup, when all the tools and lumber were locked in the barn and Floyd hitched a ride home with Tom in his station wagon, Chick handed Leo a starched nail apron, a worn leather hammer hook for his belt, a new tape measure, and a long-handled hammer with one of its iron claws chipped off. "You'll be needing these," was all he said.

They drove along the river road in the truck, Chick behind the wheel. Leo mentioned how much he was learning and how he sure appreciated having the job. When Chick didn't say anything back, didn't even nod or smile, just drove, Leo started to talk about how fast Floyd always works and how Tom really knows what he's doing and how you, Chick, *you* always know what has to happen next. Chick glanced at Leo then and Leo shut up, though Chick's expression didn't really tell him to. It was more a look of, "Oh, you're talking, how nice." And so Leo kept quiet. He had started to sound like

Floyd, he knew, talking and moving around all the time whether there was a reason to or not. But there *is* a good reason here, he thought. I'm doing it with your daughter Mr. Donovan, and I don't want to come across as nervous or anything but I can't stand sitting in this truck cab alone with you, mister.

At the covered bridge, Chick dropped him off. "See you in the A.M., amigo." Leo stood in the road and watched him make a three-point turn in the gravel, then head back towards Spoon Hill, the flatbed's tires spinning out pebbles into the brush.

On his way through the bridge, Leo stuffed the tape and hammer into the nail apron and draped that over his shoulder. As he stepped out into the light, the sun still hot on his forehead and nose, he thought that he'd like Allie to see him like this right now, see the guy in the T-shirt and jeans with the sunburned face, tanned arms, and blistered dirty hands, his heavy sun-dried work boots. Yesterday Beatrice had put her on a new shift—noon to eight, Monday through Friday—the lunch and supper crowd, which last night Allie said she liked because she got to sleep late, only she didn't care for the times when the place was full of other summer vacation kids from the high school, girls and boys she had to serve shakes and Cokes and Unidentified Frying Objects to while they played nothing but those obnoxious Beatles songs on the jukebox. When Leo asked what was wrong with that, she said, "Number one, kids don't tip. And number two, Leo, they're so intellectually inferior it's tragic. Really. Tragic."

They were sitting in the front seat of Jim's Valiant at the time. When Leo borrowed it, his father had handed him the keys and said to bring her over sometime, we should meet. Leo put on fresh underwear and brushed his teeth twice before he picked her up at Beatrice's then drove across the river past Spoon Hill to where the road forked up to the job site. He parked there and put his arm out the window. He could still smell the shavings from the two-by-fours they'd cut that afternoon. The sun was down in the Berkshires. The field grass out behind the barn was high and thick, and the spruce stand beyond it looked blue.

"Really, tragic," Allie said again.

He put his arm around her and kissed her on the lips. She kissed him back with a closed mouth. He rested his hand on her bare knee beneath the hem of her UFO Show skirt, but Allie pressed down on it. "I think we should converse this evening, don't you Leo?"

"Yeah, let's converse." He ran his nose up into her hairline and kissed the top of her ear. Allie shrugged her shoulder and pushed his hand off her knee.

"No, seriously, Leo. If we make love every time we see each other then it'll never work."

"What won't work?"

"Our romance. It won't be one." She reached over and scratched the short hairs on his neck. "We have to engage our minds now, don't you think?"

Leo was quiet. His erection was pushing against his jeans. He took her scratching hand and held it.

"My mom says lovemaking is like dancing. Once you find a part-ner you just wait for the music to start up. Well yesterday there was us and there was music and now that we've danced we can get on with more adult matters."

"What matters?"

"Don't play fencepost with me, Leo."

"I'm not, I just don't know what you're talking about."

Allie looked out the windshield and smiled. "See? This is good. We're getting into a heated debate."

"This isn't a debate, I just asked a question."

"And see how neat questions are, Leo? My dad says every question asked is an act of hope, and that we all have this natural hunger for the truth." Allie scooted to him and rested her cheek on his shoulder.

"You admire him a lot, huh?"

"How many men do you know who want to change the world?"

Leo thought of Chick thanking his three-man crew for their atten-tion after his lunchtime lecture, the way he walked quickly away like he didn't want to hear any wisecracks behind him. Leo wanted to say, "Tell me another one," or "You're nuts," but he put his hand on Allie's knee again instead.

———

41

"You have vision too, Leo. I saw it in your room."

"Under my bed?"

She swatted his shoulder. "Nope, that poster. You think Gerry Poitras has any Negro heroes on his wall?"

Leo laughed. "He calls me a nigger-lover sometimes."

"You *let* him? You let him say *nigger*?"

"I guess so. He's only kidding me. He kids everybody about everything. Besides, I just like blues music and bluesmen. I don't know much about Negroes. Never met one really."

Leo could see her stiffen. Then he heard it in her voice, and he didn't want her to get the wrong idea.

"But you do respect them, right? As equals?"

"Oh of course, absolutely."

Allie let out a breath and kissed him on the mouth. They talked and kissed a long while after that, until the moon was out and the half-frame of the new house shone pale as a skeleton. Allie didn't touch Leo below his belt, but she let him put his finger inside her.

Leo walked along the breakdown bed of Paper Boulevard. The sky had been clear and blue, but now that he was out of downtown a huge cloud bank moved in and in its shadow Leo could see red in the asphalt. He figured the rain would come from the north because the wind was carrying the smell of the paper mill with it; Ryder said it was a natural wood smell that's been turned inside out and so leaves your nose as insulted as your eyes would be if you saw that done to a kitten or a little girl. That's how he described it and he wrote a song about it called "The Inside-Out Low-Down Paper Mill Blues." But it wasn't a blues number at all. It sounded like one of those Pete Seeger or Kingston Trio songs. Ryder's harp still sounded gut-bucket true, but it didn't match his singing too well. Really, only Jim could pull that off, it seemed. To sing Negro songs without sounding like a fake.

The rain came just as Leo started down Saunders Hill. He held his hammer and apron and ran the rest of the way. Ryder's white Impala was parked alongside the pines. Leo didn't see his father's car anywhere. Jim was inside though, sitting at the kitchen table with a can of Pabst in front of him and a full iced coffee too. Ryder stood at the counter dicing an onion with a paring knife, and he wore Jim's soiled white apron around his waist.

"Hey Young Buddy, how's the carpentry business? Chick Donovan treating you all right?"

"You know Chick?"

"Ride knows everybody, didn't you know that?" Jim sipped from his beer can, then lowered it fast to the table. Ryder smiled and scraped the onion chunks off the cutting board into a bowl of hamburger meat and raw egg.

"'Scuse me, Mr. Bunyan. Grab me another, please."

"You really want one, pop?"

"How's that?"

"Do you really think you need one?"

"That's the strangest question I ever heard."

Leo pulled a can from the fridge. He saw two more untouched six-packs on the bottom rack, and he couldn't remember the last time he'd seen his father drunk.

"Grab one for yourself, Johnny Bunyan."

Leo did. He didn't really want one. He didn't want to be hazy for his harp lesson with Ryder, but Jim had never let him so much as sip a beer before, even on Wednesday nights, just Coke, so Leo set his nail apron on the floor in the corner and sat down at the table with his beer.

Ryder asked Jim where the salt was. Jim didn't answer. He was looking right at Leo, his forearms resting heavily on the table, his shoulders hunched up to his ears.

"The salt, Jim. Where is it?"

"Above the toaster," Leo said. He took a long sip off his beer and watched Ryder add salt to the meat loaf. He wondered how Jim could have gotten this far so fast after work. The beer was ice cold, though, and tasted wonderful.

Jim spoke up:

"From the moonshine harvest
  our nightwatch we reap,
  the love of our neighbors,
  our bloodkin we keep."

Leo looked at his father.

"You don't know who wrote that, do you?"

"No."

"You ought to, you sure as hell ought to, you look just like her."

"Drink some of that iced coffee, Jimmy."

"You tell me he doesn't."

Leo kept his eyes on Ryder. He knew who his father was talking about. He sipped more beer.

Ryder put the meat loaf in the oven and wiped his hands off on his apron. "Some poor fool rolled his trailer into the power station this morning, so we spent the day at the club. 'Course your old man here spent a little more than the rest of us." Ryder took off the apron, hung it on its nail, and got a Narragansett from the fridge. "Sure, I know Chick Donovan. Two years ago he was up at the mill passing out pamphlets at the gate. Remember that, Jim? Those history articles talking about unions being the brainchilds of our communist brothers and a bunch of other horseshit like that? Nice enough fellow, though. He built my gal's porch and new kitchen awhile ago. Did a damn good job too."

"Yeah, he's showing me a lot."

Jim stood all at once and stepped outside with his iced coffee. The rain gutter was full and dripping loud but Leo could still hear Jim's boots on the ground as he went around the house.

"Man, why'd he drink so *much*?"

Ryder shrugged and sipped his beer. "You know Bill O'Donnell? That good-looking fella Lars brought over here a couple times?"

"Steve McQueen."

"That's him, his boy got killed in action last week."

Leo sipped his beer.

"You probably didn't know him—he went to the high school in Holyoke. Anyhow, Bill was drinking next to your old man all day and I guess that's all it took for Jim. Young Buddy knows as well as I do how soft he can get."

"But what's the scoop anyway, Ride? He wasn't always this bad. Since last year he's been worse, like she just died. I don't get it really."

"I have a hunch."

"What?"

"What did your papa say just now?"

"A bunch of drunk *crap*."

"No, he said you look just like Katie Faye."

Leo had never heard Ryder say her name before. He said it like he had lunch with her yesterday. "Did you know her pretty well?"

Ryder nodded. He started to sip his beer, but then stopped. "You do look an awful lot like her, Leo, now that you've lost your baby fat. That's what your father's been seeing lately, but it's not what you think. Jim isn't feeling bad 'cause you remind him of her. He's scared of losing twice what he already lost once, that's all. And it didn't help him today hearing about O'Donnell's boy."

Leo swallowed and looked down at the yellow linoleum floor. The rain had lightened up outside and was coming down through the trees like wet whispers. The bark on the pines looked rust-colored. "What's this Asian conflict about anyway? I don't even know what it's about."

"That'd be a damn good thing to write a song on."

"No, really. What are we fighting over there for? I don't get it. And what is so bad about communists? If Chick Donovan's one, how bad can they be?"

Ryder drank from his beer and nodded his head as if Leo had just made a very good point. "All I know, Young Buddy, is nobody's cozy talk is worth a tune when you're out there scared shitless, and freezin', and having a loud ugly hand in human death. To this day I cannot tell you what business we had in a civil war in Korea. But like I tell your pop, you stand a damn good chance of not even having to serve. So cross your fingers and forget about it is all I can tell you."

Leo looked outside where the last of the sun had broken through, and the pine needles glistened in the branches. He pictured Jim standing on the gravel down at the river, swaying a little on his feet.

Ryder walked into the parlor, then called Leo in for harp lesson number three. He had his harness on and after he warmed up with an A harp, he pulled out a C and started to sing:

"Allie's got a neck,
A neck so fine,
I want to kiss it,
Kiss it all the time—"

Ryder began to play a riff for the words when Leo shook his head and put up his hand to stop him. "We can't do that one."

"We can't? I came up with a melody for it."

"She's my girlfriend now."

"You work fast, kid."

"Not as fast as her." Leo's face got hot and he wanted to explain what he meant but the truth was in the heat of his cheeks and Ryder was drawing it in.

"I don't mean to pry, Leo, but humor your Uncle Ryder here and let him know you're taking precautions."

"Sure thing. Hey, listen to this." Leo started right in on the fo-wah see-you combo. He used as much air as he could without ruining a reed and he went too fast at first but when he saw Ryder smile he relaxed and brought the tune down to its natural rhythm. He closed his throat and fanned his cupped hand and finished off with a long squeezed *See you you you you.*

"Hot damnit, kid, that's one *heck* of a start. Here, do it again and I'll hop in on my G."

Leo played the exact same riff and when Ryder came in after the first fo-wah with a lower-pitched solo in a stripped down blues beat, Leo felt so right with the floor he was standing on and the air he was pulling through those tiny metal reeds that at first he didn't notice Jim had come into the room, taken out his guitar, and was sitting on the stool. As Leo kept playing, he watched his father fasten a capo around the neck, nod his head, tap his feet a few times, then start picking a sister arrangement to Ryder's lead. As soon as Leo finished his last "see you" note, he went back to fo wah and repeated the whole refrain. Then Ryder really took off on some wild hand-smacking combination that Jim matched with loud strumming chords. They kept on with it until Leo's tempo was beginning to lag and that's when Ryder slowed it down, then stopped altogether so Leo could take it out for the finish.

They went straight into two more songs together. This time Leo tried back up. The first song, a mournful one by Blind Boy Fuller, was easy in a way, once he found the right underbeat to stick in behind Ryder's lead. But the second, a Big Bill Broonzy room-mover, he got instantly lost in and he settled on coming in every few counts like an echo to Jim's singing. When the words ran out, Jim wound it down with a pick that Ryder went quiet for, then they pumped it back up and ended so suddenly it seemed the ringing silence in the air was the final note they'd all been aiming for.

"Hot damnit to *hell,* Jim, listen to that kid. He's kickin' our ass."

Leo was breathing hard. If he'd ever felt this good outside of being with Allie Donovan, he didn't know when or where or how.

"Quit the teaching," Jim said. "You're making yourself obsolete." He straightened up and slipped the capo off. "Let's do a Leadbelly number."

"I can't, pop, I gotta go meet Allie."

"Who do you meet in alleys?" Jim was looking up at Leo and he didn't seem drunk until he glanced at Ryder and missed him by about three feet.

"Young Buddy's in love, Jimbo. Put that in your smipe and poke it."

"Donovan's daughter, is it?"

"So the kid says. Fine neck I hear."

Leo laughed and went into the kitchen. He took the meat loaf from the oven, cut himself a heavy steaming square of it, put it on a plate in the fridge to cool while he washed up, and changed into a pair of clean jeans, a short-sleeved shirt, and sneakers. In Jim's room, he sprinkled Old Spice cologne on his comb and ran it through his hair. In the stand-up portrait on the bureau, Katie Faye was looking right at him. She was leaning on the hood of a black Ford Ryder had owned before Leo was born. A kerchief was on her head. She wore tight high-waisted slacks and a dark short-sleeved blouse. Her legs were crossed at the ankles and she was looking right into the camera, not showy, Leo thought, or like she was thinking how she looked. Katie Faye Suther's face said, "I'd kiss you if that camera wasn't in the way." Leo went into the kitchen and ate his cooled meat loaf. Jim and Ryder's music sounded greased and steady out in the parlor, and Leo pictured fast-talking Gerry Poitras working alongside Allie up at Beatrice's UFO Show. He scraped his plate, brushed his teeth, and was booking it for Paper Boulevard just as Lars's Rambler turned down Saunders Hill Road.

8

But there was nothing to worry about. Even with half the counter stools taken and all the booths filled with boys in cuffed jeans and tennis shoes and loose short sleeves, the girls in skirts and sleeveless tops, Allie interrupted an order to rush over and kiss Leo. There was only one other waitress working the floor, and she was way at the other end of the diner. Beatrice stood behind the cash register ringing up a check, peering over her half-glasses at Leo as if this on-the-job kissing was his idea.

"I'm done pretty soon, honey heart," Allie said. "Have a seat."

Leo sat one stool down from Beatrice and the cash register. To his left were two girls he didn't know. They both had dark shoulder-length hair. The one closest to Leo had hers held back with a tortoise-shell headband. They were talking about Jayne Mansfield getting killed in a car accident down in Louisiana. Leo listened up because he hadn't heard a thing about it.

"Her poor *children*," the headband one said. "Can you imagine seeing your mother's head get lopped off?"

Her friend covered her face with both hands and shook her head real fast. Allie took two plates of gleaming french fries from the grill window and placed them in front of the girls. When she served them their Cokes, she slipped one to Leo, smiling as she walked around Beatrice and the register carrying three dishes of vanilla ice cream on a tray.

Leo leaned forward to try to see GP through the window slot, but all he saw was sweating Sidney flipping something in the smoke. The jukebox played a Beatles song called "Help" from their movie. Leo thought it sounded all right, not bad, but so dry somehow, like those four guys had only half a body of blood in them. He wondered why there wasn't ever any real blues in those boxes, not Elvis or Carl Perkins, but more like Lightnin' Hopkins, Champion Jack Dupree, and one of the kings with the Harp of the Blues, Junior Wells. Just then Gerry sat down on the stool between Leo and the cash register. He was sweating so much his white shirt stuck to him in wet spots on his chest and stomach. He took off his UFO cap and wiped his forehead with it. "Didn't see you at the big grad."

"We went."

"We?" Gerry tucked in his chin and rolled his eyes. "You mean you and Miss Groovy over there, without one—count 'em folks—*one* powwow with yours truly."

"Sorry, GP. Long days."

"Long nights?"

Leo looked over his shoulder at Allie wiping down a booth table in front of three boys, her ponytail jerking and rolling across her back. He looked back at Gerry. "You hear about Mansfield?"

"Yeah, I think she gave a little too much head playing that one." Gerry laughed enough for both of them. He reached over and took a long swallow of Leo's Coke. "You got a sunburn."

"I'm a working man, GP."

"Yeah? Let's see your hands."

Leo held them out, palms up.

"You ain't workin'." Gerry turned his hand over in his lap. There was a long red line on the skin of his forearm from his wrist to his elbow. "French fry basket. Gets dangerous in there, pal."

"Try building a house."

Gerry stifled a belch, which he never did. "You get anything in the mail lately?"

"No, have you?"

Gerry nodded. He was looking down at his Coke glass and he

———

turned it in a slow circle with his fingers, keeping his hands still. "I got my notice." He glanced at Leo. "My old man opened it before I did. He had tears in his eyes. Can you believe that shit? *My* pop?"

"Shit, Gerry."

"Yeah, yeah, yeah." Gerry spun the Coke glass a couple of times. He was looking straight ahead, nodding and squinting like he was watching something far away. "Know what I can't stand? I'm at home, right, and I go into the kitchen for some milk and I notice the trash is full so I start to walk over to take it out to the garage, but just before I get to the bucket, Betty or my pop'll say, 'Hey, Ger, take out the trash,' and man, I'm tellin' ya, I wanna explode, because I was just about to do it on my own anyway and so then when I *do* do it, it's got nothing to do with what *I* want to do anymore, you know? It's highway robbery, man. Friggin' highway robbery."

"That happens to me sometimes."

"Yeah, well, same thing here."

"Where?"

"The marines, man. I've been plannin' on going in anyway."

"When did you plan this?"

"When did you start going with Miss Bell-bottoms? You want to go in with me?"

"The marines?"

"I talked to this guy in Springfield and they got this Buddy Program all set up. We go to boot camp together, grunt it out, then wango-bango, zoom into Combat Zone City."

Leo looked down at the counter. He smiled and wished he hadn't.

"Yeah? You in?"

"I don't know, GP. I haven't even registered yet."

"Yeah but, 'member when I talked you into going out for wrestlin' and you made varsity and friggin' loved it?"

"I *liked* it."

"Yeah, anyway, same thing. Except this time it's like going to the Olympics, you know? Much better than All-State. This ain't even the nationals; we're talking *world* shit here."

"I hope you two aren't talking baseball because I find it incredibly bourgeois and boring." Allie sat down on the stool between Leo and the Jayne Mansfield girls. She rested her chin on his shoulder and said to Gerry, "You swear a lot. Don't you think that compromises your integrity?"

"Integrity? Who's got integrity? I'm trying to talk Lucky Leo here into a little world adventure. Allison's not contrary to her man rubbing up against some world adventure, is she?"

"Not if it includes me."

"That's a laugh. Isn't that a laugh, Leo?"

"We gotta go, GP. We'll talk about it later, okay?"

"Nothin' to talk about, man. You're in or you're out."

Leo stood. "I'll see you 'round, buddy."

"You got it, the *Buddy* Program. Look it up, will ya? Just go look it up."

Outside, in the white and red light of Beatrice's, Allie put her hands on her hips and looked over the parking lot.

"I walked," Leo said. "My pop's wheels are down at the Elks."

"On a Wednesday night?"

"No, he's at home."

"Did he get a flat?"

"Nope."

"So let's go get it for him."

This was a good idea, an all-around solid thing to do. Allie picked up on things fast, and when she got out of work, she talked fast too. While they walked she went into great detail about the people she'd served from noontime to now: what they wore, how they ordered, what they ate, who sat with who, what they talked about, and how they tipped. All of this Leo listened to as far as the lighted marquees of the Fremont Theater. He kept holding Allie's hand while she went on and he thought of Jayne Mansfield's head rolling over asphalt in Louisiana, then he pictured Gerry's head tumbling over pitted ground in Cong Land, a smile still on his stupid second-string face. "Look it up." *Sure,* look it up, GP. As if hauling a machine gun is the same as running around a track with a gold medal hanging off you. *Jesus.* But this wasn't it, either. This wasn't the problem. Leo knew he wasn't avoiding any of this because he was scared; he wasn't any more scared than anybody. It was something else altogether. And he

51

wasn't sure what it was except he knew it had to do with the fact that nobody really talked about the war like you would expect people to talk about wars. Sure it was in the newspaper, but sometimes not even on the front page. Bill O'Donnell's kid gets killed over there and it's like hearing about a boy who rolled his car into a tree when he was drunk and out with somebody else's girl; you're sorry, a young guy is gone, but it's not the kind of death you describe with great respect to anyone. Instead a father might find himself drinking on a stool, saying it through some kind of squeezed voice to the big-chested man sitting next to him because his mill shut down for the day and so here he is to hear the secret. Only it shouldn't be a secret. None of this should be a secret. And while Leo knew that it really wasn't—there *were* headlines about the Yanks and the Reds—somehow the newspapers just seemed to be printing it the way they knew they were expected to, or maybe the way they did when we were all fighting swastika soldiers in the snow over in Europe and everybody was daily interested in what was what over there, the way people are when there's a house burning down on their street, or when a car crashes through the picket fence into their own yard.

At the high school in the library, Leo had seen the 1942 *Life* magazine pictures of men enlisting and getting their physicals, the photo of them standing around in their T-shirts and boxer shorts. One guy had a fedora hat on his head and looked into the camera with an unlit cigarette hanging between his lips while a doctor poked a needle into his arm. Behind him were other men waiting in the line that would get them into a uniform so they could all go over there to kick the crap out of those guys. And there were pictures of highway billboards urging everybody to save rubber and metal for the war effort. Fighting Yank U.S. Savings Bonds—all that stuff. But not this; not your best friend plopping down next to you on a diner stool and asking you to go to war with him like this is the opportunity of a lifetime and not many people know about it yet, so c'mon, man, before the train leaves the station.

In the well-lit stretch between two street lamps on Paper Boulevard, Allie stopped talking. They walked holding hands and except for the occasional skid of a pebble under their feet, things were quiet. The stars were out and Leo could smell spruce and wet asphalt. Then through the trees came the scant but steady sound of Jim Suther's guitar and high, singing voice.

"Hear my pop?"

"Is that him?"

"'Fraid so."

"Why afraid?"

"I didn't mean *that* way."

"Something's eating on you, sweetie. Is it me?"

Leo looked down at her. She was smiling so he knew she was only half-serious and he was glad about the serious part. He stopped to kiss her, and she tasted like french fries. She hugged him and he held her close and very tight and, shit, everything would pan out fine. Everything would.

The light from the kitchen shone out onto five cars and Dwight's van. Through the window Leo could see Lars leaning against the counter forking hunks of meat loaf out of the dish, shoving them into his mouth. Some man with a flat-top haircut was counting out the chips. Another man was shuffling cards. Dwight pulled a Narragansett from the fridge and walked into the parlor.

"They haven't started dealing yet. Stay here, I'll be right back with the keys."

"What do you mean, 'Stay here'? I want to meet your dad."

"No, later, Allie. He got pie-eyed today. Besides, not with those guys here."

Allie puckered her lips at him.

"Back in a streak."

The kitchen still smelled like the meat loaf Lars was just finishing off. He looked over at Leo and smiled with his full mouth. "Hey, Einstein."

The card shuffler laughed. Leo waved and went into the parlor where his father and Ryder were tapering off a fast Son House number called "Empire State Express." Jim started right in with something else when Ryder noticed Leo standing against the wall next to Dwight. "*Hey,* jump in, man." Ryder's voice was a little unsteady. There were five beer cans on the windowsill behind him. Leo noticed an iced coffee on the floor next to his father's stool.

"Can't stay, I need the keys to the car so I can go get it."

Jim stopped playing. "Where's Donovan's girl?"

"Chicken Donovan?" Dwight said.

Leo turned to look straight at him.

"That bastard's got a girlfriend?"

"Daughter," Ryder said, looking at Leo.

"She a red too? Or just a fucking beatnik."

"*Hey,* shut up, she's with me, all *right?*"

Dwight nodded and smiled.

"You apologize to Dewey right now," Jim said.

"What for?"

"Do what I tell you." Jim was up off his stool, stepping towards Leo.

"No."

Jim was still holding his guitar by the neck with his right hand, the hand he did everything with, and so Leo didn't see the left which was cupped and which hit Leo hard in the jawbone making him step sideways to keep from falling over.

No one said a word. Everything was quiet. In the kitchen the stranger shuffled the deck.

Leo brushed by Dwight, then was out the door which he slammed so hard Allie jumped. He grabbed her hand and walked fast into the shadows up the road.

"What *happened?*"

"My *father's* what happened, Mr. fucking Doom and Gloom is what happened."

Someone came running. Leo spun around ready to hit Jim if he had to, but it was Ryder, and he was already breathing hard. "Sorry about all that, Young Buddy. You did the right thing telling Dewey off. Don't take it too hard though; Jimmy's still half in the can and I know for a fact he's—"

"He's a *joke* is what he is, Ryder! A goddamn joke."

Ryder held his hand out to Allie. "Ryder Stillwell. Pleased to make your acquaintance."

"My name's Allie. Likewise."

Ryder handed the car keys to Leo. "If you're still up to it. Might get ticketed or towed, I guess."

Leo drove south along the river towards Springfield and Chicopee. Paper Boulevard narrowed once they left Heywood and there were no street lamps. At first, Allie had sat right next to him but as Leo's talking got louder, as he took one hand off the steering wheel to make a point, then the other, she moved a few inches over as if he were a growing fire that needed more air.

"I'm telling you I'm *sick* of it. Know the last time a woman stepped into my house besides you? Do you? Two-and-a-half years ago when Lars's wife had to come and get him, that's when. Know why my father never goes out on dates? Never drives over to other towns where there's a woman on every block? 'Cause he's a chicken shit, that's why. He likes to feel sorry for himself. The only things that mean shit to him are his guitar and the pictures of my mom. Not even her anymore, but the goddamn *pictures.* And Ryder talks to me ten times more than *he* does. *Twenty* times more."

"My father hardly ever speaks to any of us these days."

"And even in my own house, when a guy has just insulted my girl-friend, he doesn't stand behind me? He goes *against* me? Shit."

Leo slowed down and turned right onto Longbranch Road, wher-ever that was. His jaw was sore and at first he thought it was from talking so loud. Allie put her hand on his thigh near his knee. "Thank you for defending my honor like that, Leo. I would have done it myself, but I'm happy you did."

Leo glanced over at her. She was facing him. Sometime tonight she had pulled the rubber band from her ponytail and her hair hung past her shoulders around her face. In the dim light of the Valiant's dash she looked like a girl, nine, maybe ten years old.

Leo breathed in a chestful of air and let it out. He was glad he told Dwight off. And he knew if Dewey had said anything more he would have socked him right there. Defending honor. That was good, that was a good thing to do. And Jim can just talk to Katie Faye all night about it.

Allie moved in close. The road was fresh-paved and wide enough to be two lanes but there were no dividing lines. When it dipped before a hill Leo pushed the gas pedal to the floor, keeping it there

---

until just before the top of the rise. He pulled his foot back and the Valiant sailed past the hump out into the air where the headlights lit up trees and the road curved away from them, the lights hitting tall grass now as the car jolted then rolled into a small weed field. Allie was laughing. The car bumped to a stop and Leo turned off the ignition and lights. He stuck his head out the window and looked up at the sky. The Big Dipper was off to the east. Around it were clusters of other stars whose names he wished he knew. Allie put her hand on his leg and he started to sing: "Allie's got a neck,

> A neck so fine,
> I want to kiss it,
> Kiss it all the time.
> We got a house,
> Me and her on the hill,
> It's got a porch
> Bigger than the paper mill."

He stopped and sat up straight behind the wheel. "It sounds better with a harp, least that's what I wrote it for."

"When, Leo? When did you do this?"

"'Fore school let out."

Allie knelt on the seat and took his face in her hands.

"Ow."

"Oops, I forgot."

He kissed her and wrapped his arms around her narrow back. The road lit up behind them. A pickup truck went around the corner and down the hill.

"I want to hear you play sometime."

"I was blowing pretty good with Ryder and Pop tonight. Before, I mean."

"The only thing I do with my father is fold his pamphlets. Did he tell you he's driving over to Boston this weekend to pass them out to all the rioting Negroes?"

"Good, maybe he'll save *them* and you won't have to go south."

"You are so thoughtful, Leo. You are just so thoughtful and

debonair." She sat back on the seat and was quiet. They both were. She began to unbutton her UFO uniform in the dark. She got on her knees, then sat back down to get it over her head. Her small breasts barely moved as she leaned over and slid her panties off. Leo went to unsnapping and unzipping his jeans. His erection caught a second as he pushed his underwear down. He couldn't get them past the steering wheel so he scooted over and that's when she straddled his lap. He wanted to push his pants over his knees but it was too late now; he was inside her, inside the hot slip and squeeze of her. She started moving up and down, kissing his face, and he gripped her small hips with his fingers on her bottom, his thumbs on her hip bones. A car passed along the road behind them. Its lights swept the back of their heads and was gone.

9

It was probably ten when Leo dropped her off at the cabin on Spoon Hill. The bottom windows were dark but a front one on the second floor was lit up behind cotton curtains.

"See? Mom's up waiting for Daddio."

In the woods on the ridge fireflies pulsed and faded. Allie kissed Leo's cheek. "Love you."

"Me too, Allie."

"Good night, my defender."

Leo drove all the way to Springfield and back, figuring that would allow plenty of time for the men to leave, for Ryder and Jim to tidy up, for Jim to go to bed. It was a good drive too. Except for blowing the harp, it seemed like the best way to clear the brain, driving at night when hardly a soul is out, just you and the glide of your wheels, your headlight beams the only path you need, all those stars up there, not just the age-old witnesses they feel on normal nights, but more like invitations; come-on-up calls of the Jack London wild. And the Connecticut to his left, moving pale in the same direction, swirling and spilling over in the starshine. Leo imagined jerking the steering wheel left and crashing through the puny steel cable rail on into the water where he wouldn't sink but float, him and Allie cuddled up there in the front seat with the radio playing a sweet Skip James serenade, the river carrying them out of Massachusetts, straight through Connecticut, down into New York Harbor. They'd drift south to the big city where they'd rest and make love in some downtown bohemian motel. Leo would play blues in the streets at first and Allie could maybe tap her feet and look pretty, then they'd get their own club engagements, get married, buy a mansion on the Hudson River, have eight kids.

Leo wished he'd told Allie the true words instead of the weak and stupid "Me too." Because he *did* love her, didn't he? Wasn't she the absolute prime thing next to the harmonica and the time he played it? Wasn't she the kind of woman a man could depend on through fat times and skinny? A woman with a backbone and her own beliefs? That's important. All this is important. Shouldn't a guy turning eighteen think about these things in a very serious light? How is college, or finding a trade, or—for shit's sake—going off to Asia for medals, how are any of these things more important than finding the future mother of your children, your second half, your comrade until your teeth fall out? In fact, shouldn't finding her even come first and foremost? Would a guy go on a cross-country trip with only one gas tank if he could have two? And would a guy go to war with a single pack of ammo if he could have double? But no—this part didn't make sense. Why would a guy go to war at all if he had a good woman at home? *That's* why this war isn't quite on the level like wars should be. It had everything to do with women and children because it had nothing to do with them. In the other one Hitler was wiping out millions and taking over so who could say he'd stop at the ocean? And when the Japs did their bombing riff in Hawaii, things couldn't be more clear: kill or be killed. Paint the windows black, ladies. Ration your food, kids. Men, get your guns. It all made logical sense. But not this Cong stuff. This wasn't the same at all. Guys like Gerry Poitras went because they had nothing better to do.

But I know what *I* want: I want Allie and kids and more harmonicas, Leo thought. And he knew that she was the measurement of it all, that if this were a worthwhile war, then the more he loved Allie— and man, he did—then the more he would want to go fight for her permanent safety. Leo Suther was a defender. He had defended honor tonight and it had felt so natural that even with his own father's cuff in the jaw, his body had felt strong, his blood righteous, his voice resolute. So screw you, GP. You show me a real threat, not some Asian duck hunt we're not really needed in, and then I'll give it some serious thought, then I'll look you in the eye and we can talk lies and truth, but not this All-State, Olympic medal wet dream, Gerry. Not that.

Leo rested his elbow out the window and drove into sleeping Heywood. He felt as calm and clear, warm and loose-in-the-limbs as if he'd just made love again with Allie then played his harp for an hour straight. He'd planned on getting gas at the Esso station when he drove in, but it was closed and that was fine too; if it weren't for Leo, Jim's wheels would probably be chained to a tow truck somewhere anyway.

He shut off the headlights and eased the Valiant up alongside the house. There were no cars around, not even Ryder's Impala. The outside light over the screen door was on but the house was dark, and the kitchen smelled like cigar smoke and men's sweat. Leo was tired. His eyes burned and his throat felt thick, but his hunger was worse. In the fridge was the empty meat loaf dish streaked with tomato sauce. There were different kinds of unopened beer cans and bottles on the bottom rack, half a head of lettuce above them. Leo pulled out an uncovered bowl of beans and hot dog chunks from Tuesday night's supper. He opened the silverware drawer as quietly as he could, then sat at the table and ate in the light that came through the window from outside. He thought about him and Allie making love in the car, the way she rocked herself on his naked lap.

"It's late."

Leo jerked in his chair. In the doorway, Jim's Lucky Strike glowed.

"Get the car?"

Leo nodded.

"Yes or no, son."

"It's right out the window."

"Ease it down, Leo. Just ease it down." Jim walked into the kitchen in his robe. He turned the faucet on over his cigarette and dropped it in the sink. "Did you go out with your girl?"

"Yep."

"When do I meet her?"

Leo kept eating. Jim didn't seem to be waiting for an answer. Leo heard a moth's wings beating on the light bulb outside.

"Is she good to you, son?"

"Why wouldn't she be?" Leo swallowed and wiped his mouth.

"Because that's important. They should be good to you." Jim filled himself a glass of water and drank half of it. "We aren't always good to our loved ones, Leo. It's our nature. No excuse though."

Leo dropped his fork into the empty bowl. He wanted to get up and wash and go to bed.

"Do you like the carpentering? It's a damn good trade to know. You can always find work with that one."

"I guess."

They were quiet. Jim reached into his bathrobe pocket and lit another cigarette.

"Gerry got his draft notice."

Jim took a deep drag off his Lucky Strike, the tip glowing very bright. He blew the smoke out real slow. "When?"

"This week, I think."

Jim let out a long breath. He turned and doused his new cigarette under the faucet.

"Gerry asked me to go in with him. He says the marines have this Buddy Program. I think this war is screwed up though, Pop. GP thinks he's trying out for first string again or something."

Jim walked over, took Leo's bowl, and set it in the sink. "Let's get our rest, son. Let's go to bed."

Thursday morning the sky was gray and there were huge charcoal clouds over the field and spruce trees to the east. A cool breeze came from that direction, from out behind the barn, and three times before coffee break Floyd looked straight up and said, "Don't do it, you son of a bitch. Don't do it."

Chick had paired Leo up with Tom Burrell for the day, which felt like a promotion; the farther from Floyd Leo got, the more fortunate and sophisticated he felt. Packing a hammer and a nail apron around his waist helped too, though he wasn't using them. While Tom wrote down measurements Floyd called out to him, Leo set up two sawhorses in the gravel driveway, then loaded a dozen two-by-fours across them for cutting. By the time Leo plugged the power saw into the generator, Tom had gone to work measuring. He drew straight pencil lines with a combo square, then sheared through the wood, the metal-whine of the electric blade spraying out sawdust that sometimes hit Leo behind Tom, his hands on the middle of the two-by-four, ready to carry it over his shoulder to Floyd, who was assembling the new wall frame flat on the ground. He would just finish end-nailing one stud when Leo delivered the next. This framing lasted all of about thirty minutes, but the pure, sweating efficiency of it, the precise beauty of having the exact right man doing the exact right task left Leo feeling as solid and important a part of Donovan's Renovators as Chick himself, who wasn't even on the job, but was downtown with the flatbed buying coffee and muffins from Allie at Beatrice's.

Leo didn't mind missing her either; a little break in the routine would leave them hungrier for each other later. And besides, he thought, it'll be good for her to see her old man peppy and cheerful for a change. Leo didn't know what it was, but the Chick of the past week and a half—the quiet and distracted foreman, Mr. Silence when he dropped Leo off at the covered bridge after work—wasn't around today. At seven this morning, when Jim drove Leo up Spoon Hill, Chick was already coming off the porch all smiles and light on his feet. He was at the driver's window offering his hand before Jim had even opened the door.

"Chick Donovan. You must be Leo's father."

They shook hands. "You have a super fine young man in that Leo. Works hard, he concentrates, but most important of all—so damned important—he *listens*. Now that's a rare commodity in American youth, don't you agree?"

Jim nodded and looked out the window up at the sky over the

Donovans' cabin. "Stange is on the mound today. Hope you both don't get rained out." He waved at Chick, nodded at Leo, and backed down the hill.

"Fine, fine," Chick said, tossing Leo the truck keys. "Let's build that house."

And that's what they were doing all right. After Leo hauled the last stud over to Floyd, Tom called Leo into the barn and dropped a bunch of sixteen-penny nails into his apron pocket. Leo grabbed one more handful out of the box, then met Floyd and Tom at the new wall, which was still lying in the grass where Floyd had built it. With Tom at one corner and Floyd at the other, Leo squatted in front of the middle of the frame and on Floyd's "Ready, set, *heave*" they all three lifted the wall and leaned it against the first-floor frame under the second-floor winch. Tom had Floyd and Leo climb the ladder while he tied the rope to the top plate, stepped back, then raised the frame hand over hand up to them on the second story. After Floyd and Leo had it set on the floor, Tom climbed up and held the level to the vertical stud in the corner. He closed one eye and squinted at the tiny glass bubble. When he liked what he saw, he told Leo to drive two nails through the base plate between each stud, something Leo had never done before, but which, after the first few hammer misses, began to feel strangely natural, like running up a hill or climbing a tree. While he hammered, setting the nail heads deep into the wood, Floyd let loose nailing the corner stud into the wall frame they had put up yesterday afternoon.

Then Chick pulled into the driveway. He tapped the flatbed's horn, killed the engine, and got out carrying the cardboard coffee tray, the muffin bag hanging between his teeth.

"I should leave you fellas alone more often."

"Three's a divine number, Chick." Tom wiped the sweat off his forehead with the back of his arm, then climbed down after Floyd. Leo drove two more nails. He missed the last one once but then sunk it in three swings. He stood and dropped his hammer into his belt hook handle-first. He wiped the sweat off the way Tom did and joined the men.

"Your Coke's in the cab, Leo. Sorry 'bout that."

The driver's door was still open. Leo grabbed his soda fountain Coke off the seat. On the floor of the passenger side were three tall stacks of white papers. He took the lid off his Coke and sat on the other sawhorse near where Floyd was slurping his coffee with a mouthful of blueberry muffin. Chick and Tom were talking about buttressing the second-floor walls. Tom suggested they use scrap wood from the barn, and he had a few other ideas about how to proceed, all of which Chick nodded his head in agreement to. But it seemed to Leo Tom could have said, "Let's just burn it back down and go home," and Chick would have smilingly nodded his approval to that too.

"This sky gonna open up on us or what?" Floyd lit up an L&M, then flicked the smoking match onto the flatbed.

"No, amigo," Chick said. "It's going to leave us alone right through the weekend. And speaking of weekend, have you fellas got a minute?"

"That's up to *you*," Tom said.

"Well lookit," Chick leaned into the truck cab. "I was going to wait till lunch, but you've all had a good morning, so let's do it now."

"Here we go." Floyd blew smoke out his nose, shaking his head.

Chick came back and handed each of them a white leaflet. "Take your time with it, lads. Tell me what you think."

"You gotta be shittin' me." Floyd squinted through his smoke as he took the pamphlet.

"On the clock." Chick smiled. "It's short."

Leo took a bite of his corn muffin, sipped his Coke, and opened *The Negro Manifesto, compiled by Michael C. Donovan.*

Greetings Brothers and Sisters!

Read On and Be Inspired!

Change Is At Hand!

"The history of all hitherto existing society is the history of class struggles. Freeman and *slave*, patrician and plebeian, lord and serf, guildmaster and journeyman, in a word, oppressor and oppressed, stood in constant opposition to one another, carried on an unin-

———

63

terrupted, now hidden, now open fight, a fight that each time ended, either in *revolutionary reconstitution of society at large, or in the common ruin of the contending classes."*

My Negro comrades-in-arms, these words were written over one hundred years ago by the brilliant Karl Marx and Frederick Engels in France. Guess what? *You* are the modern "leaders of a new reconstitution of society at large."

Why?

Because you, above all others, are now prepared to go to the streets to fight and take what is rightfully yours. BUT BEWARE: DO NOT BE TRICKED INTO A PETTY WAR OF RACE HATRED. True, the white man is your enemy, BUT NOT ALL WHITE MEN, ONLY A SMALL FEW: THE BOURGEOISIE!

"The bourgeoisie is unfit any longer to be the ruling class in society, and to impose its conditions of existence upon society as an overriding law. It is unfit to rule because it is incompetent to assure an existence to its slave within his slavery."

How sad it is that in the one hundred years since these words were written, matters have only gotten worse. BUT, MY BROTHERS:

THAT APPLE IS NOW ROTTEN ENOUGH TO FALL FROM THE TREE! REVOLUTION IS AT HAND!

DOWN WITH THE SLUMLORDS!

DOWN WITH THE BANKERS!

RESIST THE DRAFT AND THE IMPERIALISTIC WAR MACHINE!

DOWN WITH THOSE POLICE WHO PROTECT ANY OF THE ABOVE!

We communists have been reproached with the desire of abolishing the right of personally acquiring property as the fruit of a man's own labor . . . hard-won, self-acquired, self-earned property! Do you mean the property of the petty artisan and of the small peasant, that form of property that preceded the bourgeois form? *There is no need to abolish that;* the development of industry has to a great extent already destroyed it, and is still destroying it daily.

Or do you mean modern bourgeois private property?

The distinguishing feature of communism is the abolition of bourgeois property. Modern bourgeois private property is the final and most complete expression of the system of producing

and appropriating products that is based on *class antagonisms,* of
the exploitation of the many by the few.

MY NEGRO BROTHERS, BOURGEOIS PROPERTY IS THEFT!

NO MORE GHETTOS!

EQUAL RIGHTS FOR THE NEGRO!

NO MORE RIGHTS FOR THE BOURGEOISIE!

UP WITH THE COMMON PEOPLE, BLACK AND WHITE!

THE FUTURE IS HERE!!

LET US ALL SEIZE IT AS ONE!!!

When Leo looked up, Floyd and Tom were still reading. Chick sat
on the back of the flatbed drinking his coffee. His eyes settled on
Leo, who nodded and bit into his muffin. The silence was unbear-
able. The breeze cooled the sweat on his back under his T-shirt, then
swept up his muffin paper and sent it down the driveway.

It was Tom who spoke up first. Floyd was still in front of the barn,
craning his neck at what he read when Tom walked over to Chick,
dropped the leaflet on his lap, and said, "Grow up, Donovan. What
the heck are you trying to prove?" Tom turned and walked straight to
the house frame, pulling his tape measure out as he went. Then
Floyd either actually finished or else took Tom's move as a cue; he
downed the last of his coffee, tossed his leaflet into the cab, and
shook his head on the way to the house. Leo didn't want to look at
Chick, but as he got off the sawhorse, he did. Chick was looking
right at him, waiting for the third verdict, and his face wasn't at all
what Leo expected. He wasn't sitting up straight with his chin out,
or shaking his head with a sigh at the stupidity around him; Chick's
shoulders were slumped, his mouth was slightly open, his eyes were
big behind his glasses. Leo stepped closer, out of Tom and Floyd's
earshot. "Can I keep this?"

"Do you comprehend it?"

"I think so."

Chick nodded. "I believe you do." He slid off the truck. Tom's
leaflet fell to the ground. Chick picked it up and pointed to one of
the paragraphs inside. "See this, Leo? 'The common ruin of the con-

tending classes.' That's what's coming if there's no leadership. Tommy and Floyd are asleep at the wheel and it's partly my fault. I keep them working and I pay them more than they earn, but if they were out of a job and couldn't find one, well then they'd be in the trenches smashing windows with our Negro brothers. It's that simple, isn't it?"

Chick hadn't shaved this morning, and even though the skin of his face was tanned, he looked pale. "But there's got to be compassion, don't you think, Leo?"

"Sure."

Chick gulped some of his coffee. "And this man King is beautiful but he doesn't seem to have a grasp of your average Jack. A man down is a man mad. It's natural. A crime against one is a crime against all; why don't people just inherently know that?"

Leo shrugged. He glanced at the house frame. Up on the second floor, Tom was watching them as he held the dumb end of the tape at the corner of the north wall while Floyd checked the length of the space where the new one was to go.

"Aching to get back to work, aren't you? You're conscientious beyond your years. I'm bucking you up to two dollars an hour, Leo. Starting now."

The rest of the morning until the rain came, Leo hauled more two-by-fours from the barn to the sawhorses for Tom to measure off and cut for the north wall. But now Chick was working too, helping Floyd fasten the frame together on the ground, so Leo carried two studs at a time to them instead of one. Chick set the ends in and nailed them in no time, and Leo had to jog back and forth between the men. When they raised the frame, Chick stood on the second floor to guide it all into place, then began nailing the base plate off. He buried each nail in three blows, and as he finished one nail, he already had the next one set up in his fingers so there was never any pause, and no point in interrupting him either. Leo stepped back and watched Chick speed along much faster than Floyd, who was working on the corner studs while Tom held a plumb level up to them.

It was close to lunch and the breeze from the field had turned into a gusting wind. Leo started for the barn to get his overshirt, but then the sky buckled and the rain came down like it had been waiting weeks to do it. He unplugged the power saw from the generator and ran into the barn. Tom followed. He took the tarp from the stockpile and draped it over the generator outside. Then he took a sawhorse and wedged it legs-first over the canvas. Chick rolled up the windows in the flatbed's cab and came running inside with Floyd.

"Didn't I tell you cats? Didn't I? Rain Central." Floyd already had a cigarette lit. Leo pulled off his wet T-shirt and put on his dry button-down.

"She'll break soon enough." Chick took his glasses off and ran his hand back through his wet hair. His eyes were small and bloodshot, like he needed a month of naps.

"That's your problem," Tom said from the doorway. "You're a bad judge of weather and a even worse judge of character. This rain's been building since five this morning and let me tell you something, you try and pass that godless dirt out in a colored riot you're gonna wish you didn't."

"*Amen,*" Floyd hooted.

Chick put his glasses back on without wiping them off. He rested his hands on his hips. "I have respect for you, Burrell, but you're tiny."

"Hey now—"

"The world is not composed of you and your little clan. You think your Lord wouldn't want you concerned about the Negro and the poor? Hate to break it to you boys, but our world is on fire these days. The time is now."

"For what?" Floyd said. "You gonna burn a bank?"

"Maybe."

"You're nuts."

"I'm informed. I've tried to inform you as well. Leo here has more on the ball than you two put together."

Leo looked at the ground, his heart shifting into second gear.

"Leave him alone," Tom said. "He doesn't buy any of your malarkey."

"Do you, Suther?" Floyd said.

Leo looked out at the rain and shrugged.

"Smart kid," Floyd said. "Won't bite the hand that pays him."

"Don't count on it," Chick said. "His daddy's a union man—"

"His *daddy*? Give him his due, man. A year from now this kid'll be mowin' down reds. What branch you hopping into, Leo? Gonna be a jarhead like Pretty Boy Floyd here or what?"

"*Empty* jarhead," Chick said.

"Watch it."

"Emptier than empty, the worst."

Leo's face was hot. How all this conversation had landed around him, he didn't know. Maybe it was because he stood in the middle of the barn. He smiled and walked to the wall. He leaned against it not far from Tom, but he must have missed something because Floyd and Chick were looking right into each other's faces. Floyd's eyes were open wide, his damp forehead all ridges.

"Is there any goddamned war you'd fight, comrade?"

"I fight one everyday, kid. Guess who the enemy is?"

"You wouldn't last a day in the Corps. They'd cut you to shit."

"Mind your mouth, sonny."

"Hey, you two."

Chick shot a look at Tom. "You think this is kids' stuff, Burrell? *Read the papers.* We've lost twelve thousand boys since sixty-one! We're shipping them home every goddamned day and it's mindless shitbrains like Floyd here who tell 'em to go!"

Floyd took a lunging step to push Chick in the chest, but Chick grabbed his wrists and swung him backwards into the barn wall. Floyd's head whacked a cross brace between two studs, his eyes rolled back, his arms went loose, and in that half-breath before Chick moved again, Leo knew Floyd was about to go down anyway and Chick had to have seen it too but that didn't stop him from rushing in and slamming his right fist into Floyd's mouth. Chick set his feet and slugged Floyd in the cheek, then he pulled back and shot one into Floyd's nose, the blood squirting out in three directions as Tom came up and yanked Chick away like he was a small child.

10

Even with Floyd moaning in the back seat of the station wagon, holding a blood-soaked bandanna to his swollen face, Tom Burrell drove as slow and deliberate as he did everything else. The rain hadn't let up, but was coming down harder than ever. Leo sat in the front and could barely see through the windshield, though the wipers were going top speed. When he could see the river road, there were boiling brown puddles three or four feet wide. The roof of Tom's car was a drum.

"I'm gonna kill him." Floyd's voice sounded weak and nasal, like someone was pinching his nose though that was impossible because Floyd could barely touch it himself. "He's dead. I swear to God, he's dead."

Leo smiled at those words coming from that Mickey Mouse voice, and he remembered how when Floyd was still out, crumpled against the wall in the dirt, Chick, still breathing hard, had looked down at him and said, "I won't be in tomorrow." Then he walked to his flatbed in the rain, climbed inside, and backed as slowly out of the drive as if he were off to pick up more nails.

"Well," Tom said to the windshield, "I'm through after this job. I've had it."

"How long have you worked for him?"

"Till today I've always taken his politics with a grain of salt because he's been good to me, number one, and because I'm a Christian, number two. But he's off the deep end now. I don't want anything more to do with him."

"He's a dead man," Mickey Mouse said from the back.

"Three years, Leo. Floyd's been with him for two."

Leo felt strangely wonderful and he wasn't sure why, but as Tom drove through the dark dry comfort of the covered bridge, then out again into the rain, Leo knew he had to see Allie. "You going to Holyoke Hospital?"

Tom nodded, though he looked like his mind was still deeply on Chick.

"Mind dropping me off at Beatrice's?"

In this pelting wet gray, the red and white lights of Beatrice's UFO Show stood out like bright electric hope. Except for a man in a short-sleeved shirt and tie sitting in a back booth with a cup of coffee, the place was empty. Allie stood at the register reading a book propped on the open cash drawer. She didn't look up when Leo walked in, his hair dripping onto his forehead. Leo could see around the corner through the grill window. Sidney was in the way-back talking to Gerry and a girl in a waitress dress. The girl was doing something with her hands, cutting potatoes probably.

"*Hey*," Leo whispered. Allie looked up, and blinked once before she smiled. Leo pecked her on the cheek, then he pulled her to the door, out of Sidney's sight, and kissed her a good one.

"Ooo, what's the occasion?"

"You're the occasion, you are. Guess what your old man did today?"

"Uh, let's see, he gave you the day off because of this bummer rain."

"Nope. He beat the crap out of Floyd Starrett."

"You're pulling my toe, Leo."

"Nope. Floyd went after your pop for calling him a mindless shit-brain, and Chick put him up against the wall and knocked him out."

"Knocked him *out?*"

"I think he broke his nose, too."

"Wow."

"Excuse me, Romeo and Juliet." Gerry stood at the counter with his arms folded across his chest. His UFO cap stuck out his back pocket like a tail. "You still need a ride home, Allie?"

"You were going home?" Leo turned back to Allie.

"It's going to be a dead lunch. Gerry was kind enough to offer me a ride."

"In what?"

Gerry smiled. "Betty sold me her Corvair. You comin'?"

"Of course he's coming." Allie turned to Leo. "We're going to your house, right?"

The short ride to Saunders Hill Road took twice as long in the rain. Leo sat in the rear. It felt strange seeing the backs of his buddy's and girlfriend's heads up there together. GP must've misunderstood what Allie'd said because when they got to the house, he turned off the engine and got out of his car too. In the kitchen, he went straight to the refrigerator. "Just look at all those beers, won't you?"

Leo took a close look at the post-Wednesday-night variety: half a six-pack of Narragansett, one untouched case of Miller cans, a full six of Pabst, and an unopened quart of Budweiser.

"What're you gonna offer your guests, pal?" Gerry's wide cheeks went into a tight smile that was absolutely without warmth. Leo grabbed the Narragansetts, set them on the table, and opened one for Allie and another for himself. He handed the bottle opener to Gerry, then went into the parlor after Allie.

GP followed. "What, no toast, Leo? Rude, man. Very rude."

"Yeah, let's toast." Allie was squatting on the floor in front of the record player, thumbing through all the blues records so fast she couldn't possibly be reading the names of any of them. She picked up her untouched Narragansett and joined Gerry and Leo standing at the window. The rain ran down the glass panes in small clear rivers, and there was a fine mist out in the trees.

"You're the host."

Leo held up his bottle, glanced at grinning Gerry, then settled his eyes on Allie. "To Truth City."

Allie smiled and drank.

"To *what?*"

"Just what I said, GP."

Gerry Poitras guzzled his beer. On his way into the kitchen, he burped.

"You really think he's kind?" Leo whispered.

"When did I say that?"

"At Beatrice's."

Allie cocked her head. "You're not getting into an ownership trip here, are you, Leo? I mean, I don't have to start watching what I say, do I?"

GP came back into the parlor sipping from the quart bottle of Budweiser.

"Why don't you just make yourself at home, Ger?"

"Don't mind if I do." Gerry sat on the couch and propped one foot on Jim's guitar stool. "Here I am, a *graduate,* with two high school kids. *Man.*"

"Lonesome, isn't it, Gerry?" Allie sat down next to him.

Leo put on a 1938 Big Bill Broonzy record with Albert Ammons on the piano. As soon as Big Bill started in C with "Louise, Louise," Leo zipped to his room and got his harmonica. He came back and turned up the record player in case he made too many mistakes, though he didn't think he would. Ammon's piano and Broonzy's guitar were already doing backup, so Leo hopped in as a harp echo to Broonzy's crooning. He kept his eyes closed, like Ryder, and when he was sure he was in the groove with Big Bill, he blew the reeds as loud as he could. He wanted to open one eye to catch Allie's face, but he couldn't without looking showy, so he kept them shut and pictured himself playing to one of those crowded and dark little coffee houses Ryder had once told him about jamming in. But Ryder had bluesed in a club in Springfield and Leo was thinking Chicago all through the number. At the finish, he drew out a long wah, wah, wah right up into the intro of the next song. When he opened his eyes to the blue and brown shadows of the parlor, he felt like he'd just blown up three balloons and he needed to sit down. Allie was smiling at him, but Gerry was nowhere in sight. "Where's GP?"

Allie said something Leo couldn't hear over Broonzy. He got up and turned the record way down. "Gerry?"

"He was sort of rolling his eyes while you played. I think he left."

Leo walked through the kitchen to see for himself. GP's Corvair was gone, all right. Rainwater had already filled his tire tracks.

Allie came up from behind and kissed Leo on the neck. "You're pretty good. Better than I imagined."

"You should hear Ryder."

"I just want to hear you."

"You don't want to hear Gerry sometime?"

"What?"

"You know, tell his jokes and stuff."

"Oh just kiss me and be quiet."

Under the wise hungry eyes of Big Bill Broonzy, in front of the chest of drawers, Allie got naked. She did it slow but without putting on a show. She unbuttoned her dress to her flat belly, slipping first one shoulder out, then the other. She shimmied the dress down her hips, stepped out of it, then laid it neatly across the top of the bureau. When she reached back to unhook her bra, her eyes caught Leo's and they stayed there until she turned to place her bra and panties on her dress. Leo got out of his shirt and jeans much too fast, he thought, but he couldn't stand there completely nude like her, not with an erection pointing at the ceiling. He slid under the top sheet and light blanket of his bed, holding the corner up for her to get in too. And there was no hurry, no rush. They had almost three hours in front of them before Jim came home. This was the sort of afternoon other boys only dreamed about, but other boys didn't have Allie Donovan, Leo thought, just him, just Leo, and everything about the way she kissed his forehead, the top of his nose, both cheeks, his chin, the way she licked his lips open, then ran her tongue in past his teeth, said this fever was for keeps; these fast shallow breaths, these open legs, this faint smell of hers, the river's mud at noon—and then this—oh, man, this: her heels nudging the backs of his legs as he pushed into the wet sheathed heat of her.

And this could end and they could rest and do it again, but this one was going on a long while, and for most of it their mouths were pressed together, their tongues curled and locked inside, the rain whipping the roof of the house. Allie turned her head and took a heaving breath. She straightened her legs, arched her bottom slightly off the bed, then trembled and nodded as she breathed out, "Baby, *oh.*" Leo began to shudder, then he released what had been building all day.

There was no more wind outside; the rain came down steady through the trees onto the roof of the cabin. Leo and Allie lay in bed together and listened to the muffled hit of it on the shingles above them. There were fewer shadows in the room than before. Leo was on his back and Allie on her side. She was humming a Joan Baez song Leo had heard on the radio before about being a thousand miles from home. When she ended it, he could hear the river down the hill. It was gushing. There would be flash floods all over. Allie hummed another song, a sweet one she didn't finish because he turned and started kissing her, was inside her before she was even on her back.

They took a bath, and with Jim coming home soon and all, even with the rain, they were careful not to wet their hair. Leo dabbed suds on Allie's nipples. She laughed and sculpted a soap beard on his face. After, Leo dressed back into his work clothes while Allie stood at the bathroom sink in her bra and panties and scrubbed tiny fry stains from her UFO dress. She wanted to use the iron, but Leo didn't know where it was. Jim used one sometimes, when Leo wore a button-down shirt to school, or those rare Sunday mornings when he and his father drove up to the St. John's Church in Holyoke for mass, where his mother was buried. So Allie hung the dress on a hanger from the shower curtain rod, turned the water on as hot as it could go, then shut the door on it and steamed the wrinkles out.

When Jim pulled his Valiant up to the screen door, the rain had stopped and the sun was burning a hole through the clouds. The water trickled off the ends of pine branches. It ran out the gutter and splashed onto the gravel of Saunders Hill Road. Leo threw away the empty beer bottles and stood at the counter with Allie so they could watch Jim as he leaned into the front seat for his metal lunch box and a bag of groceries. Either his hair was wet or he'd gotten it cut today, Leo couldn't tell, but it was definitely closer to the sides of his head. His black moustache looked thick as ever.

"He's so handsome, Leo. God, how do I look?"

Leo pushed open the screen door.

"Get rained out at work, son?"

"Yep."

Jim stepped sideways to squeeze by.

"Hi, Mr. Suther. I'm Allie."

Jim almost took a step back. "Well." He set the groceries and lunch pail on the table, then shook her outstretched hand. "Finally we meet. You're lovely. She's lovely. Why didn't you tell me?"

Allie laughed and glanced at Leo as she let go of his father's hand.

Jim said they were having lasagna tonight and won't she join them. While Leo set the table for three—something that only happened on a rare Wednesday night when Ryder ate something—he watched and listened to Jim and Allie as they worked alongside each other at the counter. Jim had changed out of his mill overalls into a clean pair of Sunday slacks and a short-sleeved shirt. Allie had insisted on helping, and even though she was still in her UFO uniform, Jim said that he'd take it personally if she didn't wear his apron. While he browned the hamburger in a skillet, Allie diced up two onions and scraped them in on top of the meat. Jim pushed the tomato sauce can and opener over to her. "Those onions don't bother you?"

"Nope, never have. Besides, I like it here too much to get wet eyes."

Jim smiled at Allie on that one. He took the tomato sauce she'd opened and poured it into the sizzling meat and onions, making them quiet. He stirred and asked Allie to fill another pot with hot water for the noodles.

"I've never liked that word, have you?"

At first Leo thought she was talking to him, her voice was so calm and warm and at home, but she was looking at Jim. "It sounds too much like poodles," she said, "and I just can't tolerate those little creeps."

Jim laughed an honest-to-God laugh. He took the box of dry noodles, opened it, and handed it to Allie. "You're right. They are little creeps. 'Poodles, Those Little Creeps!' We should do a song on that one, Leo."

"After supper." Leo walked up and leaned against the counter.

"How 'bout right now?" Jim handed the wooden spoon to Allie. "If you will look after the sauce and the poodle noodles a moment." He bowed his head slightly, then left the kitchen.

Leo moved up behind Allie and wrapped his arms around her waist. He kissed her on the neck and cheek. "This is amazing, Allie. *You're* amazing."

Jim came back from the parlor tuning up his guitar. He winked at Leo and smiled at Allie. "This is a blues house, young lady, but we can do this song in any form you'd like."

"Oh, I love blues music, Mr. Suther."

"Jim. Please call me that."

"Okey doke, how do we start?"

———

Leo stepped in and sang a standard blues intro. "Lord, we got a poodle that sits on your lap."

Jim zipped in with a railroad track picking in G. He nodded and smiled at Allie at the stove. Her face was flushed, but she held up her wooden spoon and in a sweet flat voice sang, "All it ever does is go yappity yap yap."

Jim and Leo laughed. Jim built the chording up to his intro. "If you think that's bad then, Mister, you ain't got a clue."

Leo hopped in, "'Cause what that dog does next is take a poodle crap on you."

Allie laughed and whacked the wooden spoon on the skillet, splattering some sauce on the wall. Jim bent over laughing while he played. Leo pulled his harmonica from his back jeans pocket and came in with almost the same lead riff they were singing. Jim nodded in time, then struck some back-up chords as he dovetailed in with a high-crooning chorus:

"He'll take a crap on you,
  He'll take a crap on you,
  Lord, Mister, I ain't lyin',
  That creepy little poodle will do a
  Poodle little doodle on you!"

They were all laughing, and Jim tossed in a mix of lead chords, really picking away, before he toned it down for his son's harp, the two of them taking it out together, drawing it out on the same bent note.

After supper Jim brewed up a pot for his iced coffee. He offered Allie some and she asked for a hot cupful. Black.

"Just like Chick likes it, huh?" Leo said in the parlor.

"Nope, just like my *mother*."

Jim walked in holding Allie's coffee cup and saucer with two hands. She stood to take it from him.

"Would you like to see some pictures of Leo's mother?"

Allie said she'd love to.

If Leo had ever seen his father like this, he didn't know when. A dream, maybe. Even just now, when Jim mentioned Katie Faye, his voice stayed up, his face too. He smiled at them both as he left the room.

"Allie honey, I'm about to pass out."

"Why? What's wrong?"

"Jim is never like this, ever. The only time I even saw him close to this was a night he kept winning at poker and he was feeling no pain anyway. He loves you, Allie; I'm not kidding."

"He's so sweet. I can't imagine him getting mad at you."

Leo leaned over and kissed her on the cheek as Jim came in carrying a Heywood Paper Products cardboard box. "I got more poems here than pictures. Why don't you sit between the two Suther men, Allie?"

Jim rested the box on his lap. Suther *men*. Leo let that one echo through him. A beer last week, Suther men tonight. He laid his arm on the couch back behind Allie's head, his fingers touching his father's shoulder.

"Our good friend Ryder took this one."

Allie held the snapshot in front of her. Jim and his wife stood in a brick alleyway in the daytime. Jim wore a dark tie and overcoat that looked too small for him. Katie Faye was in a blouse, dress jacket, and skirt. She wore dark lipstick. Her hair was pulled up tight on one side of her head. They had their arms around each other and they had either just stopped laughing, or they were about to start.

"Where was this taken?" Allie said.

"Fifty-seventh Street, New York City."

"No way," Leo said.

"Sure, you were there, too. Sleeping in this." Jim handed Leo a picture of the same Ford that was in the bedroom dresser portrait of Katie Faye, only in this photo Ryder sat on the hood with a bottle of beer between his knees, smiling skinny-necked at the camera. His cowboy boots stuck out from his legs and made him look bonier than ever. He wore a string tie and a white shirt under an aviator leather jacket.

"Is that the man I met the other night?"

"Yeah, that's Ryder," Leo said.

"We heard some good sessions down there that time. Some jazz we never even *knew* about. But once we got up into Spanish Harlem, boy, we didn't want to leave." Jim took out another picture. He and Katie Faye were sitting on the bottom concrete step in front of a brick building. Above them were Ryder and a small Negro woman with a city man's hat on her head, big round earrings on her ears.

"Where's Leo?"

"Sleeping again, I think. Probably up in that girl's place above us. I forget her name. She loved Leo's Uncle Ryder, though. We met her at a club up on 131st Street. See, Ryder got drunk and hopped up on stage to play with Joe Alvin Brown. Before we knew it he was up at that microphone blowing his harmonica to Joe Alvin's guitar. That little girl came up to our table afterwards. Stayed with us the rest of the weekend."

"Your wife was beautiful."

Jim looked at Allie. He looked at the picture again, then reached into the box and unfolded a sheet of red-lined notepad paper. "This is called 'Man in his Buick.'

> Surely it was the uniform, you say
> that pulled me in that day
> or it must've been his big hands
> and little feet,
> the way he parked at the
> curb and
> got out so sweet.
> He played the guitar
> or so everybody said.
> He'd walk down the street
> and all the gals would drop dead.
> But it was none of these things that made my heart crack;
> it was when this man Jim,
> drove down the road, in that shiny big Buick,
> that Buick so black.

Allie laughed. "That's really good."

"I'm glad you like it."

Jim reached into the box again. Leo looked across the small room and out the parlor window. The sun had burned through the clouds on its way down behind the Berkshire Mountains. The pine trunks and branches glinted wet.

Jim took out another poem. "She wrote a lot her last year. Most of them sounded like this." He cleared his throat. His hand trembled slightly and he handed the paper to Allie. "I can't read that one, I'm afraid."

Allie held it so Leo could read it too, both to themselves:

When I Found Out

When I found out, I already knew—
like wet grass drying in the sun
like snow falling down instead of up
like beavers building nests in
water, there was no other way for things to go,
and when I found Jim,
I already knew my path would now hold two—
we made love under dogwoods,
we woke and dressed and ate
our days—
it wasn't my breasts, tender to touch,
it wasn't the mornings, squeezing me
in, it wasn't my cycle, gone upriver;
when I found out about my Leo, I already knew:
my path would now hold
three.
When he was five
things weren't right with me, and I already knew—
before the spells when I couldn't
sit or stand,
before the pains sent
me to my hands
before the doctor told me
the news—

Better me than my baby Leo
Better me than my wonderful Jim

When I found out,
there was just no other way for things to go
it was the earth tilting
the trees swaying
window panes that crack in winter,
Lord,
I already knew.

Allie lowered the poem to her lap. Leo swallowed before he spoke. "How come you never showed me this?"

Jim was looking straight ahead. He sipped his iced coffee and shrugged. "It wasn't time." He gently took the poem from Allie and put it back in the box with the pictures.

"Was it cancer?"

Leo's father folded the box flaps together so they stayed shut. He nodded once. "She was twenty-six."

They were quiet a few seconds. Leo wanted to get up off the couch and go walking alone. The river wash was louder than before and the birds—starlings maybe, or sparrows—were making all sorts of noise down there.

"I see you've been listening to Broonzy."

"Leo was playing his harmonica with it."

"He's learning fast."

"Hey, why don't you guys do another song together?"

"No, Allie. I'm not good enough yet."

"You are so."

"Tell you what," Jim said. "We'll do a slow one. We'll do 'Blues in G' by Mance Lipscomb. Just give me a few minutes to say my prayers down the hill and we'll get started." He stood up with the box and looked down at Leo. "I'll put this in your room in case you want to go through it."

*   *   *

By midnight the river still gushed, but not so loud Leo couldn't hear the gurgle of it over low rocks in the eddies. There was no wind, no moon. The air was heavy and he'd thrown off his sheet. A mosquito flew low at one ear, then went quiet before it feinted at the other. Outside smelled like wet wood and earth, and something he couldn't name, a flower of some kind, blue dogwood maybe, or lady's slippers, just the hint of diesel gas, though he didn't know why. He didn't know anything, he'd decided; he didn't know his father, he sure didn't know Katie Faye, he probably didn't even know Ryder like he thought he did. Skinny Ryder with the pointed cowboy boots, who was almost always clean shaven and carried four or five Heywood Paper ballpoint pens in his front shirt pocket. Nobody would look at him and say that this man has slept with a Negro woman in Harlem, New York City. But then nobody could look at him and know what a king with the Harp of the Blues he was either.

And Floyd Starrett. Who could've called him going down so fast and easy? With his veins and leathery muscles, the Marine tattoo on his neck, those gray flames-for-eyes? Who can ever really know anything about anybody unless they're just told straight out? Like Jim saying to give him a few minutes to say his prayers down the hill. Now why didn't he ever say that before? He never said he prayed down there. If Allie hadn't been here—so warm and funny and sweet—would he have put it that way at all? Or would he have just walked down to the river without a word? The truth is, Leo thought, if Jim hadn't taken to her, that box full of Katie Faye would have stayed in his room, and then when would it be time?

Leo thought about that one awhile. He understood what Jim meant about waiting to show him, but why tonight? When they weren't alone? Is that why women are needed in a house? Maybe that's why Gerry Poitras and his old man are so chummy; they've got Betty in the house with them. Mr. Poitras is a positive pole, GP's the negative, and Betty's the wire. Something like that. A tree connecting the leaf to the ground.

The room was so dark Leo saw the same blackness whether he

closed his eyes or kept them open, but he looked in the direction of the bureau anyway, in the direction of that Heywood Paper Products box.

Better me than my baby Leo
Better me than my wonderful Jim

Leo thought of that picture of Jim and Katie Faye in the alley in New York City, the one of them hugging. And that was the thing of it. Tonight, after watching how cordial, charming even, Jim had been with Allie, it didn't take much work to picture him being a husband. A lover even, to picture Jim Suther being a lover.

Leo closed his eyes. The mosquito lit in around his head again but it never landed and he began to hear it as a high treble to the river's rushing bass. He remembered how this afternoon, before he and Allie took the bath together, she had walked naked into the kitchen for a glass of water, her blond hair swinging, her bottom pale and perfect as she disappeared around the corner. His penis grew heavy. It ached slightly and he rested his hand on it, but that was all.

He was breathing long now, and soon he saw birds down in the trees by the river: blue jays and cardinals, hummingbirds and ravens, blackbirds and crows. It was dusk and Jim was down on the bank yelling something up at them or the sky or both, then one by one the birds flew up out of the branches and headed east, but they flew strangely; their wings seemed to flap higher than they needed to and their feathers fanned out in a huge hump behind their little heads. Then Leo was up there with them and it was clear why they flew the way they did: each bird had her beak tucked in tight to her chest as if she was carrying something very precious there, something Leo just could not see.

11

Theresa Donovan stood at her front bedroom window and watched the green Chevy station wagon take the turn for the climb to their house. It was a quarter after six. The sun hadn't come up yet, and down the hill the river was wide and a deep brown, not a boulder in sight. The trees in the national park beyond Heywood looked purple. Chick stepped off the porch to meet the car. He was carrying three cardboard boxes of his manifesto pamphlets, the top box almost reaching his chin. He wore a clean pair of dungarees, boondocker boots, and a faded button-down work shirt open at the collar. Two college boys hopped out of the car. The driver had short bristly red hair and a patchy beard. He wore corduroys and a plaid shirt and Theresa felt hot just looking at him. The other student was tall with wide shoulders, a deep chest and a belly that hung over his beltless denims. He wore a white sleeveless T-shirt. His arms looked like stuffed sausages as he took the boxes from Chick and walked around to the rear of the station wagon. She thought he looked like a football player, and she smiled and almost laughed at the irony: a communist on the gridiron. God. She watched as the big one slid the boxes into the rear of the station wagon, closed the door, and climbed into the back seat so Chick could sit in front: their guru, their king. The bearded one backed the car, then drove down the gravel drive of Spoon Hill. It was still wet from yesterday so no dust shot up behind them as they turned right and disappeared into the trees.

Theresa lifted the hem of her afghan and walked downstairs for coffee. She poured the last of Chick's brew, black as roof pitch. She usually made her own: weaker, more sane. On the back porch, she sat and watched the first amber band of light come over the ridge through the trees. A robin landed on the clothesline pole in the field, then took off just as quickly. To her right, Chick's heavy boxing bag swayed slightly on its chain. She'd heard him punch it two or three times just before he left. His barbell was on the floor up against the porch railing, four different-sized iron plates on each end of the bar. He had exercised with it yesterday, though that wasn't one of his normal days for doing so, and he did it in the rain, in his work clothes, at noon. She had been preparing two plates of crackers, cottage cheese, and sweet pickles for her and Christopher when the flatbed drove up. Christopher had just resumed drawing color pictures on the floor and he had finally stopped crying after being interrupted so Theresa could drive Allie to work. Chick walked right around the cabin, his glasses so wet he couldn't possibly be seeing much in front of him. She heard the light clanking of the barbell plates as he stepped off the porch, and she noticed he didn't do his usual warm-up movements with a broomstick but went directly to work pushing the loaded barbell over his head, lowering it, then pushing it back up at arm's length again and again. The rain soaked him and dripped off the iron bar, the corners of his glasses, the tip of his nose. She heard thunder south of them and she thought of her husband as nothing but an invitation for a lightning bolt. She walked to the back screen door and called out to him that if it was too wet to work then it was too wet to do that, sweetheart, come inside. But he didn't even glance at her. He rested the bar on the ground, bent his neck sideways as if to work out a kink, then he squatted, hoisted the bar to his shoulders, and went back to his lifts and grunts in the rain. She watched him. She thought how she would tell Allie: "Your father's dead. He was hit by lightning. He wouldn't listen to me." Then she felt Christopher's little arm around her leg, saw him peering through the screen. He said, "Daddy out. See?"

"Let's eat. He'll be in pretty soon."

But he wasn't. He was out there for over an hour, and when he was through, he stepped back up on the porch, put on his leather gloves and punched that canvas bag, the rafters shaking whenever the chain jerked on its hook.

Tess sipped her coffee as a flash of orange came over the ridge. The sun came after, and even with the hardwoods and brush in front of it, she had to look away. She got up and walked through the house. Chick's sheet and pillow were still on the couch. She stepped out front and sat on the porch steps. The light was bringing out the blue in the river, and the tree trunks on the national forest hill were more red now instead of purple, the pine branches yellow. All of Heywood was still in shadow, its buildings brown and gray, and Theresa took a deep, shuddering breath. Her eyes filled and emptied themselves down her cheeks. Not so long ago she would have felt grateful for such beauty, for her witnessing of it to enter her like a lover. She would have breathed it in and later, when she was still full, she would go to her easel and paint. She still painted. When Chick wasn't asking her to proofread or to type, or to collate, she did it three or four mornings a week. Her latest landscapes were stacked against the walls of their bedroom, which doubled as her studio. And Lord, that was it. It wasn't much of a bedroom at all any longer, not where a man and woman rest together, talk, make love. It was where Chick crash-landed after a full day of carpentry and a long night of meetings with the Communist Workers Brigade in Amherst. *Workers.* My God, they were kids. But the irony was that's where Chick should be in the first place, behind some university lectern using all that wonderful charisma of his to *teach* this dark history of his he reads like gospel. Last night in the bedroom, when she read the final copy of his manifesto pamphlet, he stood at the open window in his boxer shorts and waited. He had taken off his glasses. One hand was on his hip, his shoulders were slumped, and for the first time in weeks he didn't look so sure of himself, which is why she worded her opinion the way she did. She told him how she didn't think it was a good idea to start voicing his ideas in the city, he could get hurt—

"*My* ideas, Tess?"

"Yes." She didn't even hesitate: "They're not mine."

He was quiet. He seemed to be studying her. "What are yours then, Tess? Andover?"

"Don't patronize me, Chick. I didn't volunteer for this craziness of yours, and neither did Allie or Chris."

He stood still a moment, watching her. Then he walked over and lifted the pamphlet from her as carefully as he would a loaded pistol from a small child. He took his pillow, pulled a sheet from the closet, and started down the open stairwell. He stopped after three or four steps, and looked at her. "You're weak, Tess. You're weak."

She hadn't said anything, just watched him disappear beneath the floorboards. And she wasn't angry, then or now. She was past that, back to where she started, which was dumbfounded, really, still blinking in amazement at just how far Chick was taking all this. It had started out barely three years ago as a few night courses to "quench his thirst." One of them was labor history, and he began to learn more about that dreary mill town of his youth—Lawrence, Massachusetts—and the role its textile workers had played in the making of the unions. He would come home after class, his cheeks flushed with enthusiasm, and he'd pace the floor and recite some new historical fact. Sometimes Allie was still up when he came in, and he would speak a little slower, and clearer, already sharing and teaching what he knew. And when he began to study Marxist theory, he became even more animated, sometimes still talking in bed after Tess had turned off the light.

"You see? The more screwed over a group of people get, the more they realize just how they're getting it and who's doing it and that's when they realize they're all in it together: *class consciousness.* That's the first step, hon. Isn't this guy beautiful?"

"You're beautiful." And soon she would be sliding beneath him and he would thrust as fast and wild as a boy, as if perhaps she herself carried the answer to all things inside her.

And she meant it; he *was* beautiful, this Chick Donovan whom she had met eighteen years ago at a party at her sister's house in Andover. He was Patty's boyfriend's friend, a boxer, so Theresa had expected a thug, not the thin boy in the baggy chinos and flannel shirt who looked like Robert Taylor and kept his eyes down whenever she spoke to him. One night out he drove her to Salisbury Beach and they went on the roller coaster. On the first and steepest rise, he put both arms over his head and kept them there until the final, jerking curve of the ride, a strangely satisfied smile on his windchapped face. Later, they sat on the sand against the creosote stilts under Lena's Dance Club and drank beer out of bottles. The moon was low over the ocean. He told her then that he had a sea of respect for his father but he didn't want to be at all like him, punching a time card down at Malden Mills, working for a man he'll never meet. When she asked him if he was thinking of college, he laughed.

"Nope, it's the trades for me. Then I can take you around the world, if you want."

And that was his calling for a while it seemed, after they were married: travel. When he began building for himself, they followed the work: Triangle, West Virginia; Temple, Texas; Salinas, California, where she delivered Allie; Tacoma, Washington; LeRoy, New York; Kittery, Maine; and now Heywood, Massachusetts, where Christopher was born. Chick had his sights on Jackson, Mississippi, next, and that one had come out of the blue. It wasn't even in the form of a question.

"We're going south, Tess," he'd said one Sunday morning after three hours of drinking that black coffee and reading four newspapers, Frederick Engels and Karl Marx. "That's where the fruit is ripe, that's where we're needed."

Allie was reading a novel on the couch with her hair tied back, eating an apple. She sat up. "Oh yes, Daddio, and we'll live in a mansion like *Gone with the Wind*."

Chick laughed, then gently corrected her with bourgeois this and proletariat that, and their talking kept Tess from having to speak. When he did bring it up with her that night, she smiled and said, "Fine, Chick," and after that he simply referred to the fall and the move south as something thoroughly discussed, decided upon, mutually agreed to, and believed in.

But there had been no reason for Theresa to bring it up because she was not going and neither were her children and she didn't want to fight about it because she wanted Chick to go and she should have known what was coming when, last spring, her overly sincere and passionate husband discovered Marx's line, "The point is not to understand the world, but to change it," when Chick began living his days like those born-again people for whom ambiguity is a dirty word for they have found the parted seas of the black and white, all the answers are at hand, and you doubters best beware: to straddle the fence is to hesitate, and to hesitate at the calling hour is to side with the enemy—and make no mistake, the enemy will be vanquished. You will all be vanquished.

The sun glinted off a small plane far above the Berkshires. Tess tossed the last of her coffee, and remembered the stillness she had felt yesterday when she imagined her husband lying electrocuted on the ground. There was a quietness to it, a calm that seemed needed, one she knew for an instant she could slip into easily, if she were alone, if there weren't her children's grief to contend with, but

mainly if there weren't Allie's, that bright darling girl who loves her
crazy father so much.

12

Tom Burrell shook his head and drank coffee from one of Beatrice's
cardboard cups. "His cheekbone's broken too, not just his nose."

"His *cheek*bone." Leo spit out a chunk of ice from his Coke. They
were sitting inside the walled skeleton of the second floor. The sun
was already clearing the roof of the barn and Leo knew when it got
over the driveway and the road it would be lunchtime. The field
grass down the hill was thick and green and a slight breeze blew it in
uneven waves. "Did you mean what you said yesterday about quitting?"

"With God as my witness."

"What will you do?"

Tom looked off in the direction of the road a moment. "My
brother-in-law runs a crew in Chicopee. I don't care for him much—
he drinks like a catfish—but I'm going to have to make an exception
right now."

Leo leaned his head back and closed his eyes to the sun. "You
think Chick will really move to Mississippi?"

"Who said that?"

"Allie."

Tom's eyes stayed flat on the previous subject.

"Chick's daughter. We're going together."

Burrell nodded, then sipped more coffee. "What did she say about
Mississippi?"

"Nothing much. Chick wants to renovate Southern mansions or
something."

"Something?"

Leo looked away and drained his Coke. He could feel the lie in his
face, though he knew he only stopped short with the rest of the truth.

"Allison?"

"Yep."

"Billy had a crush on her awhile."

"A lot of boys like her. Not like I do, though."

Tom smiled and stood up. "You going to marry the boss's daughter, Leo?"

"Maybe." And he knew when he said it he meant it.

"Well, good luck on that one. I just hope Chick lives to walk her down the aisle. Floyd's not the kind to call a lawyer, I'm afraid." Tom buckled on his tool apron and turned it around so the clasp was in back and the nail pouches, tape measure, and hammer were in front. "Let's hang some sheathing, Leo. The faster we finish this house, the better."

Leo woke Saturday morning to the whine of cicadas in the trees, the smell of frying bacon. His sheets were damp. A sun shard reflected so bright off the wall he couldn't look at it. Jim and Ryder were talking out in the kitchen. He showered and dressed in cut-off shorts and a T-shirt and ate breakfast at the table with the men: three eggs over easy, four strips of bacon, and two pieces of buttered Wonder Bread toast. He drank a cup of coffee with milk and three sugars while Jim bragged to Ryder about how well Leo played lead on Lipscomb's "Blues in G" Thursday night. Jim mentioned Allie and what a polite young girl she was. Ryder winked at Leo and nudged his knee with the point of his boot. The conversation quickly turned to the Red Sox and how damned good they look in second place, how they're starting to get mentioned as actual contenders for the pennant. "And boy we're going to fry at Fenway if we end up in the bleachers," Ryder said. He asked Leo to come with them but Leo smiled and said no thank you, he had a date.

Which he did. He and Allie had planned to picnic somewhere in walking distance from Spoon Hill.

"Take the Valiant, son. Ryder's heap needs a few city dents."

After the men had gone, each laughing at something the other had said, Leo took his work cash from his drawer and counted it. He had a little over $150, and with Chick's seventy-five-cent raise, he could figure on getting eighty bucks a week instead of fifty. He took three twenties and stuffed them into his shorts pocket.

On the drive to Springfield he thought about Allie and what he would buy her. Something fine. Or imported. He thought about that Bob Dylan song of a man bringing his woman a pair of boots of Spanish leather. But it was too hot to think of boots. A summer dress, maybe, with flowers on it. Some French perfume. A scarf made in China. Or jewelry. No, that was out. There was only one jewel to buy her, and he was going to wait until he knew it was the exact right time.

The sun shone bright off the river to his left. The water was still high from yesterday and most of the boulders were submerged. Near the Springfield city limits was a small pebbled beach. A pickup truck was parked there. Two girls in one-piece bathing suits were wading in waist deep. On the ground in front of the truck sat a man about Floyd's age, maybe younger. His hair was buzz-cut the same way, and Leo wondered if he was a soldier, home for good, sitting there watching his wife and sister swim, thinking about combat.

Leo walked in and out of a Rexall drugstore and two boutiques before he saw Tony's Musical Suite under an awning next to a barber shop. The inside was dim and hot and smelled like rosewood. Behind the glass counter stood a man in a green T-shirt. He was clean shaven and his black hair was long and hung to his shoulders. "Beautiful day in the world."

"You sell harmonicas?"

The man had three turquoise and silver rings on his fingers, and when he patted the counter top with his palm, they clicked against the glass. "I only carry Marine Band, but I move 'em in every key."

Leo looked down at two blue felt-covered shelves. The top one had guitar picks on it; a juice harp; a red-, orange-, and green-flamed guitar strap rolled up like a sleeping snake; and a tuning fork. On the bottom shelf was nothing but harmonicas in three neat rows, shining silver in the light of the display case.

"You play?"

"Yep."

"Local?"

"Heywood."

The man handed Leo a Tony's Musical Suite business card. "Ever groove to Anthony and the Holy Roaders?"

Leo nodded, still reading the card.

"That's us. We just lost our harp to Uncle Sam. You want to bend 'em sometime, buzz my horn."

Leo said sure thing and bought four harmonicas: a G, a B-flat, an A, and one in D. While Tony took them out of the case and boxed them, Leo looked again at the Mexican guitar strap on the top shelf. He pointed at it and said he'd take that too. He wanted to get something for Ryder but Ryder had two harps in every key so it had to be something else. Leo walked over to the book rack and flipped through some jazz song books, folk books, then the blues. He pulled out a thin book with a picture of Huddie Ledbetter on the cover. He dropped it on the counter, and Tony told him twenty-eight and change. Leo handed over two twenties. "What kind of music do you guys play?"

"R & B funk. The clubs dig us."

"You play in clubs?"

"Every weekend. Give me a call, man, we'll throw together a session."

Outside, the sun shone so bright Leo had to shield his eyes with his hand. He pictured himself in a dark nightclub up at the microphone with his harp like Ryder in New York City. Only Leo wouldn't be drunk and he'd be getting paid. For *playing*. He ducked inside the drugstore again and bought himself a pair of aviator shades with blue lenses. Then he bought sunglasses for Allie too, the green horn-rimmed kind with white plastic frames like Marilyn Monroe used to wear. He stepped inside a store called Delores the Florist and bought a dozen long-stemmed roses from a woman with dyed red hair and a slight mustache.

"Are these for your sweetheart?"

"My fiancée."

"Well good for you." She put her glasses on to ring in the money. On the wall behind her was an electric clock shaped like a daisy. It was already close to eleven and Leo was supposed to meet Allie at noon. These roses were taking a bigger chunk of money than he'd figured.

"God bless you, son."

"You too." He put on his new shades and stepped back outside. Across the street, in front of a red brick building, was a man in a wheelchair. He had a green army cap on his head. A black band was tied around his upper arm, and on his lap was a big cardboard sign, but Leo couldn't make out what it said. He climbed back into his father's Valiant and drove out of town.

13

It was awfully hot, late July already. Allie kicked the sheet away and pulled her T-shirt off. The house smelled like coffee and paint and she could hear a warbler outside in the woods. Chris was out in the kitchen talking to their mom. His voice was nose-blocked and most of his sentences ended on higher notes than they started. She reached between her legs and felt her panties, though she knew if she really wanted the straight scoop she'd have to pull them down and look. But even if there was a blood spot, she would have to wait and see if her period showed up, if it was going to.

She thought about Billy Burrell last year. He was so sweet, too sweet even, and not too smart. It took all of October and half of November to find that out. But by then she had let him be the one, partly because of his wide neck and those mocha-brown eyes—that mix of muscle and soul—but what really cinched it was the dual knowledge that she had just turned sixteen and if girls like Nancy Titcomb were still virgins, she wasn't going to be. So on a blanket on the floor of Billy's father's work shed she let a boy inside who had the good sense to pull on a rubber first. And that was a problem too: Billy's good sense. From his sound homework habits—one hour right after classes, another hour after supper—to his insistence that

Allie eat three meals a day, to his always wearing a hat in cold weather so he wouldn't miss any school; boy, he got obsolete fast. Leo wasn't big like Billy was in the back and arms, but looking into Leo Suther's eyes, green like hers, she knew something was going on in there, and not just thinking, but *feeling,* so much of it.

Allie pulled her panties down and saw white cotton, not even one drop of dried blood. She remembered that poem Leo's mom wrote when she found out her body had pulled a mean fast one on her. And that part about her breasts being tender to touch, her cycle going up the river. Gosh. Allie wondered if she'd pulled a mean fast one on her own self. She had been late once or twice before, but her breasts didn't feel bruised like they do now. She knew what her mother would say about all this: "Oh Allie, how awfully, awfully foolish of you." Then Allie could count on being driven to whatever doctor— no matter how far away—who got rid of problems such as this.

She thought of that line she'd written down last week from *Fables of Conquest* by Vega Menudo about how average men look at all things as a blessing or a curse while to the warrior all things are a challenge. That was more like it. That was how she felt. This wasn't a problem yet. She rested her hand on her belly, so flat, and she imagined it swollen and ripe with new life. That would mean wearing dresses instead of jeans. Maybe she could just leave her pants unbuttoned and wear one of her dad's shirts. No, that was out; Daddy was strong but he was still small. How would he think of that? Thirty-nine and a grandfather. A super fine picture came into her head. She would run off until her eighth or ninth month, then walk through the front door of her house big as two women, a wide smile on her face as her mom and dad—but primarily her dad—soaked it all up, that his little girl had things going, big plans, something he couldn't *not* look at, no matter what the world was up to.

He would want her to get married, of course. Which was strange, really. He had her read a book about labor organizers at the turn of the century, when that doomed Swedish songwriter Joe Hill was hopping trains all over the country, and a lot of them didn't believe in marriage. Daddy did, though. At least he seemed to, being married and all. Then she started to think of Leo again and she thought it sort of odd that she wasn't really imagining him being a part of all this. Except as a lover. It was easy to see him that way. Thursday afternoon in his room, while it rained outside, as she gripped his long sweating back, thunder had rolled from her knees to her face and when it got to her ears, she lifted her butt off the bed and everything let go in a downward fall right out her toes. She could have said I love you like she'd said it before, and meant it like she meant it before, but her breathing was short and anyway how could she have felt all that if she didn't truly love him, so why say it a second time when he hadn't really said it to her once yet?

But anyway she herself started everything. She knew she was going to Mississippi in the fall, and she knew she wanted to do at least once with Leo Suther what she'd done three times with Billy Burrell. Tall, skin-tight Leo with his smooth cheeks and dark hair, his songwriting and harmonica-playing, his being mad at his lonesome father. We're in it now, she thought. Nothing to do now except go to a picnic, laugh like a warrior girl, and wait for a bloody moon.

Leo stood waist-deep in the water of Empire Lake and took in the sheer climb of the Berkshires on the other side. Their slopes were thick with blue spruce, interrupted only by an occasional slab of granite in the sun. Up near the peaks the treeline ended, opening up to dots of brush, more rock, then a few narrow patches of earth. Above that, the sky was more blue than the lake, and as a curl of cloud moved by, Leo felt a little dizzy. He dove forward into the water and came up facing the grounds. Allie was helping her mother lay out the chicken salad sandwiches, potato chips, and Cokes on a picnic table under the trees. Leo side-kicked a few yards. He could see Christopher teetering over to where another family sat eating on a quilt.

At first Leo didn't like the idea of the whole Donovan family— minus Chick—coming along. He had planned on just himself and Allie because he'd wanted to give her the roses at the lake when they were alone. But when Allie told him on her front porch she didn't want to leave her mom with Chris all day, Leo led her to the car and gave her the long white box from Delores the Florist right then. Allie let out a little whimper when she opened it, then she French kissed him there under the sun in front of her cabin. Leo followed her into the house, and as soon as he saw Chick's pretty wife smile up at him from her sandwich work at the kitchen table, as soon as he heard her praise the flowers and then him for bringing them, he figured today would fit two more in all right. They stopped at Trudy's Grocery for Cokes and ice. Mrs. Donovan tried to give him some money, but Leo wouldn't hear of it. It was his car, it was his treat.

On the drive through the national forest, Allie put on her new sunglasses to match his. She checked her face in the rearview mirror, then sat closer to him. Leo thought she looked older in them, more like a woman, and he glanced in the mirror at her mother. She held Christopher in her lap, the both of them looking out the open window at the woods going by. Chick's wife was nice to look at with her long brown hair and that wide mouth she'd passed on to Allie, but her eyes always seemed to be in a squint like there was something bright and dangerous near her. It made her look tired. Anyway, she didn't seem to notice, or mind, her daughter sitting this close to him.

When they got into lake country Christopher craned his neck to see better and said, "It's ocean, look. Ocean."

Allie turned around smiling. She looked pretty with her hair hanging loose around her shoulders. "No, Pooh, that's a lake. We're going swimming in it."

"That's a *lake*." Mrs. Donovan kissed her boy on the back of his head. Leo took Allie's hand in front and squeezed. He rested his driving elbow out in the warm wind that smelled like pine and somebody's barbecue charcoals and he took a deep breath because, man, this all fit so good; better than a sixteen-penny nail in a toe plate, more like the sweet Harp of the Blues in his hands, but most, like him inside Allie—'cause from that comes this: him and her sitting up front, their own little boy and girl in back, the four of them heading for sunshine and mountain waters, a chicken Allie'd cooked, and a picnic ground crowded with other happy families.

Leo swam to the raft anchored out in deep water. There was a four-foot-tall diving platform built on one side of it and three boys about twelve or thirteen years old were taking turns trying jackknife dives. Leo stayed in the lake and held on to the corner of the raft to watch. One of the boys was real thin, and his dives were the worst. When his head hit the water he was still touching his toes, and Leo could see a whole network of blue veins all the way down his thin legs. Farther out in the lake a speedboat cut its way through the water. Two water skiers, a man and a woman, skidded a swath behind it, and the man had muscles like Chick Donovan's.

Leo looked back at the shore and saw Allie wading into the lake in her cut-off jeans and a white T-shirt. She waved to him and was about to dive in when somebody called her name and she turned around to two boys wearing shorts and no shirts. It was GP and some kid named Logan who was on the football team with him but played first string instead of second. Their hair was so short they almost seemed bald. But something else was stranger than that. Leo didn't know what it was at first, then he did; GP didn't have a belly anymore. His stomach was about as flat and hard-looking as Logan's. Allie turned and pointed to the raft. Both boys looked out at it, then ran and dove into the water. Allie waded in and followed them stroke for stroke.

Leo climbed up and sat on the hot boards. He clasped his hands around one raised knee and tried to look as disinterested as he could. The thin boy's friends started back for shore and Leo watched the kid do a flying cannonball, leaving hardly any splash at all. Logan made it to the raft first. He pulled himself up the ladder, walked past Leo to the platform, and dove in, his knees bent, his feet spread apart.

"What's happenin', Lucky Leo?"

Gerry stepped up onto the raft. He was breathing hard, but not very.

"What's new, GP?"

"You tell me, pal."

"You're not fat anymore."

"An A for Suther."

Allie's face popped up between the ladder rails. "Hello, boys." Her hair was slicked back, all wet. Her T-shirt stuck to her shoulders and breasts, and Leo could see the color of her nipples. When Logan came up the ladder behind her, Leo stood and put his arm around her, pulling her in close so her chest was facing his. She kissed him on the cheek, then followed Logan off the diving platform. Gerry watched her go in.

"How'd you get so skinny all of a sudden, GP?"

Gerry's bristly head glistened in the sun. He was either squinting at Leo or smiling a tight one; either way Leo didn't like it.

"All of a sudden? Me and Logan been runnin' the bleachers all summer, man. Where you been?"

"Working, GP. I work for a living."

"Yeah, I can see that." Gerry nodded at Allie as she came up the ladder in front of Logan, her small breasts showing pink through the wet cotton of her shirt. She smiled at Leo, then sat cross-legged with her back to the beach. Logan stayed low on the ladder and looked right at her. Leo stepped into his view. "You going into the marines, too?"

Logan nodded, keeping his eyes where they'd been.

"I can do sixty-five straight push-ups, buddy. Logan can do over a hundred, but that's cool 'cause I can do more sit-ups than him."

"How many?" Allie said behind Leo.

"Three hundred and fifty, Allison Baby. Three-five-oh. Straight."

"That's nice," she said, "but have you read any books?"

"As a matter of fact I have, Miss Groovy. *To Hell and Back* by Audie Murphy himself. It's as thick as Leo's head here."

"You're the one with the thick head, GP," Leo laughed but it sounded as forced as it felt and he knew it. He glanced back down at Logan who was looking up at Gerry with a stone face.

"This time next week me and killer are gonna be sweatin' bullets in the Corps," Gerry said.

"Good for you, GP."

"Yeah, who actually cares, Gerry?" Allie said. "Leo doesn't have anything to prove."

Logan laughed and pushed himself off into the water. He surface-dove backwards and as he went under he squeezed his legs together perfectly straight, his toes pointed like one of those gymnasts.

"What a homunculus," Allie said.

Leo laughed again. Gerry was looking at him with a slightly cocked head. His face had lost some weight too. He had cheekbones and no double chin. His hands were resting on his hips real relaxed, like a pitcher between throws. He shook his head once. Then he climbed the platform, ran and dove out into the air with his back arched and his arms held out straight like wings. Leo hoped he would belly flop for certain, but he didn't. GP's arms and head cut in not far from where Logan was treading water waiting for him, his eyes on Allie's wet back. When they reached shallow water, they walked up onto the sand and straight into the trees.

"They really think they're the end-all, don't they?" Allie said.

Leo didn't say anything. He took a breath and let it out.

"What?"

"What the hell's wrong with you?"

"Me?"

"You're practically naked, for Christ's sake. They were staring right at your *tits*."

She stood up fast. "Oh don't be a jerk, Leo. They're *my* tits."

Leo looked down at the raft boards. He didn't know what to say; she was right, but then again somehow she wasn't.

She stepped over and took his hand. "I'm famished. Let's go eat."

They jumped into the water. Allie hit first, then Leo. He sank deeper than her, and when his arm jerked at hers underwater, he didn't let go.

14

The air was so still and heavy Monday morning Leo smelled the pulp pools all the way up to the job site. The sky was the color of tin, and from where he stood on the second floor, he could see two squirrels on the roof of the barn, a fat one chasing a skinny one right along the ridge to the back where Leo couldn't see them anymore. He saw a willow branch dip as one or both of them took hold. It wasn't even coffee break yet and his T-shirt was sticking to him all over.

"All set?" Chick stood below. He held up an eight-foot-long, four-foot-wide plywood sheet for Leo to take. Leo grabbed it by the corners, pulled, then stepped back onto the next joist and the one behind it. He turned the plywood on its edge, then Tom took it and with a heave and a swing dropped it onto the stack against the north wall. Chick already had another sheet held up as Leo stepped back to the header. When Leo bent over, gripped the plywood and pulled, he was looking into Chick's face a second but Chick wasn't looking into his; his eyes were on the sky as he grunted air out his mouth and pressed the wood over his head. He had whiskers like he hadn't shaved since Thursday when he punched out Floyd, but he'd been working as steady and business-like as always, even though Tom talked to him first thing this morning just outside the barn. Leo was gassing up the generator and he heard Chick say, "That's that, I guess," just before the two men went to work.

Tom was pushing pretty hard. With each new plywood sheet, he seemed to step in and take it a little faster, heave it higher, and toss it with a vengeance onto the stack. Leo thought it was because Chick shrugged off Tom's news like he would a stubbed toe. This morning, when Jim had dropped Leo off at the Donovans', Chick was already in the truck, sipping a coffee. He waved at Jim and he was so damn cheerful as he drove Leo down the river road to the job. Leo wanted to know about the weekend, about how it went over in Boston with those pamphlets, but Chick didn't leave any room for him to speak. He didn't mention his trip, or last Thursday; he was talking about picnics in Washington State when before Christopher was born and Allie Cat was a little girl, he and Tess would drive her out to a park outside Tacoma where there was nothing but hills of long grass, "*Green* grass, Leo. There's so much rain up there in the Northwest, their grass is emerald. *Emerald.* And you should've seen Allie running and jumping through that stuff.

"I used to do this thing, where I'd have her hold on to my neck, and then I'd go rolling down one of those hills, using my elbows so I wouldn't crush her, and Jeez, she loved that. Even when she got dizzy, she kept wanting to do it."

As Chick had talked, driving much slower than Leo would have,

99

Chick's whiskers looking almost blue in the gray light of the truck cab, Leo winced at the idea of his getting hit with the news that he didn't really have a building company anymore. But if Chick was bothered, he didn't seem it. Not by Tom's news anyway. And something was up. After they finished hauling the plywood, Chick pulled himself up onto the header and told Tom in a friendly voice to go ahead and lay out the floor with Leo and tack down the sheets. He was still breathing hard when he said it, his hands on his hips, and Leo noticed he went into a kind of stare at the plywood stack, his eyes a camouflage curtain of retina, cornea, and pupil, just sitting there in the sockets so a riot of other things could go on behind them. He was sleepwalking really; nothing here mattered. And as Leo took one end of the top sheet and followed Tom to the far corner, stepping from one joist to the next, he thought about that emerald picnic Chick told him about and he changed his mind about Chick being cheerful; true, his voice had been full of steam for so early in the morning, but when he smiled it had looked like that same curtain, and now Tom's news seemed to be just one more fly on his back that Chick was too busy, or too tired, to swat.

It was numbers night at the Elks so Leo decided he would clean up and change his clothes before taking a relaxed walk to the UFO Show for a cheeseburger with Allie as his waitress. After his shower, he went naked into the parlor and put on a Howlin' Wolf record. The first song was in C so he picked up his new G harp and sucked out what sounded like back-up chords to Wolf's lead. This new harp felt solid and hard-cornered in his hands, its reeds stronger than the ones in the harp Ryder had given him.

Jim and Ryder seemed to like their presents. Leo had left the guitar strap and Leadbelly book on the kitchen table before going to bed Saturday night. He wrote on a torn piece of grocery bag: "This strap's for you, Jim. The book is for you, Ride. Hope you can read music!"

The two men woke him up sometime after midnight. Ryder sat on the side of the bed so close to Leo the sheet pinned him down before he turned free of it. Jim stood in the middle of the floor, rocking slightly on his feet. Those Sox won again, in extra innings, and ol' Boston was in deep need of a Jimmy/Ryder Romp.

"Which we gave it," Ryder said. Then he leaned forward and kissed Leo on the cheek, his whiskers brushing a scratch on the tip of Leo's nose. "Thank you for the song book, Young Buddy. You big rascal, you."

Jim squeezed Leo's foot. They both left the room, and as they made their way down the dark hall to the light of the kitchen, Leo heard Ryder whisper, "Good kid, good goddamned kid."

Leo tried out the rest of his new harps with Mr. Wolf until he got to his D. None of Wolf's keys matched it, so Leo turned off the record player and blew it alone. He was getting the hang of the note-bending pretty good, but it was mimicking tunes he was even better at. Last Thursday night, when he followed Jim's singing in Lipscomb's G, Leo hit most every note right the first time. What Ryder said was true: you have to *feel* it, not think it. Whenever Leo found himself trying too hard, he'd hit a wrong one. And trying wasn't the same as con- centrating either. Concentrating was really just listening to the river of music you're sitting in, letting the current take you and having faith you won't get ducked. He sang the first verse of "The Love Abode," then he raised his harp to his mouth and went in tongue- blocking the low notes, pulling in on the high, he fanned his right hand as fast as he could and shit if he didn't sound like a bluesman. He picked up his B-flat and tried the same in that key, this time saving his woo-wah tremolo for the end. Then he grabbed his G, danced around the parlor and didn't sing a word, just played the whole num- ber start to finish, his penis and balls bouncing and swaying as he dipped and turned, threw in a few forced trills and flutters, then ended it all at once at the window where he opened his eyes. He was breathing fast, sweating, and he felt wonderful. He looked through the trees down at a section of the river running pewter under that heavy sky he couldn't see.

He gathered up his harmonicas and went back into his room where his penis got instantly hard; he was thinking about Allie again, the way she undressed in this room and made love and walked around naked. Man, how good it was to have this whole place to themselves. He lay back on his bed and began to stroke himself, but then he stopped. Big Bill was giving him big eyes from the wall. And for good reason. Leo walked over to Katie Faye's box on the dresser. He put it on the bed and pulled out some of the pictures they saw last Thursday. Underneath loose papers was a square of cardboard. Written in his mother's small neat print was a recipe for Mexican chili. On the other side was:

And so then, my Lord, baby Leo could be a piece of oak leaf a thousand years old—or the splintered hoof of a daddy goat who died on a Pyrenees peak—he might be the first drop of blood to trickle down my great-grandmother's leg, or maybe he's the sweat on Jim's papa's upper lip as he stoops to lift a bridge timber—No. Leo goes back further than that. My baby is hot dust blown from Mercury, cold light from the moon. He is the fish who flies into an Ecuador village. He is the blanket on which Sitting Bull sleeps. He is my mother's mouth and my father's ears. He is Jim's penis and my face. He is staring at me right now as I write these words. Those green eyes that look at me with such a quiet love. He sits in the very center of the rug like a Pygmy Buddha. And the air holds the truth of the matter out to me: my baby Leo just pooped.

15

Because Allie woke up sick Monday morning she heard the whole fight start to finish. She had been dreaming of Jayne Mansfield and Vega Menudo in Beatrice's kitchen. They were standing around the fryolator watching Sidney cook onion rings. Sid looked very proud of himself. He kept glancing over at Mansfield, who was wearing a navy blue sequined evening gown that pushed her milky cleavage right out there. Vega Menudo wore sandals and was dressed in a plain cotton work shirt and pants like Mexican farmers'. He was the guide of the tour, no Beatrice in sight. As soon as Allie realized this, she also realized she was standing very naked on the other side of Sidney. He lifted the fry basket out of the hot grease and when he started to shake it, Allie stepped back so she wouldn't get burned. She covered her crotch with her hands, her breasts with her upper arms. Jayne Mansfield saw this and started to laugh. Sidney gave Allie a look like she was spoiling his show, and when he dumped the onion rings under the heat lamp, Mansfield put a hand on each side of her laughing blond head, lifted it off her shoulders with no blood whatsoever, and placed it lovingly into the sizzling grease. Allie thought she was going to throw up and she woke up feeling the same way.

It was very quiet in the house. Outside was just getting light. She got naked out of bed and walked to the open window. She took a deep breath of very still and warm air and out it came, splashing out the window onto the grass. For the second surge, she knelt on the floor and rested her arms on the sill. On the third, nothing came out but brown liquid and she knew that was it. She went into the bathroom and brushed her teeth, then got back into bed just as a car rolled over the gravel out front. A door slammed and her father's voice said, "Adios."

She wanted to go see him, but even with the toothpaste she knew she still smelled like throw-up. While he was making coffee, she heard her mother come down the stairs and go into the kitchen. They must've hugged and kissed at first because there weren't any words for a good two or three minutes. Then came the doozies. Her father was going on and on describing this liquor store that got looted while its roof was on fire. This Negro kid, whom Chick had just given a manifesto, rolled it up, put it in his back pocket, then ran into the store through its missing front window. He came out carrying a case of wine. The back of his T-shirt was smoking and the pamphlet burned like a candle in his back pocket.

"And that's about how it went, Tess," he went on. "They weren't even looking inside them. Even when I read it through a megaphone in the street, they sort of plowed by us on the way to the loot. Yesterday Big Toby got his tooth knocked out with a brick. They looked at us like we were either the enemy or a sideshow. We stayed clear of the law though, hon'. We parked under an overpass and slept in the

103

wagon Friday and Saturday night. Last night we climbed a tenement and threw the manifestos off the roof. We planted the seed, Tess. That's all we can do. The South will be easier, you watch. They're already organized down there, they're ready—"

"We're not going."

Wow. Allie sat straight up at what her mother just said.

"What did you say?"

"I noticed something this weekend, Chick. You didn't call home once. Not once."

"*Who's* not going?"

"Your wife and children, mister. That's who."

Allie heard two steps, the slap of something hard hitting something soft, then her father yelling louder than she'd ever heard him, "You'll goddamn go where the hell I tell you and that's fucking that! Do you *hear* me?! Do you fucking *hear?!*"

Then her mother was screaming back all kinds of things like what a pathetic man Chick Donovan was, what a fascist bully phony shit of a man—"You're so fucking *impressionable!* You are a *child,* and I am sick to *death* of being your *mother!!*"

One of them walked right out the back door, then outside and off the porch. Allie knew it was her dad because her mom started to cry in the kitchen, the same kind of weepy sighs building to gasps she let out when they made love. Christopher was bawling in his room next to Allie's, and she thought about going to calm him down but didn't move.

Soon things were quiet again. Her mother had gone straight to Chris's room and Allie could hear her cuddly-sounding sentences, then a song Tess's mom used to sing to her, some old Irish ballad about Erin and a potato crop and a penny in the grass. The back screen door closed quietly on its spring. Allie heard her father pour himself coffee and taste it. He went upstairs a minute, came down, drank more coffee, then went outside and started up the flatbed. She could hear the steady rumble of the engine a good fifteen minutes. She got into her UFO dress and went out to the living room window. Her father was sitting in the truck cab looking straight out the windshield down at the river. He was just sitting there. Allie heard the rocking chair in Christopher's room. It sounded sort of heavy on the floor, which meant her mom was holding little Chris in her lap, probably pressing his wet cheek to her breast. Who did she think she was, saying Allie was not going without even asking her? But gosh, how could Dad have hit her like that?

The sky was such an ugly smear of gray, it looked like it was about to get sick with rain. A shiver went through Allie's chest and that's where it stopped because the Warrior Girl doesn't cry over things like this. Just then, the Suthers' white car drove up the hill, and as its front started to level off in the driveway Allie felt things level off inside her too. Leo was in the passenger side, sitting taller than his father, and his hair had a cowlick in the back from sleeping. He glanced at the house but didn't see her, even though she waved.

Her dad was waving too, at Leo's father. Before Allie could move, Leo got right into the truck and she watched it and the car drive down the hill, the flatbed taking a right, Leo's father taking a left. And all day at Beatrice's she pondered in which direction she had to go.

As she served hot coffee and cold blueberry pie to milk truck drivers and men in suits, a few burgers to a handful of boys who whistled at her as she left them with their food, she wasn't even there. The cosmos had presented her, Allison Marie Donovan, with the following: pretend your family is not breaking up in the rough seas and about to go under—or—take up your spear, and do something fast. So in true Warrior Girl fashion, she found herself looking to the very thing that seemed at first to be the anvil in the boat, this queasiness in her belly that the coffee and muffins and grilled-meat smells of Beatrice's had only made worse, sending her twice to the restroom where she threw up orange juice the first time, stomach-heaving air the second. Sidney let her go home after the lunch rush, and on the walk home Allie made herself think the words: pregnant, expecting, with child. Of course she really could just have a touch of virus, and might simply be late with the moon, but her small breasts said differently. She was more aware she *had* breasts, that they occasionally rubbed against her uniform in a way that didn't feel far from a cool wind hitting a bad tooth.

Of course this isn't what she had planned. Not to say she had any plans. Other than Mississippi. Allie was used to going where the signs—or her mother and father—pointed her. But not this time. They weren't going to catch her up in their big fight net. She had something big of her own, as natural as grass fires, winter flus, and spring floods.

Allie climbed Spoon Hill sweating herself thirsty. As she got closer to the top, she imagined a Suther-Donovan household. Oh, days could be very copacetic for all; Leo and her father could renovate the cabin, add a big section onto her room for her and Leo and their baby; a room or two out back for Jim Suther, a larger studio upstairs for her mom to paint in. Jim could still work at Heywood Paper, and Leo and her dad could build houses during the day. Some nights, her father could preach his politics down off the gazebo on Thompson Green while the Suther men played blues music in between speeches. And of course Leo would be happy about all this, wouldn't he? The question hung behind her face like a rigged bomb, and she thought of the dozen long-stemmed roses that still sat in a vase on the kitchen table. He seemed to like working at the carpentering. And maybe someday he could take that harmonica playing of his and do something with that too. There was no doubt he was a reliable man. Her father had even said so to her one night in only the second week of the summer. "Your beau's a good hand on the job, Allie Cat." What more proof was there of innate character and strong provider potential? Not that Allie Donovan would just be married to a house and child. She could get a scholarship and take night classes at the university, maybe be a teacher, or an anthropologist, or a film star. Why not? She did look sultry in those sunglasses Leo give her. And actresses have babies too.

As she reached the top of the drive she thought of Jayne Mansfield again, of her frying head, and Allie had to kneel on one bare knee in the gravel and take a deep breath, which was hard to do from the climb. She wanted a cold cola on ice, that, and a long talk with her mother. No need to pretend Allie was in the dark about things. But Tess was asleep on the sofa beneath the ever-watchful eye of Mr. Marx. She was wearing one of Allie's dad's button-down shirts and a pair of shorts. Her legs were long and smooth, still very appealing, Allie thought.

Chris's door was open. He was sleeping in his crib, his bottom sticking up in the air. Allie pulled a glass bottle of Coke from the fridge. She opened it quietly, took a huge sip, and went into her room. Both windows were open and there was no breeze whatsoever. She could smell a sour touch of this morning's evidence, even though not a drop had fallen inside. She stretched out on her bed and fell asleep in her UFO dress.

She woke hours later. The trees outside her window were in a gray, smokey light. Her father was out in the living room talking silly with Christopher, who was laughing so hard he sounded like he might pass out. The house smelled like frying chicken and roast potatoes. Allie sat up and rubbed her eyes and began to cry, hoping to God she was just late and had only taken on a morning bug, that her mother and father had fought an overboard fight they now regretted, that the four of them would be driving down to Mississippi in a month to a gorgeous place among all those cypress trees where Leo could send her letters, if he truly cared to. Gosh, he could even visit.

16

The sun showed itself for the first time all week on Wednesday afternoon. It shone through in patches at first, but soon the sky opened up and the sun's heat was everywhere. Tom stood spread-legged, balancing himself on the top plate of the north wall while Chick straddled the ridge pole of the roof skeleton fifteen feet or so above the plywood platform of the second floor. Leo stood there and his job was to pull the twelve-foot rafters up one at a time to Tom, who was taking them real slow. He made sure his feet stayed firm on the plate, then he lowered the notched end of the rafter behind him out over the ground two stories below so he could feed the other end to Chick up on the ridge. Leo looked up at Chick but that's where the sun was, just over Chick's left shoulder. Leo looked back down, blinking green.

It was slow going. Chick had cussed himself for lending out his ladders and he made a point of telling Leo this wasn't the best way to lay out rafters, ball-hugging an inch-and-a-half-wide ridge pole, trying to nail from up there too. But he was doing it. It was just taking a while, maybe five to eight minutes a rafter.

Leo held one end of the next board to go up. He looked through the framed wall down to where the road disappeared into the trees, and it was good seeing the sun on things again, but he was thinking about Allie acting like someone else ever since this past weekend when he gave her the roses and sunglasses. Well no, actually, she was all right Saturday. Sunday night seemed normal too. Chick wasn't back yet then. Leo had borrowed the Valiant and he and Allie went driving along the river all the way up to Hadley where they pulled over into the dark of a plumbing supply store and kissed a while. She wouldn't let him touch her breasts and other than hugging and kissing, she didn't touch him anywhere. But that was okay really. After a time, Leo sat back behind the wheel and played her some meandering blues riffs, first in B-flat, then in C.

But Monday night at Beatrice's, he found out from Sidney that Allie had gone home sick in the afternoon. Leo called her house from the UFO Show and she told him she'd rather see him some other time. "Some other time." What the heck kind of words were those to be using with him, Leo, who she saw practically every day? And last night, Tuesday, when Jim lent him the car again, she didn't even want to go anywhere. She said she was tired and couldn't they just sit on the porch awhile and talk? And that was fine except Allie didn't do any talking. She just sat on the steps with her elbows on her knees and her cheeks in her hands, looking at the ground a few feet in front of her while Leo tried bouncing around from one subject to another. He talked about Katie Faye's writings. He didn't know it until he said it, but he felt special—and his cheeks got hot when he said that word about himself in front of Allie—but he did, he felt special when he read his mother's words about him. Allie actually looked at him for that part; the light from the living room window fell on the side of her face, her eyes were unblinking, her

108

lips in a soft slight pout. She looked full of caring, but sadness too. Which is why Leo kept talking. Sad about what? *Him?*

So he turned his talk to the job and Tom quitting, and Chick— who wasn't home—working like a demon, but kind of distracted too. And that's when Allie looked down at the ground and seemed to go off someplace else without walking anywhere. Finally Leo shut up and took out his new D harp. He played the first few notes of "The Love Abode," but he didn't feel the number inside him at all. Besides, the D was too high and whiny for the lyrics. He would have to write a song to match that key. He played "Mary Had a Little Lamb," then put the harmonica in his back jeans pocket. When he said he should get going, Allie stood up right away, kissed him on the mouth with her lips pursed together, and went inside without a word.

"Let's go, Leo." Tom held his hands out for the next rafter. Leo gave it to him too quick.

"*Easy.*" Tom pulled the two-by-twelve to him until he held it at its middle, then he turned at the waist and pushed the top end out to Chick, who caught it though Leo couldn't tell for sure because of the sun. He heard Chick drive a nail, then his voice, "I was on one of my first jobs, flat-roofing over in Lawrence. We were gooping up a fresh layer on top of this mill, five, six stories up." Chick drove a second nail, and Leo heard him reach into his pouch for another. "This old guy slipped and went right over the edge."

"Oh Lord."

"You said it. He lived about three days. Next day of work, foreman lines us up and says, 'Any a you fall off this friggin' roof, you're fired on the way down.'" Chick grunted out a half-laugh and drove his third nail. 'Start of my education right there." He slid another sixteen inches along the ridge pole. Leo fed a rafter up to Tom. Just as Burrell took it, Leo heard the open-throttle scream of an engine down the road, the knock and tap of loose gravel up under the chassis. There was an easing up on the gas as a blue Chevy van drove slowly out of the trees into the sunlight. Leo recognized Dwight right away and before he could check himself, he waved. If Dwight saw, he didn't acknowledge it. He had a white painter's cap tilted back on his head.

———

109

His face was sunburned. In the shadow of the passenger's side was somebody wearing a white hanky around their nose and mouth. No, the mouth was showing. Only the nose was covered. Above that were small dark sunglasses. Dwight looked over the job then hit the gas again, squealing his tires over the gravel, spraying pebbles and dust out in a wide arc as he took the turn down toward the river. Leo picked up another rafter.

"Have you subbed out the painting yet?" Tom said.

"Nope, and we're not hiring that swinging dick, that's for damn sure." Chick's hammer echoed off the ridge as he missed a nail. He swore, then drove it in three swings.

For supper Jim barbecued hot dogs and hamburgers out on the grill in the driveway next to his car. Leo had just showered and sat shirtless in a pair of jeans on the kitchen stoop. He held his D harmonica and watched his father turn over the meat patties, leaning back and squinting his eyes at the smoke. The sun was still high over the trees up Saunders Hill, and when the smoke drifted into the pines it showed the twilight in slanted rays, and for some reason it made Leo think of the Civil War, of muskets and cannonballs and torn Confederate flags.

"You seeing your sweetheart tonight?"

Leo shrugged. "Maybe."

"I bet she likes baseball. She seems like she would. Invite her over to watch the game."

"Poker?"

Jim shook his head and turned the four hot dogs over. "Change of pace. Lars is bringing over one of his television sets. We're starting to smell a pennant race, son. Bring her over."

Leo put the harp to his mouth and sucked out a long bent five-hole note. He fanned his cupped hand for the tremolo, then dropped to the one- and two-holes for some train-chugging back-up. He repeated that twice and lowered the harp. "Is it wrong to give a girl a dozen roses?"

"Hope not. I used to give them to your mother all the time."

"I read some more of her stuff."

Jim glanced at Leo, then tapped the spatula on the grill.

"She had a good imagination."

"Yes she did."

"You must miss her a lot."

Jim nodded. "Why'd you ask about the roses?"

"Nothin'."

Jim turned over two patties. Orange and green flames flared up into the grease drippings of one of them.

"I read this one where she was talking about me being a dead goat and an old leaf."

"That's her." Jim took a tin platter from the hood of his car and flipped the smoking hot dogs onto it. He turned over the burgers again and pressed down on them with the spatula. "Your mother believed when we pass on, we all go back to where we started and live again. That's why she doesn't want us wasting our time up at the St. John's cemetery."

"Oh."

Jim glanced at Leo, but only looked as high as his knees before he turned his attention back to the grill and flipped the patties onto the tin.

"You should go out on a date."

"You think so?" Jim didn't look up and his voice sounded relaxed and respectful, the way it did around Ryder and his buddies.

"You might have fun."

"I already did, son. I already did."

They ate in the parlor in front of the window fan. Jim looked over the paper as he chewed. Leo finished off a hot dog and a hamburger and was reaching for another when Ryder walked into the kitchen carrying two six-packs of beer and no harmonica harness. He said Lars would be along in a minute with the TV so let's make it fast, Young Buddy, you play and I'll listen.

Outside, Leo sat on the hood of Ryder's Impala. It was hot under his legs and felt good. He played "The Love Abode" for him in three separate keys, then sung and played it in two more. Ryder stood back in his short-sleeved cowboy shirt, his thin arms crossed in front of his chest, and he studied Leo's face and hands as he played. On his exit riff Leo threw in some flutters and a couple of hand-smacks before he capped it all off as loud as his lungs and the harp would let him. Ryder went right in with instruction. Leo had noticed that the better he got, the more picky Ryder was getting with his teaching points. Today it was Leo's left hand, his holding hand. Ryder said when he got carried away on the high notes, his pinky finger stuck out like a boner, letting precious air out of his fanning cup thereby throwing off his tremolo. "And your hand-smacks are all wrong, Young Buddy; you want to hit them on your off-notes, not the other way around." Ryder took up Leo's new A harp and showed him what he meant. He let out a woo-wah-ing shotgun of a riff that zipped out into the trees like sound shrapnel. "You want to top 'em on the downside. That adds juice to your high notes, which can already cut through the bull. Got it?"

Leo thought that he did, though he didn't feel up to trying it out right now. He heard a car coming down the hill and turned to see Lars's Rambler pull up behind Jim's Valiant. Two of Lars's regular buddies were with him. Leo could see TV antennas sticking up in the back seat next to a man finishing off a can of beer. Lars put his head out the window as he shut off the engine. "Einstein good as you yet, Stillwell?"

"No way," Leo said.

"How 'bout it, Slim. Should the kid keep his day job?"

"Not for damn long." Ryder squeezed Leo on the shoulder, held the door open for the men, and followed them inside.

Leo put his harmonicas back in their cases and he wondered if Ryder had meant it. He sounded like he did. Leo pictured himself being so good he didn't have to get up for work in the morning like every other man but could sleep late because he wowed the crowds in the clubs at night with his Harp of the Blues. Ryder was crazy for not doing that. Once this summer Leo had asked him why he didn't and Ryder said, "If my passion becomes my work, Young Buddy, then what do I do for fun?"

"You could have fun while you work."

Ryder had confused the question by explaining to Leo that *passion* in Latin means to suffer and so there's no way he could have fun at work if Mr. Harp of the Blues is his passion.

"So you suffer every time you play?"

"You got it."

"But you said you had fun."

"That's right too."

"So how can you suffer and have fun at the same time?"

"Good question, Leo. Write a song on it."

Right this minute Leo wanted to walk through Heywood, over the bridge, and down the river road to be with the Allie he used to know before this week, the one full of heat and sparks. But he knew if he did, he'd probably find the pursed-lipped quiet girl instead, and his feeling good would fall to suffering in no time.

There was a song there for certain, but he didn't see himself writing one on a Wednesday night in his house, not with loud Lars and a TV set and a bunch of men's voices. And he sure didn't see himself walking all the way up to Beatrice's, or later to the Donovans' to get treated like a stranger either. Maybe a little mystery about Leo Suther was in order here. Maybe Allie would miss what she didn't know she was taking for a given. Tonight was men's night and Leo was going to find Gerry, maybe get in his Cornet, drive to Springfield and slip some guy a buck to pick them up a six-pack or two. Or maybe he'd walk to the Poitrases' just to sit on the couch and eat some of Betty's chewy cookies, watch some television. But this picture was all wrong.

How GP had stopped being a friend Leo wasn't sure, though he knew he hadn't been missing him much. He thought of Gerry's new lean face at the lake when GP had insulted Leo in front of Allie. Gerry was being his usual rude self, but behind that disgusted shake of the head before his showy dive, he looked sort of hurt. Gerry didn't have a girlfriend, and Leo was sure he'd never made love before.

There was a new movie down at the Fremont, *The Warlord* with Richard Boone and Charlton Heston, the *Ben Hur* actor. Leo thought about catching the 7:00 show but that would mean going downtown and he didn't trust himself to avoid that quick walk to Beatrice's to see Allie, so he went inside, grabbed a Coke, and went into the parlor to watch baseball with the men.

After the Sox won, Lars and his two friends pulled up chairs at the round card table Ryder and Jim were setting up for a game. Leo stood by the fridge with the *Boston Globe* and he scanned the local news about the city riots over the weekend. The national news section said there was one still dragging itself out in Newark, New Jersey. He got himself a left-over hot dog from the fridge. It was completely dark out. Around the outside light above the screened kitchen door was a swarm of moths and flies, some mosquitoes, a couple of june bugs too. Jim sat on his stool tuning his Dobro steel slide guitar, while Ryder took cash and coins and passed out chips. Lars put the deck in front of Ryder to cut.

"When's Jimbo gonna let Einstein piss away his pay?"

Jim slid his finger thimble down along the guitar neck. Without looking up, he said, "He turns eighteen soon and he can do whatever the heck he wants. Right now he watches."

One of Lars's taller friends glanced up at Leo and looked him over. He picked up a dime chip and threw it into the ante in the middle of the table.

Leo wiped mustard off his face. "I'm going to GP's. Be back later."

The smell of the mill was everywhere tonight. Leo was sweating when he stepped up to the lighted porch and rang the buzzer. Gerry's father answered the door. He wore a white V-necked T-shirt and a pair of plaid golf shorts that went right to his knees and were unsnapped just under his belly. "Well, *Leo.*"

"Hi, Mr. P." Leo stuck his hand out, thinking a handshake was in order. Mr. Poitras was slow on the take, though.

"Gerry home?"

"Gee, you just missed him, Leo. We put him on the train with his friend Logan this morning."

"To the *marines?*"

"You bet. We won't see him for thirteen weeks anyway. What's that, middle of November?"

"Boy, I saw him Saturday. I didn't think he was leaving till later in the week."

"No, 'fraid not."

Leo could see Ruth lying on her stomach on the rug watching the TV. Betty wasn't in sight.

"Come on in, Leo. Catch us up on things."

"No, thank you very much, but I have to get home. Do you have Gerry's address?"

"Sure thing, I'll go get it."

Ruth was watching "The Virginian." She wore shorts that hugged her good-sized butt. A tremor rolled through Leo's groin. He was surprised he'd asked for GP's address.

Mr. Poitras came back from the den wearing his glasses. He handed Leo a small folded sheet of paper. "Regards to your father. Don't be a stranger, now. Good night."

When Leo got to the street lamps of Paper Boulevard, he unfolded the paper and read the address:

> Pvt. G. Poitras
> #304-48-6329
> 1st Recruit Training Battalion
> Platoon 1210
> Marine Corps Recruit Depot
> Beaufort, S.C. 29904

Leo stuck it deep into his shorts pocket, and walked home.

17

Allie hadn't told a soul, but sometime between Monday night and now, Wednesday night, she had started to think of herself as the Warrior Woman instead of the Warrior Girl because girls don't have babies. All week at the UFO Show she kept sipping cold glasses of Coke and she held her breath whenever she passed the fryolator window. She joked with Sid and Beatrice and served all her lunch and dinner customers as quickly and well as she could. The whole time, though, she thought of Leo and the shoes she wanted him to fill. God, confusion was too small a word. It was a dog's situation and green-eyed lanky Leo seemed such a puppy. Tonight he didn't come by or even call. It was also the first night since the weekend that her father skipped driving out to the university to regroup with his comrades. Allie knew she was with her mother on that one: change the world, yes, but keep to your family hearth, mister. That's what her parents were talking about now, though Allie had only heard the start of the discussion because she was in her closed room and soon they moved upstairs to theirs.

That's what it was, too. A discussion. In the kitchen, her father had sounded tired, her mother sad but hard about it, like whatever had made him so tired had also brought them to where it would never be the same again and they both knew it and now had to figure out what the new picture would look like.

"Bourbon?" her dad said. Her mother just nodded yes, and after they had gone up with their drinks and somber voices, Allie tried to read a book she pulled off one of the shelves after dinner, *The Naked and the Dead*. The title seemed to match something she knew, but the actual words she found herself reading over and over again while she thought of taking that drive with her mother—who still didn't know a thing—to whatever doctor hollowed out the promise of what she carried. After a while, she could hear the muffled gasps of her mother's lovemaking, and it was a sound she took with her straight to sleep.

18

The van moved slowly from the north over the sun-dappled road along the ridge in the trees. Earlier, it had rained and now, two hours after noon, the gravel was the color of cinnamon. The man in the passenger seat held a pair of binoculars to his face. He was careful not to rest them on his nose, and when he saw beyond the junipers what he wanted to see, he said, "Right here," and the man behind the wheel steered the van over a bed of pine needles under light branches that dripped rainwater over the windshield, that scraped the van's roof until it came to a stop.

The man in the back belched and took an immediate sip of his Narragansett. He was sunburned and blond like the man behind the wheel, but much bigger in the chest, arms, and belly. On the inside of his right forearm was a tattoo of a long blue mermaid with flowing hair and outward-curving breasts. The man in the passenger seat ducked his head and aimed the binoculars through an opening in the branches over the sun-bright field to the wood frame of the new house. He could see the kid working on the north face of the roof. His shirt was off. He was driving nails into the plywood sheathing, probably missing his rafters too. A rope flew out from the south face of the roof the man couldn't see, uncoiling itself to the ground where Chick Donovan caught it and tied it around a roll of black roofing paper.

"There's the son of a bitch, that's him."

The man in the back leaned forward between the front seats.

Through the binoculars Tom Burrell came into view as he leaned out and pulled up the roofing roll hand over hand, his thick shoulders and arms gleaming with sweat. The kid had hit a good rhythm with his hammering, four whacks a nail. The man behind the wheel pulled a can of beer from its cardboard case on the floor. The man in the back belched again. The engine ticked with heat.

It was a day that couldn't make up its mind on how it wanted to go. First rain in the morning, then hot sun through lunch and after, then, at a half an hour to cleanup, came gray clouds again, a short wind, and a few splatterings of cool rain that felt good on Leo's upturned face but when they touched his sunburned back he got instant shivers and he climbed down Chick's new ladder to find his shirt.

Chick and Tom were in the driveway discussing whether to quit now or later. If they quit now, Chick said, half of the roof will be tarpapered overnight and the other half won't. Tom got in his two nickels about there being some wind. Who can say what it'll do later? Better to have half a roof of paper blown away than the whole thing. Chick agreed he was right and they decided to stop for the day.

Leo got the wheelbarrow and went to work picking up all the wood and paper scraps on the ground around the house. When he had a full load, he aimed for the dirt path that led around to the back of the barn. He stopped there, squatted under the wood handles, and flipped the wheelbarrow upside down onto the debris pile that had grown five or six times since that first week cleaning out the ash basement. He was glad they were knocking off a little early. And none of this pride stuff today; he was going to walk straight to Beatrice's. Business there was slow about this time of day and he was going to get Allie alone in a corner and just ask her flat out what he did wrong. He was just going to put that question to her pretty face and handle what comes.

The sky had darkened and a warm wind blew east from the fields. Leo rolled the wheelbarrow into the barn next to the generator, then he and Tom pulled the tall sliding door shut and padlocked it.

"You did a good job nailing off that roof today," Tom said. "Some fellas can't function up off the ground like that."

"I like it."

"'Course you do." Tom started his station wagon and backed out of the driveway. He kept his eyes on the road and waved a big hand at Leo and drove off.

Chick yelled down from the second floor to ask if Leo had seen the leather notepad he kept in his back pocket. Leo said no, he hadn't seen it. He could hear Chick walking over the plywood, then saw him lower himself feet-first through the stairwell opening. Chick held on to the header, swung once, then dropped square on his work boots to the first floor. He wiped his hands off as he walked towards Leo and the truck, his eyes scanning the ground. "Tomorrow's materials list is in there. I'll have to drop you off and come back."

"I'll help you look."

"I appreciate that, but I got enough people picking up after me as it is." Chick climbed in behind the wheel of the flatbed and started her up. Leo was barely in with his door closed when Chick had the truck in gear and was heading out.

"How do you mean?"

Chick glanced over at Leo. The right lens of his eyeglasses had a speck of tar in the upper corner. "You're very fond of Allie Cat, aren't you?"

"Yes sir, I am."

"Good. That's good." Chick kept the flatbed in second gear as he drove down the hill to the river road. He was clean-shaven and tanned in the face. He didn't look nearly as tired and distracted as he had at the beginning of the week.

"It's hard to carry a torch when you're head of a family, Leo, that's all."

Leo could see the river through the trees at the base of the hill. He nodded and looked out his open window. They were passing a deep stand of poplars. The wind made their leaves twist and flutter, their silver undersides showing till they shimmied back around. Leo liked that Chick had said good, good; that must mean he's got warm feelings about Leo and Allie together and how could he have those if he wasn't getting at least half of them from Allie at home? "I guess a family is all I really want in life, Chick."

Chick put on the brakes so fast Leo slid forward and hit his elbow on the dash. He looked out the windshield and saw "Call Dwight—He Paints it Right" on the side door of Dwight's Chevy van. It was twenty feet from the flatbed, taking up the whole width of the road. Dwight must've gunned it out from the trees and Floyd was jerking open the passenger door, stepping out with a wooden baseball bat in his right hand, an aluminum splint and a patch of white gauze taped across his nose. Chick took off his glasses and stepped out of the cab. Leo stepped out too. He saw Dwight come around the front of the van just as Floyd rushed over and slammed the bat down on the truck's hood. Floyd turned to face Chick. His left cheek was purple and yellow. He was breathing hard through his mouth, the gauze flaring out and sucking in at his nose.

"Have we got a problem, Floyd?" Chick's voice sounded squeezed, but in no hurry.

"*You* got the problem, red chicken mother*fucker*!" The veins stood out on both sides of Dewey's throat. Somebody was yanking on the inside handle of the van's side door. Dwight reached over and let out his younger, bigger brother Olin, who Leo had seen at poker

Wednesday once before. He had said hardly a word all night, drunk almost three six-packs, and had only red eyes to show it. His eyes were red now. They moved from Chick to Leo, then back to Chick, where they stayed.

"Can't get it up alone, Starrett?" Chick's voice didn't sound squeezed anymore. Floyd's breath made a slight whistle out his nose and clenched teeth. His gray eyes had a bonfire in them, and he was holding the bat above his right shoulder, gripping the handle with both hands.

"Squash him." Dwight looked at Leo and raised his eyebrows like he was about to smile. There was a droning in Leo's ears. He clenched his fists to quiet things. His palms were slick and his mouth had gone so dry he couldn't swallow. Floyd's bat came down like it was attached to a spring. Chick dodged to the left but Leo saw and heard it crack into his right shoulder. Chick's eyes teared up and his right arm hung loose and stiff. He got his footing and lunged up with a hooking left that hit Floyd in the ear and snapped his head to the side, sending him sideways against the flatbed where he dropped the bat. Olin grabbed Chick by the throat and walked him backwards as Dwight grunted out half-words and threw punches over Olin's shoulder into Chick's face. Chick kept hooking at Olin's head with his left, but Olin stuck his elbow out to block the blows. Leo started around Floyd but slipped on the gravel and fell just as Floyd was reaching down for the bat. Leo got his hand around it, pulled it free, and stood up. He grasped the handle and raised the bat over his head facing Floyd who blinked twice and didn't move. Leo took a running swing at Dwight. He brought the bat down in a sideways arc that caught Dewey under his punching arm in the middle of his rib cage. Leo felt the tip of the bat go in, heard all Dwight's air leave him in a rattle as his feet slid out to the left and he hit the ground. On the other side of Olin's shoulder Chick's face was almost purple, bleeding, his eyes squeezed shut, and he had stopped swinging his left, was just holding onto Olin's wrist with it. Leo raised the bat over his head. There was nothing else to do; he aimed for Olin's thinning blond hair, but Leo's arms were jerked backwards, there was a sharp pinch in his lower back, then the slam of the ground. Floyd stood over him with the bat. Leo rolled over and jumped to his feet.

"He's killing him, Floyd! He's fucking killing him!" Leo took a step toward Olin when Floyd's bat swing nicked Leo's shoulder and he stepped back.

"Hit the road, man." Floyd held the bat high, ready. Dwight pulled himself up on his elbow and got enough air to let out a long groan before he coughed and tried to catch his breath again. Olin still had Chick by the throat. Both Chick's arms were hanging at his sides now and the muscles in his blue face were relaxed, his eyes only partly open. Leo turned and ran around the van. When he reached the bottom of the road he was going so fast he couldn't make the turn without falling so he slid on purpose, scraping his left leg on the gravel. He pushed himself up and was going again, and he had never run so fast or so hard and still it wasn't enough. He could see the covered bridge down the road through the trees, the police station just on the other side of it, but Chick's face had looked so bad, there wouldn't ever be enough time. For a heart-streaked second Leo thought of a dive and swim across the river to the floodwall behind the courthouse, but he didn't want to slow himself thrashing through the trees and brush down to the water so he kept running, his lungs screaming heat as he finally reached the bridge, hit his shoulder against the frame, and headed through to the other side, up the road, around the corner, and over the courthouse steps.

Sergeant Mike sat at his desk behind the wood counter and partition that Leo half threw himself on, gulping air and nodding his head, trying to speak as the new cop in town came over from the other side of the room.

"They're ki—, they're *killing* him."

"Show me." The officer's nameplate said F. PETRUCCI and that's all Leo got a look at because the cop was already walking fast through a side door to the parking lot where the cruiser was. Leo ran after him out into a wind that had made it down the hill and across the river to whip warm rain into his face and chest. He pulled shut the cruiser's passenger door and yelled for the young officer to take a right over the bridge and he would want his gun because there's three of them and they've got a bat and they're killing my boss.

121

19

Officer Petrucci put on his blue lights but left the siren off. He drove fast over the bridge planks, but took the turn slow, sped up for the river road stretch, then took the right up the hill slow again, too slow, Leo thought, still breathing so hard his breath misted a spot on the windshield that was already hard to see out of with all the rain. The flatbed was up ahead with both doors wide open. No blue van though. No Floyd, Dwight, or Olin.

And no Chick.

Leo opened the door of the cruiser and stepped out before it came to a full stop. The rain pelted his face and head. The wind jerked the poplar tops at the edge of the road where he ran but didn't see Chick anywhere. He looked at the small clearing the van had to have come from. He waded through the brush at its border, the thicket branches pulling against his legs. He peered into the trees and started to go in when the cop yelled something and there was Chick lying on the road behind his truck on his back. The cop was squatting beside him, holding two fingers up under Chick's jawbone. When Leo got close he felt something rise and fall in him all at once; Chick's eyes were closed and his face wasn't blue anymore, just very pale, and wet, the rain washing away the blood around his nose and mouth. But something looked wrong with his arms and legs. His right elbow was square and turned out, and his wrist was almost as wide as his hand. His left pant leg was stretched out at the thigh, while his right wasn't.

The cop put his ear to Chick's chest, saying words Leo couldn't hear over the rain. He squatted at Chick's splayed feet, hoping to Jesus the policeman wasn't saying what he thought he was. "*What? What did you say?*"

The cop was up and running to his car, his supply belt and gun holster bouncing. Leo closed his eyes and when he opened them the policeman was back, trying to lay a blanket out on the road next to Chick, but the wind picked up the corners and rolled it back. Leo jumped up to hold two of them down. The cop slid his arms underneath Chick's back, letting Chick's head rest on his forearm. He tucked his other hand under Chick's armpit, then pulled him onto the blanket. Leo reached for Chick's feet.

"Careful, he has breaks all over."

"They had a bat, they had a frigging bat."

The cop came around, then gently lifted Chick's legs over onto the blanket that was so wet now there were puddles in the folds. He went back around to the other end and grabbed the blanket at its corners. *"Lift when I say to, and watch where you step."*

Chick wasn't heavy at all. This didn't seem right. Both rear doors of the cruiser were open. The cop told Leo to back through one door and exit the other and don't bump anything as we lay him on the seat. When Leo stepped backwards out of the car, leaving Chick laid out in the back seat, he could see Chick's stomach move a little with his breathing, but not much. The policeman got an orange rain slicker from the trunk and covered Chick with it. Then he shut both doors, got in behind the wheel, and called in on his radio, telling Sergeant Mike he was going straight to Holyoke Hospital. The blue light on the roof turned back and forth in its globe. He pulled the door shut. *"Get in."*

"I can't leave his truck here; is it okay if I meet you there?"

The cop hesitated a second, then put the cruiser in reverse. *"I'll see you there. No malarkey."* He backed all the way down the hill in the rain and the siren came on as he hit the river road and headed for the bridge.

The thing is, Allie looked like her old self when Leo rushed into Beatrice's wetter than water itself. She was ringing up a check for two older women who wore those see-through plastic scarves over their hairdos, and she was smiling as she handed them their change, chatting about a waterfall she'd read about, and so Leo was the party-wrecker and he knew it, and when she saw him and smiled even more, he knew he was taking joy in being about to smash what's been missing between them through no fault of his own, and as soon as he knew all this he felt immediately worse because all this hinged on Chick, who wasn't playing any kind of hand here at all, who was hurt so bad he was maybe beyond help.

———

Something along these serious lines Allie had to have seen because her face changed, and even though the place was busy, Leo took her hand and led her to the door.

"You've got to come with me right now, Allie; your dad's messed up."

On the way to Holyoke, the flatbed's wipers going top speed, the road water sluicing out and away from the truck, Leo described the whole fight right up to him going back in the cruiser to find Chick laid out on the ground. Allie sat still and looked straight out the windshield as Leo talked. When he told her about Chick's blue face, her mouth became a flat line, her eyes shallow.

This was a reaction Leo hadn't figured on. He was hoping for more softness, some tears maybe, something he could put his arm around. He should've pictured this, but he hadn't, not Allie looking like she could kill someone.

"The shit *bastards.*" She put both hands on the dash and clenched her fists. For reasons he couldn't begin to explain to himself, he had an erection.

"They did it because of his pamphlets, didn't they?"

Leo shrugged. He reached over to put his hand on her leg, to squeeze it once as some kind of answer, but she was right up against the door and he didn't want to lean to do it. "I think it was Floyd's revenge, that's all."

"With a *bat?*"

They were climbing a rise, and down and off to the right Leo could see the wide and rain-dimpled Connecticut River. He pictured a funeral procession going along that river, a black hearse followed by Chick's wife's black Star Chief, her inside it with little Chris and some relatives. Tailgating them would be Leo and Allie in Jim's Valiant, Leo dressed in clothes he wore once or twice a year up to Katie Faye's grave, a gray tweed jacket that didn't fit anymore, white shirt, black pants, and a maroon silk tie with little half-moons embroidered into it that you couldn't see unless you looked real close. He pictured Allie in some black dress, a red flower in her hair.

"My mother refuses to go to Mississippi, Leo. I've been meaning to tell you that."

Leo downshifted, then looked over at her as they cleared the rise. "Is that why you've been so far away?"

Allie unclenched her fists and sat back against the seat.

"Huh?" Leo took the left up another hill. On both sides of the road water flowed so fast in the culverts most of it was splashing right over the street grates. He could see the hospital up ahead.

"There's so much I have to tell you, Leo." She was looking at him now. In the gray of the cab her cheeks looked blueish and she seemed very tired.

20

But she didn't tell him a thing. How could she? With the policeman talking to him? And her mother on the way with little Chris? And her father up in something called an Emergency Triage Ward?

The policeman was as wet as Leo. He was young and handsome and he had very black short hair. Allie could see them both from the waiting area where she sat. They were sitting at a small pink Formica table inside a glassed-in cafeteria called the Care Canteen. The policeman kept licking the tip of his pen as Leo talked. Allie had asked to be included but he said he had to speak with Leo alone.

Across from Allie sat a man and woman. They were both old, probably thirty. The woman had curly red hair, and her brown eyes looked puffy from crying. The man held her hand. He was skinnier than Leo's harmonica teacher, with sideburns as long and wide as Elvis Presley's. In his seat he was half-turned towards his wife, but he was looking up at Allie's bare knees which were spread about a foot apart as she was forever forgetting a dress wasn't a pair of jeans. She stood and walked to the rain-streaked window to look for her mother, who had sounded so strangely distraught on the phone. Her voice had gone from sleepy, to sharp and clear, to a sort of whimper, like this news was exactly what she'd been expecting and God, how awful that it's all finally come to town.

The whimper part surprised Allie; it was the kind of throat sound that can only echo off a lake of devotion. And sitting next to Leo in her father's truck, hearing him tell of taking the bat and cutting down that man Dwight like a tree, Allie had felt something close to devotion, she was certain. She sat there with a fullness inside her that ached with softness for Leo but then turned when she heard about her father's blue face. She wished she'd been there herself, she would have swung that bat down on their heads and split them open like pumpkins.

Outside thunder rumbled hollow through the Berkshires, and Leo's father drove up the hill with his headlights on. Allie watched him cross the parking lot in the rain in his coveralls and short-sleeved shirt, his arms so thick, his mustache already dripping as he made his serious and so wonderfully solid way to the doors. She met him there, and Jim smiled as soon as he saw her, a big one that changed his whole face. She wrapped her arms around his neck and found herself crying into his wet clothes that smelled like denim and sweat and those sour pulp pools outside of town.

By dark the rain hadn't let up and the wind tore parts of branches from the trees, some falling into the river that swirled them on past black mudbanks and over boulders where they snagged only a moment before being whisked out to the center of the current again, heading south. Veins of lightning flashed out over the mountains, and the rain became a spark of mist against the hills. In town it battered the tin backs of the street lamps, the roof shingles of the houses, the tops of cars, the asphalt of Paper Boulevard. There was such a steady smacking of water, people inside turned up the volume on their televisions and radios. On the Springfield station an announcer with a scratchy voice warned about standard flood heights being reached before midnight.

Tess sat on a wooden chair beside her husband's bed in a curtained cubicle lit only by a small square nightlight in the wall near the floor. The rest of the Intensive Care Unit was one large room with twenty or so cubicles along two walls. It was dimly lit and quiet. She could hear the rain and wind outside, the tubular wheeze of someone's respirator a few beds down.

Chick's shoulder and chest were wrapped in some kind of tape. His right arm and left leg were each in a cast, and the leg hung in a sling from a metal frame over the bed. His head and face were swollen terribly. Earlier in the night, his cheeks and forehead had looked as yellow as oleo, and Theresa didn't know how long she could wait for the knowledge of what that man's hands had done to him.

Both his doctors said it wasn't uncommon to stay unconscious after sustaining a severed clavicle, a crushed elbow and wrist, a broken femur, and a sprained neck. And God, if all that wasn't enough, it was the neck that worried them, the bruised handprints on each side of it, that, and Leo's description of a blue face, of that big one not letting go. If he squeezed off the artery flow for longer than four minutes, they said, just 240 seconds, then her husband could be in a coma. They were watching for any swelling of his brain.

Chick's good hand was swollen too. Tess held it with both of hers. It was moist and callused and frighteningly warm. Leo had told her the whole story twice, and she was glad he had tried to do something to stop those men; hearing that made it easier to see the boy appearing so healthy and untouched. The policeman said it looked like one of the men had stood over her husband and swung the bat when he was already unconscious, once down on his elbow, once down on his wrist Then the man—Floyd Starrett, she was sure—must have stepped back to really put his weight into the last one, the one that actually cracked the long bone in Chick's thigh.

Tess took a deep breath, and when she let it out she was crying again. Exactly a week ago she had watched Chick push that barbell over his head in the rain in the backyard on top of Spoon Hill. And there, with the sky tearing itself open with electricity, she'd let herself linger on a rumor of solitude, let herself hear the news she would bring to her children that their father who had drifted so far away wasn't going anywhere anymore.

She wiped her eyes and put both hands on Chick's left forearm. She could feel the blood pulsing in it. She prayed for it to bathe his brain, to send it as much as it would ever need to bring him back to his old driven self. She hadn't talked with God since she was a girl.

127

She did it now with her eyes closed, her face resting on her out-stretched arms.

Allie said she had so much to tell him, but she was quiet all night and Leo couldn't blame her. At the hospital Mrs. Donovan had thanked him for his help and told him to use the truck to take Allie and Christopher home. The boy kept asking how high was that ladder Daddy fell off of, and when he was in his pajamas in his small bed he began to cry and he only calmed down after Allie and Leo took turns reading him Rudyard Kipling stories, then he was asleep.

In the living room Allie hugged Leo a good minute or two with her cheek pressed to his chest. She turned off the light without a word and soon they were making love on the couch while the rain slapped the window panes and the room sparked blue with lightning. Leo squeezed his eyes shut when he came and he saw Chick's plum face, its muscles unnaturally relaxed, his eyes like the moist slits of turtles. After the final shudder, he said into Allie's salty neck that he loved her. He opened his eyes and lifted his head. "I do, you know."

Allie held his neck in her hands. Her eyes were pockets of shadow. She hugged his back and squeezed very hard. Leo was about to say more but Allie began moving again so he moved too, letting this take them where they didn't need to talk at all.

It was almost midnight but the kitchen light was on and Jim rose from his chair at the table to look out the window. Leo turned off the engine and sat still a minute. The wind had picked up and was blow-ing the rain sideways at the house, and he heard the muffled crack of a dead limb as it fell through the trees. He locked the truck and ran inside. The kitchen smelled like coffee and cigarette smoke. On the table was a bottle of Jim Beam bourbon.

"Did you get everyone home all right?"

"Yeah." Leo took a dishrag and toweled his hair. He pulled off his shirt and wiped himself dry.

"You want coffee?"

"I'll never sleep."

"You won't be working tomorrow; this is supposed to keep up till Saturday."

Leo opened the refrigerator. At the hospital around seven Jim had bought him and Allie a macaroni and cheese plate—which Allie didn't touch—but Leo was hungry again. There two hot dogs left from last night. He sat down at the table across from his father and ate them both.

"I called that Tom Burrell for you. He wasn't surprised at what happened. He said to keep him posted and he hopes to see you on Monday." Jim poured bourbon into his coffee. He sipped the coffee quietly, then lit up a Lucky Strike. "Remember when you skinned your knee open wrestling?"

Leo nodded and swallowed. He had lent GP his knee guards and hadn't gotten them back in time.

"Then and tonight are the two times I've stepped into that hospital since your mother passed on." Jim took a pull on his cigarette and squinted through the smoke. The rain was loud against the house. "Allison's mother had that same look."

"What look?"

Jim raised his cup and looked straight at Leo. "You saved a man's life today, son. I'm proud."

Leo's face felt suddenly loose in its moorings, and he had to hold his breath so he wouldn't cry. He stood and went to the fridge for a Coke. He didn't know why he felt like this.

"Get yourself a beer."

Leo did. He sat back down and drank off a third of it. "I thought they were going to kill him."

Jim sat sideways in his chair with his arm resting on the back, his cigarette smoking between two fingers. He was staring off in the direction of the kitchen sink, and Leo asked him if he'd told Ryder about what happened.

"He came over an hour ago. He's got a new name for you."

"What?"

"The Louisville Kid. He said of all the men in town in need of a stomping, you gave it to the first in line."

Leo laughed and sipped more beer but his heart had picked up its tempo. "Think he'll come after me?" He immediately wished he hadn't said a word. He shrugged as if he didn't care anyway, as if the question was a small one that didn't need to be answered.

"He's not that foolish, son." Jim screwed the cap back on the bourbon bottle and stood to put it in the cabinet above the fridge. Leo burped and thought of Gerry and his Coke belches down at the UFO Show, the marines.

Jim sat down and smoked some of his cigarette. "That Allie's a fine one."

Leo sipped his beer.

"She's got a grown woman's eyes for you." Jim cocked his head, like he was listening for something out in the rain. "Are you sleeping with her?"

"C'mon, Pop."

"Good, that's right. I expect you to be a gentleman." He went to the faucet and ran water under his cigarette. "I'm just going to take it you make regular trips to the drug store."

Leo leaned his head back against the wall. He could feel the rain on the other side, and he wanted to be with Allie; he wanted to be lying in her bed next to her right now. "You think Chick's in a coma?"

Jim walked over and picked up his cup. "He'll be all right. You just take it slow and easy, son." He touched his cup to Leo's can. "To Allison's family."

"To Chick." Leo bottomed up his beer, keeping his eyes on his father's eyes until there was nothing left to drink.

21

The next morning Leo slept until seven. Jim was already gone but he'd left a pot of oatmeal covered on the back burner. The rain had stopped and there was no sign of the sun. While he ate in the kitchen, Leo could hear the river outside. It was washing out the way

130

it did during the spring after the last snows, when the dancing water seemed full of mischief and couldn't wait to get out of the hills and down through Connecticut to New York Harbor and the Atlantic. Now though, halfway through summer and first thing in the morning, it didn't sound right; it howled over the boulders and gushed through the mudbanks like it had just been betrayed.

On the way to Allie's house Leo stopped off at the police station, but only Sergeant Mike was there, drinking a coffee at his desk. He told Leo to keep them up to date on Donovan's condition. If he doesn't come around soon, then you, young man, will have to press charges on probable cause. We can't let this one slide.

Leo drove the flatbed over the covered bridge, his arm out the open window, and the river was so loud he would have had to shout if he wanted to tell anybody anything. But he didn't want to tell anyone a thing, especially anybody in a courtroom with Floyd, Dwight, and Olin looking at him from their seats across the floor.

The air was warm and heavy, the sky gray, and Leo could smell the pulp pools all the way up Spoon Hill. Mrs. Donovan's car wasn't anywhere in sight. Leo walked up on the porch as Allie came to the door in a T-shirt with a white pair of panties underneath. "I just called you. I want to go to the hospital."

Leo told her that's why he's here. He bent to kiss her but she turned her head and took it on the cheek. He smelled the mill in her hair. Nope, throw-up.

"You sick?"

She shook her head. "My mom stayed there last night. They want to hook him up to a brain machine."

"Is he awake?"

Allie shook her head again, this time biting her lower lip. Behind her, Christopher was at the picnic table in the kitchen quietly eating a bowl of cereal.

Only sixteen-year-olds and above were allowed in the Intensive Care Unit room, so Allie left Chris with Leo in the small waiting area outside the door. They were two floors up in a section of the hospital where there weren't many windows, just yellow cinderblock walls. Hanging above the empty seats across from them was one of those framed Norman Rockwell paintings of a doctor giving a little bare-assed boy a shot. The boy looked like he was trying to be brave enough not to cry, and Leo thought of Allie's mother's pictures back at their house. There weren't any people in them, but still, they were a lot better than this stuff. One of her paintings was of the national forest across the river from Spoon Hill. She must have used six kinds of purples and greens and browns to get those trees. She could have used even more, and it looked like she knew it but ended up letting the woods be what they were because that was truer than the way she *thought* would look good. This guy Rockwell didn't do that. All his pictures were cute, as if everybody in the world but him was a kid.

Christopher sat in his chair with his coloring book open on his lap. Leo had his C harp in his back pocket, but this didn't seem to be the place to practice. And he wasn't about to pick up one of those magazines only to have Allie walk out of that closed room to see her beau skimming through a story about bass fishing in Maine. So he waited, and watched the boy draw, sometimes standing to stretch, walk down a hall or two, then come back and sit in a new chair. After a while, Allie came out. Her eyes were wet and she was biting her lower lip again. When she looked at Leo it was like she was seeing past his eyes into his head but wasn't interested in being there at all.

Christopher said he wanted to see his daddy. Allie knelt and put her hands on his knees and coloring book. The ICU door opened and Chick's wife stepped out. Leo stood. Christopher raised up his arms and she lifted him over Allie and kissed and held him, turning slow from side to side.

"Daddy fell off a big ladder."

"Yes, he did."

"I want to go in the room."

"No, the doctors don't let children in there; they work very hard in there."

"Fixing daddy? Right?"

"That's right."

Mrs. Donovan didn't look as pretty as usual. There were dark smudges under her eyes. Her long hair looked thick and dry, a little wild. Allie sat in Christopher's chair. "Do you want me to get you some food, Mom?"

"Coffee would be nice."

"I'll get it," Leo said. "Black?"

"Please."

"I'll come with you," Allie said.

When they were halfway down the hall to the stairs, she stopped, covered her face with both hands, and cried. Leo hugged her and she cried harder. He patted her back. A middle-aged nurse walked by them and he nodded at her reassuringly, though she didn't seem much interested either way. Allie sniffled and took a deep breath. "He looks so awful. They have wires taped to him for his *brain*."

Leo didn't know what to say, so he didn't say a word. He pulled her close again, then kissed the top of her head.

22

Real waiting is doing absolutely nothing until what is expected happens. This was so clear to Allie Sunday night that calling in sick to Beatrice's was the only thing to do. And someone could live a whole lifetime without ever really waiting once. She knew this to be true. She also knew that Friday morning in the hallway of Holyoke Hospital, while she cried into Leo's chest, she almost told him everything. With each sob she felt the words move up her throat to the back of her tongue, but even after talking about her father, then crying some more, Leo's arms holding her just right—not too little and not too much—those two words wouldn't come out, three if she addressed him right to his face: "Leo, I'm pregnant."

But even this reluctance didn't come as a surprise to her, because Thursday night with him on the couch pointed to it going just that way, when, still on top and inside, he told her twice that he loved her and she hugged him with a gladness that felt automatic, sort of outside herself, and instead of blurting out the news, the two of them lying there together talking about the baby that was coming, she began making love with him again, and while she did, the rain slapping the roof, the lightning opening up the room, she had never felt so truly alone and yet completely herself; Leo Suther's love was immaterial. Which could only mean one thing, she thought. I don't love Leo.

It was a phrase she allowed herself as soon as he'd driven off in her father's truck that night. It came as she sat on the toilet and let his sperm slide out of her into the water. I don't love you, Leo. Sorry. I sure like you, you're very sweet and good. But I don't love you, Leo. I don't.

She did before, though, she was certain. That night after they made love in his father's car, when he drove her back home, she meant it then. But something happened almost as soon as she said it. Like saying it was the same as letting it loose in the woods to run around on its own and maybe never come back.

She'd flushed the toilet and gone to her room. There was a storm outside, and her father was hurt, but a big piece of Allie Donovan had just fallen into such a clear and steady place, sleep came very soon, but then she woke to Christopher crying, she felt sick again, and when she saw her swollen-faced unconscious father behind those grim curtains, the last thing in the world she wanted was to be out of love with the boy who held her in the hallway, who stayed with her and her baby brother and mother all weekend long, who bought them fried chicken and ice cream, who just tonight told her again he loved her and don't worry, honey, Chick will be fine, I'll see you in the morning, good night.

In Leo's dream, Big Bill Broonzy was dancing across the floor with Katie Faye. They were all in a nightclub of some kind, dark except for a small spotlit platform stage. Jim was on it, sitting on a stool playing his steel slide guitar. His eyes were closed and he was singing Ryder's "Inside-Out Low-Down Paper Mill Blues." Katie Faye wore the same dark blouse and slacks outfit as in the bureau portrait in Jim's bedroom. But the red kerchief was tied around her neck this time, the triangular part pointing down her back. Broonzy was in denim coveralls, barefoot. His eyes were closed too. Only Katie Faye's were open. As she danced slow, her cheek resting on Broonzy's chest, she looked in Leo's direction, studying the floor in front of him. It was the same way she took in the sidewalk in that picture of her and Jim, Ryder, and his new girlfriend in New York City. And Leo knew she wasn't seeing him as he sat there at a corner table sipping a Coke through a straw, watching her like he'd never watched anybody in his life. But that was all right. He probably wasn't born yet and it was good enough she knew to look hard at that empty table and chair while she danced with Broonzy, her husband playing for just them. She looked away as Big Bill danced her all the way around the tiny floor, never opening his eyes, all ears to Jim Suther's music. Then it was Jim talking, gently slapping the bottom of Leo's bare foot.

"Phone's for you." Jim turned and headed back down the hallway to the kitchen. Leo sat up. His room was still dark and he smelled coffee. He zipped his jeans up over his erection and got the telephone in the parlor. It was Tom Burrell. He told Leo to meet him at the job site in a half hour, they needed to chat.

It was odd driving Chick's flatbed to work without him, and an hour earlier than usual too. On the other side of the river the waterline was only a foot or so beneath the level of the road, the bases of the poplars covered. Jim had walked down to the bottom of Saunders Hill over the weekend and said the river was four feet into the trees on both sides. And it might rain again today. It sure looked it. The sky was gray as tin, the air cool and weighted.

Burrell's station wagon was backed up to the open barn and Tom was setting the generator on the tailgate, then pushing it up into the rear of the car, where Leo could see more tools. He parked the truck and got out. Tom walked by to grab two sawhorses. He laid them on the wagon's roof rack and began to tie them down.

"I guess we're not working today."

"I will be." Burrell pulled a slipknot tight and walked around to the other side of the car.

Leo followed. "I'm sure Chick wants us to keep working on this house."

Tom tied another knot and pulled it snug. He pushed on a sawhorse to check it. He put his hand on his hip and wiped his forehead with the back of his arm. "Floyd came around last night."

"Was Dwight with him?"

"Who?"

"One of the guys who jumped us."

Tom shook his head. "Floyd was as scared as I've seen him, too. He's afraid he overdid it on Donovan. He's worried about him passing on."

"He should've thought about that before."

Tom crossed his arms. "Probably the darn hardest thing He ever told us to do."

"What's that?"

"The cheek business, it goes against all the instincts."

"Where will you be working?"

"Chicopee today. I can't wait around for Chick to get better, I'm afraid. If he comes around—and I pray he does—then I'll finish the job with him like I said I would. Looks like you're out of work for a while."

Leo shrugged. "I got some saved."

Tom said good and walked around the car to swing the rear door shut. He got into the driver's seat and looked out the window at the road. "I just wanted you to pass this all on to Chick, or whoever." He started up the engine and smiled. "If you marry that daughter of his, I expect an invitation."

"Sure thing." Leo watched the station wagon pull away and turn right down through the woods for the river. Tom had left the barn door open, an all-around selfish thing to do, Leo thought, considering a stack of fresh lumber and all of Chick's tools were still in there. He pulled the door closed and padlocked it, then walked inside the half-finished frame of the new house. There were wet spots on the plywood floor, and the place smelled like sawdust and rainwater. He sat down on the floor in the corner.

These few weeks he'd worked alongside Tom and Floyd and Chick helping to build this house, he had imagined the owners to be a big family: a husband and wife with five or six kids, all of them cramped in an apartment somewhere waiting for their home to get done. But now, Leo felt certain there was no family attached to this place at all. It probably belonged to some old bachelor dentist, or accountant, somebody with enough money for a country house to come putter around in, maybe die in.

The air was so quiet there was a light ringing in Leo's ears and he couldn't nail it down with anything solid but he had never felt before such a sureness about the coming of something either truly horrible or else changed for good, no matter what he had to say about it. He reached around for the C harp in his back pocket, hoping to blow this all right out of him in a popwailing riff, but his pocket was empty so he started up the truck and drove straight to the Donovans'.

On Spoon Hill a scattering of droplets blew across the windshield, and down below, the river moved wide and fast through Heywood, the water skimming only a foot or so from the top of the concrete wall behind the buildings on Paper Boulevard. Allie's mother's car was parked next to the cabin. Leo backed the flatbed right up to it the way Chick would. It was barely 7:00 and he hadn't counted on Chick's wife being home. On the way over he'd imagined himself tiptoeing through the house into Allie's bedroom. He'd kiss her awake and they'd maybe make some quiet love before Christopher woke up and they all drove to the hospital. When Leo actually stepped up on the porch and smelled coffee, he thought about getting back in the truck and driving home, but it wasn't his flatbed anyway, and if he could catch smells through the screen door, Mrs. Donovan had probably already heard and seen him at least once. He opened the door and stepped inside. Allie's mother was sitting at the picnic table in the long red and orange cotton robe she wore that first night he met her. There was a coffee mug on the table in front of her. She yawned into her hand, then rested her face sideways on her wrist. "He woke up at three this morning."

"Who? *Chick?*"

She lifted her head and smiled. Her eyes were wet.

"What happened?"

"He couldn't talk at first but we discovered that was from his mouth and throat being so dry. After a glass of water he seemed better."

"He *was?* This is wonderful, this is so good. Does Allie know?"

Mrs. Donovan nodded and went to the cabinet for an empty mug. She poured it full of coffee and asked if he wanted milk and sugar and Leo said okay. Allie's bedroom door was closed. Leo walked over the knit rug in front of the fireplace and sat down at the table in the kitchen. He heard some birds calling out in the trees on the ridge. They sounded different from the ones down on the river, who seemed to whistle and shriek more than anything else. This was some news about Chick. Leo watched his wife walk over with the coffee. She had small breasts like Allie. They moved just a little under her robe as she set the coffee in front of him and sat down across the table.

"So he wasn't in a coma then?"

"Yes. He was."

"Boy." Leo shook his head and sipped his coffee. Mrs. Donovan didn't touch hers. She was watching him with those almost tired, nearly squinting eyes. It was an expression of sizing up. She probably looked at one of her own paintings with that face: not warm or cold, just deeply interested in knowing more about what was really in front of her. He sipped his coffee again, staring at the wood planks of the table top.

"I wonder if I could ask you a favor, Leo."

"Sure thing."

"This family's going through a rough time right now, as you know, and I think it's best if you and Allie don't date for a while. At least until her father is back home and doing better."

Leo didn't know what one had to do with the other. His mouth and chin felt funny, like Mrs. Donovan's stare was eroding the foundation of his face. He shrugged. "I think I can help out."

"Oh I'm sure you can, Leo. And you have. I want this family to have some privacy, that's all. People heal better that way." She reached over and rested three fingers on his wrist. "You've been a big help all weekend, thank you."

Leo sipped his coffee so her hand would fall away and it did. "Allie knows, I guess."

"No, I'll tell her when she wakes up. It will only be for a week or

138

so. And that includes phone calls, of course." She tilted her head to the side. "No distractions of any kind." She smiled again, stood, and put her half-full mug in the sink. "Just give me a minute to change and I'll drive you home."

"That's all right, I'll walk."

"But it's going to rain."

"Thanks for the coffee." Leo stepped off the porch and walked with a full stride over the gravel drive. When he was halfway down he cut into the trees and headed up the hill. He ran through the underbrush, ducking limbs all the way up until the ground leveled out and he was squatting in the woods across from Allie's bedroom window. He was breathing hard. He got into a three-point sprinter's stance, then leapt out of the bush and ran across the side yard to Allie's window. He leaned against the logged wall, keeping his head under the sill. Okay, he thought, a week's not forever but I'm going to kiss her goodbye.

Then he heard talking. It was Allie's voice. He straightened up and looked inside. Allie's bed was made and her door was wide open. He could see her crossed bell-bottomed legs from the knees down as she sat at the picnic table. She was barefoot, bouncing the top leg, and she wasn't talking anymore. The faucet was running in the kitchen. Then it turned off and Leo heard the sliding clink of plates underwater. Allie kept bouncing the back of her calf on her knee. Her moving foot looked pale as plastic. He turned and walked out of the yard and down the hill.

23

He was harmless, actually. A very sweet boy, really. Tess Donovan's eyes burned from lack of sleep and as she washed another one of the plates Allie had let pile up in the sink over the weekend, her sixteen-year-old sitting at the table, so quiet and jittery, Tess thought about hot air balloons. Two summers ago the town committee hired three balloonists to hover over Empire Lake on the Fourth of July as a Come-Discover-the-National-Forest stunt. There were three separate balloons, each dyed a different primary color. After they found their spot over the middle of the lake, the man in the red balloon did something in his basket to make it float higher than the blue and yellow until all three formed a pyramid. Then the men in the two lower balloons unfurled a banner between them that read: "Heywood—Summer of '65!"

At the picnic ground, while Chick and Allie swam and baby Christopher slept in his diapers on the blanket under a tree, Tess had watched these men up above. What was so compelling was how they could all float so perfectly still, staying in pretty much the same spot, and remain a pyramid all day long. It was the sandbags that helped pull it off. Each basket had a dozen or more of the solid canvas sacks hanging from ropes off the sides. Nothing overly scientific about that. Apply the same pull to a push and motion stops: and that's precisely what happened before dawn this morning when Tess drove home so fast she almost went off the road twice, once on a curve near the river, the other in the middle of Paper Boulevard at the Heywood town line where she swerved to miss a shadow in her headlight path. The street lamps were still lit, but not another light in all of town. As she drove through the black of the covered bridge she knew she would wake Allie, perhaps even Christopher. At the bottom of Spoon Hill she pushed the accelerator to the floor and felt stones knock under the car all the way up to the ridge where through the trees was the light blue smear of daybreak. She got out of the car, and her eyes filled at the thought of seeing Allie's sleepy face when she would hear that her father was okay, he was going to be all right. But the living room lamp was on and Allie was not in bed asleep, was instead standing near the couch holding a novel closed on one finger to mark her place, a place she forgot all about as Tess told her the news and Allie dropped the book, hugged her mother crying, then sobbed into her hair and shoulder, "Oh shit, Mom, I'm going to have a *baby*."

Allie the weight. Doing her mom a favor, keeping her close to earth where nothing is simple and with the sun comes sunburn. But also I drove home like a drunk and if Icarus hadn't flown so high he wouldn't have fallen so far, so there you have it, she thought; I'm right where I should be, in the thick of this striving little family, my sleeves rolled up, my hands wet, my head still, and my heart calm.

Allie had stopped bouncing one leg against the other. She sat against the table with her arms folded, looking across the living room out at the awful gray sky. Tess dried her hands, took her daughter's, and led her to her room. While Allie undressed and got into bed, Tess checked on Christopher, who she knew would be up very soon. For now though, he was still asleep on his stomach, his little fists loosely clenched out and away from him on the sheet. Tess walked quietly over the floorboards, picked up the rocking chair, and carried it into Allie's room. She set it down with her back to the open window so she could look at her daughter's face. Allie's green eyes were cloudy with fatigue, and her lips were pursed in the sort of pout Tess hadn't seen on her in years.

"Don't you feel better getting that secret out of you?"

Allie shrugged her shoulders against her pillow.

"Well, until we go to Boston we don't know anything for sure."

"*I* know for sure, Mom. It's not fair to Leo either. God, I wish I told him."

Tess took a deep breath and let it out very slowly. Allie was looking at the ceiling, her blond hair spread out on the pillow around her. A tear had rolled along her nose and stopped at her lip. Tess imagined Leo looking down at that loveliness. "I was twenty years old when I first made love."

"I turn seventeen in October."

"Yes, and you'll be a senior in high school and you certainly won't be bulging with a baby, either."

Allie's eyes moved to her mother's, stayed a moment, then turned back to the ceiling. Soon they closed and Tess rocked awhile. She'd thought she would come in here to sing her pregnant daughter to sleep, but no song was coming now. Allie's breathing slowed and deepened. Tess heard the hollow tapping of a woodpecker out on the ridge, then the thrash of something large leaving the brush, a jackrabbit, or a pheasant. She thought again of Chick's story about his great-grandmother back in Ireland poaching food off her landlord's property, a very serious offense. At dawn, she would hike out to the tall grass with a fishing pole, bait the hook with a raisin, toss it out in a clearing where she spread more raisins, then hide in the grass and wait for the big sly birds. Once she had one, she'd give the line a yank, then wade into wildly beating wings with a knife. She was usually back home before the sun was half an hour old.

It was a story Tess thought of often, one she knew she would tell Allie because Allie needed to hear the kinds of things a mother must be prepared to do. Of course, Allie would probably end up romanticizing hunger with her strange Warrior Girl talk and become even more inspired to give birth to the infant Tess knew she could not begin to consider her grandchild. Not for one moment, even this one.

Leo spent the morning lying on his bed in the quiet of the house. The walk home could have been worse, but not much. On the river road he had felt a thickness in his throat so severe he let himself cry and as soon as he wiped his eyes it was over, but not enough that he thought he could carry on a conversation with one of the cops at the courthouse; he wanted to tell them about Chick coming to so they could go talk to him and leave Leo Suther out of it. On Paper Boulevard things got worse when he saw a van—not even blue, but white—in the morning stream of cars, and he started to run and didn't stop until he was on Saunders Hill Road.

Something was definitely, horribly, undeniably wrong between him and Allie. How could she keep her door closed and pretend she was asleep the whole time her mother was telling him to get lost? Was she embarrassed to tell him she wanted to be alone with her family? Or did she really not give two shits about him whatsoever?

Chick's wife said people heal better in private, but Leo didn't believe that was true at all; people need people around them the way music needs ears. And not just any ear, but one that can appreciate what it's hearing. Like Ryder hearing Jim's guitar and Jim hearing Ryder's harp. None of those poker men were up to that kind of listening. Maybe Lars on a good day, but that's about it. Jim would be lost without Ryder. And who knows, Leo thought, maybe Ryder needs Jim just as much.

Leo thought of GP, the way he walked out of the parlor that day when Leo was jamming with the Broonzy record. That was the kind of buddy he didn't need. At the same time though, Leo missed him. He missed the way Gerry looked at the world like nothing in it should be a surprise to anybody, it's all a rat hole in one way or another so grab some fun while you can, boys. Leo wondered how much fun GP was grabbing down in South Carolina right now. He fell asleep thinking about it.

It was raining soft on the roof and in the trees when Leo woke up. He was hungry and knew he'd slept a long time. The thunder sounded close; it always did because of the mountains. Sometimes there would be a storm fifty miles north you would never think was that far because the thunder rolled itself down along the range to carry the news. Leo had an erection. He unzipped his jeans, gripped himself, and closed his eyes to that picture of Allie on his bed with her skirt pulled up, her panties off, and him sinking in. When he came he caught it in his cupped palm and opened his eyes to the wall. He thought of Katie Faye's box on the bureau. He got up without looking over there and went to the bathroom where he washed off his hand and splashed his face, then walked right to the parlor and called Beatrice's UFO Show. Sidney answered. He said that Allie had called in sick for the week and how come *you* don't know this?

Leo hung up. This was bullshit, he thought. All of it. If she can call Beatrice's, she can fucking call me. He picked up the phone again but then hung up. No, mister. No way was he going to be the confused little poodle begging for a lap. If she hasn't got the guts to tell me she wants to be alone, then she can just try being alone alone. Shit.

It was past four on the kitchen clock. Leo looked at it twice to make sure. Jesus, the whole day gone. He got himself a Coke from the fridge. There was half a tuna casserole in there Jim had told him to heat himself for supper. Leo sat at the table with the Coke and a box of Saltines. He thought about walking up that hill again, rain or not, Chick's wife or not, Allie or not; this just wasn't the way he deserved to be treated. Nope. He wasn't going to do that either. He

143

was going to stay right here and eat and practice his harmonicas and he was going to be nobody's dummy. Maybe he'd even write GP a letter, tell him all about last Thursday with Dewey, Olin, and Floyd.

Something was driving down Saunders Hill Road and Leo stood up quick to see. It was Ryder in his Impala. There were a few green leaves stuck to the wet of the hood. Ryder tapped the horn and waved at him to come on out. He rolled down the window as Leo poked his head out the door.

"Get in, Young Buddy, you got to clear something up down at the club."

Leo hadn't been inside the Elks club since the wrestling awards dinner last year when the Woodies made it to the state championships down in Springfield. It was a one-story cinderblock building, and the high school had rented the Very Important Persons Quarters for the occasion, a white paneled room just past the shuffleboard table in the main lounge. Mounted on the VIP walls were moose antlers, a couple of deer heads, a store-bought bobcat, even a wild boar, its eyes closed and its mouth part way open like someone had shot it as it slept. There had just been the team and their families, all seated around the room at small folding tables decked out in black and blue tablecloths and napkins. At first Jim and Leo had a table by themselves, but when Betty Poitras saw that, she insisted they put their two tables together like one big family. After the roast beef, the awards ribbons were passed out and everyone got something. Gerry got a ribbon for Fastest Quarter Nelson. Leo stuffed his in his pocket: Most Improved Man on the Team.

The rain wasn't soft anymore. When Leo got out of Ryder's Impala, the drops were fat and heavy and they came down hard on the top of his head. Ryder didn't give him much information on the way over. He just said, "Your old man needs the Louisville Kid and that's all you need to know." Leo followed him inside. He smelled cigar smoke and Lestoil. There was some talking going on in the back. Up at the bar on the left side of the room stood ten or eleven men and a couple of women playing their numbers as the bartender called out cards. The bar ran almost the full length of the room. Hanging over the bottle shelves was a long cloudy mirror, and above that, framed behind glass, the American flag. All along the window-less walls were black and white photographs of the Elks softball team, going back forever it looked like, some Red Sox pennants, and a few posters billing boxing matches between men with names like Sonny Kidd, Gus "the Fighting Swede" Gustafson, and Fist McCarthy.

Ryder and Leo walked over the hardwood floor towards the pool tables and shuffleboard. Back against the wall, near the door to the VIP Quarters, were a half dozen drinking tables, only two empty, the rest full of men from the paper mill. A lot of them wore the same kind of coveralls Jim did. Some played cards. Others looked up from their beer glasses and smoking ashtrays as Ryder and Leo walked to the far corner table where Jim sat with his back to the wall. In front of him were seven or eight empty glasses and two full ashtrays. He looked up at Leo and pulled the chair out beside him.

"Where did Larsmouth go off to?"

Jim nodded in the direction of the bar. He reached over and lightly pinched Leo on the arm. "You want a Coke?"

"I think Young Buddy deserves a beer, don't you Jimmy? Nobody'll see him back here." Ryder went to the bar. Jim lit up a Lucky Strike. One of the numbers men called out that he had a winner so hold the damn deal. Behind Leo, shuffleboard pins clattered.

"How come you're not playing your number?"

"Work today?"

Leo shook his head. "Burrell quit. But guess what? Chick came out of it."

"Dewey and his brother left town last night."

"*Dwight* did?"

"He told Lars he had a big job somewhere, which is odd, son, because Dwight can hardly walk. You broke five of his ribs." Jim held up his open hand to make the point. He smiled, and it was such a rare thing for his face to do, it was like seeing something very private that you almost had to look away from. Leo couldn't tell if Jim was a little drunk or not. They sat quietly a few minutes. Leo wanted to ask why Ryder came for him, but it didn't seem to be the thing to do. Then Ryder showed up with a full tray he set on the table.

"Hope I didn't overstep protocol, Jimmy." Ryder put a glass of beer and a jigger of something brown in front of Leo. He did the same for Jim and himself, then held his full shot glass over the table. Jim and Leo followed suit.

"Not only have you got the music, Young Buddy, but you got the balls to roll it up that hill and back." Ryder clinked his glass to Leo's. "To the Louisville Kid."

Leo downed the jigger and immediately sipped his beer to steady the heat chills in his neck and face. He wanted to cough and shrug his shoulders but he swallowed more beer instead. He heard the bartender call out a number that got one of the women slapping the bar, shrieking too. That seemed to be the end of that round because most of the men were heading back for the tables. One of them was Lars. He was walking with O'Donnell, the dead soldier's dad, and both of them carried a glass of beer. Somebody put an Elvis Presley song on the jukebox, and he was singing sweet and low about fools rushing in when Lars and O'Donnell got to the table and Lars squeezed Leo's shoulder until it almost hurt. "Einstein going to set the record straight, or what?"

"Sit down," Jim said. "Bill, have a seat."

Lars motioned for Ryder to move over so he could sit next to Leo. Leo didn't like how quickly Ryder did just that. O'Donnell walked around the table and sat next to Jim. His face looked softer somehow, his eyes dim. Even in the darkness of the lounge, the other men's eyes caught some of the electric light around them, but not O'Donnell's.

"Go ahead, son. Tell him."

"Tell who what?" Leo's voice shot out of him on its own, like he was talking in his sleep. He'd gotten beer-drunk with Gerry a handful of times, but it never came this fast.

"Hey kid, I'm not wild about my brother-in-law. Did he kill anyone is all I want to know."

"Tell him what you just told me, son."

Leo looked from his father to flat-topped Lars. His lips were parted like he was waiting for a punchline to let loose at. Elvis went into his first refrain about how he can't help falling in love. "Chick Donovan's not in a coma anymore. He came out of it last night."

Lars's face didn't change for a beat and a half. "So. What's the good

146

news?" He laughed as soon as he said it, whacking the table with the palm of his hand. His own beer glass started to turn and Ryder caught it. Leo noticed nobody else was smiling. O'Donnell didn't even seem to be listening.

"No, seriously you boneheads, wouldn't that be a gas to watch Dewey squirm under a murder rap?"

Ryder smiled and shook his head. Jim was looking at Leo. "Tell him the rest."

Leo shrugged and drank from his beer. It was cold and once it got to his whiskey-streaked throat, he couldn't taste it anymore.

"I told you, Suther," Lars said, "Donovan put it to Dewey just like Dewey said he did."

Leo sat forward. "Like who said?"

Lars smiled at the men around the table and jerked his thumb in Leo's direction. "Now he wants to talk, look at him."

Leo couldn't believe what he was hearing. "Dwight said *Chick hit him?*"

"With a bat, Einstein. You beg to differ?"

"The only guy Chick got a chance to hit good was Floyd Starrett," Leo said. "He knocked him right on his butt, too."

"I hear he's running scared," Lars said, raising his eyebrows at nobody in particular.

"Yep," Leo said, "and he should 'cause Chick'll go after those guys with the cops."

"So what did Einstein do?"

"Call him by his name, Lars," Jim said.

"I always call him Einstein."

"Not now." Jim smiled.

"Lookit, all I know is Dewey says Donovan swung a bat at him so the smear brothers went after Chicken in self-defense."

Leo drained his beer glass, shaking his head. "Those three jumped us. Chick punched Floyd *after* Floyd hit him with the bat. Then the other two were all over him."

"*In steps the Kid.*" Ryder shook his head and laughed. Leo couldn't help smiling himself. Jim glanced at Lars and nodded at Leo to finish up.

"Floyd dropped his bat so I picked it up and got Dwight, that's all." Leo fingered his empty glass. The Elvis song was ending.

Lars kept his eyes on Leo, then he sat back and looked around the table. "Now that makes a hell of a lot more sense." He laughed louder than ever, then he squeezed Leo's shoulder again, softer this time. "My round." He picked up the empty tray and went to the bar. A new song came on the juke, the one about the girl with the flower in her hair, and Leo thought of Allie right away. Maybe he'd ask Ryder for his car, go up to Spoon Hill and settle things face to face.

"Why did you stop them?" O'Donnell stood up. He looked from Ryder to Jim. "He shouldn't have stopped them." Then he looked down at Leo, his eyes wide and lightless. He pushed in his chair hard, then turned and walked past the shuffleboard players and out the door. Lars showed up and put the full tray on the table. "What scared Billy off?"

"The understandable." Ryder took two full beer glasses and pushed them both in front of Leo. "We'll let Louisville have his."

24

The rain had stopped and now Allie heard the squawk and caw of crows out in the trees. Two or three, it sounded like. Which seemed strange after dark. She couldn't remember ever hearing them in the night before. Morning, yes. And noon, especially then.

That's what time her mother woke her today to say she'd made an appointment with a doctor down in Springfield and they had forty minutes to make it. Her mom hadn't gone to bed yet then, either. Her breath smelled like coffee and the rest of her had that kind of corn husk scent real tired people give off. And gosh, she certainly was riding high on these family events; starting to make Allie's bed almost before she was out of it, going on about the great visit Christopher and their father just had at the hospital, how Daddy might be home end of the week, and Allie honey, don't you worry about a blessed thing; really, don't.

It was a part of her mother Allie had always seen but never really noticed: Theresa Donovan loved a good catastrophe, preferably a bunch at once. Her own brothers and sister did too. One of Allie's uncles was a doctor in a state prison, the other a helicopter pilot for forest fires out west. And Allie's Aunt Pat had three kids of her own who seemed to disappoint her if they weren't sniffing after some kind of harm or another. The one or two times a year Allie got together with her younger cousins, she could see it in their faces. Their eyes, brown and hazel, looked at her with, "Yeah? What else? Hurry up."

But there were no crows down that narrow street of one-story houses where Queen Chaos drove Allie and her little brother in the rain. In the doctor's front yard was a short round tree all blossomed out in white flowers. There were petals on the grass, and the rain was sending more fluttering down. Allie had expected an oldish man, very thin probably, with a few budding liver spots on the backs of his hands. But what walked into the examination room where the nurse had given Allie a johnny to change into was very different: Dr. Trudeau was a small woman, no more than ten years older than Allie. She had fine red hair and freckled skin. When she smiled her teeth were white and very straight. Her eyes were as dark as Billy Burrell's.

"Your mother tells me you expect a pregnancy. Is your period late?"

Allie nodded.

"Is your partner using a prophylactic?"

Allie almost said yes, but then she shook her head and looked down at her toes.

"Okay then, lie all the way back for me, please."

The examination table was cool and sticky against the backs of Allie's bare legs. At the foot of the table were two metal posts with U-shaped pads on top. The doctor called them stirrups and had Allie scoot down and put a foot in each one. Allie felt a twinge in her hip but it went away as the doctor stepped in and folded the johnny up onto Allie's stomach. She stayed up on her elbows and watched the doctor fit her hands into see-through rubber gloves.

"Lie back, Allison. I don't want your stomach muscles contracting."

The ceiling was white plaster. The doctor's finger went all the way in, touched the very center of the Warrior Woman, moved lightly in a half-circle, touched again, then slid out.

"Did that hurt at all?"

"A little."

The doctor pulled off her gloves and dropped them into the wastebasket.

"Have you had any morning sickness?"

"Yes, but sometimes it comes at night, too. Whenever there's food really." Allie smiled. She wanted to take her legs down and sit up. Dr. Trudeau folded her arms and looked down at her with a face Allie thought seemed suddenly sad.

"How old are you, Allison?"

"I'll be seventeen in October." Allie thought the doctor was very pretty. Beautiful, even. "I am, huh?"

"Yes, but we'll take a urine sample to make sure." She gently lifted Allie's left leg from the stirrup, and Allie pulled the other one out herself. She sat up. The doctor had her hand on the doorknob, looking at her. "You have an intelligent face. Here's a thought: no protection, no affection." She smiled and left the room.

Now the crows were quiet and from her bedroom Allie could hear the faint hum of the refrigerator, the dripping of rainwater off the roof outside. She lay on her bed and tried to read *The Naked and the Dead*, but it wasn't a night for soldiers at all. After the finger examination, Allie had watched Christopher take apart a Tinker Toy on the floor while her mother and Dr. Trudeau talked a good fifteen minutes in the office. Allie didn't have to guess about what, either. As soon as they got back home, Tess called her sister in Boston and got the number she was looking for. Allie picked up the newspaper and acted like she wasn't listening when her mother made the appointment for the day after tomorrow: Wednesday, August 18, at 2:00.

Two days from Leo Suther's birthday that's how she'd been regarding him the past few days, she noticed. Not as Leo, but as the full name she knew him by in Mr. Jewett's class before they actually met in the kitchen of Beatrice's UFO Show. A kid's name, like all the rest.

Not that she thought he was like Gerry Poitras and Logan Wright, or AnnaMaria Slavitt, Nancy Titcomb, and Billy Burrell, because she didn't and he wasn't. She just couldn't afford to think of him as sweet Leo right now. Her mother had told her once that loving someone is sometimes letting them take a big crap in your lap. Her mom didn't talk that way often. Usually when her painting wasn't going too well, Allie noticed. But boy, she had shown some mother's love today, letting her daughter blubber out her bad news right on top of hearing Dad's going to make it. Allie wanted to see him right this minute, though she knew her mom was right, that he probably needed a couple more days' rest before the whole family squeezed in around him in that cubicle. And for the fifteenth time she heard again what Leo had said this morning on the other side of her bedroom door, his voice so thoughtful and alert as he said sure thing to her mom's requesting the favor of kicking him out. Allie had wanted to open her door right then, but not enough. Obviously, not enough.

25

His sleep had been one long thirst and Tuesday was half gone when Leo got up, pulled on cut-off shorts, and walked barefoot down Saunders Hill Road to the river. He had to walk only half as far as usual because the water was high in the trees on both banks. He squatted and splashed his face, then he cupped his hands and drank water the color of dead leaves. When he was full he splashed himself again. The birds were chirping up a storm, but the river was quiet. The bigger it got, the less noise it made, and Leo thought of Dwight's brother Olin. He remembered Jim saying how they left town. Then he remembered the bourbon, and his stomach seemed to float out and away from him and his mouth filled with spit. He took a few deep breaths and the nausea went away.

Out in the middle of the river the sun sparkled and hurt Leo's eyes. Nothing was floating downstream like it would in the spring;

no trees, no boards, no drowned dogs. One year, a live chicken swept by. Leo was nine or ten years old and he'd walked down the road with his father after supper. It was probably April, and cold enough he wore a coat. Jim was in his coveralls with a wool shirt underneath. Leo could see his breath in front of him, but still Jim was sipping an after-dinner iced coffee. When the chicken came by, Leo almost missed it. It was all white, but yellow around the beak, perched on the corner of a wooden box that turned slightly as it floated downriver, and the chicken could not have looked less worried. No little jerks of the head. No spreading wings. "She's out for a drive," Jim said, and Leo laughed.

Now he turned and headed back for the house. How some men could call Chick Donovan chicken, he didn't know. A real chicken wouldn't have gone down to a Negro city riot to pass out communist pamphlets, a real chicken wouldn't have jumped out of his truck to face a beating. And man, that was a punch and a half that Chick hit Floyd with. There was a beauty to that kind of move; seeing it was like watching someone do a flawless dive into the water, or skate on ice with their hands behind their back. Watching Ryder and Jim play together fit in there somewhere too. Leo hoped he hadn't soaked up too much of that Louisville Kid stuff last night. He thought of Bill O'Donnell again, the way he walked out on them like Leo was bad news. But the thing is, Leo didn't think he'd done near enough that day; he should have tried harder to get the bat back from Floyd after snatching it. Floyd had still been woozy from Chick's hook, but Leo ran, and they broke Chick's bones and put him in a coma, and now Chick is on the mend and Allie is a complete Mystery Girl.

But no way in heaven was Leo Suther going to do anything about that. He walked into his kitchen, pulled two bottles of Coke from the fridge, grabbed the window fan, and went to his room. In fact, he couldn't wait for this week to hurry up and get over with so she'd know he wasn't calling not because her mother said so, but because Leo was pretty damn busy with other things. Like his music. Even last night, so drunk he had to close one eye, he played well enough in the parlor to keep up with his father and Ride. Honest-to-God blues till past midnight. They played a lot of Leadbelly, real street cracker tunes that Jim sang as loud as if he had a big audience instead of just the three of them. Ryder blew the reeds like he wanted to take off and fly, and Leo found himself playing a happy one-eyed backup, the harp-playing Leweyville Kid.

Leo pulled the shade, turned on his bedside lamp, and sat on his bed in front of the fan with a notepad and pencil. He thought he was going to try throwing together another song, then come up with the music too—he'd call it "The Mystery Girl"—but what came out instead was a letter.

Dear Gerry,

What's new? I'm hung over and unemployed. You'll never guess what happened last week. Allie's dad and I got AMBUSHED on the way home from work. It was Floyd Starrett with a bat and a couple of painter brothers I don't think you know. One of them was huge. Anyway, Chick put Floyd down with a left hook to the head, then the brothers starting creaming him. I swiped the bat from Floyd and whacked one of the painters in the ribs. Knocked him down too, but then Floyd got it back from me and started swinging. Anyway, Chick was in a coma for three days, but we hear now he's going to pull through.

So, I'm taking my first break of the summer. Allie's doing great. We'll probably get married one of these days. No lie.

Leo stopped. Where the hell did that come from? He looked up at the black and white poster of Big Bill Broonzy looking down at him. He glanced at Katie Faye's box beneath it.

Anyway, miss wasting time with ya. Keep me up on World Adventure.

Your friend,
The Louisville Kid

He tore out the page, found the piece of paper Mr. Poitras had written GP's address on, and copied it onto an envelope. He got up, took Katie Faye's box from the bureau, and turned it upside-down on the bed. All the pictures and poems and two notebooks fell out in a cool pile on his legs. There was more paper than pictures. He unfolded what looked like a piece of a brown grocery bag. On it was his mother's handwriting: small, neat letters in pencil.

> Coca-Cola
> butter
> rice
> bread
> corn
> pads
> Lucky Strikes

The other side was blank. Leo lifted the list to his face and smelled it. He picked up a loose-leaf composition notebook and began reading the first page:

February 11, 1955

Jim and I had a horrible fight last eve. I could say I started it but that would be inaccurate because what I really did was set about finishing what he started, which is his blind and deaf performance. I told him he's a musician who's not facing the music; it's time to prepare for the inevitable. Oh God, such a hard word for Jim. Fighters get so lost when it comes to things they can't stop. And Jimmy is a fighter. That old line about some men being lovers and others fighters does not apply to my husband. It seems one part fuels another and it all comes out in his singing and playing.

Yesterday, we all went to Sunday mass at the St. John's Church in Holyoke. (Such a strange word, like Sacred Eggs.) It's built on a hill overlooking the river. And behind it is a cemetery laid out in front of a pure stand of white oak trees. I had thought for a while that I'd like to be buried with my folks in the Texas panhandle, but yesterday morning, with the sun on the trees and grass, the entire valley stretched out below, I knew that hill was meant to have a stone with my name on it. Last night, after we put Leo to bed, I told Jimmy. I tried to do it in an offhand sort of way, but I suppose that was the worse route I could have taken on this point. He's convinced the next operation will be the last and we'll have beaten this thing. But I know I won't see Leo turn six.

Some days this knowledge can send me howling into my pillow where Leo and Jim can't hear. But other times, like now, when for some reason there's not much pain to speak of, I can feel almost okay about having to go so soon; I'm convinced there's something ahead for me I'm supposed to get to, and the only way I can escape feeling heartbrokenly guilty about this belief is by telling myself that lightning won't strike twice in the same family and that when I'm gone, my husband and baby will live long and glorious lives, and when they're done they'll join me and I will have had plenty of time to prepare them a heavenly home.

But the abdominal pains change everything; I imagine Jim remarried, maybe with more children, and Leo a grown man with his own family, and then who would I be making a heavenly home for? My husband's new wife? Their kids who I would be no kin to? I'm forced to adjust my vision, which isn't hard because my view is not at all fixed—not a common trait in a Baptist girl from Texas.

What I truly believe is that no sooner am I put in this earth, than I will be of it again. Like so much milkweed. Daddy would turn over and do push-ups in his grave if he knew I thought this. Mama too. Sometimes I think of joining them and I'm elated and bemused all at once; I think of those long quiet nights on the porch outside Hartley under so many stars so close to the ground I thought one night I could see the rings of Saturn. Mama used to fan herself with the almanac cover and Daddy would smoke his cigarettes and rock back on the legs of his cane chair. When they spoke at all, which was seldom, they talked of the heat, Mama's allergies, George and Gracie Burns, current events like who bought a new tractor.

Once puberty struck me, they referred to me in the third person, even when I was sitting on the porch with them. Daddy would say, "Katie did her share of work in the barn this afternoon."

Mama would say, "So why's that girl take to washing her hair every night if she's goin' to be doing that in the day?

"Katie's a multiplicitous girl." And he would lean forward and nudge me with his shoe. Daddy's formal education went as far as the fifth grade. But that didn't stop him from looking up a new word in the Oxford English Dictionary every day and repeating its pronunciation and usage until he had it. Sometimes the usage didn't always fit.

Days before he died, when he was still in bed resting from the first attack before the second and last, I sat at the foot of his bed sharing my iced tea with him. I was sixteen. There was a breeze that afternoon that blew Mama's curtains away from the window, and I remember smelling manure and the eucalyptus tree out in back. My father had lost a lot of his color but none of his cheer. He'd been using his resting time to learn more words and was working on ten a day. That afternoon he used three on me from the L's: "Katie, not only are you loquacious, but you're a damn sight lubricious, not to mention lovesome."

Which meant I talked too much, was a tad slippery, and inspired love in others. This I knew just from hearing the words and when I told Papa this he stopped smiling and sat up against the headboard: "Don't marry a farmer, Kate. Go to one of the cities and get yourself an education, and find a man who loves you so much he wouldn't think to make you a farmer's wife." Or something like that, and he said it with such a still face and tight voice I knew that he knew he was going to leave us soon, and I spilled my iced tea on the floor as I leaned forward to hug his bigger-than-you-would-think chest.

He was wrong about the loquacious part, though. The only one I ever talked to like that was him. After he died, so did my talking. Mama and I moved down to her mother's place in San Antonio then. And it was there that I became more slippery and I seemed to inspire love in a host of public school boys. A lot of them were tall and blond like the German boys up in New Braunfels. I liked them fine and admired them more for being Junior Farmers, but I couldn't give them the time of day and still be true to that afternoon with Papa, so what was I to do except keep quiet, do the homework I loved doing, and spend nights in front of the radio with Mama and Gram, who was also widowed. Me and the widows.

It was those nights, in the second floor bedroom of that stucco house off Bandera, that I began writing my poetry. The first ones were sweet and sincere and hideous as I recall, all about baling hay with Daddy, and baking biscuits with Mommy. Then I composed my war trilogy. Only instead of writing about the war I knew, the one with rations and black windows and the loaded .410 Papa kept by his bed in case of an invasion of the panhandle, I made it all happen in France and Germany. I was the girl who tramped through the snows to the barbwired death camps. I was the maiden who hid with other children in the haystacks outside the Black Forest during combat, I was—oh, it was passionate and worthless stuff. Then I began my love sonnet period, an utterly fatuous exercise until I began to stick in passages about Ramos Herrera.

Ramos was tall and thin and quiet. His hair was longer than any I'd ever seen on a boy. It was black and went all the way to his shoulders. At lunches Ramos sat alone. Not with the fifty or sixty other Mexican boys he could have sat with, not with the blond Junior Farmers. One day Ramos walked into the classroom with no shirt on under loose overalls and he was told to go home. He didn't hesitate, just went. I think that was the first poem I wrote about him, "Smooth-skinned Ramos, Walking Home."

The more I wrote, the harder it was to be in the same room with him, even two desk rows apart. I was much more at home with him in my dream world, and I believed, if he had a choice, he'd have picked my poems over his real life too; he was a matador in some, a portrait painter in others, a brain surgeon on the battlefield, my beloved in all of them. Some mornings when he would walk so straight and tall, almost feline, to his desk, I would practically shake my head in amazement that Ramos Herrera was actually flesh of this world. He was famous to me then. Those last two years of high school we never met or spoke to one another even once. How could I? I had whole notebooks to burn if he opened his mouth and turned out to be dumb. Papa used to say that if he was any dumber his heart would stop. But he became the physical measure by which I judged young men, at least in the just-looking stages.

After graduation I had it firmly in my mind that I was going to be a poet, and how could I be that without going to Paris, France, like Gertrude Stein. I'd read her book *Three Lives* as well as a long *Ama-*

157

rillo Gazette insert on her when she died in '46. I would obey my
father's plea and go to that city for my education. Only who's to say a
university is the sole place to get learning? I would enroll in one or
two of those literary salons and there'd be no stopping my pencil
then. To make this all float out of the airy realms of my head down to
the hard world beneath my feet, I took a night job behind the
counter of American Flyers Tenpin Bowling at the corner of Mendez
and Texarkana, near Schnabel Park. I rented out shoes to the boys
from Lackland Air Base, I drank Coca Colas, studied the French book
I bought second-hand, and planned for Paris.

Mama and Gram—to whom I told nothing—were sufficiently
worried; I wasn't dating near enough. So once every five or six
weeks, I'd go to the show with one of my regular customers. Two or
three of the fellas I liked well enough. None of them were real
amorous on Lovesome Kate, which is how they knew I wanted it. My
favorite was a boy my age at the time—nineteen, I believe. His real
name was Jacob Goldstein, one of the only Jews in San Antone, but
he went by the name of Jack Gold, which didn't suit him at all
because he was pale, short, and thin with wrists that were a sight
loose in the joint. He wore glasses and when he came to American
Flyers three nights a week, it wasn't to bowl or shoot billiards, it was
to drink Cokes and read war books, preferably by Ernie Pyle.

He was my favorite because he spoke less than I did. I think one
night he tried to kiss me as we walked home from a picture show. My
memory is hazy on that one. I do remember his hand on my shoulder
as we walked, however. Walking along like that, you would have
thought I was a frail creature needing advice, or else he was working
towards a pivoting, spin-on-his-toes kiss on the lips. In the summer of
'48 he stopped coming into American Flyers and I heard later he'd
hitchhiked out to one of the other bases in town and signed up.

By then, I had enough saved not only to fly to France, but to live
there four or five seasons at least. This I had every intention of doing.
Then one fine quiet night in early August, as I was renting out shoes
to a very large woman named Ruth Lee Howard, in walked two soldiers dressed in the pea-green khakis of the U.S. Army. I was in the
process of shrugging them off when a third soldier came through

the doorway behind them and I looked so intently, I hit the wrong key and jammed the register. Not since Ramos Herrera had a boy turned my head so much. They looked nothing alike. This one was short with a wide neck and Popeye forearms. I immediately took him for a wrestler, asked myself what on earth I was gawking at, and went to fixing my register. But I kept watching him anyway. As the three of them went to the billiards tables, that one looked over the tenpin alleys and the people playing them with the softest dark eyes you'd ever want to see. And I realized that's what had me. The same with Ramos. Right away I thought of Daddy and big game hunting. He hated it, but he had to do it at least once to truly know that. That one time was with me. His friend Buster was planning a four-day trip to the Big Thicket down near Houston to hunt deer with his son, Buster Junior. So Papa took his .410—which Buster Senior disapproved of greatly—and me.

Buster Senior ended up killing what they call a ten-point buck. Daddy and I tracked something to a water flat in the trees where we lost it. She didn't lose us, though. She was in eight-foot-high grass in the clay bank. She bolted out and as she passed in front of us Papa raised his .410 and shot her in the neck. She went down right at our feet. He must have hit an artery, because the blood came out in pumping squirts onto the trail. She was looking right at us. There was enough muscle left in her neck that she could still use it and she held her head up off the ground, her wet nose pointed up at our faces. If it was not for all that blood, you'd have thought she'd been asleep and just woke up startled. My father and I were both quiet and still as we watched her watch us, her eyes so brown and unblinking and with an intelligence so primitive and simple, she looked like she forgave us on the spot. I recollect I began to cry. Then the doe's hind hooves dug sideways into the trail, she blinked and rested her head on the ground and was dead.

And this is the thing that came back to me like a smell on the wind when I saw Guitar Jimmy walk into the American Flyers that night. That's how his friends referred to him. I know this because I broke routine, grabbed myself a billiards brush, and went to the tables to clean them off. I was wearing a plain cotton dress and no makeup

159

whatsoever. My hair was tied off to one side. I thought I looked fine, but not fine enough to garner the instant attention of the first two soldiers. Though they couldn't have been more than a year older than me, they went right into a pathetic display of patronizing bravado, a chorus of sweetheart this and darlin' that, as if they were anything more than privates in an army of penny-per-pound lunkheads. Then the one who just referred to me as darlin' introduced himself.

"I'm Toby, and this rascal over here calls himself Rex, and this one"—he was pointing his thumb over his shoulder at Popeye Dark Eyes—"he doesn't call himself anything 'cause he's so darn shy and retirin' but we call him Guitar Jimmy. Shoot, if y'all had a stage he could lay a mile of tunes for you right now."

Needless to say I was intrigued. And stayed that way through August and into September. Toby, Rex, and Jim came in every Friday night to shoot three-man eight ball. Toby came up to the counter and bantered with me more than I would have liked. But never Guitar Jim. Sometimes his eyes would catch mine while he stood at the table with his cue stick, waiting for his turn, and I would smile but he never did. He didn't *not* smile either. He seemed to receive it without any internal need to send anything back, not mean, just solitary, it seemed.

One afternoon, while shopping with Mama down on Texarkana I saw him drive by in a black Buick with "U.S. Army" stenciled on the door. That night I wrote my first poem about him, "A Buick So Black," and after I finished it I almost tore it up and threw it away, because the last thing I wanted was to make an unapproachable Ramos Herrera out of Guitar Jimmy. That night, as I lay in bed and listened to Gram sighing herself to sleep in the next room, I vowed to take this man to the moving pictures before I flew to France. That very week I had taken the bus down to Longhorn Travelers and directed a Mrs. Biddle to prepare an itinerary for my trip to Europe, something about which I had yet to tell the widows. I thought early autumn would be a nice time to do it, then adios mi madres, au revoir mes amis, life on the Seine. I vowed to write no more about Guitar Jimmy, and then I threw in that I would kiss him too, a real kiss, the kind I had yet to do. That sort of event could only better prepare me for my coming adventures in the European Theater of Poetic Operations.

That Friday Rex and Jim came in alone, and then not till after ten. Fourteen out of fifteen alleys were rented out and bustling with recreational business. All you could hear was the constant roll of bowling balls over wood, through pins, then the boys out in back heaving them down the chute, all at different times and paces. That and the high-pitched ya-hoo of an occasional winning wife all added up to my feeling jumpy. When perfectly fine people paid for shoes, I gave them their change with hardly a word, never mind a smile. Today, with the benefit of hindsight, I see that I was living one of my first premonitions—no, that word is too supernatural, melodramatic—I was feeling the current of my true flow, or at least sensing where the river was, and that alone was enough to throw me; suddenly, at least that night, my living in Paris seemed about as likely as Guitar Jimmy walking over to start up a conversation.

Then he did. And I felt better and worse all at once.

"Feel like renting me and Rex some bowling shoes?"

"Shoot, you fellas never bowl." Or something cowgirl swift like that!

Guitar Jimmy shrugged, then he smiled right at me, those deer eyes honing in on me at the same time they were staying put. I squatted behind the counter to rummage for shoes but I hadn't asked sizes. Then I heard his voice right over my head. I looked up, and there was his face at the counter's edge.

"Ten wide for me. Give Rex nines, I think." His face popped out of sight and I knew right then was my only chance of the evening, what with Rex off in the bathroom or wherever.

I stood up with the shoes. "Saw you in a black Buick t'other day."

He looked for a moment like he didn't know what a Buick was. Then he smiled. "Oh. Yep."

"They let you use it whenever you want?"

He shook his head.

"That's fine, we can walk."

He smiled again. "Where will we walk to?"

"The moving pictures? Tomorrow night? *Oliver Twist* is playing."

Rex came up to the counter then. He was a long-nosed young man with eyes close together. Without Toby around he seemed fairly tame. He waved at me, even though I was standing right there. I looked at Guitar Jim, waiting for his next word so that my wildly stalled heart could start up again.

"Till then, I suppose." He took both pairs of shoes and walked off to the alleys with Rex. I treated myself to a deep breath and a trip to the ladies' room.

Leo kept his finger on the page. He reached into the pile and turned over the pictures until he found one with his mother in it. It was one of the New York City photos, Jim and Katie Faye in that alley. But in this one, instead of laughing they were kissing, and Katie Faye's hand was raised to her cheek like she was trying to catch her hat that was half-covering her face but Jim's arms had her locked in and so were their lips.

Leo didn't know how much more he should read. This wasn't mother stuff, it was woman stuff, and she had put in so many details he thought he might get hit with something very private before he knew he was on it. But how could he stop? He looked over the pile, then took out the other notebook and any paper with writing on it. Most of those looked like poems. Some were written on pieces of grocery bags, others on napkins or envelopes, and two were on the backs of paper plates. He thought the words must have come out of her as unexpected as a sneeze so she had to reach for whatever was closest.

The other notebook was only half written in. It was white with metal spirals and on the cover in ballpoint was his father's handwriting: *Memoir Book #2*. There were no other notebooks, just photographs and poems, which Leo stacked back neatly in the Heywood Paper Products box. He finished his second Coke and went back to the fridge for another. How men could drink whiskey, he didn't know. On the way back to his room he stopped in Jim's. He stood at the foot of the small double bed and stared at the wedding day portrait over the headboard. Katie Faye was looking deep into the camera with just the shadow of a smile on her lips. Her gown made her seem pretty skinny. Her breasts were small, like Allie's and her mother's. Katie Faye appeared so damned serious in most of her pictures, in practically all from her wedding. Serious and weak, that's how Leo had always thought of her. But he was very mistaken, Katie Faye was funny and strong. Damn. He walked back into his room and sat on the bed with the notebook. He leaned back against the wall and kept reading.

Jimmy was tardy meeting me at American Flyers so our actual date didn't seem to begin until after the movie, which I remember Detesting with a big D. I'm afraid I made the mistake of expecting something close to what Charles Dickens had built out of words in his gorgeous book. This I told to Guitar Jimmy as we left the theater, something I recall immediately regretting for every manner of reason, the first being I wanted to kiss him, and my teen-age idea of a romantic date was a wordless face-gazing one culminating in lips colliding. Also, I didn't want to be disappointed in anything he might have to say and thereby not want to kiss him at all. And thirdly, I didn't want to sound like the snob I knew I was.

But, it was too late. I'd already said it. We were walking down Las Lomas for an eatery on Texarkana. It was a warm September night. Jim was looking dapper and squarely built in his uniform. I wore ruby-red lipstick, my hair was folded in a demi-bun just above my neck, and Gram had lent me one of her old cotton dresses, circa 1910. It had tiny lavender wagon wheels printed all over it; it hugged my waist and left my breasts pockets of air.

"I'm not much of a reader," Jim said finally, sounding a mite apologetic as we walked. I almost said I wasn't either, but I kept my mouth shut instead. I remember telling myself to be quiet and ladylike; the goal was to get kissed by Guitar Jimmy and who cares if he doesn't read?

The sidewalk along Texarkana was crowded with strolling Saturday night couples, loud groups of snatch-butt soldiers, and an occasional shoeshine kid. One of them, a local *chico de zapato*, was ahead of us lugging his kit up to four uniformed men standing around a parking meter. The boy was nine or ten years old, dressed in blue jeans that were rolled up six or seven times but were still too long and he stepped on them with his bare heels as he walked. He wasn't wearing a shirt. On his head was a fairly new-looking straw ranch hand hat with a rawhide strap tied around the crown. When he got to the soldiers one of them took the hat off his head and put it on his own. The boy jumped for it and of course the men laughed. We were walking by then, Guitar Jimmy on the street side, when the boy hauled off and kicked the soldier in the shin with his bare foot. The other soldiers laughed harder but the kicked one lifted his arm to backhand the boy. Then my date—without taking an extra step—grabbed the soldier's wrist and held it there in front of the soldier's face. They locked eyes and Jim took the hat off the man's head, lowered it to the boy without glancing down at him, looked into the bully's eyes a moment longer, then let go and began walking beside me again as if we'd never stopped. I remember hearing the snorts and laughter of the men behind us, the swearing of the bully, but Guitar Jimmy didn't turn around and neither did I and when we got to Locos Caballos to eat, neither of us mentioned it.

But it left a hum in me as we ordered iced teas and read our menus. It wasn't the strong cowboy part of it—though the soldier was taller, Jim easily outweighed him by twenty-five pounds and that's what the mean one must have felt behind that grip on his wrist—it was the way Jim had moved so swiftly, instinctively I'd say, to help a street-wise little Mexican. *That* I had not seen much of in my young years. And my admiration for this sort of kindness left my face feeling wooden with shyness. I looked down at my menu and read the English side of the page even though I'd already decided on a guacamole salad.

I had been to the restaurant twice before, once at lunch with Gram, and one weekday night with Mama after a show. It was small and square with low stucco ceilings, the walls papered with bullfight posters, a short candle in red glass at each table. The waiters were middle-aged Mexicanos. They wore white shirts, black bow ties, and gold lamé cummerbunds that were half covered by the soiled white aprons around their waists. Our waiter was close to fifty, a thin bald man with a bushy gray mustache. He bowed slightly, tilting his head as he listened to our orders. It was a formality I liked; it matched the stiffness in my face.

Our table was near the back. I remember hearing through the

kitchen doors a man shouting something in Spanish about onions and oil. Behind that was the static patter of an announcer at a night baseball game. For some reason, it put me in mind of Ernest Hemingway and Spain and then Gertrude Stein in France. I smiled at dark-eyed Jim, who was looking at me, then I sipped my iced tea and before I knew it I'd put down my glass, dabbed the tea at my lip, and said, "I'm flying to France come November. I'm sure I'll live there many years."

It was such an odd way to begin! I hadn't told one beating heart about my life's plans and here I was cracking them open on the table in front of a big-necked soldier they called Guitar Jimmy. But things got even more amazing: as Papa would say, Jim didn't "miss a whisker." He sat there nodding his head slightly, the smile gone, that warmth still in his face. He was waiting for me to continue, and there wasn't a solitary hint of one derisive bone in his body about a nineteen-year-old girl from Hartley County flying herself off to Europe. Then I said, "I want to be a poet, Guitar Jimmy. I write all the darn time."

He nodded again, his lips pursed in reflection. It was the sort of quiet respect I was accustomed to getting from my father only. I sipped my iced tea to settle myself. Then Jim said such a wondrous thing.

"All I think about is music, Kate. I don't believe I give anything else a thought."

And that was that; we were off, or, I should say, I was off. Our food came and I kept talking. While Jim ate his quesadillas, looking at me and nodding while he chewed, I talked over my guacamole about things I didn't even know I had a thought on, about San Antonio and how city life disagreed with me as much as it concurred; I didn't like the streets staying lit up at night. Through my bedroom window off Bandera, I told him, came the orange glow of the neon laundry sign across the street. Up in the panhandle there had been nothing but pure night out my window. From my bed, I used to crane my neck and look out past the roof overhang to a spangle of stars. Many nights there'd be nothing, just a blackness so black my lightless room had color to it. I talked about Mahatma Gandhi getting shot to death that year; I mentioned dead Papa, who was always kind; I went on about meanness for a long while, saying how much I despised it, though I don't recall what precisely I referred to. I do remember ending the point on him, on the way he took a chance for that *chico de zapato*. Jim was, and is, a very humble man. That was the first time all evening his cheeks got red. He tried to hide it, pointing out how hot the jalapeños were in his quesadillas, but no go, Joe.

This sounds like such a cliché, but it is unfathomable to me that James Suther and I have only been together seven years; I've known Jim since he was a babe in another life, I'm convinced. Not a string of cosmic muscle on his bones can have escaped my senses. But, getting back, I made myself shut up by forking guacamole and lettuce into my mouth. I let Jim talk. Not much came out, so I asked him where he got that funny accent that sure wasn't Texas. Massachusetts is the last place I would have guessed. My notion of this state was Paul Revere and the Boston Tea Party and rich Yankees called Brahmins. Guitar Jimmy looked like Montana to me, or Maine perhaps. He said that his father was also gone, killed when a half-built bridge he was pouring collapsed. Four others died with him, their bodies floating underwater all the way down the river to the Connecticut border.

"How old were you?" I asked.

"Sixteen."

"Me too, Jim. I was sixteen when Papa died." It was the first time all night we let our eyes linger. I was meeting that other half of me that was a man, I was sure. Him too, the other way around. And how could we have heard tell that four years later our mothers would die a week apart, mine in San Antonio, his in Amherst, Massachusetts? Mine of lonesomeness, his of high blood pressure. Leo was such a sight at Ma Suther's funeral. He was big at three, with a thick head of hair and my eyes, Jimmy says. I had nothing fitting to dress him in so I checked with Jim first, then drove to Springfield and bought that tiny gray suit with the clip-on bow tie. He already had a white button-down shirt. I dyed his shoes black and Jim polished them up when he did his own. At the funeral home in Amherst, Leo found a spot on the flower arrangement bench behind the casket. He sat between morning glories and dahlias and stayed there the whole time in his suit, his little face resting on his hands as he watched the legs of the grown-ups file by the coffin.

Oh, I cannot put off talking with him much longer. I will talk about heaven and love and how fast time can seep by, and more love.

Leo read ahead. He could see she was getting back to her first date with Jim and he wanted to know the rest, but he wanted the whole notebook to last too. One thing he knew already, though: they got married in October 1948, and Leo was born that next summer, and Jim went off to war the summer after that.

He thought of the war that was going on now, the one his best friend was going to out in Cong Land. Then he thought of Allie. That night she was over for dinner, she had liked Katie Faye's poems and pictures so much. He wanted to show her this stuff, too. Then he didn't. He didn't know why, really, he just didn't. But still, he wanted to see her. Maybe he'd catch her hanging around downtown not far from the police station, where he was about to go, or up at the hospital, where he was headed next. Mrs. Donovan didn't say anything about staying away from the hospital, and it was time for Leo to visit Chick for himself. Short of Katie Faye Hewson Suther, there was no one else he wanted to see.

26

No wonder he hadn't seen even a branch floating downriver this morning: things were all bogged up at the covered bridge. There was barely six inches of air between it and the water, and a whole poplar was pinned on the upstream side. In the tree's branches were wood planks, a track tire, half a white styrofoam cooler, an upside-down easy chair, and a gray rowboat, its nose wedged past a full branch into that space under the bridge. Leo took his blue sunglasses off and looked over toward the parking area behind the courthouse building. A green army truck was parked next to two police cars.

The canvas at its back was rolled up past the metal frame and stacks of sandbags were inside. There were stacks outside too, all along the concrete river wall, six or seven rows high. Leo dropped GP's letter in the mailbox in front of the Hungry Pioneer Inn, crossed the bridge road, and climbed the side steps into the police station.

"So then Farrell tells the captain he's gonna break his own friggin' record."

A man dressed in camouflage shirt and pants leaned against the counter listening to Sergeant Mike. Two more soldiers sat on the bench near the front entrance. These men were younger, in laced boots, probably twenty or so, Leo thought. They both held empty green Coke bottles and watched Leo as he came in, their faces flushed and wet.

Sergeant Mike glanced over at him and kept talking. "'Course the cap's all for it. He licks his pencil tip, right? Resets the old stopwatch. Now I'm standing there, and I'm getting a funny read on all this, you know? It's not right; the guy's got a three-year standing record for Most Accurate on a Draw but those little milliseconds are keeping him up at night, right? So anyways, Farrell holsters his piece and digs in his heels and I swear I knew what was going to friggin' happen right when Farrell slaps leather and discharges his weapon. I'm thinkin'—Jesus, nobody's gonna beat that for speed." Sergeant Mike shook his head to hold back the laugh. "Only Farrell never got around to raising his damn barrel, and there's these two, smokin' .38 holes in his friggin' leg. Entrance and exit!" Sergeant Mike slapped the counter, and all the soldiers were laughing, the younger ones shaking their heads.

Leo stepped up to wait his turn. He could see the river through the office windows in the back. From here the sandbags looked pretty thin in front of that wide water. He thought about Toby, Rex, and Jim in his mother's bowling alley in Texas so many years ago. A toilet flushed and Officer Petrucci stepped out of the men's room behind the counter gate.

"I came to tell you something," Leo said to him.

"Shoot, Leo."

One of the soldiers laughed from the bench.

"Chick Donovan came out of his coma."

"That's right, I saw him this morning."

"They let you see him?"

"Sure, he's out of Intensive. You haven't been?"

Leo shook his head. "Not since the, you know, last Thursday."

Officer Petrucci picked a walkie-talkie up off the desk behind him and put on his visor cap. "You want to go black this time, Sarge, or goop it all up?"

"Gimme the goop."

The younger soldiers laughed again. The older one at the counter looked at the work boots on Leo's feet, his bare legs, then his shoulders and face.

"Come on," Officer Petrucci headed for the side door. "We'll both talk some sense into him."

The cruiser smelled like air-conditioning and spearmint gum. As they drove by the UFO Show, Leo looked past the young cop's face to the lot, the glare of the sun on the windows.

"So why won't he press charges? You think he's scared?"

"I don't know why." And Leo didn't. Chick didn't seem to be the type to let a bygone be a bygone, especially from men like Floyd, Dwight, and Olin. But here was the young handsome cop saying just this.

"I don't know," Leo said. "I'd sure be mad. I am, really."

They left downtown and drove along the wide high river, the sun shining off its center. At a low curve before the Holyoke line were more sandbags, stacked on a fresh wall of earth. Leo could see bull-dozer tracks in the ground in front of it. He was thirsty and wished he'd bought himself a Coke at Beatrice's first.

"This happen every year?" Officer Petrucci pointed at the river as they drove up a rise.

"Only in the spring. Where're you from? I mean, you're new here right, officer?"

"Call me Frank. Worcester. My wife has family in Springfield, so we're out here now."

They drove up a side road away from the river. The car was cool and one of the air-conditioning vents was pointed at Leo's chest. He thought how he could curl up right here on the seat and sleep away the ache in his eyes, the dried whiskey puddle in his stomach. The cruiser reached the top of the hill and Mrs. Donovan drove by on the left. Christopher sat in the front, his little head barely level with the dash. Leo jerked around in his seat to glimpse Allie as the car headed down the hill. She sat in the back seat but he could only see her blond head through the rear window. Then the sun hit it and he couldn't see anything. He felt like he might throw up.

Officer Rank pulled into the parking lot of Holyoke Hospital and drove under the awning reserved for ambulances, but kept the engine running. "It's none of my business, but you don't want to get in too deep with those people."

Leo opened his door.

"You believe in God, Leo?"

"Sure."

"Well, they don't. I can't go along with what those guys did to your boss, but stay away from the radicals, pal. They're no damned good."

Leo started to nod but then stopped himself. "Thanks for the ride, Frank."

"See what you can do."

"Sure thing."

At the Care Canteen Leo bought two large Cokes and three Hershey bars. The woman at the switchboard directed him to the second floor, a long hallway called the Secondary Unit. Chick's room was at the end, to the right of a small window with a view over the hill down to the river. Leo knocked once and walked in. There were two beds side by side. The one farther from the door was empty and stripped of its sheets. Chick Donovan lay in the nearer one sleeping. He wore a white johnny and his left hand was resting on the cast of his right arm across his stomach. His entire left leg was in a cast too, propped on four pillows at the foot of the bed. There were crumbs on his chest, and a yellow stain that looked like egg yolk. So did his face, Leo thought, yellow as eggs. Purple and blue around his closed eyes, even some green in there. Leo thought of Floyd's face, how he had the same colors in his.

Leo set the Cokes and candy bars on the bedside table, then sat in

170

one of two folding metal chairs. He wondered which one Allie had been on.

"Hey." Chick's voice was low and whispery, his eyes still closed.

"Hi, you look good."

Chick opened his eyes. He got up on his elbows and pressed a button on the bed frame. An electric moan raised the head of the bed until he was sitting up. There were two bits of toilet paper stuck to blood spots on his lower chin, and Leo asked if he'd forgotten how to shave. Chick squinted at Leo like he was a bright light in his face. With his good arm, he took his glasses from the table and put them on. There was still a speck of tar in the upper corner of his right lens. "Tess gets overexcited."

Leo smiled. He wondered if Chick knew about his wife telling Leo to stay away for the week. He put a straw in the iced Coke and handed it to him.

"You saved my ass, buddy."

"I wish I'd done more, but I just couldn't get past Floyd. He was crazy."

"They all were, especially me."

"You didn't do anything."

"That's right."

"No, I mean you could've if you'd had your other arm to use."

"I'm not referring to that." Chick sipped through his straw. "You want to get a good handle on things, get yourself put in a hospital. It's the Big Brake, this place. Leo, I've been a fucking idiot." Chick's voice broke on that last word. He shook his head.

"You've been doing what you think is right. That's good, isn't it?"

"What's good is being more than just the Invisible Man."

"But everybody in town knows who you are."

"To laugh at, or swing a bat at maybe."

Leo looked at the casts on Chick's arm and leg. He thought of Allie; he wanted to see Allie.

"I'm not feeling sorry for myself, Leo, but my strategy has been very stupid. When I was a kid, maybe a couple years older than you, all I knew is I wasn't going to be my father, I wasn't going to be machinery in some fucking mill. No offense. It just wasn't me; man, I was Golden Gloves Champ. Anyway, the beauty is—and I don't know if it's the painkillers they're pumping into me or what, but—something came to me today I forgot I knew. My first carpentry boss was this big Frenchman in Lowell, a fight fan. He saw me in a couple of fights, took me under his wing on the job. I was loving it, too. Working under an open sky. Building something I could drive by a year later and point to, all of it. It fit the plan."

Chick took the cap off his Coke and drank it all down until the ice hit his teeth and he winced. "One morning, the Frenchman and I were unloading tools from his truck onto the sidewalk in front of a three-story. The sun was out. I was feeling on top of things. I set the sawhorses down and hopped up in the truck for more tools and I notice the Frenchman is studying one of the sawhorses. I didn't think much of it, except that maybe I had screwed up somehow. Then he reached over me, gets himself the long sledge, and I watch him break the horse into five flying pieces. He looks up at me and guess what he says?"

"What?"

"'If you don't trust a horse, break it.'" Chick smiled. He lay his head back on the pillow and let out a breath. "Do you comprehend it?"

Leo said sure, it made sense.

"It only did to me this week. You see, if a man is going to organize, he'd better goddamn instill some trust in his followers. Floyd was my student, I thought I was his teacher, but I gave up on him, insulted him, even hurt him. Jesus, you can't screw up more than that."

Leo didn't say anything and he wondered why Chick was telling him this. Chick pointed to pots and vases of flowers on a wall shelf near the window. "From the kids I huddle with at the college. Couple of them have offered to blow up Floyd and his buddies for the cause. None of this brings me joy. It is not lost on me that my truest believers are kids. *Why?* If the fruit Marx talked about is really ripe, then there should be no need to yank it from a limb, right? I'm tired of yanking, Leo. A man trusts a sawhorse when it works for him. And when he's got a wobbler on his hands, he doesn't want some Jack

---

172

showing him *plans* of a better horse to use, he wants the damn horse. You understand?"

Leo could hear the loud voice of a nurse in another room. He looked down at his fingers. He wanted to open a Hershey bar, but now didn't seem to be the time to do it.

"I met this man in Boston. Lives in this community up in Vermont. Seven families all living the word, dealing out of Adam Smith and into the earth, living by *example*. They don't push their scene on anybody. Comprendo?" Chick's bruised face seemed to get more red as he spoke, especially in the forehead. "Next to farmers, who do you think these people need most?"

Leo said carpenters, probably. Chick started to smile again but it seemed to hurt his swollen lip so he stopped.

"You okay?"

"Never better, kid. I'm glad you came. You just missed the family, too."

Allie didn't think it was sleeping weather in the least. Her bedroom window was wide open, and the cicadas out there seemed to agree with her; the sun had shone on the wet valley all day and now the night air was steam and people weren't supposed to breathe steam. People weren't supposed to do a lot of things, she thought. People weren't supposed to vacuum up their babies like so much floor lint. That's how her mother said it would probably be done tomorrow, a quick suction. She had said it with such authority Allie had to wonder about any brothers or sisters she of course wouldn't have heard of.

She thought of Leo and wished he were here now, drinking iced tea, talking, maybe playing his harmonica. Her mother had taken everything Allie told her and was now going to go get rid of it tomorrow; all Allie had to do was show up. And she would; she knew that. But before she did, she was going to see Leo. Tonight. Right this minute.

Leo lay on his bed. His legs felt tired and heavy from the seven or so miles he'd walked from Holyoke Hospital, and he was thinking about Katie Faye and Texas. After supper, he'd come back to his room and started reading her notebook again, but then stopped; he already knew how the story ended and he wasn't going to gobble and rush all he was going to get of her, so he read again up to where he left off earlier today. He looked at some of the photographs awhile, then he put everything back in the box and played his C harp. He'd been working on his train rail chugging riff the last few days. Tonight he'd combined it with a few hand-smacks that bent the notes in a jolt, like the train was heading over a trestle.

Jim came in before going to bed. He wore his white tank T-shirt and light blue pajama pants. He must've been standing in the doorway awhile, listening, because he was there when Leo finished up the riff, taking it out on a high wail he squeezed to a fade. Jim's right arm was resting on the door jamb above his head, his wrist and hand relaxed. Leo hadn't heard him pick up the guitar all night, but his father looked kind of tired and peaceful anyway.

"Good night, son." He turned down the hall and was in his room before Leo could say much. He undressed to his underwear, turned off the light, and lay there in air that was hard to breathe. The river made hardly a sound as it moved high in the trees behind the house. There were moonlight shadows on the wall, and he thought of fall coming. He thought of his whole senior year without Gerry. Without Allie. Because Chick was serious. He was packing up and driving his family up to one of those communities in Vermont. Leo remembered what Allie had said about her mother not believing in Chick anymore, not wanting to go to Mississippi, but Leo thought she might go to Vermont. Allie was too close to the situation to see, but her mother was devoted. If she wasn't, why would she have given Leo the boot for the week? Why would she visit her husband every day? And shave him, and all that? Nope. They were definitely going. The top of Spoon Hill would be empty of them very soon. They were almost gone already.

Leo heard a car or truck pass by up on Paper Boulevard, and he thought of Gerry and his Corvair, the way he just had a car one day, and then was gone for World Adventure the next. GP wasn't as thick as he seemed. He was going to do things, probably be a businessman like his pop, but richer, and he'll marry another Betty with big breasts. But not me, Leo thought, I'm going to play the harmonica all the way around this globe, and he saw himself up on the stage in nightclubs like the one in his dream with Katie Faye and Big Bill Broonzy. New York City, London, and Paris.

He got up and stood in the moonlight in the middle of his room. He turned on the overhead light and counted the money in his drawer. Over $600. He looked up at Big Bill's wide-eyed sweating face in the poster. Such a bluesman. What was better than being called that? Nothing, that was it. That was the only way to go.

"Hey."

Leo jumped at the whisper. The doorway was empty and he couldn't see past the screen because of the light over his head. He hit the switch and saw only darkness for a second.

"It's me. Open up, it's Allie."

The moonlight came clear again and he could see the outline of her head, of her long blond hair that right now looked ghostly. He pushed the screen up its track. Allie was halfway through the window before he could even offer his hand. She took it, stood, then placed her hands on each side of his neck and kissed him on the lips. Her breath was bad. He kissed her back, but didn't hug her or anything.

"Howdy, long lost boyfriend. Miss me?"

Leo felt "yes" coming so he turned and pulled on his work shorts, then sat down on the mattress and switched on the bedside lamp.

"Well?" Allie had her hands on her hips. She was barefoot, wearing shorts and one of Chick's T-shirts. Her legs looked brown but very skinny. Leo hadn't realized how long and skinny her legs were.

"Are you *mad?*"

"Whisper. My dad wouldn't like this."

Allie crossed her arms and looked down at him. A strand of hair came loose from behind her ear and hung in front of her face. She left it there, and kept looking at him. "Why are you mad at *me?*"

Leo kept quiet. He liked the way this was going. He sat back against the wall and crossed his ankles. She was actually a plain girl if you really studied her. Long arms and legs, a mouth too wide for the cheeks on each side of it, and her hair wasn't exactly Jayne Mansfield thick and blond either.

"So you are mad."

Leo almost said yes, but held off. He looked off in the direction of the doorway. Where this was headed he didn't know, but he liked that she had come here and he was only going to push a little bit more.

"Oh screw you then." Allie stuck one leg out the window and bent forward to squeeze through.

Leo grabbed her around the waist. "Who do you think you are even coming down here? You weren't asleep when your mother told me to get lost, I snuck around to your window to say good-bye and I saw, so screw *you*, Allie, you're the one who should be screwed."

Leo held on a second longer, then let go. Allie looked like somebody had just slapped her with a wet sponge, not really hurting, just shook up, not sure if she was going to hit back laughing, or hit back crying, or else sit down and wait for it all to go away. Leo watched her do all three. She smiled up at him like she'd just had the last word. She walked by him, sat on the bed, looked at the floor between her bare feet, and began to cry. Softly at first, then pretty much out loud.

He didn't feel a thing watching her, not at first. He was wondering how she got here; he hadn't heard a car engine. Did she walk? He imagined her hobbling barefoot under the moon over gravel down Spoon Hill, then along the river road and through the covered bridge that was close to washing away. All of that to see him. Now here she was. Crying. Shit.

He sat on the bed next to her. He put his arm around her shoulders, but he felt like a daddy, so he pulled it away and rested his hand on her warm and narrow knee. That seemed to bring more crying out of her. Leo looked at the doorway and saw Jim step into it in his pajama bottoms. Jim's hair was already sticking up in the back and he was squinting from the lamplight or else from trying to make sense of what was happening there in front of him. He scratched his leg, his eyes on Leo, then he turned back into the darkness of the hall.

Allie hadn't even looked up. "You have no *idea,* Leo." She took a half-breath, then another. "It's not *fair.*"

Leo got up and closed the door. He took a work bandanna from his bureau drawer and handed it to her. "He's going to be okay, Allie. I saw him this afternoon, he looks real good."

———

Allie's eyes were already swollen underneath. She wiped off her cheeks and blew her nose. She let out a long breath and looked up at him. "I'm pregnant—"

"You are?"

She nodded, keeping her eyes right on his. "Yes."

Leo sat down, then stood up again. He walked to the bureau, leaned on it with one elbow, looked at her, then walked over to the window and sat on the sill.

"I'm getting it fixed tomorrow. I just wanted to tell you."

"Fixed?" Leo thought of dogs, bitches in heat getting spayed. Dirt tools. No more puppies. Now Allie. Now this. "Did you take a test?"

Allie nodded. Her face was tilted down, but her eyes were looking up at him. She sniffled and Leo stood again. "How long have you known this?"

Allie wiped her nose.

"Huh?"

"A while."

The Mystery Girl.

"It felt awful not telling you, Leo. I mean, you're so material to the situation. I just couldn't do it, for some reason."

"What do you mean 'fixed'? You mean kill it? I thought that was illegal."

Allie rested her elbows on her knees. She looked straight ahead at the drawers of the bureau. "It is. My mother's doing it all."

"Your *mother?* With *what?*"

"No, she's taking me to a doctor in Boston. He did one for my aunt."

"Does she know I don't know?"

Allie nodded.

"Chick knows?"

"No, and you can't tell him, Leo."

Leo walked over, squatted on the floor, and gripped both her calves. "I got a question for you. Do I get a vote here?"

"No!" Allie pulled on his wrists but he squeezed more.

"Say something else."

She pulled harder. He could see she was scared. He let go, and she jumped up and climbed out the window. He let her go. He stood

177

there a second looking around his room, but it felt about as familiar as an African village. He was on his own, but he wasn't going to let her do a thing without him. He ducked out the window, landed barefoot on wet pine needles, and ran around the house. He could still see her in the shine from the light over the kitchen door, stepping as fast as she could into the darkness up Saunders Hill Road. Her mother's car was parked facing downhill and he caught up to her as fast as if he'd been running over grass. Allie pulled open the driver's door and climbed in. The car was too close to the trees for Leo to open the passenger door, so he climbed in the back seat just as Allie started the engine and put it in reverse, looking out the rearview mirror like his head wasn't even there.

She stopped. She looked at him in the dim light from the control panel. "Don't you dare ask me to marry you or something hokey like that, Leo."

"Hokey?"

"Phony, contrived, not real, *hokey.* Don't be a fence post."

"Don't insult me, Allie. I've never treated you bad. Never. So ease up."

Allie turned around and shut off the engine, the lights too. Leo could hear the moths flitting into the outside bulb through the trees. The air was so heavy he smelled a touch of the mill. He leaned forward and rested his arms on the top of the back seat. "Why's it make you so sad, Allie? What's so lousy about having a baby?"

"I'm not sad."

He touched her shoulder. She didn't stiffen, but she didn't lean into it either.

"I'm mad, Leo."

"At me?"

"No, me. I wasn't using my head."

"Me either. I should've worn something, I guess."

"No, I don't like those."

Leo took his hand away. "How many guys have you done it with, Allie?"

She looked at him, looked away, then looked at him again. "It's none of your stinking business, but I'll tell you anyway—ONE."

178

"Who?"

"How many girls have you been with?"

"Answer my question."

"Answer mine."

"Just you."

"See? We're way too young to have a baby, you're the man and you're practically a virgin."

"You sound like Gerry Poitras, Allie. What does any of that shit have to do with loving a little baby?"

"You would?"

"Wouldn't you?"

"We shouldn't even discuss it. It's been decided."

"*Not by me.* By *you?* Have you decided?"

"*No,* and quit yelling at me, I haven't decided anything!"

"I thought you said you did."

"My *mother* did."

"Well screw her."

Allie took a long breath and let it out. Leo swung his leg up over the back seat, grabbed the dash, and pulled himself down into the front.

"What are we going to do, Leo? I don't want anyone sticking a vacuum cleaner in me."

"That's how they do it?"

"One way."

"Don't people die from those, Allie? Gerry told me about this girl up in Hadley who went and had one in some garage and died."

"I bet she didn't see a doctor, though."

They sat quiet for a couple of minutes.

"Let's go someplace," Leo said. "I can't think here."

"I don't want to drive. I feel a little sick."

"'Cause you're pregnant?"

"No. Yeah. I don't know, maybe."

Leo drove into town, heading for the light of the Fremont Theater and the UFO Show.

"Don't go to Beatrice's. Sid thinks I'm sick."

"You didn't tell him about your dad?"

"Would you?"

"Why not?"

"It's not easy being a communist's daughter, you know."

"I thought you liked them."

"I like my dad. Communists are too serious."

Leo took a right at the courthouse and drove through the covered bridge. "The cops know about Chick. That new one from last week? He told me I should stay away."

"What did you say?"

"I told him it was none of his business."

"Good, Leo. Good."

Leo's cheeks were hot with the lie. He stuck his elbow out the window as he drove down river road past Spoon Hill, then up the fork to the job site. The headlights lit up the house frame as he pulled in and shut the engine down. The moon was high over the field down the slope. The two-by-four walls of the second floor shone pale as a skeleton. Leo got out of the car and walked to the barn door. In the moonlight he could see the padlock looked fine, but he jiggled it anyway. It was a manly picture of himself, he knew. And it wasn't such a big lie. He hadn't sucked up to the cop or agreed with him or anything; he'd just changed the subject by thanking him for the ride.

"You guys did a lot." Allie stood in the driveway in front of the house. Her T-shirt really stood out in this light, so big and loose on her. Leo imagined it bulging out tight with their baby.

"It makes me sad, Leo."

"What?"

"To see you guys stop working on this house. The doctors don't want my dad to work for a long time. What if you never finish it? When I think of that, all these new boards make me sad."

"And a new baby doesn't?"

"Please don't give me that shit, Leo Suther. Oh you men are so superior about your orgasms. I mean, that's all this is." Allie put both hands on her flat stomach. "I'm carrying around your wad. You guys never have to carry around ours, and if you did, you sure wouldn't let it get you so big your chest and back started to hurt and then you had to poop a Volkswagen out of you."

"I would," Leo said before thinking about it, but now that he said it he was pretty sure he meant it. "I would. I'd carry yours."

"I don't believe you." Allie walked through the side doorway up onto the plywood floor. Leo waited a second before he followed her. He could still smell sawdust. Something flew over him, an owl, or a bat. He stepped into the house. Tom Burrell had cut a square opening in the plywood of the north wall for one of the windows. The moon shone through it, laying a light path across the floor. Allie sat there with her legs crossed, her back straight, looking up out the window. Leo sat down against the wall beside it. He could see her face pretty well, and he thought of Katie Faye telling Jim on their first date how she couldn't see stars out of her window in the city.

"What about love, Allie? Maybe a woman carries a man's love inside her too. Ever think of that? All you're talking about is coming."

Allie kept her eyes on the window opening. "Why do you say maybe? You're not sure, Leo?"

"I didn't say maybe."

"You most certainly did."

Leo kept quiet. She was right, he knew. He wasn't sure if he loved her like that, not in the way a mother and father are supposed to love each other. But he had missed her, and he was glad they were together tonight even if she was testy and pregnant here in this half-built moonlit house.

"Jim gave me some diaries of my mom's."

"Changing the subject?

"*No.* Christ."

Neither of them spoke for a minute or two.

Allie said she couldn't see him at all.

Leo stayed where he was.

"C'mere."

"No, now I'm mad."

"Again."

"You don't give me enough respect, Allie. You should've told me about this when you first found out."

"I know."

"So why didn't you?"

181

Allie looked down at the floor, then up at him again. In the moonlight, her hair looked almost white. "Have you read any of those Vega Menudo books about Juan Perez?"

"No," Leo said. "Changing the subject?"

"This is very material to our situation, Leo. Please."

"Okay, what?"

"This book *Fables of Conquest,* it's really something, Leo. This man Juan Perez is very wise. One thing was so good I wrote it down: 'The basic difference between an ordinary man and a warrior is that a warrior takes everything as a challenge while an ordinary man takes everything either as a blessing or a curse.' See? And he didn't mean just men, but women too. That's how I want to live my whole entire life, Leo. Not lying down for anything, but rising up to everything. You know, a Warrior Woman."

"But you're going to go lie down tomorrow, Allie."

Allie didn't speak. Leo heard the flap of wings outside again. Had to be an owl, a hungry one. Leo scooted forward into the light and rested his hand on Allie's leg.

"That's what I knew as soon as I saw you tonight, Leo. That's why I cried. A true warrior takes responsibility for her actions. I've been taking this like a curse."

"And it's a blessing."

"*No,* it's neither. It just *is.* And what I do about it determines what I become. See? But I'm not going to become anything if I ignore the challenge, Leo."

"What about me? You keep saying 'I.'"

"Well, I mean 'we.'"

She squeezed his hand and Leo remembered her mother doing the same thing to him. "So, you want to have it?"

Allie shrugged her shoulders. "I want to do it on my own."

"Do what?"

"The true thing."

"You're starting to sound like Ryder when he's drunk."

Allie pulled her hand away and stood up. "You are such an embryo, Leo. That's why I can't marry you."

"You keep talking about marrying me. Did I ever ask you to marry me? I don't care what you think, or your whole damn family, always telling people what they are. I wouldn't marry you if *you* asked *me!*"

Allie turned and walked out of the house. Her bare feet made a light scuffing sound as she went. Leo got up and stood in the doorway. He watched her get in the car, pull the door shut, and sit behind the wheel. Embryo. She probably thought he didn't know what the word meant.

He walked to the car. He put his hands on the roof. He looked down at her between his arms. "Still feel sick?"

"No."

"Your mother's not going to cream our baby."

"If you want to argue, Leo, change the subject."

"Let's you and me take care of it."

Allie looked up at him.

"We'll do like you said, we won't ignore our problem. You have it and we'll both take care of it. I have some money already and I can make a lot more by then. We don't have to get married to be good people, Allie."

Allie moved her lips like she was repeating to herself what he just said. "Mean it?"

"Yeah, I mean it."

As soon as he closed the passenger door she kissed him, her hands on each side of his face. "I love how unpredictable you are, Leo. I'm sorry for being so tempestuous."

"Let's go tell your mother."

"In a minute." Allie slid her tongue inside his mouth. Leo pulled her to him, though he didn't know if they should be doing this or not. Allie sat back, unsnapped her shorts, and pulled them and her panties off. She did it very quickly, but with great concentration. Leo knew she was right; they'd be a stronger couple in front of her mother after. He knelt on the floor on the passenger's side and pulled his shorts and underwear to his knees. Allie slid over. She swung one leg over his head and left the other where it was as she held his penis and pulled him in. Leo felt things building very quickly, but this time he'd pull out. For all he knew, a pregnant girl wasn't supposed to do this at all.

———

183

27

Tess Donovan sat on the front porch sipping iced tea. She had turned off the living room lamp so she could better see the lights of the town down the hill across the river, though at this hour, that meant the movie house, the diner, and the streetlights only. The moon was high behind the house and the whole hill looked underwater. She thought how she had never painted a night scene before, never even tried. Perhaps some evening, after Chick is home, she would set up her easel on the porch and paint Heywood as it looks now: like a brief three-in-the-morning sandwich stop for bus passengers on their way to somewhere else.

Headlights lit up the river road from the north, then the car turned up Spoon Hill Road and came very slowly. Tess had watched it leave from her bedroom window. Now she watched Allie come home. If she went and saw her boyfriend, then that's all right, Tess decided. Tomorrow's going to be a big and awful day. I'm not going to push her into any more of a corner than she already is in.

The car drove over gravel and parked next to the flatbed, but when two doors opened and closed, Tess stood up and walked through the shadowed house to the kitchen. She pulled the string to the overhead light above the table, leaned against the counter, and waited. It was Leo all right. He held the screen door open for Allie, who ducked under his arm and walked in. As she got closer she seemed to still be ducking. It was the boy who walked so tall and sure of himself behind her, and it was he who first opened his mouth to speak.

Tess held her hand up. "What do you think you're doing, Allie?"

Allie pulled the picnic table bench out and sat down. Leo stayed standing behind her.

"Answer me."

"We're going to have the baby, Mrs. Donovan," Leo said.

"*We?* There's no we here, just a she, and *she's* not having anything at sixteen years of age."

"Seventeen, Mom. You know I'll be seventeen then, and Leo turns eighteen next week."

"What are you saying, you're going to get married?"

"No, Mom."

"We want to be responsible about it," the boy said. Tess looked at him, at his long tanned arms, his curly hair that needed a trim. There was just a hint of a man around his mouth, but not his eyes; he had the damp, green eyes of a child.

"I'm glad you want to be responsible, Leo. You can pay for the procedure. Lord knows we'll be getting enough bills."

"We don't want a procedure, Mrs. Donovan. I'm sorry, but—that's final really."

"Good night, Leo."

"Mom."

"Go home, Leo. *Now.*"

Allie stood. "This is *our* problem, not *yours*. You can't kick him out; it's his baby too!"

"Baby? Where's a baby? I see two in front of me, which is why there won't be a third, do you understand? No more talk."

"You can't make her do it."

Tess walked over to the wall phone and picked up the receiver. "Do I have to call the police to get you out of here?"

Allie turned and walked through the living room and out of the house.

"Come back here."

The boy stood there. "Nothing personal against you, Mrs. Donovan. We just want to do the right thing."

Tess hung up the receiver. "What's this 'right thing,' Leo? Are you going to work down at that awful paper mill? Never go to college, or travel freely? How bright can you be to sign up for this?"

"You did, though."

"I was a *grown* woman, marrying a grown *man*. And just what do you plan to do if you're not going to marry?"

The boy looked down, then back up just as fast. "I want to marry her. She doesn't. She wants to do it all on her own."

Outside, Allie paced the front porch like some female mountain lion in a cage. To Tess, everything was suddenly so clear. "Please leave now, Leo. We'll all talk later, all right?"

"I didn't mean to be rude."

"I know you didn't. I'd appreciate it if you convinced her to come back inside." Tess watched the boy walk out to the porch where he immediately put his arm around Allie's shoulders and kissed her on the forehead.

Mrs. Donovan dropped him off at the top of Saunders Hill Road, then drove off without a word. Leo didn't mind that at all. This was a lot better than the smiles and pats on the arm that left him feeling like a cub scout who had just missed earning his first badge. Now was different. Those kinds of manners were obviously used for children, and how could he be considered a child when his seed was growing inside Allie and, man, he was going to be a father?

A *father.* And Jim a *grand*father. Jesus, Leo hadn't given much thought to Jim. Now, as he walked down the road towards the light of his house through the trees, he wanted to run. Not to the house, but past it. He'd dive into the river and swim across to the woods on the other side. He'd crawl around until he found a big enough pine to sleep under. In the morning he'd get up and set about building a hut out of branches and logs and river mud. The next night, he'd creep into GP's neighborhood and steal the welcome mats off front porches to use as rugs and wall coverings on the inside. He and Allie would raise their baby there like Indians, no matter what Jim or the Donovans had to say.

The kitchen light was on and Jim sat at the table smoking a cigarette. Leo picked up his walking pace and went right in. He closed the door, kept his back to the table, and took a bottle of Coke out of the fridge.

"She all right?"

"Yeah." Leo leaned against the counter and sipped his Coke.

"You two having trouble?"

"A little."

In front of Jim was an empty milk glass and a crumb-covered plate.

"Burrell called a few minutes ago. Apologized three times for calling so late."

"What'd he want?"

"He's a man short on some roofing job. Wanted you to work

tomorrow." Jim got up and carried his plate and glass to the sink. His forearm brushed Leo's. "I told him you would."

"What time?"

"Six-thirty. Looks like you'll be working down in Springfield."

Leo drank his Coke fast, the bubbles rising up his nose, popping somewhere behind his eyes. He coughed, took a breath, then sneezed.

"You all right?"

"Yeah, I'm fine," Leo said. "Everything's fine."

It was a steep roof on a hill not far from Springfield Center. From where Leo stood he could see the chimneys of houses all the way down to the flat store roofs on Main Street. The morning sky was clear and the sun hit him square in the face. He reached into the nail bag that straddled the ridge of the roof, and he wondered which of those one-story buildings was the music store. He put two handfuls of roofing nails into his apron, then he stepped flat-footed down to where Burrell was laying the third course of shingles from the edge. His brother-in-law's crew was on another job over in Chicopee and Leo was glad it was just Tom and him working together.

They were a good team. Burrell had the know-how, Leo had the drive, and when it came time for Tom to show Leo something, he taught him slow, almost gentle. He was as good a carpentry teacher as Ryder was a harp man. And these—carpentry and blues—were two activities Leo was thinking of almost without a break; senior year was gone, no doubt about it. Instead he saw himself working with Chick for maybe the first year or two, but no more than that. By then his harp playing would be good enough he could start getting gigs either by himself, or with a band. And he'd have to come up with a name. Something as catchy as Big Bill Broonzy, Champion Jack Dupree, or Homesick James. He thought of his birthday coming up this Friday, how that made him a Leo. Leo Leo, GP called him for almost a year. So how about: Leo "The Lion of the Blues" Suther? Nope. Too long.

At coffee break, as they sat on the ground against the house, Leo almost told Burrell everything. But then Tom brought up the river and how he hadn't seen it this high in the summer since he was a boy. Leo mentioned that his grandfather had drowned in the Connecticut building a bridge and Burrell said he seemed to recall hearing something about that accident. They talked of hurricanes and tornadoes, earthquakes and tidal waves. Tom quoted something from the Bible about Armageddon as they went back to work.

Leo refilled his nail apron and followed Tom. They'd found a good system: Burrell laid down a shingle, put in one tack to hold it, then moved on with another shingle while Leo hammered two more tacks into the first one. It was a real close feeling working with a man like that, Leo thought, almost like wrestling practice. A lot of sweat, a few grunts, both of you doing, or trying to do, the same thing. No, wrestling wasn't it, really, it was more like bluesing in a jam with different instruments, setting out to build a song that won't fly unless everybody's working on the same thing in separate ways: Jim on the guitar and lyrics, Ryder on the lead harp, Leo on the backup, people building things together not because they're all alike doing the same things, but because they're all separate doing things different, but with their eye on the likeness of what they're heading for.

Leo got to thinking of Ryder's speech about music being a bridge to Truth City, and he thought of lying, which reminded him of lion again. Then he had it. As he moved to a new shingle and set his nail next to Burrell's he had it: the Leo Ain't Lying Blues Show. With this one, he could go out on a stage alone, or else with a whole band, *his* band. That kind of life Allie would surely go for, the Warrior Woman marries the Bluesman, travels the world with him, carrying their child in a Indian knapsack. And that brought up a whole other challenge of the day; naming their little one. If it was a boy they sure weren't going to name it Chick or Jim. Too dull. Too over and done with out of the mouth. Maybe their grandfathers had had better names. He wondered what Katie Faye's dad's first name was. He already liked the family name, Hewson. Man, that wasn't bad at all: Hewson Suther. Sounds like a rich rancher, or a movie director, a playwright even. Not really like a boy, though.

Besides, that wouldn't be fair, taking all the names from the same side of the family—because there was no question what her first name would be if it's a girl—Allie could even stick her last name on there if she wanted to: little Katie Faye Donovan, daughter of Leo and Allie who aren't married but love each other anyway. And that'll change too, Leo thought as he walked back up to the ridge for more shingles. She'll marry me just to feel more grown up and ready for the whole thing.

By noon, Tom and Leo had finished the east face of the roof and half of the west. Burrell wiped the sweat off his forehead, blew his nose, and suggested they work straight out till they're all done, then take a late lunch and call it an early day. Leo had had a Coke for breakfast, a coffee at break, and still food wasn't a thing he'd considered, so that was all fine with him.

Tom was humming a tune as he worked. He'd hum some of it, then whistle, then hum some more. It was that cowboy one about hearing the robin sing and being so lonesome you could cry. He was doing such a nice job of it, Leo tapped the nails in lighter so he could hear better. But in the middle of the song, Burrell switched over to a new one. Still cowboy music, but this one had religion in it and Leo pictured a bunch of cowboys standing around a grave with their dusty Stetsons in their hands, their heads bowed as the preacher spoke. Wedding or not, the baby would have to be baptized.

Leo was going to ask Ryder to be the godfather. Allie could come up with a girl for the godmother, though he didn't know who that would be because she didn't have any girlfriends. Maybe Allie's mother could be a grandmother and a godmother at the same time. Well, whoever, it was all going to have to happen up on Katie Faye's hill at the St. John's Church in Holyoke. No question there.

Soon they reached the ridge of the roof and had only the cap along the seam to nail off. Burrell knelt down, took his razor knife, and cut a full-sized shingle into three equal rectangles. He handed them to Leo, said to watch out where he was backing up, then went to work cutting more caps. The sun was gone now, and with the clouds came a breeze that smelled like the mud along the river. The air had turned cool by the time they were done. While Burrell tied the ladder to the roof rack of his station wagon, Leo finished tossing the old shingle scraps into the rear. He slammed the gate shut and they drove down the hill to Springfield Center and parked in front of the post office and municipal building.

As Tom got out, he nodded at the red brick building behind him.

"Billy came and registered last week. He's off to Fitchburg State in the fall. Did I tell you that? Taking up engineering."

"That's good."

They looked both ways, waited for two Chevys to pass, then crossed the street.

"How about you?"

"I put in my name next week."

"I meant the college. After your high school." Tom stepped onto the sidewalk and headed through the open doorway of a sandwich shop. Taped to the plate-glass front window was a three-foot-tall sketch of a cup of coffee, its steam rising up, then floating its way through the hole of a donut beside it. Leo told Burrell he'd be right back, and he walked down the street a block to Tony's Musical Suite. The door was locked, and beneath the CLOSED sign was taped:

Anthony and the Holy Roaders are on tour! See you after August 21!   Tony "Anthony" Delvalle

Leo turned and headed back to the sandwich shop, and he remembered what Tony had said about losing his harp player. He walked up to the counter where Burrell stood. Behind it, a balding black-haired man took a knife and slit open a bread roll. The place smelled like raw onions and cooking meat. Burrell asked Leo what did he want. Leo stared straight ahead at the man's fast hands, at the way the oil on them glistened in the kitchen's light.

"Everything, Tom. I want every damn thing in town."

28

Allie hadn't expected the doctor's office to be across the interstate from Fenway Park in a very public place called Kenmore Square. The sun was shining off the cars in the street, and when she pulled the

Star Chief into a two-dollars-all-day lot, she suddenly felt as if she'd forgotten something, but didn't know what that could be.

She wore sandals, her denim skirt, and one of her mother's sleeveless flowered blouses. Before she left Spoon Hill she'd tied her hair up, but here in Boston, near the ocean, the air was cooler and she pulled the rubber band free as she stepped into the foyer of the stone building. Dr. Robert Boyd was on the third floor and there were no elevators. Allie walked up carpeted stairs, which she noticed needed vacuuming in the corners. Her mother had never mentioned it either way, but Allie had hoped the abortionist would be a woman. Robert Boyd was a young man's name. Everyone probably called him Bobby, Bobby Boyd.

She had felt okay driving in, but now, as she reached the second floor and started up the stairs for the third, her mouth was dry as sawdust and she felt certain she smelled bad. Last night, when Leo was back home, her mother had said only one thing to her on the porch before going upstairs to her room. "It's your life, Allison, do what you want. I've got enough on my hands with your father and brother." This morning Allie had gotten up early, before eight, but her mother and Chris were already gone. On the table was a note: "Took the truck for a tune-up. Visiting Daddy after. The kitchen floor could use a wash. Mom."

Not far from the note were the keys to the car.

In the shower Allie avoided getting her hair wet and she found herself thinking of her aunt's written instructions about no food or water after midnight. She tried to remember whether she'd gotten up to drink any water last night. She definitely hadn't eaten anything, and so far this morning nothing had gone into her mouth. She turned off the water, looked straight ahead at one of the wet square tiles, and watched a water drop gather above it and then run all the way down to the next. In minutes she was dressed and starting up the Star Chief, her aunt's folded directions between her teeth.

Dr. Boyd's office was the first one in the hallway across from the stairwell. The door was open. Sitting at a corner desk was a woman about Beatrice's age, forty-something, Allie thought, wearing half-glasses on a strap around her neck. She looked up over the lenses as Allie walked into a reception room full of chairs but empty of people.

"Miss Donovan?"

Allie nodded.

The woman took off her glasses, stood, then walked over, closed the door, and locked it. "Come with me, please."

Allie followed her down a narrow corridor past a bathroom and a small examination room to a larger one at the end of the hall. The window shades were drawn but the room was bright with fluorescent light. The woman told Allie to sit on the exam table. She put a thermometer under Allie's tongue, then wrapped a rubber pad around Allie's upper arm and inflated it tight by pressing an air bulb. She let the air out and wrote something on a clipboard. She checked Allie's pulse, pulled out the thermometer, and wrote down more things. "Five weeks, correct?"

"I think so."

"Yes or no, dear."

"Yes, I'm sorry."

The woman opened a closet door and pulled out a white cotton johnny, the same kind Allie had seen on her father at Holyoke Hospital.

"Take off everything and put this on. Do you have payment?"

"My mother didn't tell me about that."

"Her name?"

"Theresa Donovan."

The woman put her hands on her wide hips. "Who referred you here?"

"My aunt."

"Who?"

"Patricia Roach."

"Oh, yes. Get into the johnny, please."

Allie stepped out of her sandals and undressed while the woman set up a round gray machine at the head of the table. There was an upside-down glass jar connected to it. A clear tube ran from that to a triangular mask the woman set on the table. Allie pulled off her underwear and folded it inside her skirt. She slipped on the johnny and was tying it tight in the back when a young man dressed in white shorts and a red-striped short-sleeved shirt walked in.

"I took her vitals. She's five weeks." The woman reached into the closet, then carried over two stirrup stands that she placed at the foot of the table. The doctor picked up the clipboard, then put it down almost as fast. He had short blond hair and blue eyes. His face was tanned and the hair on his forearms was sun-bleached and curly. He patted the table. "Right here, Alice."

Allie sat on the end of the padded bench, then lay back slowly. She crossed her ankles and kept her legs straight. The woman unlocked a door, and rolled out a table with a square white machine on it. Attached to the machine was a coiled white hose. At its end was a long plastic cone that reminded Allie of an anteater's nose. "Can I have some water, please?"

"Afterwards." The woman lifted Allie's right foot up into a stirrup. She did the same with the left. The johnny fell back onto Allie's stomach. The doctor walked over to a window, lifted the shade six inches, and pulled the window up that much too.

Allie lay her head back. The ceiling light hurt her eyes, but when she closed them she felt dizzy. Now the woman's face was over hers and she held the clear plastic mask in her hands. "No ether reactions, correct?"

"I don't think so."

The woman's breath smelled like onions and cigarette smoke.

"You'll have cramping for two or three days. You should feel fine after that."

Allie heard something creak and roll over the floor. The doctor's voice came from down between her legs: "This office is closed every Wednesday afternoon, Alice. When you come to, I'll be back on the Charles River and that's where I'll say I've been. Okey doke?"

"Yes."

Outside, cars and trucks passed by on the highway, and Allie heard a far-off train moving heavily along its tracks. Down on the street or sidewalk, a man yelled somebody's name but then the traffic got louder and Allie couldn't hear him anymore. The woman lowered the mask over Allie's nose and mouth.

"Breathe deeply. Count backwards from twenty."

The woman was pressing harder on the mask than she needed to. Allie breathed in the sweet plastic smell and began counting to herself. *Twenty, nineteen*—the machine near the doctor started up, a loud whir that turned into a steady, high-pitched hum—*eighteen, seventeen, six*—

Burrell dropped Leo off at the top of Saunders Hill Road and paid him in cash, a $20 bill. He said thanks, we'll do it again, then he drove down Paper Boulevard under the clouds. On the ride back they had been quiet and Leo was thinking about all the grown people he would have to tell. Jim and Ryder mainly. And Chick Donovan. Jim was going to be the toughest, and Leo decided he would tell Ryder first, then face Jim with a backup right there beside him. And maybe Allie's mother had already told Chick. That would be a better way for things to go. Leo knew Chick liked him. In fact, of all the grown people, even Ryder, Chick would probably take this news as good. Leo just hoped Chick wouldn't ask him to move up to Vermont with them. But Leo didn't think that would really be a problem, not with Allie wanting to do so much of this on her own and everything.

Leo wanted to see her again before he told anyone. Maybe she could come over and they'd make love in his room, snuggle up and map it all out before Jim and Ryder showed up. Yep. It would be better to tell everyone that way, the two of them standing together side by side.

Leo walked into the house to the parlor and called the Donovans. Allie's mother answered and Leo was glad. He wanted to talk to her some more about last night; he wanted her to know how much he respected her and Chick and the family and how she didn't have to look at this in such a bad way; him and Allie would be going places, she'd see, baby and all. But Mrs. Donovan almost sounded like she understood this already and there was no need to discuss last night. She said Allie had gone out, she wasn't sure where, then she mentioned that Chick was coming home tomorrow morning. Leo said that's wonderful, please tell Allie I called, and say hi to Christopher for me.

194

Leo hung up. Man, if she can take it, then Jim can. He ducked his head into the kitchen and glanced at the wall clock. He had almost an hour before his father came home to cook and get ready for Wednesday night poker. Allie would probably call and be able to come over by then, but even if she doesn't, he thought, I can do this alone. In fact, I *should* do it alone. No Allie, no Ryder, just me and Jim.

He took a shower and changed into clean jeans and a button-down short-sleeved shirt. He combed his hair back, pulled on his sneakers, then yanked his G harp off the bureau and went right into Mance Lipscomb's "Blues in G." But instead of playing it slow like it was written, Leo bluesed it up in a double-time tempo; he hopped around the room on one foot while he blew out a chord note, then sucked in for a long fluttering trill he capped with a hand-smacking pop. He put down the G harp, picked up his D, and went right into "Burning Fire" by Otis Spann. He did this one fast too, then he ditched the D for his C. He kept the medley going with Mississippi John Hurt's "Moanin' the Blues," and he slowed it way down. Then Leo surprised himself: he lowered his harp at the crooning cue and he began to sing:

"No, no Baby, I don't want to go,
 No, no baby—"

He kissed the harp and fanned out a heart-cracking tremolo.

"Why'n't you do me like you
 did before?"

He raised the harp again, tongue-blocked a long high wolf-cry of a note, then brought it back down to a four-reed bass chord he used to launch right into "The Love Abode." He lowered the harp and closed his eyes and sang as loud and as in key as he could:

"That Allie's got a neck,
 A neck so fine,

I want to kiss it,
Kiss it all the time.
Me and her,
We got a house on the hill,
It's got a porch
Bigger than the paper mill.
Sometimes when we hug
I feel like I'm gonna explode,
But then we do what we have to
Up there in our Love Abode—"

He raised the harp and zipped right into a lead echo off the last line. He pulled back for a chord buildup, fanning his hand for a solid tremolo that he drew out so long he knew the following single note would prick it like a needle and set any audience to clapping. But when he finally pulled out of the tremolo and went to the lead, two notes came out instead of one, so he dropped the tongue-blocking method and pursed his lips for the final draw that didn't sound near as pure as he wanted it to. He'd have to work with Ryder on that one tonight. He tapped the spit out of the harp into his palm. He did the same with the D and G, then he wiped them all down with a clean pair of underwear.

A car door slammed shut outside. Leo tucked in his shirt and walked right out to the kitchen as Jim came through the doorway carrying a full grocery bag. He was looking down in front of him and didn't notice Leo right off. When he looked up his eyes were a little bloodshot, like he wasn't sleeping enough. "Hey, son." He put the groceries on the counter, then pulled a loaf of Wonder Bread and three cans of creamed corn from the bag. He reached in for a carton of eggs and held them out to Leo. "Check those."

Leo popped the lid and looked inside. The eggs were fine, but he wasn't; he felt soft in the legs and when he opened the fridge, he thought for sure it was a better idea to tell Ryder first.

"How was the roofing?"

"Good." Leo took a Coke from the fridge and opened it. "What's on the menu?"

"Fish."

"Lars won't go near that leftover."

"No game tonight."

"How come?"

Jim pulled a casserole dish from the cabinet, unwrapped the fish, and laid it in. "You and Allison have birthday plans Friday?"

"No."

"Invite her down. Ride says he's going to bake you a cake."

Leo was starting to feel better. He sat at the table. "I guess Chick Donovan's coming home from the hospital tomorrow."

"Good news."

"Yep." Leo breathed deep. His heart was really going; when he let out his breath, he could feel the beats echo from his mouth like smoke rings. He sipped his Coke and looked out the window at the trees. The sun was out again. A breeze blew through the pines and made the skinny branches bob and sway. "I got some other news too."

Jim turned from his work at the counter. He was smiling, though his eyes looked tired, sad even. Leo thought how much he looked like a Mexican really.

"What is it?"

"Allie's going to have a baby."

Jim didn't move. His smile vanished. He kept his eyes on Leo and he looked like he was about to go off into a stare but then he blinked twice and shook his head. "When?"

"Eight months from now, I think."

Jim reached into his coverall pockets for his Lucky Strikes. He shook one out and tapped the end on the flat of his lighter.

Ryder's Impala pulled up behind Jim's car. He had the radio turned up on a talk station. He shut down the engine but let the news play a few more seconds. The announcer's voice was deep, talking about the Red Sox game to be played in Boston tonight. Ryder shut off the radio.

Jim lit the cigarette as he walked in.

"You brewin' coffee yet, Jimbo?" Ryder rested his harp harness on the table and put his six-pack in the fridge.

Jim blew out smoke, shook his head, and looked back at Leo. "Tell him."

"Bad news?" Ryder said.

"No, it's not, Dad. It's not bad news."

Jim dropped his smoking cigarette and stomped on it. A plate slid from the dish rack into the sink and Jim pointed a thick trembling finger at Leo's face. "Do not, give me, any lip."

Leo glanced down at the table, then out the window. He wanted to stand and walk outside, run through the woods, but he wasn't about to move in front of Jim the way he was right this second.

"Go ahead and tell me, Young Buddy. Did you get in another fight?"

Leo looked at Ryder's lean smiling face. He felt like smiling too but he held it off and said the words as serious as he could: "Me and Allie are going to have a baby, Ride."

Ryder's eyes shot from Leo, to Jim, then back. "Is this before, or after the wedding?"

"Before, I hope."

"Hope?" Jim said. "There is going to be a wedding, and damn soon."

"Allie doesn't want to get married, Dad. She just wants to have the baby."

"I b'lieve he means adoption, Jimmy."

"Is that true?"

"No, I want to marry her. She told me she wouldn't, but I think she will. She's confused."

Jim leaned back on the counter and crossed his arms. "Does Donovan know?"

"We told her mother last night."

"How'd she take it, Young Buddy?"

Leo shrugged. "She wanted Allie to get an abortion."

"Over my cold body," Jim said.

"No, it's all right. I talked to her today and everything's fine. She knows it's up to me and Allie."

"Why hasn't she called me?"

"Allie?"

"No. Her mother should call me."

Leo sipped his Coke.

Ryder smiled and shook his head. "Look at him, Jimbo. A boy daddy."

"No. You're wrong. He just kissed his boyhood good-bye." Jim looked at his son. "You know that, don't you? After supper, we are driving up to the Donovans."

The sun had dropped down in the Berkshires. The breeze was gone too. Leo sat in the passenger seat of the Valiant and looked up at the orange and purple streaks in the sky over the hills just before Jim drove quiet through the dark of the covered bridge and turned left onto the gravel. The water was still high in the poplars but the road was dry. Leo felt more calm than he had in days. Things were really coming together now: Allie wasn't a Mystery Girl anymore, Chick was coming home, Dwight and Olin had left town, and Jim knew everything.

When they drove up Spoon Hill Leo's heart picked up some, but not much. The Donovans' cabin looked peach-colored in this light. The Star Chief was parked in front of the flatbed, and on the porch sat little Christopher in a shirt and diapers, pushing a small toy truck back and forth in front of him. He didn't look up as Jim and Leo got out of the car. Leo tucked the back of his shirt into his pants and followed Jim, who stepped around Christopher and knocked on the frame of the screen door. Leo's mouth was dry. He squatted and put his finger in front of Christopher's truck. The boy smiled up at him, then laughed, pulled the truck back, and rolled it at Leo's hand. Leo could smell chicken frying inside. He heard it sizzling too. Then he heard Mrs. Donovan's voice at the door saying, "Oh. Please, come in."

Allie's door shut as they walked inside. Mrs. Donovan was wearing that long African-looking afghan again, the one with all the sunset colors in it. Her hair was pulled up on top of her head and she wore no makeup whatsoever. Leo was glad his father had changed out of his coveralls into good pants and a short-sleeved shirt. They followed her onto the knit rug in front of the fireplace. She turned on the lamp next to the couch.

"Have a seat, I'll just shut off the fire. Would you like anything to drink, Mr. Suther?"

"No ma'am, thank you."

Jim and Leo sat on the couch facing the empty hearth. Jim folded his hands in his lap and looked up at the bearded man's face over the mantel. Leo watched as Chick's wife turned off the stove and then walked right into Allie's room without knocking. She closed the door behind her and Leo hoped Allie would hurry up and rise to this challenge like he knew she wanted to. The hard part was over; Jim already knew. I probably should have called her first though, he thought, so she'd know this already.

Jim stood and walked over to look at one of Mrs. Donovan's paintings that hung over a bookshelf next to the fireplace. It was another one of the hills down across the river. Jim had both hands in his pockets, and he was bending over, looking real close. Allie's door opened and Leo stood up so fast he almost fell back on the couch. Mrs. Donovan came out, then Allie. She held her hands crossed in front of her. She was barefoot and wore a nice blouse tucked into a blue-jean skirt. Her hair hung loose around her shoulders. Her face was pale, but Leo couldn't remember her ever looking so pretty. He smiled and waved. Allie smiled back.

"Hi, Jim."

"Hello, Allie. Looks like we have a situation going, huh?"

"Yeah," Allie said. Mrs. Donovan sat in the rocking chair near the fireplace and Allie sat on the couch right up against the arm opposite Leo. Leo sat down too, but Jim stayed standing near the mantel.

"Allison?" Mrs. Donovan said.

Allie crossed her legs at the knees and started bouncing the calf of the top leg against the shin of the bottom.

"Leo filled me in on the whole story," Jim said. "Let's go from there."

"I wish it were that simple, Mr. Suther," Allie's mother said.

"You can call me Jim if you like."

"Thank you. Allie, go ahead now."

Leo looked over at her. She was bouncing her leg pretty fast. Her arms were crossed too.

"My father came up here to talk, Allie."

"Allison," Mrs. Donovan said. "If—"

Allie uncrossed her arms and legs and stood up. "It *is* simple. There's no baby, okay? I drove myself to Boston, and I saw a creepy doctor, and that's that! *Okay?*" She looked down at Leo. "All right? I did it. *I* did it. Not *you,* not my *mother,* ME!" She slapped her chest with her hand. She looked quickly at Jim, then turned and ran through the kitchen and out the back door.

Leo jumped up and started after her but Jim grabbed him from behind at the waist and Leo jerked his elbows back and charged outside to the rear porch where he tripped over a barbell plate and fell forward over the steps onto the ground on his knees.

"*Allie!*" He yelled her name before he knew where she was, but now he could see her: straight ahead beyond the grass, she was in the trees at the ridge, still running, her blond hair and white blouse giving her away. He got up and ran over the yard into the hickories and spruce. He tripped over a root, skinned the palm of his hand, and kept running. He couldn't see her anymore. Then he did. The ridge gave way to the other side of Spoon Hill, a long steep pine-tree slope that ended in a runoff gulley, still wet and muddy from the rains. And there she was, running down to it. She held her arms out and let the trunks slap her hands as she headed for the bottom. Leo did a fast roofing sidestep down between the trees.

"*Leave me alone!*"

It was a shriek, like a cat on fire, but Leo didn't stop. He watched his feet and let the hill take him fast to the gulley where he slipped in a damp mound of pine needles. He caught his balance and walked fast over mud and rock after Allie, who was swinging her arms, walking barefoot down the shallow ditch, the bottoms of her feet shit-colored. "Stop! God *damn* you!"

She did. She kept her back to him. Her hands hung loose at her sides and her shoulders began to shake with her crying.

"You're crazy. You're *fucking* crazy. How could you *do* that?" He stepped forward and jerked her around to face him. Her hair spun and some of it stuck to her wet face. She kept crying, looking right at him, and the meanness slipped out of him but nothing came in to take its place; he didn't feel a thing, really. Back in the cabin *he* had felt like crying, and when he ran after her he only wanted to catch her and make her hurt, push her, or punch her, even. But now, breathing a foot in front of her, he felt nothing. It was like blowing into a harp hole where the reed inside it is bent or twisted and you get no sound at all: He didn't care how much she was shaking or how wet her face was; he saw that one of her hands was bleeding and he didn't care about that; he noticed how steep the gulley was behind her, how he could give her a two-fingered shove and she'd fall and roll over backwards easy, but there was nothing for him in that either, so he didn't move, and he didn't speak. He stood there and stared at the blond strand across Allie's filled-up eyes. He heard his father call his name up the hill, but he felt even less about that.

Her crying slowed to a sniffle, and soon she stopped altogether. She pulled the hair free of her face, then she squatted and blew her nose into a bush. She stood, wiped her eyes, and said, "So, am I a witch now, Leo?"

Leo turned and headed across the gulley for the back of Spoon Hill. He was feeling things now, his throat for one: it was thick and all balled up. If he opened his mouth to speak, he would cry for sure. He started up the hill but the pine needles on the ground made him slip, and he had to pull on the tree trunks to keep moving.

"Last night we were just being brave, *Leo!*"

Her voice sounded like it was coming from two feet behind him, though he knew she hadn't moved from where she stood. The sky at the ridge was purplish, almost dark. A lightning bug flashed off to his left, another one right in front of him.

"You're such a *hypocrite!* I know you're *relieved!*"

Ryder was gone when Jim and Leo drove up to the house. On the kitchen table he'd left a note under a half-full Pabst bottle.

> Guess I'll go dust off the wedding tux. Call me if you want to play.
> Uncle Ride

Jim had said only one thing on the drive home and that was when they pulled up onto Paper Boulevard, all lit up with street lamps and the light from the theater. "Damned baby-killing bastards." Now he took the note from Leo's hands and crumpled it up.

Leo let out a long breath. The newspaper was on the table and the front-page story was about another big war protest down in New York City. Jim walked into the parlor and began tuning up his Dobro. Leo leaned back against the fridge and closed his eyes. He couldn't remember ever feeling this tired. His arms and legs were concrete and he couldn't stand up straight. He heard the squeak of Jim's capo, then the slide of the finger thimble up the neck. Leo pulled the kitchen light string and headed down the hallway to his room. Before he got there, Jim stopped tuning. "I don't want you going near that family again. You hear?"

Leo thought of Chick coming home tomorrow, of his wife's cheerful voice telling Leo that he would, cheerful because she knew where Allie had been all day, what she was doing.

"Leo?"

"Yeah, I hear."

Jim was quiet, his guitar stool squeaked, then he launched right into a fast and heated "How Come Hell Came Calling, Lord? How Come?"

Leo left the door open. He lay down on his bed without taking off his sneakers, and he was asleep before Jim hit the first refrain.

29

Thursday was hot and dry and sunny. No rain, no floods, not even a cloud. The sky was a mammoth blue that Leo tried to admire from the roof of the old job site, the job they'd all abandoned, but when he looked for too long he felt the house move beneath him and he had to squat right away to keep from falling. Twice that happened and twice he pictured Allie sitting at his bedside holding his hand as he lay there with his legs wrapped in plaster.

No one had asked him to lay shingles on the new roof, and he wasn't even sure he was doing it right, but no way in red hell was he going to sit around Saunders Hill Road all day after last night. He was awake before Jim this morning but didn't get up until his father was gone, the house creaking, the birds down on the river chirping up a frenzy. He drank the last of Jim's coffee, then walked out of the house in the same clothes and sneakers he'd slept in. He swung his arms in a march as he went, and he was past downtown and through the bridge in no time. He knew where he was going and it wasn't the Donovans'. As he passed Spoon Hill, he glanced up it for just a second. Their cabin used to look good in the early light, the logs pinkish, the porch dark, the windows darker, everything inside warm and loving. But there was nothing in there now except coolness and no caring at all.

He wondered what Chick would say about all this. Leo didn't care really. And he sure wasn't off to work on the house for *him* either. While he was drinking coffee back in the kitchen, two pictures had come into Leo's head. The first was of the unfinished house, the framed roof and walls covered with new plywood that had already turned brown and gray under the rains; and there was all that material in the dark barn, the stack of drywall, the leftover two-by-fours, the wrapped shingle bundles near the door. Then the second picture had come to him, Allie lying on a bed, her legs spread for some man who stuck a vacuum cleaner nozzle inside her and turned on the machine that sucked up their little one, probably tearing it to pieces before it ever got to become the whole thing we all end up being. And Leo had to know. Was it a boy? Or was it a girl? Was it a Hewson? Or a Katie Faye? And this was just too much to ask. He dumped his coffee in the sink, wiped his face, and set out walking to at least shingle the roof before the whole damn house started to rot brand new.

It took all day but Leo had covered both sides and he was capping off the ridge when he heard a car coming down the road from the north. The sun hung low over the hills of the national forest across the river. The trees looked gold in this light, the road too. Leo stood, but the ground began to swing up at him, so he sat down on the ridge. He had taken off his shirt early and kept it off. Now his bare back felt skinned and he was glad the sun was finishing itself up. He figured the dizziness was from no food and no break, and the chills he felt were probably from no water which he felt stupid for not bringing because he had carved out an early thirst just by walking up here and tearing the padlock off the barn door with a two-by-four scrap from out back.

The car wasn't a car at all, but a truck, a white Dodge pickup with an empty steel rack fixed in the bed. Its windows were rolled up. The radio was turned on loud inside and Leo could hear that new good song about the guy coming along so far just to sit on the dock of the bay. The truck drove by, slowed at the turn, then stopped, backed up, and stopped again. The window rolled down and there sat Floyd Starrett, his nose splint gone, looking up at Leo, bobbing his head to the song.

"Hey, killer," Floyd said.

Leo rested his hand on the hammer handle. Now his head felt hot, almost as bad as his back. The radio clicked off and Floyd stepped out of his pickup, the engine still running.

Leo tried to see if anyone else was in the cab, though it didn't look like it from here. Floyd's hair had grown out to about an inch long and stuck out all over his head like he'd put his wet finger in an open fuse box and didn't give a damn. His nose was still wider than normal, but his gray eyes looked less like slits than before. He walked up the drive. "You alone?"

"Maybe."

"Maybe?" Floyd stepped inside the house. Leo placed a shingle cap on the ridge and nailed it down on both sides. He could hear Floyd's boots walking loud over the plywood floor below. The last time Leo had seen him, Floyd was swinging a bat at him while Dwight and Olin went to work putting Chick in a coma, and no doubt Floyd was the one who broke Chick's arm and leg later, but still, Leo didn't feel mad. All he felt was feverish and a little shaky, two things he was feeling before Floyd showed up.

"This job went to hell without me, I guess." Floyd was back in the driveway, smiling up at him. He lit up an L&M.

"Where'd you get the truck?"

"My brother's. You like?"

Leo shrugged and nailed off another cap.

"Your line's off."

"How come you're not on the run like your two buddies, Floyd?"

"Never run if you can walk, I say."

"Walk where?"

"It don't matter where. What happens happens, man."

Leo had two more caps to go. He laid them down and nailed them, then he twisted around for the leftover bundle draped over the ridge and dropped it off the side to the ground.

"You can catch a ride with me if you want. The air conditioning's free."

Floyd handed Leo a cool can of beer as soon as Leo pulled the door shut. The top of the windshield was tinted and Leo felt like he was sitting behind a big pair of shades. Cold air blew over his pants to his bare stomach and chest. He put on his shirt but left it unbuttoned, then popped open the beer and drank off half of it.

"You should play ball." Floyd took the turn down the hill for the river. Leo asked him what he meant.

"Your *swing,* man. If Dewey was a stitch ball, he'da scored you a fuckin' homer."

"He all right?"

"Nah, those busted ribs are gonna kill him dead." Floyd laughed and drove faster.

The skin of Leo's back felt pinched and he had to sit forward and put his hand on the dash. "I got too much sun."

"Drink a six in a cold bath. Free advice from Pretty Boy Floyd."

Leo finished off his beer. He remembered taking that bath with Allie after making love all afternoon. He dropped the empty can down on his sneakers. "You almost killed him, man."

Floyd stopped the truck at the bottom of the hill. He rolled the window down and blew smoke outside. "Eye for an eye, man. Teeth for teeth."

"Oh sure, he breaks one thing of yours and you break about *five* of his."

"Yeah well, you mess with the best, you lay with the rest. You know?" Floyd handed Leo another beer. Leo drank off half right away.

"So how come I haven't heard from the smokeys? Chick coming after me himself, or what?"

"Forget it. Chick told me he feels bad he ever hit you."

"You're dickin' me."

"No way, soon as he's better, he's moving up to Vermont. The whole frigging family's moving up." Leo swallowed more beer. He thought how Floyd was right, a cold bath was going to feel good.

"Your girlfriend too?"

"Hey I don't give a shit. She fucking does what she wants anyway."

"She fucking does?" Floyd stuck his finger in his closed hand and pulled it out and pushed it in slow. He raised his eyebrows, making ridges all up his forehead.

Leo smiled. "Does a saw cut wood?"

Floyd laughed so hard he coughed. He lit up another cigarette, then he switched on the radio, got a news announcer, and switched it back off. "So Chicken Little is calling off the dogs then?"

"Yep."

"And I can call up my boys and tell 'em?"

"What about Dewey?"

"What about him? You got his attention, but I can tell you first hand, he don't have much of an attention span."

They both laughed. Floyd put the truck in drive and spun out gravel as he turned onto the river road. Leo drained the last of his beer. He rolled down the window and threw the empty can out into the trees.

In the dream Leo's back was on fire. He stood in a parlor that was half like the Suthers', half like the Donovans'; there was the empty fireplace and the portrait of the bearded man above it, but off to the right, instead of the Donovans' kitchen, was the Suthers' parlor window overlooking the woods down to the river. And it was the river Leo wanted to get to. Nobody seemed to notice the fire. Jim and Mrs. Donovan stood over by her new painting, talking about it. Allie sat on the floor reading a book. She wore a T-shirt but no pants or underwear. Her legs were spread apart and Katie Faye Suther was wriggling out of her. His mother was dressed in a blouse and skirt and her hair was pinned up to the side of her head. She looked up at Leo and smiled, her red lipstick catching the light from the flames licking over his shoulders.

Then Leo was outside lying by the river on his back in the snow. The flames were out, and the burning had dropped to a sizzle that was sputtering down to a cool fade. Above him was gray sky and the bare branches of trees. Allie's crying face was over his, her hair hanging in front of her wet red cheeks. Leo asked her where his mother was but Allie kept crying as if she didn't hear him, or even see his lips moving. A raven, or a crow, flew over her head for the river and Leo wanted to get up and watch it but the snow held him down. Now Allie was gone and Jim was talking, but Leo couldn't see him anywhere. He could feel the river, though. It was moving under him, and he was beginning to float—

"You slept right through supper."

The bedside lamp was on. Half of Leo's face was in his pillow and he could see a glass of water on the table. Jim was rubbing an ice cube over his back. Leo tried to swallow, but his throat was too dry. "I think I have a fever."

"Sunstroke. Drink that water."

Leo turned around and sat up. He drank the water and looked at Jim. "I dreamt I was lying in snow by the river."

Jim took the empty glass and had Leo lie back down on his chest and stomach. He cracked another ice cube from the tray. "I was just down there praying to your mother."

"She was in it, too."

Jim ran the ice along his son's back from his neck to where his butt began. "I told her to meet that tiny baby at the station. I know that she will."

Leo held his breath. His stomach muscles tensed and something caught in his throat, then shuddered back down.

Jim rubbed the cube over Leo's skin until he had to get another one from the tray. "They say when a child dies she becomes an angel. Yours didn't make it to being a child, so I'm certain she's been conjured into something better—a muse, I think."

"What's that?"

"A muse is a goddess, son. Zeus had nine daughters and I believe each one of them looked after a different kind of art. Your mother's favorite was Erato because Erato like to preside over the poems. But ours is Euterpe. She sits in the lap of all musicians." Jim pressed the towel down on the wet sheet. "That's where yours is, out there with Euterpe, looking to help a bluesman try on a song."

Leo felt the towel on his back. It burned, and when he shut his eye, a tear squeezed out onto his pillow.

"There's plenty of time for children, son. There's better fish in the river too."

Leo slept through the night and straight till noon. On the kitchen table was a note from Jim.

Don't make any plans. We got a birthday to celebrate. Take some aspirin for that back.

Leo stood shirtless near the fridge and drank down two glasses of orange juice. He ate three bowlfuls of Cheerios one after the other, then he made himself a peanut butter and honey sandwich and finished it off while he heated up the last of Jim's morning coffee. He took a full cup out to the stoop and sat down.

The sky was gray but a little too bright to look straight up at. The air was heavy and warm again and the mill smelled stronger than the pines. Leo drank his sugared coffee. A car horn honked up on Paper Boulevard. The skin on his back felt dry and tight, but it didn't sting as much. Yesterday didn't seem real. If somebody came and told him the roof at the job is naked of shingles just like before, Leo would almost believe them. Being with Floyd happened, though, sitting in that air-conditioned truck, letting him off the hook about Chick, letting Floyd talk about fucking and Allie in the same breath—Jesus.

Three brown birds, swallows maybe, flew out of a pine and over the house. Leo sipped his coffee too fast, spilling some on his chin. He remembered what Jim had said last night about children and angels, about there being better fish in the river. And that was sad to hear, because Jim and Allie had liked each other so much. Leo could still hear her voice shrieking through the trees at him as he climbed the back of Spoon Hill. She was wrong though; he didn't feel relieved, he felt scooped out, which was strange when you think it was Allie who got scraped clean of what they'd both conceived. But he felt so suddenly hollow, when the day before he'd been so full, that he was almost light-headed in the nothing he felt.

He wanted to take back what he'd told Floyd, though. And no matter what Allie had done, she wasn't proud of it; Leo wished Jim could have seen her crying as hard as she did.

He drank the rest of his coffee and he thought, here he was, eighteen years old today, and life isn't what he felt like celebrating at all. He stood and went inside and read what Katie Faye had left behind.

But I'm straying from my and Jimmy's first date. Over a wedge of flan we shared, Jim decided he would have to play for me. We took a taxi straight to the base and Jim had me wait at the guard booth while he went on in for his guitar. I tried to make conversation with the boy on duty, but even with an MP band around his arm he was about as shy as they come. After a long twenty minutes, Jim drove up to the gate in his captain's black Buick, the guitar neck sticking up in the back seat. Then we drove on out to Calaveras Lake and parked in a clearing among the trees by the water. We sat on a boulder at the lake's edge, and while Jimmy tuned up his guitar, I remember looking up at the stars I hadn't seen near enough of from downtown San Antonio. I felt more like myself than I had since Papa died.

Jim started out playing a folksy instrumental. His fingers moved fast but relaxed, and he tapped his shined army shoe to a perfect beat. But it was when he began to sing that Guitar Jimmy emerged so beautiful. His speaking voice was your average manly alto but when he sang he became what I believe they call a tenor, a gut-bucket tenor. He was just discovering the blues then so he did quite a few Leadbelly numbers. He played the more gentle ones, and when he sang a line about dragging a cotton bag or hopping the rail, it sounded as natural as could be and I knew it wasn't because Jimmy was a good mimic; he didn't have to live a sharecropper's life to guess at the hurt that came with it.

As he sang, I clasped my hands around my drawn up knees and

---

watched as much of his face as I could see. Kissing him was now no longer simply an adventurous notion, but a bodily need as necessary to me as taking my next breath. When he paused to tune what he told me was a too-tight E string, I got on my knees, put both my hands on his meaty shoulders, and pressed my lips right to his, the guitar lodged between us. He smelled like sweat and Old Spice cologne and he tasted like jalapeños and chocolate. I pulled away as soon as I realized our mouths had opened some and I said, "Don't be fooled; you're the first boy I ever kissed." He didn't say anything back. He put that guitar off to the side and we stretched out on that rock and kissed and hugged and talked for a long while, until pink dawn spread out over Calaveras Lake and we stared into each other's faces. We were privy to fate then, and we knew it. Jimmy broke into a smile and laughed out loud, then he pulled me closer and said he hadn't planned on it but here he was AWOL and don't count on seeing him for a time.

That time was only two weeks but it could just as well have been two years. Funny enough, the captain who belonged to the Buick thought highly of Jim and lightly of his crime and helped him get short stockade time and only one demerit. They let Jim have his guitar in there, too. He wrote me three songs, my favorite being "Kate Made Me Late, but I Love Her Anyway." Leo likes that one. I asked Jim to play it for us last night and he did. We were all snuggled on the couch in the parlor. I lay back on the arm opposite Jimmy. Leo lay with his little back against me and I put a pillow between us to try and ease the pain in my stomach, his short legs sticking out between mine. I hugged him to me and as he laughed at the funny lines of Jimmy's song, I felt his strong little body jiggle against me.

How strange this dying is. Everything becomes so god-awful clear. Watching Jimmy's big handsome head sing away to his family, I saw the whole spinning web of how we three got there on that couch.

Jim proposed on our third date. We'd gone strolling together down on Bandera. There was a warm breeze and I remember smelling fried corn tortillas from an eatery. There was an open farmer's market near the theater and I could hear the cluck and cackle of live chickens. Jimmy insisted we buy one for my mother and Gram though they didn't need a chicken and he hadn't even met

211

the widows. I stopped at the sidewalk and wouldn't go in. The smile left his face and he held my hand in both of his. "All right. Marry me then, Katie Faye." He looked down at the sidewalk a moment, then back at me, and it took every bit of my panhandle-girl resolve not to bust out and cry right there like a child. I couldn't speak so I nodded yes and Jim hugged me so hard and so long I don't remember feeling my feet lift off the ground.

We were married two weeks and a day from that night, on October 14, 1948. Mama insisted on a church wedding so we made it official at the base chapel. Jimmy's mother and an uncle came down from Massachusetts by train. Our best man wasn't Toby or Rex, but Jim's bunkmate of one year, Ryder "Harmonica" Stillwell. Gram sprung for a photographer, a German from New Braunfels who took such care with each shot, I took to calling him Vinny Van Gogh. Before long, in the early days of December, I spent mealtimes feeling sick. It was the same week Jimmy's enlistment was up, so two hours before my husband wasn't a soldier anymore I went to the base doctor and was given that wonderful news, courtesy of the U.S. Army.

We moved into a boardinghouse a block from where I still worked three nights a week at the bowling alley. As Leo grew inside me, I worked my regular shift while Jim walked the sidewalks from Bandera to Texarkana looking for nightspots in which to give a humble show. We spent the afternoons together making love, and I still talked of Paris, I still thought it possible for our little family to go to France. Jim seemed neither for nor against the notion, simply preoccupied with getting work. Soon he found it, a Friday- and Saturday-night gig at a honky-tonk not far from Schnabel Park. I don't recollect the exact name of the place, though I do remember Horse or Stallion being part of the sign. Jimmy lasted only two weekends there, as the tavern's clientele were far more inclined to hear the twang and moan of some boy mocking Bob Wills or Patsy Cline, not some big-headed ex-soldier singing colored music from the cotton shacks of Louisiana. On that second and last Saturday night, I sat in the front sipping a Coca-Cola when an empty whiskey jigger hit Jim in the shoulder just as he was finishing up a rousing Lightning Hopkins song. I jerked around to see a tall sunburned ranch hand stand up and call my husband a nigger-lovin' son of a bitch. Next thing I saw was Jim. He'd leapt off the stage with his guitar and was standing there in front of the tall drunk cowboy.

"That's not a kind word. Don't say it again."

"I said you was a damn—"

Jimmy rammed the guitar neck at the man's chest, stepped back, then swung his only guitar crashing down over the cowpoke's head, sending him to the floor. A week after that Jim re-enlisted.

It was a hot bright day in August when Leo James Suther came into this world. The women in my family have always had small hips and Mama fretted about the delivery, but my Leo cooperated by weighing in at a very agreeable six pounds, five ounces. I squeezed him out like a pumpkin seed. Jimmy got a marriage subsidy from Uncle Sam so we were able to stay living off base. In late September we took what we had in savings and bought Jim a new guitar, a better one than he'd ever had. A Mexican man off Guadalupe ran a pawn shop and in the back of the store he kept a few high-quality items. He had a fox hair coat, a fine crystal decanter set, even a Civil War cannon without its wheels. The guitar hung by its strap on the wall. The man said it was handmade in Spain out of rosewood. We paid a month's rent for it, and the Mexican was so pleased, he threw in that Dobro steel slide guitar for three extra dollars.

It was a wonderful first year. Jim's army duty felt like a regular day job. He'd leave the house at 6:30 and be back by 5:00. I'd have cold beer in the fridge and a hot meal on the table. We rarely touched the beer till late, though. Jimmy has always preferred playing his music as clearheaded as possible, which I understood and understand. After supper, he'd hold baby Leo until it was time for me to put him to bed. Then Jim would break out his new guitars and work on his songs. I'd brew us a small pot of coffee—which Jim has always wanted iced—and while he picked and hummed, I'd take out my writing and go to work at the kitchen table. I wrote a lot of wife and mother poems then, some of my best, I think. Jimmy thought so too. Most every night he'd ask to read or hear something.

Weekends I let Mama and Gram babysit, and Jimmy and I would go dancing with Ryder and his girl-of-the-moment. I liked Ryder from the get-go. Skinny men can't help being adorable, and when you throw in Ryder's talent with the harmonica, his big straight teeth, his way of laughing at most everything everybody else forgets to, well then I couldn't help but look at him as the bony brother I never had. One night, after two-stepping ourselves silly at the Wrangler, a road-house across the San Antonio line right at the edge of the plains, we three gathered in front of Ryder's car and made a vow to each other. Ryder still had the giggles from losing his date, a breasty blonde girl who it turned out was only fifteen, a point of information delivered to our table by her angry large brother. Ryder stood, bowed like a gentleman, then gave up his intended roll-in-the-hay with a straight face. We danced some more, then went outside to cool our sweat. From the Wrangler's parking lot the sky looked magnificent. Jimmy said he was going to stand on the roof of Ryder's Ford and pick me a whole galaxy. We all laughed.

"Heck," Ryder said. "I thought she was *four*teen." He pulled out his harmonica and played a triple-time "When the Saints Come Marching In."

Jimmy and I sat on the hood. Ryder stood in front of us. When he finished playing we went quiet for a few minutes. Jim had managed to walk outside with a full bottle of Pearl beer. We passed it around. I took a wonderfully long cold chugalug. It was Jimmy who brought up the vow.

"Listen, you two." He had his arm around me. He reached out and lay his hand on Ryder's shoulder. "Let's never quit. We should swear to each other that we can't ever quit."

"Quit what, Guitar Jim?" Ryder still had a smile in his voice.

"Just that. My guitar, and your harmonicas, and Katie Faye's poems. We should just keep marching ahead. You know?" Jim looked at me, then pulled me close. "I think I'm figuring out once you start you're not supposed to ever stop."

"Should we draw blood?" Ryder said.

"No," Jimmy said. "Let's just promise we won't let each other quit."

"I promise," I said.

"Throw me in there." Ryder sipped the Pearl. "But when I start sounding poor you should promise to *make* me quit."

Jim raised his right hand. "I promise to keep you, Ryder, playing and you Katie, writing. I also promise to lie to both of you when you're not sounding good anymore."

I laughed and hugged Jimmy with both arms. Ryder took out his mouth harp and played a down-home wedding march in half-time.

And in July of the next year, 1950, marching is what they did. We'd been hearing about the possibility of a civil war in Korea for months. On June 25, when Leo was ten months and five days old, the North Korean communists attacked the south and two weeks later Jimmy and Ryder and thousands of other soldiers were on their way. For two months Leo and I stayed at our boardinghouse apartment behind American Flyers—the army was paying the rent—but then the widow terrors set in and I found myself moving in with Mama and Gram, the only real widows I knew.

Lord, how wildly unpredictable this living is. Jim was gone seventeen months and in all that time only five of his letters got through to me. Meanwhile, hundreds of boys were coming home dead, and the last thing I would have believed then was that Jim would be burying me.

March 7, 1955

(It occurs to me I should have been dating all these entries.)

Last night, I talked with my five-year-old. I was too sick to eat—Jim's a wonderful cook but the smell of his lasagna sent me to the john. I was still breathing hard, kneeling on the floor and resting my head on the toilet lid, when I heard Leo's high quiet voice. He asked me if I threw up and I told him that I did. He was wearing his baggy blue jeans and the green sweater I knitted for him last Christmas. The sleeves were rolled up over his tiny wrists. His round face looked full of worry. I've lost a horrible amount of weight, and these past few days, after the nurse has come and gone with the morphine shot, when the absence of pain begins and leaves me feeling almost giddy, I've fretted in front of the mirror about my looks, mainly to avoid scaring my son as much as I obviously do.

In the bathroom last night I asked him to come closer. He walked over and stood in front of me.

"You know, you're right, I won't get sick anymore."

"You won't?"

I shook my head and told him when you die, you can't get sick.

"Me too?"

"Everybody, honey."

"Everybody won't get sick?"

"Not after they die."

"How do they die?"

Lots of ways, I told him. Leo was quiet a moment, then he cocked his head and asked if I was going to die like the pretty leaves.

"You can look at it like that."

"But I don't want you to turn orange." He laughed and I put my hands on his hips, my fingertips almost touching. I said that people die different, that they just lie down one night and don't wake up. Their body stays, but their spirit flies away. He was quiet for a half minute, then he perked up. "So you'll come back to your body when the snow's gone? Like the leaves?"

I hugged him and I didn't think I could continue, but Jimmy was washing dishes in the kitchen and this was as good a time as any other. I kissed my son on the forehead and held him at arm's length. I looked right into eyes that may as well be mine and I told him how we bury our bodies so they can help the ground grow the trees that grow the leaves. I told him he didn't have to look so scared because it doesn't hurt. It's like being real sleepy and cuddling up under warm blankets. When you wake up, your spirit is in another place.

"But when will I die?"

"After a long happy life, honey." I wanted to tell him more, tell him not to worry, our lives are over before we know it. I wanted him to know I'll be back to see him in whatever way I can, but his big eyes showed just how saturated his little head was, so I stopped there. Jimmy stood in the doorway drying his hands on a dishtowel. I don't know how much he heard. He looks so handsome with his new mustache, and it was that I concentrated on.

"When are you going to die, Daddy?"

"Not for a long time, goofy." He looked at me, his eyes suddenly wet.

This morning I woke up weaker than I've felt in days. Jim dressed Leo and cooked us all scrambled eggs and toast. I sat near the window, had tea, and watched them eat. It came to me then that my time is very short. And I'm convinced the approach of my grand exit was hastened by my talking with Leo last night. That was the last and most precious bag to be packed. I'm free to go.

I've always been unpoetically anal about trips, though. On the way back home, I have to sit and review all that has happened so it takes root in me as deep as any seed Papa ever sowed in the panhandle soil; I don't want to forget a thing.

Jimmy came home two days before Christmas in '51. He spent three days in California getting discharged and he never called because he wanted to surprise me. Kill me is a better word. The widows' doorbell rang just after supper. Of course I was standing barefoot on the arm of the couch trying to hang a Christmas cookie on the highest bough beneath the angel. Mama opened the door and gasped, then started crying. I could hear Jimmy's voice but I was still shaken from the gasp and now I somehow thought Jimmy was dead even though I could hear him and when I turned around and saw him walking towards me, twenty pounds leaner, I screamed and fell back against the tree and he caught me and it.

If I lived to be a thousand I would never have another holiday as wonderful as that. Right away I took my husband upstairs to show him sleeping Leo. He lay on his stomach in his crib next to the bed in my old room, which Leo and I now shared. We could see him in the light from the laundromat across the street and Jim reached down and rested his big hand on our son's back, then Jimmy began to cry and we hugged each other for twenty straight minutes.

Later, after coffee, pie, and some brandy Jim brought us from San Francisco, Mama and Gram left us alone in the parlor. I could hear them upstairs rolling Leo's crib into their room. On the couch,

217

Jimmy gave me a small wrapped package and I opened it to find a pearl necklace from Japan. A belated third anniversary present, he told me. He was still in uniform, his tie off and shirt collar open. He sat on the couch next to me looking so different, yet so the same too. He'd lost a lot of his chest and neck thickness, but it was his face that seemed so foreign. His cheeks went in where they didn't used to, and there was more of a line to his jaw, which made him seem less big-headed. But Lord, his eyes hadn't lost a bit of their softness. In fact, they seemed deeper set and more brown than ever.

"I lost track of Ryder four months ago. We were out at Pusan together. I don't suppose you've heard from him?"

I said I hadn't and I reached over and ran my fingers across the short hairs at the back of his head. "Was it just horrible over there, Jimmy?"

He barely nodded, his eyes on the tree. I got up and turned off the lamp so we could better see all the tiny lights. I curled my feet up underneath me and rested my head on Jimmy's shoulder. We sat and stared at that tree like it was a crackling fire.

"I won't be talking about it much, Kate. It'd be like kicking a bruise."

I said I understood but I felt scared about him having had such a big thing happen to him and me not knowing a whit about it.

"Remember I wrote you that a GI let me use his guitar south of Kaesong? He lost both hands under a tank tread he was cleaning, so he let me have the guitar. You can't believe how many dumb accidents happened over there." Jim was sitting up straight and tight. I began to knead his arm and shoulder muscles. I was working my way to his neck.

"I think Ryder was at Heartbreak Ridge. We needed everything north of Yanggu, and I think that's where he went, Katie Faye."

"I guess you'll be talking about this more than you thought."

Jimmy smiled, then stopped just as fast. I asked him if he wanted me to bring him his guitars. He turned and kissed me on the lips and said a Korean word that he told me meant tomorrow. We made love on the couch, and as Jimmy let go inside me I opened my eyes and saw the bright angel looking out across the room from the top of the tree, and I remember offering her a prayer of thanks for my husband and I believe I asked for Ryder's safe return too.

Jim soon got a job building fences with a small company from La Vernia. A truck came for him every morning at seven and he wouldn't get home some days till after dark. It was only a three-man outfit he worked on and cattlemen's acreage went on for miles. That work and the widows' cooking gave Jim back his twenty pounds, plus another five. At night he'd play his guitars. More and more he was favoring his Dobro, and he just loved hearing how that was sort of the first word Leo ever said. Jim had only been gone to war a month then. I was feeding Leo oatmeal and milk one morning when he grabbed the spoon, splashed the oatmeal on the floor, and screamed "Bobro!" then laughed himself silly. I do believe that story alone got Jim favoring the steel slide over that pricey rosewood.

Jim put a down payment on a used Chevrolet sedan, and three weeks later he put a month's rent on a one-story house in the fields out near Calaveras Lake. We moved in on January 12, 1952, a cool sunny day. That night we had Mama and Gram over to eat fried chicken and potato salad on the porch with us. Leo had drunk a whole bottle of Coca-Cola and was so giddy I let him stay up until the widows drove home. The upshot of all this is that two weeks or so later, almost February, Ryder "Harmonica" Stillwell walked up onto that porch at 8:00 on a Friday night, half drunk, laughing, limping, a little *belly* hanging over his buckle. His cheeks were fleshed out too. Jimmy picked him up in a hollering hug and kissed him right on the lips. I ran over and hugged the both of them and we made such a racket Leo woke up crying so I went and got him and reintroduced him to his Uncle Ryder.

We spent the weekend together. Ryder had indeed been at this Heartbreak Ridge. Apparently a supply truck was blown up not far from him and he took pieces of it in his legs and hips. He spent ten weeks in a hospital in Yokohama, Japan, sleeping and eating, he said. The doctors told him he'd probably always have a limp and arthritis would settle in at a young age but otherwise he'd be fine. That next Monday morning, Jim signed Ryder on with the fence builders. By Tuesday night we decided Ryder should live with us till he knew what he was doing next. I had a large pantry I hardly used. There was a single window in the rear wall. I hung a curtain there and a sheet over the doorway to the kitchen. Jim bought an army surplus cot. I put a little throw rug on the floor and Ryder rested his folded clothes on the empty food shelves above.

By day they worked, by night they played. Sometimes in the kitchen, most times on the porch. After a couple of months they were really coming together, so good that they knew it and felt inspired to do something about it. But Jim wasn't even up to trying San Antonio again. He said country music was fine if you preferred cardboard to oak, and this was a cardboard town. We were sitting on the porch, as I recall. They had finished and were sipping cold Jax beers. The night was quiet save for a few hundred springtime crickets out in the grass. The sky was ablaze with stars. I didn't see that we had any choice: "We have to go to Paris, y'all. The French know oak when they see it."

I remember Ryder laughing, but Jim was as straight-faced as ever. He walked over to my chair, squatted, and put his hand on mine. "I haven't forgotten about that, Katie Faye. If you think we should go there, then boy, why not?"

Ryder said he'd already been overseas and barely got out alive. Jim said, "And here we're barely living."

Ryder took a long chugalug and wiped his mouth. "Then I'll go where my guitar man goes."

It was decided. Jim and I made love half the night. Before we went to sleep we figured out a savings plan and how many weeks we would need in order to fly to France: twelve, at least. My travel money was long gone on diapers and grocery money with the widows, but I still had three or four dollars in the account, enough to keep it open and tilt the boat full speed ahead.

But what happens fast in this world obviously is not up to us. Jimmy's mother had a heart attack the first week of summer up in Massachusetts. A day later Jim had to dip into our Eiffel Tower money to take a train to see her. He stayed a week. When he got back he was quiet and blue, looking scared, I thought, of soon becoming an orphan. One evening a few days later, after he carried sleeping Leo to his crib and laid him down, Jimmy came into the kitchen where Ryder and I sat at the table with my French book and a map of Europe. He leaned up against the refrigerator and folded his

———

220

arms across his big fence-building chest. He caught my eye, then nodded his head for me to follow him outside. But Ryder saw all this too. He chuckled, then stood and said he needed to go breathe some good Texas air to clear his french fried brain.

I should have known what Jim had on his mind, but I honestly did not see it coming.

"I can't let my mother have another heart attack all alone, Katie Faye."

I think I sighed or something because he immediately dropped his arms and looked angry. I stood, walked over, and held his wrists. "You want to move up there?"

He nodded. "I'll get you to Paris, Kate. I swear it."

The surprising thing is, I took to Massachusetts like a horse to hay. I could never have imagined there being so many hills and trees, rivers and lakes in one place. My only sadness, besides postponing Paris, was leaving Ryder and the widows. Ryder took the news with a smile, then said he didn't mind his guitar man being a Yankee but he wasn't up to becoming one himself, thank you very much. He and Jim had quite a few howling blues sessions the two weeks before we left. Ryder liked the house so much, he stayed to take over the rent and he said he'd go find himself a señorita to move in and split the bills with him.

Mama and Gram didn't receive the news of our moving well at all. The day we left we drove up to their house to say good-bye and only Mama came out: Gram wouldn't leave the kitchen. Mama stood there on the porch in front of our Chevy sedan and loaded trailer with her arms crossed tight as if she were cold, though it was almost ninety-seven degrees under a eucalyptus tree. Jimmy walked up and hugged her. I heard him apologize for taking me so far away. That's when Mama let loose crying. I ran up and hugged her, then whispered her something low but truthful: "She'll pass on real quick, Mama. We won't be gone more than a few months."

But it was Gram who passed on so fast, that very July while Jim was working his first week at Heywood Paper Products and I was hanging curtains in the parlor here on Saunders Hill. Gram and I never talked much but I loved her and felt terribly low that we

---

221

couldn't afford to go down to the funeral. I sent Mama a telegram and Jimmy borrowed money from his mother and wired a bouquet of lilies.

Jim's mama was a lot like him, big-chested and quiet, though she had auburn hair and blue eyes. It was Jimmy's father, Francis, who gave him the good looks. There was a photograph of him standing on the riverbank under the half-built bridge that eventually killed him. He's wearing a hard hat, his hands are on his hips, and his legs are spread slightly apart. What threw me was the smile. It was enormous. His eyes were shadowed under his hat, but you could see how dark and deep-set they were.

Mama Suther had that picture framed and kept it on the mantel in her living room. We fell into the habit of having Sunday dinners over at her house. Most times I cooked, and rarely a Sunday played itself out without my mother-in-law reminding me or Jim that she wanted the picture of Francis buried with her. I thought it very moving at first, and even tried writing a poem from the viewpoint of the photograph. But after a while it got tiresome, especially in light of how upset Jim got every time.

Last spring, Ryder visited. The drive up through New York City thrilled him so much, he talked Jimmy and me into driving down for a long weekend, Leo too. It was a wonderful trip! Ride is coming up again this week from North Carolina. He's been living there the last six months, working in one of those cigarette factories in Winston-Salem. He wrote us that he's been playing his harmonica with a Negro blues band out in some small town in the woods. It'll do Jimmy good to see him. Ryder says he's going to talk us into another excursion to the city, but he hasn't seen me as I am now.

I hear my little boy walking down the hall from his nap. It's warm for a New England day in March. The sun is high and I hear all those birds in the trees outside. I think I'll bundle him up and see if I can't work up the strength for a walk to the river.

Leo turned the page, but the next one was blank. And the next, and the next, for the rest of the notebook. He stood up, then he sat back down. He stared at the floorboards. He didn't remember any of these things his mother had written about. He thought he should remember some of that talk with her in the bathroom, but he didn't. All there was in his head were a few shadow pictures of her pretty face looking at him, or laughing at something Jim had said or done.

30

Leo took his C harp and went back outside to sit on the front step. The sky was bright but gray, and the air felt too dry to rain. A squirrel paused at the trunk of a pine to look Leo over. It sniffed the air, twitched its tail, then turned and skittered up the trunk until Leo couldn't see it anymore. He wondered what Allie was doing right now and he kept seeing her face as she cried there in the rain gully behind Spoon Hill, her blonde hair sticking to her wet cheeks, her eyes never leaving his, though he must have looked very blurry. He raised the harmonica to his lips and sucked out a quick tremolo. Jim would be home in a couple of hours. Leo didn't want to be by himself until then. He thought how strange time is. Two days ago Allie's tears left him feeling zero. Yesterday on the roof, if he felt anything at all, it was anger. He would remember how Allie stood in her living room and shouted out how she had done everything on her own, for *her,* and he'd swing the hammer so hard he left moons in the shingles. But today all he felt was sorry, sorry Allie didn't trust him or love him enough to take him to Boston with her in the first place, to let him have as big a part in the whole day as he deserved. And he knew that was it. *That's* what left him feeling so kicked in the chest, as much as losing the baby and with it the plan of him and Allie being a family within the year: it was Allie counting him out.

Leo lowered his harp, raised it back to his lips, then lowered it again. Which means she was half right when she screamed I'm a hypocrite. He stood and went inside to the parlor where he picked up the phone. He waited half a minute for his heart to slow down, then he dialed the Donovans' number. But he got the loud drone—

pause—drone of a busy signal. He listened to it for a long time before he hung up.

Leo was lying on the couch listening to a Howlin' Wolf record when he heard two cars pull up outside. He went into the kitchen to see Jim and Ryder slam their doors and walk up to the step. Ryder's harmonica harness hung over his shoulder. Under his right arm was a box wrapped in dark blue paper with a silver ribbon. He carried a full case of Pabst cans under his other arm, and Jim carried a white-and yellow-frosted cake covered by a clear plastic dome. Leo could see it was one of Beatrice's. The dome was shaped like a flying saucer and so was the cake. Leo pushed open the screen door for them, then stepped back into the kitchen. He was still barefoot and wasn't wearing a shirt, just jeans. He felt suddenly shy and found himself looking right at the floor.

"There's my Young Buddy, by God." Ryder put the package and bag on the table, then he walked over and hugged Leo to his chest. One of the harmonica corners poked him in the shoulder and when Ryder patted Leo's back with his bare hand, Leo pulled away. "Ow, ow."

"Oh shit, I forgot about that burn. Let's see it."

Jim put the cake on the counter, winked at Leo, and went back outside.

"Man, you got cooked, all right." Ryder looked him straight in the face. "You gonna live?"

"'Course."

"I mean about that other thing. I was damn sorry to hear what that gal did. You all right?"

Leo nodded. He felt his face getting hot. He looked out the window behind Ryder and he wanted to say something good about Allie, about how she's not so bad and he, Leo, should have been more careful in the first place. But nothing came out of his mouth.

Ryder went into the parlor and turned up the volume on Howlin' Wolf.

"Don't look in the back seat," Jim said as he came through the doorway carrying a grocery bag. "How's grilled steaks sound?"

"Good." Leo put his hands in his pockets and watched his father pull the potatoes and wrapped steaks from the bag. His coveralls looked clean and new, though he'd brought some of the smell of the mill in with him.

"I read the rest of her notebooks."

Jim turned and looked at him. In the gray light of the kitchen his hair and moustache looked black as ever. Leo could see what Katie Faye meant about his eyes. "Well?" Jim said.

"She was funny, I mean, you know, lively."

"Yep."

Howlin' Wolf sounded good and low down in the parlor. Ryder came into the kitchen and loaded the case of beer a six-pack at a time into the fridge. Jim dumped the potatoes into the sink and started to wash them.

"You brief your son on the festivities?"

"Go ahead."

Ryder pulled three sweating Pabsts from the fridge and opened them on the table. He put one on the counter next to Jim, then handed the other to Leo. "We figure your watching days are over, Young Buddy. Me and your daddy say tonight entitles you to drink beer and play dealer's choice with Lars and the boys who we expect around seven."

"On a *Friday* night?"

"Hell, yes." Ryder clinked cans with Leo and took a long pull, his Adam's apple making three trips back and forth.

Jim turned off the water and dried his hands. "Don't worry, I didn't tell them it was your birthday."

"Now listen to your Uncle Ryder. If you sit with ten dollars and lose it, then you're finished playing. If you sit down and that lady shines on you, then put that original ten in your pocket and try not to touch it again. You dig?"

"I dig."

"How's the back?" Jim was slicing potatoes on the cutting board. Leo told him it was better and he sipped his beer. He didn't know if he wanted to do any of this or not. In fact, he knew he didn't. What he wanted was to be with Allie Donovan, curled up somewhere alone with her. He did. But he could not think this and look at Jim at the same time; not while his father stood there slicing potatoes for

225

him, tapping his foot and moving his head in time to Howlin' Wolf singing how he's built for comfort, he ain't built for speed. Jim sometimes licked his lips when he concentrated on something he was doing with his hands, and when he did it now, Leo's heart spread out in his chest and he had to walk fast to his room.

He changed into clean jeans and a striped short-sleeved shirt, then he went to his bureau, reached into Katie Faye's box, and pulled out the black and white picture of his mother and father all dressed up, standing in that alley in New York City, his mother wearing dark lipstick, the two of them smiling into Ryder's camera. Leo pulled a thumbtack from one of the bottom corners of the Big Bill Broonzy poster and tacked the photograph to the wall at the head of his bed. He put on his work boots, combed his hair, then pulled a ten-dollar bill from his wad in the top drawer. The money in his hand felt like it belonged to someone else. And it did; he didn't know how much the vacuum doctor had cost the Donovans but it couldn't have been more than $600. Whatever it was, he wasn't going to let Allie have that satisfaction. Tomorrow he would walk up to Spoon Hill and hand the cash right to her mother, maybe even to Chick, who probably didn't know a thing about it.

"Don't show Larsmouth that kitty." Ryder stood in the doorway smiling. "I can hardly say 'lesson' with you anymore, Young Buddy, so how 'bout a short set 'fore we eat?"

While Jim wrapped presents in his bedroom, Ryder and Leo played alternating lead and backup to a Lightnin' Hopkins record with little or no harp in it. Leo was just beginning to learn which keys you could marry and which you couldn't. If Ryder picked up his C, Leo would grab his G, but not his D or B-flat; they just didn't go. On the third song Ryder backed way off on playing lead, so Leo took his cue and swept in with his best single-note wailing right behind Lightnin's crooning, careful not to wash out Hopkins while he did. He ended the number with two throat pops, a hand-smack, and one long tremolo wah-wah.

Ryder was shaking his head, smiling. He pulled the needle off the record. "Are you done out there, Jimmy? 'Cause I gotta give this boy his *present*."

"Go ahead." Jim stepped into the parlor carrying in front of him two newspaper-wrapped boxes. The one on the bottom was long and rectangular, the other short and square, and Jim set them on the coffee table.

"Here," Ryder said. "Open mine, it's prettier."

Leo took the dark blue box and sat on Jim's guitar stool. The room was suddenly quiet and he could hear the late-Friday-afternoon traffic up on Paper Boulevard. "You didn't have to get me anything, Ride."

"Just open the damn present."

Leo untied the silver ribbon, ripped off the paper, opened the box, and pulled out what he thought at first was a carpenter's apron. But then he saw the new-metal-shine of a harp in one of the sheaths. "Oh *man*." He lifted the harness free of the box and let it uncoil from buckle to buckle. It was dark brown and shiny and he could smell the dye fresh in the leather.

"It'll hold eight harpoons, Young Buddy. This gal I'm seeing, her brother hand-tooled it for me."

Leo wrapped it around his waist but the buckles overlapped each other a good six inches.

"No, lookit." Ryder draped the harness over Leo's left shoulder so the harp sheaths hung against his back. Then he reached under Leo's right arm, grabbed the other end of the harness, buckled the straps together in front of Leo's chest, and pulled down on them until the sheaths swung around to the front. "See kid, it's a bandolero."

"A blues bandit." Jim laughed. Leo did too. The new harp was in the top sheath right between his nipples. He pulled it out fast and sucked out a high fluttering train whistle. Ryder took Leo's harmonicas from the window sill and stuck them into the harness, one beneath the other.

"This is your all-American steer hide, Young Buddy."

Ryder was squinting a little as he pushed the last one into place. Leo hugged him so hard he felt one of the vertebrae in Ryder's back crack into place. "I *love* it."

"Squeeze any harder and you're a solo act."

Jim laughed and put the smaller package on the guitar stool. "Open this one first."

227

Leo patted the harmonicas at his chest, then he opened Jim's present and pulled out a Delta circular saw, a short paint-splattered power cord hanging from it.

"It's only a year old. Burrell bought it for his son, Billy. But I guess he never took to the carpentering like you."

The saw felt heavy and balanced in Leo's hand. It was just like the one Burrell used on the job near Spoon Hill. Leo said thank you, but didn't look into Jim's face.

"You can build me a porch," Ryder said.

"Sure thing." Leo placed the saw on the floor at his feet.

"Here," Jim said. "This one's brand new."

Leo pulled the newspaper wrapping off the rectangular box. On top of white tissue paper lay a Sonny Terry and Brownie McGhee album. "The *men,*" Ryder said. Next to it was a small beige envelope. The card showed a painting of a barn wall covered with hanging tools and some coiled rope. Inside was no store writing, just Jim's:

Work's the best cure, son. Happy Eighteen.

Yours,

Pop

Leo looked up at his father, and when Jim winked at him, Leo felt his throat thicken so he looked down and pulled the tissue out of the box to see a folded white dress shirt and a wide gray tie with red stripes. Beneath those was a dark navy blue suit jacket with gold buttons.

"It should fit, if your shirt does, anyway."

"Aw, *thank* you." Leo meant it this time; he didn't own a jacket that fit anymore, that he could wear a shirt and tie with. He pulled it out of the box and tried it on.

"He looks good, Jimmy."

"Sleeves are too short," Jim said.

They were, but not much, an inch tops. If Leo shrugged his shoulders a little bit, the sleeve hems touched his hands right where they were supposed to. Leo buttoned the jacket and turned from side to side. "Pretty slick, huh?"

Ryder smiled and glanced at Jim, then he picked up the new

album and slit the plastic covering open with his pocket knife. Leo held the tie to his neck and looked at his father. "I can wear this up to St. John's next time."

"I thought those gray pants of yours would go well."

"Yeah, they will."

"Mountain Blues" came out over the speakers. It was a Sonny Terry solo, and Leo thought how that blind man could play better than ten Ryder Stillwells and twenty Leo Suthers all at once. Jim picked up the boxes and papers and started out towards the kitchen. He stopped at the doorway. "You listen to those two, they've been touring together for years. I'll cook those steaks."

"Pop?"

"Yeah, son."

"Thanks a lot."

"Thank the union. Who wants a beer?"

They ate grilled steaks and fried potatoes at the kitchen table and when it came time for cake, Ryder opened three fresh Pabsts, though Leo wanted milk. Outside, a light rain fell through the trees and steam rose from the barbecue top next to Jim's Valiant. Jim cleared the table and set the cake down in the center. He pulled off the plastic dome, stuck in eighteen candles, then lit them with his lighter. "Now, wait right here."

Leo could hear the two men in the parlor, the echo of Jim's guitar box, and he pictured his father slipping the Mexican guitar strap over his head. He heard Ryder whisper pretty loud, "C?" and he thought of the two of them with Katie Faye in the parking lot of the Wrangler in Texas, giggling and hugging and promising each other how they'd never quit. He thought of how wonderful it was of his mother to write all that down, and then Jim walked in playing his rosewood guitar, singing "Happy Birthday," Ryder following behind with a sweet Harp of the Blues backup.

Only Lars and his cousin Cody showed up, but that was fine with Jim and Ryder, who had said many times before that a five-man game was ideal. It was past eight and getting dark. While Jim set up the round card table under the overhead kitchen light, Ryder broke out the red, white, and blue plastic poker chips and sold them at a nickel, dime, and quarter to the men and Leo. Leo bought five dollars' worth after he saw Ryder do that for himself. Lars took his usual chair close to the refrigerator door. His bald head shined and he was tanned from a week-long vacation he said he'd just taken with his wife and kids out there on Cape Cod.

"Spent all day in the sun drinking cold ones, you boneheads." He finished shuffling and passed the deck to his right for Ryder to cut. "When are you guys taking some damn time off? That friggin' mill work's taking its toll on us."

"I don't know how you fellas do it." Cody sat between Lars and Leo.

"My cousin here's an authority on indoor work. Teaches high school all day."

Jim sat on his tall guitar stool between his son and Ryder. "I used to build fences in Texas. Working through wind, rain, and that damn sun never thrilled me. I'll take a clean dry job any time."

Ryder pushed the deck back to Lars, who started dealing.

"The game's five stud, nickel ante."

"Red's nickel?" Cody looked up and scanned everyone's faces. Leo didn't think he looked much like his cousin. Cody had thick brown hair he kept short on the sides and puffy on top, and his brown eyes had a gentle light in them, smart too.

"Red, white, and blue," Ryder said. "Nickel, dime, quarter. Easy as that, buddy."

Jim leaned down and whispered in Leo's ear that this game is one card down, three up, and one down. Lars said, "No coaching," as he finished dealing everybody their first card down.

"It's his maiden voyage," Jim said.

Leo wished he hadn't put it that way.

"His birthday, too." Ryder winked at Leo and sipped the Pabst he was keeping between his legs.

"Well Happy B, Einstein. Sweet sixteen, yet?"

"Eighteen," Leo said, and he took a pull off his beer.

Lars dealt them each their first card up. "Jack bets."

"That's you, son."

Leo looked around the table. The second-highest card to his jack

---

230

of hearts was Lars's nine of spades. Leo dropped a blue quarter chip onto the red chips in the middle of the table.

"Ooo, look out," Lars said. "High roller."

"What?"

"You did fine, Young Buddy."

Jim leaned closer and told Leo you generally want to start out slow.

"Don't listen to him, Einstein. Hell, throw us all your money."

Everybody threw in a blue chip and Lars dealt the second up card. Leo got a nine of diamonds. He lifted his down card and took a look, a queen of clubs.

"Pair of fives bets."

Ryder dropped a red chip and a white chip onto the table. "Fifteen big ones."

"I see it and raise you a ten spot." Lars reached behind him, opened the fridge, and got a beer. Cody dropped a blue quarter chip on the ante pile. Leo glanced over at Ryder, then up at Jim.

"Ten and fifteen means twenty-five to you, high roller." Lars took a short pull off a Budweiser quart bottle. Leo dropped in a blue chip and watched his father do the same.

Lars dealt the last up card. Leo got an eight this time, an eight of spades, though Lars called Leo's eight, nine, and jack "nothing" as he dealt Jim a four, Ryder a king of clubs, and a ten to himself. "Oh boy, pair a tens. I'm new boss on the block."

"So long." Jim turned his cards over and pushed them to the side. Cody too.

Leo looked over at Ryder's king and pair of fives. Even if Ride had two more kings, Leo was pretty sure a straight beat a full house, though he wasn't positive. The thing is he needed a ten, what he'd heard them all call "drawing an inside straight," and Lars already had two tens right in front of him. Jim had had a four, an ace, and a seven. But damn, Leo hadn't even glanced at Cody's cards before he folded.

"Twenty to you, Einstein. Are you with us?"

"Be nice, it's my birthday."

Ryder laughed. Leo threw in two white chips and asked if he could raise. Jim said yes so Leo added a nickel to the pile. Ryder rubbed a blue chip between his thumb and forefinger. His eyes went from Leo's cards to Lars's nine and pair of tens. Ryder picked up a dime chip and dropped it in with the quarter.

"You dummies." Lars put in his thirty-five cents, and Leo dropped in another dime. Lars dealt the last card "down and dirty as doodoo."

Leo didn't want to look. He lifted the beer can from between his legs like Ryder and took two big swallows. His father whispered, "Let's see it."

Leo picked up the card and, without looking, handed it to Jim. Jim squinted at it in the light, then turned up the corner of Leo's queen card and peeked at that. His face didn't change at all. He handed Leo the card, a ten of diamonds. Leo held his breath and looked over at Lars looking at him.

"You get what you wanted?"

Ryder held his two down cards in his hands, studying them.

"Pair of tens still rules, Lars," Jim said.

Lars kept his eyes on Leo. Then he smiled and flipped his up card over. "Well tens quit."

"Uh oh," Cody said.

"It's up to you, Uncle Ryder," Jim said.

"Two bits to my Young Buddy." Ryder tossed a blue chip into the pile.

Leo added one of his own.

"You calling?"

"I don't know, am I?"

Lars laughed so loud he had to tilt his bald head back to get it all out.

"If you're not raising, you are," Jim said.

"I guess I am, then."

"I'm gonna smoke ya." Ryder spread out his two fives. He pushed the king next to them, then quickly turned over his down cards: two queens. "Two pair, lady high. Now show us that wonderful bluff of yours, Young Buddy."

Leo couldn't help smiling. He started to giggle as he laid out the cards one by one in perfect order, first the eight, then the nine, he turned over the ten card and put it in place, he slid the jack next to that, then he took a breath and made himself get serious for the unveiling of the queen.

232

"It's a six, I know it," Ryder said. "Show me that silly little six."

Leo flipped the queen card over so fast it fell back down on its face again.

"What was that?"

Lars was already laughing, Jim too. Leo turned the queen over and slid it up against the jack. He smiled up at Ryder.

"*Nobody* gets a queen high straight in the *first* hand of the *first* game of their *life!*" Ryder shook his head and smiled right at Leo. "That's it, now. No more presents from me."

Jim pushed the chip pile over to Leo and told him to keep it slow.

"Don't listen to your old man," Lars said. "Get as sloppy as you want."

While Cody collected the cards and shuffled the deck, Leo stacked his chips. He wanted to count them but there wasn't time with Cody already starting to deal and talking about what the game was, five-card draw.

Cody won with a full house he didn't really need because the next-highest hand was Lars's pair of nines. "Sorta feel like I went bird hunting with a cannon." Cody pulled in his chips, smiling that warm smile of his that reminded Leo of Chick Donovan.

"Who you calling a birdy, cuz?"

"A bald birdy," Ryder said.

"I have *never,* balled, a birdy." Lars said it with his face so composed, his voice so solemn, Leo thought at first he'd missed something. Then everyone laughed, including Jim, and Lars went right into a joke about a truck driver and a horny parrot and a rig full of chickens.

31

Allie Donovan switched off the headlights of her mother's car, turned down Saunders Hill Road, and parked well back from the Suthers' cabin. She sat there a moment. The trees were silhouetted in the light from the house and she could see the tops of three cars. Behind her belly button, a cramp turned over and let go. The cramps were better today, the tenderness in her breasts was gone, and by Sunday, the lady had said, there would probably be no more spotting in her underwear. Today was her first shift back at the UFO Show and she only felt a little queasy and that was from the fireflies in her stomach every time the door opened and she looked up hoping to see and hoping not to see Leo. And she thanked God she was out back helping Sidney make hamburger patties when Leo's father walked in and bought a cake from Beatrice. He glanced through the food tray hole once, but Allie turned her back in time, almost dropping her new patty to the floor.

Now she took the small wrapped box beside her and walked down the gravel drive in her white uniform dress. She heard laughing and so stepped into the woods, creeping over pine needles that stuck to the soles of her shoes. When she was just outside the spray of light from the kitchen she leaned one shoulder against a wet pine trunk and she saw Leo, framed there in the first window, sitting next to his father laughing terribly hard at something a large bald man was saying. They were all laughing, and it was terrible, for it was the last thing she could have imagined Leo doing just two days after that standoff behind Spoon Hill, when he had looked so hurt and she had felt so dirty, then angry for feeling dirty, then guilty for feeling angry when Leo was so hurt. Now she watched him laugh. He sipped from his beer can and was still smiling as his father dealt cards around the table.

Allie took a deep breath, but there wasn't enough air in the woods. She could hear the river moving over rocks down the hill. She put her hand to her face and smelled fryolator grease. She heard one of the men laugh again, and she wanted to step out of the trees and throw Leo's present right through the glass window. But the fireflies in her belly had moved into her arms and legs and face. She felt so suddenly weak, all her strength could be gone in minutes. But she would not cry; she'd cried enough. She dropped the wrapped package to the ground and walked back to the road. Her hair snagged once on a branch, and the hem of her UFO skirt caught at the backs of her legs.

* * *

It was early Saturday morning and Leo was walking down Paper Boulevard in his new suit. His striped tie felt tight at the throat, his dress shirt was a little baggy at the waist, and he could only hunch his shoulders for so long before his hands hung at their natural place a good inch out the sleeves of his navy blue jacket with the gold buttons. Earlier, after Jim drove off to work a weekend shift for Bill O'Donnell, Leo had shined his own black dress shoes. But they were a year too small and now they squeezed his feet like clamps.

There was a new James Bond movie playing at the Fremont. As Leo walked by the Hungry Pioneer Inn, a small boy and girl in the back seat of a passing car turned around and looked at him out their rear window. Both had blond hair and they smiled, but didn't wave. The sun shone through a thin veil of clouds and left the air hazy. He cut down the side road, passed the police station, and walked through the covered bridge. It was dark, and Leo heard the flap of wings above him. He watched a robin settle herself into a straw and mud nest perched in the center of a collar tie just beneath the ridge of the roof. He remembered kissing Allie here, and he knew he'd kiss her here again. Man, he'd kiss her all over town. Because what's done is done, he thought. As soon as I balance the books with Chick and her mother, as soon as Allie sees that eighteen-year-old man in the suit taking care of things, taking care of *her*, then she'll know she's not alone and that doing it alone gave her no satisfaction at all.

The sun had cleared Spoon Hill, and as Leo walked the long steep drive, he couldn't raise his head without being blinded, so he stared straight ahead at the gravel in front of him. His gray slacks were sticking to his thighs, and he could feel the cash wad straining against the inside of his front pocket. He was sweating beneath his new shirt but he wasn't going to take off his jacket and spoil the look. When he reached the top of the hill, he adjusted his tie knot and stepped into the shade of the cabin.

"There's my buddy." Chick's voice sounded farther away than it was; he sat in his wheelchair on the porch. He wore boxer shorts, and his left leg was in a full cast, his right arm too. His chest was

---

235

wrapped in white tape, his throat was a wide purple bruise, and he had two or three days of dark whiskers on his smiling face.

Leo was still breathing hard from the climb. He walked up onto the porch and shook Chick's left hand.

"Running for office, Leo?" Chick gestured towards Leo's outfit.

"No, I just, you know, I got these yesterday." Leo sat down on a wood stool beside him. "Allie home?"

Chick nodded. He didn't look like himself with those casts on him. He seemed smaller out of the hospital. Even the muscles in his good arm were small, the veins less pronounced.

"I'm a mess, aren't I?"

"No. I don't think so." Leo heard someone washing dishes inside. Chick took off his glasses and wiped his forehead with the back of his left arm. He kept them off and looked over the rail out at the river and Heywood below, the wooded hills of the national park beyond.

"It's funny. In the ring I could always take a good shot, but I wasn't one to take a good beating, comprendo?"

Leo nodded.

"A straight right to my chest here, a good hook to my head there— I could take them if they were spaced apart enough. So I was always jabbing my ass off to keep my man from setting himself for those kind of punches. You hungry? Thirsty?"

"I could use a Coke."

Chick called out for Tess. His voice sounded reedy and not as loud as it should have. Leo wondered if she'd heard him. The screen door opened. Allie wore cut-offs and one of Chick's white V-necked T-shirts. Her hair was tied back in a ponytail. Leo stood up.

"Look who's here, honey."

"Hi, Allie."

Allie looked at Leo's suit, then at her father. "What did you want, Dad?"

"A couple Cokes on ice? Thank you, sweetie."

She disappeared into the house. Leo sat down and swallowed. He felt like the biggest fool on earth sitting there in that suit.

"What was I saying?"

"Boxing."

236

"Yeah, the hits. They were never a big problem because I could duck and back off if I had to, but that wasn't my style; I was a headhunter. Anyway, I had a lot of knockouts. My last fight I got the crap kicked out of me though, and that's why it was my last fight, because I got hurt. This French kid—short and tubby too—somehow he could just hit me at will, all to the head. A straight right, another right, an uppercut, then two left hooks. I was out half an hour that time." Chick put his glasses back on. He looked at Leo, blinked twice, then smiled and looked away. Allie stepped outside carrying a glass full of ice in the cupped palm of one hand, two bottles of Coke by the necks in the other. Chick took his glass and bottle from her. Allie handed Leo his, though she kept her face pointed at Chick. "Let me know when you want to shave."

"Thanks for the Coke." Leo sat up as straight on the stool as he could. Chick glanced over at him, then smiled up at Allie as she walked to the door.

"Sweetie, I'm going to ask Leo to do it if that's okay. He's had some practice." Chick turned to him. "You mind shaving another man's face?"

Leo shook his head and he caught Allie looking at him just before she went inside. Her lips were parted as if she'd just stopped talking in mid-sentence and now wasn't interested in talking anymore. Her eyes were such a dark green they almost seemed brown. The screen door pulled shut on its spring after her and Leo sipped his Coke.

"Tess and I fight all the time, Leo. It can be good. Like pruning a tree." Chick poured his Coke over ice. Leo heard the bubbles and he watched a lone crow glide out over the hill towards the river. The sun glinted off the water down near the bridge and sandbag wall behind the police station.

"We're not fighting, really."

"Oh, fighting, I didn't finish my point. I lay in bed for two days after getting beaten up and you'd think I'd be feeling down and I was, but only in the body. You see, I knew the gloves were over and as soon as I saw that, a whole other feeling came: wide open freedom, Leo. Options." Chick drained the Coke from his glass in four swallows. The screen door popped open again and Mrs. Donovan came out carrying a folding TV dinner tray and a leather shaving kit. She wore a sleeveless white blouse and a dark blue skirt and no shoes. Leo stood and said hello.

"Hello."

"Country gentleman, isn't he?"

Chick's wife smiled a quick cool one, and she set up the tray and shaving things. She went back inside the house and no doubt about it, Leo thought, Chick doesn't know a thing.

"Anyway, I hate to be running off at the pump but you're a damn good listener, Leo. And don't forget what E. M. Forster said: 'How the hell do I know what I think until I say it?' or something close to that. So think of yourself as my verbal journal, comprendo? My soundboard."

"I don't mind. You remind me of Ryder sometimes."

"Stillwell?"

"You know him?"

"We've met."

"Yeah, you both have brains that don't leave you alone, I guess. Ryder's a harp man. He says he's a feeler but he thinks about things an awful lot. Chick, I gotta talk to you about something."

Mrs. Donovan stepped out with a red mixing bowl full of water. Her left bra strap was halfway down her shoulder. She set the bowl on the tray, then straightened up and fingered the strap back beneath the blouse. "Leo, would you mind coming inside a sec to reach a pan for me?"

"Oh, I'll get it." Chick leaned forward like he was going to stand up. Tess said very funny and Leo followed her inside. He smelled coffee. There was a hospital bed set up on the knit rug between the couch and the fireplace. On the picnic table in the kitchen were two egg-yolk-streaked plates, a half-eaten piece of toast on one of them. Allie's door was open, but he didn't see her in there.

Mrs. Donovan switched on the faucet in the sink, then left the water running and turned around to face him. She folded her arms beneath her small breasts. "I heard what you said out there. May I ask what you need to talk to him about?"

Leo slid his hands into his pants pockets, his right fingers stopping at the cash. "He doesn't know anything, does he?"

"Do you know how hurt that man is?"

Little Christopher laughed out in the backyard. Leo could see him through the rear window chasing after a bright red ball Allie had just kicked him. Her back was to the cabin. The sun made her hair shine, and her T-shirt hung down past her cut-offs. Her legs were tanned and skinny as ever. "Can you ask her to come in here a minute?"

"You have to get back to the porch."

Leo pulled out the cash. "I have six hundred dollars."

She looked down at the money as if it were a small animal Leo had just killed to give her. She glanced back towards the front of the house, then she looked back down at his hand, her face changed. "It cost half that."

Leo stepped forward and put all the money on the counter next to her. He looked right into her face, into her eyes that were nothing like Allie's, were deep and dark and unblinking. He turned and headed back out to the porch, the water still running.

"Get it down okay?" Chick said.

"Yep." Leo picked up his stool and set it in front of Chick's good leg, the one that was bent and allowed Leo room to get close enough. He took the bowl from the tray and held it so Chick could splash his face with his cupped left hand. Some water dripped on the gauze around his chest and turned it gray.

"What'd you want to tell me?"

"I shingled the roof of the job Thursday."

"You're pulling my cast."

"Nope." Leo squirted Old Spice foam into his palm and started to lather Chick's bruised throat.

"Have you done that before?"

"Not every morning. Four or five times a week, though."

"You're a funny one. I meant roofing."

Leo said that he and Burrell did one in Springfield last week. He smeared a streak of cream beneath Chick's nose, and remembered Floyd telling him how his ridge line was crooked. Leo rinsed his hands off in the bowl and picked up the razor. Chick tilted his head back to the side and Leo started just beneath the sideburn and pulled slowly down to his chin.

"So, I owe you some money."

"No." Leo dipped the razor in the bowl. He wondered if Mrs. Donovan had shown the money to Allie yet. He hoped she had.

"Well thank you. I won't feel so bad about leaving that house in the weather now."

Leo shaved the right cheek, rinsed the razor, then started working on the left. It felt funny being this close to a man. He didn't want to look into Chick's glasses; he felt Chick was watching him. He rinsed the razor.

"Boy, I haven't let myself think about that other stuff yet."

"What stuff?" Leo waited.

"How many Marxists do you know with medical insurance?"

"You're the only one I know."

"You're half right, I'm still a Marxist, but we don't have a dime's worth of insurance." Chick tilted his head back so Leo could finish up his throat. Leo brought the razor up in quick light strokes all the way to the tip of his chin.

"Good news for you, though; your girlfriend's family can't afford a trip to Beatrice's, never mind Vermont."

"What are you going to do?"

"Embarrassed to say."

Leo tapped the razor on the side of the bowl, then dipped it in water.

"Tess's family has some money. We'll have to borrow it and pay 'em back. Problem is, that community up in Vermont is all barter so we're anchored here till we're clear. Man, I don't want that hanging over us."

"You shouldn't be embarrassed. It's not your fault."

"That's where you're wrong, Leo." Chick cleared his throat. "'Sides, a real Marxist would never even pay the hospital."

"Oh." Leo raised the razor and shaved beneath Chick's lip down his chin. He could hear Christopher laughing out back, and he wished he was there kicking that red ball to him with Allie. Then he saw Tess in the living room. She walked up to the screened window behind Chick, put her hands on her hips, and made like she was looking out at the valley.

———

240

Allie watched him leave. She'd left Christopher with their mother, then climbed upstairs to her parents' room just as Leo started down the long drive, his arms swinging, his hands sticking so pathetically far out the sleeves of his suit jacket. He looked like such a boy, eighteen or not. Why wear a suit?

When Allie had gotten the Cokes in the kitchen, her mother had said she knew why he was here, and that young man had another think coming if he thought he was going to tell Chick any of his problems when her husband had far too many of his own. Allie had stood dead still for all this, to think Leo would come up here to tell her father and shame her even more. And as much as she'd been trying, she couldn't match what happened in Boston with the show she'd put on in the living room for her mother and Jim and Leo; true, she may have gone to the doctor for herself, but now she felt finished with something she only knew from having feared it. And as soon as that blond doctor in shorts opened the office window, she knew she'd made a mistake, that whatever her path was, this wasn't supposed to be where she paused long enough to get gassed. But then she *was* gassed and when she woke up, only the lady with glasses was still there. She took Allie's blood pressure, made her lie still in that room for an hour, then told her what her body would feel like for the next week and said she could go any time. But it was seeing the hurt in Leo's face down behind the hill that lifted Allie and dropped her all at once; lifted because she could see he'd been sincere about raising their baby, and dropped because now it was too late and she wasn't sure if she ever really knew whether she wanted it or not. But it was the memory of his fallen face, looking down at her as she cried, that sent her off to Springfield yesterday to buy him a birthday present, to hopefully gain his attention long enough for her to say she was sorry she'd done it all behind his back.

But it was him, Leo, doing all the lying.

In only a day and a half he would be drinking and laughing and playing cards with a gang of men from the mill. And today he marches up here in a suit to tell my father the horrible thing I did. In a *suit!* As if that kind of thing ever impressed my father. Leo says he's a musician, but he's wrong. Leo Suther is an actor, and he should get an award for that kicked-in-the-teeth look he gave me in the woods.

Allie watched now as he reached the bottom of the hill in the sunshine, turned his head back towards the cabin, then walked down the road for the covered bridge. She sat down on the windowsill and heard the screen door open downstairs, her father's voice, then her mother's grunt as she pulled the wheelchair up into the house.

After a while, things were quiet. Her father and little brother were asleep for mid-day naps, and her mother was walking barefoot up the stairs. Allie didn't like the sleeveless blouse she wore. Her upper arms had too many moles on them for that. Tess switched on the fan at the foot of the bed and lay down. Then, as if she'd forgotten something, she reached into her skirt pocket, pulled out what looked like a lot of money, and held it up for Allie to see. She sat up and turned off the fan. "Six hundred dollars. Leo insisted I take it."

"He *gave* that to you?"

Her mother nodded.

"Today?"

"Yes."

Allie stood. Both her fists were clenched and her fingernails pressed into her palms, which were still skinned from yesterday's run down behind the hill, away from Leo and his father and her mother, away from them all, but especially from Leo. Her body felt heavy and light at the same time. She shook her head more in wonder than surprise. "God, Mom, I hate him so much."

32

Leo hung his suit in the closet, then changed into his blue-jean cutoffs, a white T-shirt, and work boots. He borrowed the extension cord from the record player in the parlor, fed it through his open bedroom window, then grabbed his Delta saw and went outside to the back of the house.

The air was hot, and patches of sunlight lay on the ground in the stand of pitch pines near the cabin. The lower limbs of four or five of the trees had grown too close to the windows and the side of the house, and Jim had talked about trimming them last spring but never got around to it. A circular wasn't the right tool to use, Leo knew. A chainsaw or axe, even a machete would be better, but none of the branches was more than five or six inches think. He set the Delta down beneath his window and tied the two cords together at the plugs. The blade was new and the first branch dropped off almost as fast as he pulled the trigger. The whine of the machine was all he could hear. Sawdust and bits of bark sprayed out against Leo's bare arms and legs, and he wondered if Allie could hear this up on Spoon Hill. When he'd glanced back up at their cabin, the sun bit him in the eyes, and he saw green spots all the way to the bridge. Still, things were so clear; Allie never did show herself again after she brought out the Cokes, but that was okay because the nail was driven, the cash was where it belonged and now, late or not, he, Leo, had a say in all this. And that say combined with Allie's sad, crying face would equal her knowing she didn't have to be hurting by herself, that she could count on him after all. Now it was just a matter of staying busy until she found out about the money.

The blade began to smoke with burning sap. It smelled a little like the mill, and he thought of Jim saying he didn't want Leo going near the Donovans again.

Leo finished cutting all the limbs he could reach, then began to drag them one or two at a time down the road to the rim. The water had gone down some but was still high, covering the lower part of the road and the bottom three feet of the hardwood trunks at the bank. If he dropped the pine limbs in here they'd wash up against the trees, so he was going to have to wade out to where the road used to meet the river. After he had piled enough branches by the river bank, he sat down on the dry gravel, unlaced his boots, and pulled off his socks. The water was mud-colored and almost red out there where the sun shone. He wasn't wild about the idea of stepping into it after a flood, and he wasn't crazy about his father telling him who he could or could not see, either. He stood, gripped two branches, and stepped into the cool water. He dragged the limbs behind him and walked over fine grit and small stones that for all he knew could be turtle shells, or the skulls of squirrels. When he got to the open river the water reached halfway up his thighs. He swung the branches around, then pushed them out into the quiet current. Both sank a little as they flowed out and away from him, and he felt the sun on his face and shoulders. Even with his T-shirt on, the skin of his back felt raw in that light. He turned and waded back to the shadow of the road. He dried his feet with his socks, put on his boots without them and headed back up Saunders Hill.

It was the kind of half-assed dressing move Jim would shake his head at, but Ryder would smile and get a kick out of. "Boy Daddy," Ryder had called him. But Jim had said no, his boyhood's over for good, you know that don't you? And Leo did: no baby or not, I'm eighteen years old and if I want to see Allie again, I'll see her. He stepped back into the trees behind his house. He squatted for two more limbs, but then grabbed a third and a fourth, and jerked them all out onto the road.

The air had cooled and the sun was over the Berkshires when Jim, Ryder, and Leo pulled into Beatrice's parking lot in Jim's Valiant late Saturday afternoon. There were so many cars in front they had to park up alongside the white rail fence of Thompson Green. Out on the lawn between the trees, families sat on folding chairs or lay stretched out on blankets around the gazebo where there was a six-piece brass section of men in their Am Vets uniforms. The tuba player was very thin and wore a shiny metal helmet with an American flag decal stuck above the visor. None of the others even wore a hat, but they were all dressed in the same dark green uniforms with a single black stripe down the side of each leg, gold tassels on the shoulders, and a puffy white ascot at each of their throats. At the base of the gazebo, sitting on chairs facing the green, were the seven or eight women from the Ladies Auxiliary League. They wore blue slacks and white blouses. Pinned in their hair were small bullet-shaped blue and white caps, and draped from each of their right shoulders down to the left sides of their waists was a satin blue sash with big white letters: LAL. They had music stands in front of them, and all the women held wind instruments like the flute or clarinet or other long thin ones Leo didn't recognize. He did recognize Betty Poitras, though. She sat close to the middle of the second row holding a simple recorder to her lips, ready to go, the first L and the A of her sash swelling out nicely. In front of the women stood the conductor, who was talking to the crowd, though Leo couldn't hear what he was saying. He held his white baton in one hand and he was dressed in a robin-egg-blue tuxedo with tails, a long dark blue stripe up each leg, around each cuff, and around the border of the collar and both wide lapels. The shirt was all white ruffles at the chest, and his bow tie was black to match his shoes. It was the same kind of ugly suit GP had worn to the senior prom last May. The conductor smiled, turned his back to the audience, tapped his baton on his music stand, then raised both arms and swung them down in half-circles; the band began playing "Strike Up the Band," and Jim, Leo, and Ryder went and sat at a picnic table near the UFO Show's front door.

There were other tables too, most of them taken. Ryder picked a paper plate up off the ground and used it to wipe french fry crumbs off the table top.

"I'll go order for us," Leo said. "What do we want?"

"No," Jim said. "I'll go in."

"Burger, Coke, and onion rings for me." Ryder tapped three fingers in time with the band.

"Me too." Leo watched Jim go up to the door. He was still wearing his work clothes, and a V of sweat ran from his collar down to the middle of his back, where it disappeared into the rear bib of his overalls. "She doesn't even work on Saturdays, Ride. What's he gonna do, follow me around all the time?"

"I wouldn't think you'd give him cause, Young Buddy."

Leo watched a man on a motorcycle pull into the lot. His face was shaved clean and he had long hair past his shoulders. For a second, Leo thought it was Tony from the music shop in Springfield. "She's not a bad person, you know. She just got scared. You should've seen how sorry she was the night she told us. I never saw anybody cry so hard before."

The band finished the number with a long off-key tuba note. Leo turned just as the Ladies Auxiliary League started up a high flutey "When Johnny Comes Marching Home." Betty Poitras sat very straight in her chair, and she was giving the music sheet in front of her her full attention. Leo glanced over the crowd for Gerry's father and little sister Ruth, but everybody looked the same in their shorts and skirts, in their fold-out chairs and on their blankets. Officer Petrucci was standing against the fence near Paper Boulevard. His black hair was freshly cut, and he wore dark aviator sunglasses. He stood there with his feet apart, his hands crossed in front of him, and it looked like he was watching the conductor, though with those shades on, Leo thought, his eyes could be pointing anywhere.

Ryder tapped Leo's arm. "Was that a rhetorical question?"

"What?"

"About your old man keeping an eye on you."

"Yeah, I guess."

"Because there's nothing wrong with that; he's just lookin' out for your heart, Young Buddy."

"I'm eighteen, though."

"He'll do it when you're sixty." Ryder smiled. There were red day-old whiskers on his cheeks and chin, and Leo remembered the way Chick had smelled as Leo shaved him, like cast plaster and damp gauze and hair that needed washing. "I never knew you lived with us in Texas."

"Oh hell, yes. We were quite a threesome, really. Foursome, counting you."

"Hi there, Leo." Mr. Poitras stopped at the table. He was wearing baggy shorts and a striped shirt that made his gut look bigger than it was. Around his neck hung his big boxed camera. Leo stood and shook his hand. "Ryder, this is Mr. Poitras, GP's dad."

"Bob Poitras, good to meet you. Hey Leo, have you heard the latest from Ger?"

"Nope."

"They're calling him Stick now." Mr. Poitras smiled at Ryder. "Parris Island. The Marine Corps."

"Stick?"

"That's right, he's the big champ with the pugil stick. Knocks

———

246

down all comers. The wrestling team, all that exercise he did before-hand, boy, it's paying off. His drill instructor calls him Stick Poitras. Can you believe it?" Mr. Poitras laughed and shook his head. "Hey look, it's been a pleasure meeting you. Got to get that Ruthie a chocolate shake. Don't be a stranger, Leo."

Now the band was playing "Dixie," which Ryder let out a holler for, though Leo thought it was a strange number to do seeing the park was named after a bunch of boys who got killed by Confeder-ates down south. Jim brought the food and Cokes out in a cardboard tray and set it down. They ate slowly and listened to the band's med-ley which they all agreed would sound pretty okay if it weren't for the tuba player. Two girls from Leo's high school walked by the table. They leaned their heads together as they went, talking in low, excited voices. They both wore high shorts and Leo saw Ryder look long at their butts as they passed.

"I'm worried about O'Donnell, Jimmy." Ryder wiped his face and pushed his paper plate away.

"What's wrong with him?" Leo said.

"He tried to join up yesterday in Springfield," Jim said.

"They wouldn't take him, Young Buddy, so he went down to the club and drank till he dropped." Ryder dipped two fries in ketchup. "I s'pose you'll have to put your name in now."

"I'll go do it this week."

"Well, you got some luck of the draw in cards, so you're probably already ahead of the game."

Leo looked at Jim. "That's why you worked for O'Donnell today?"

Jim nodded and lit up a Lucky Strike. "Hey. Let's go to the early show of *Thunderhead.*"

"*Thunderball.*"

"I'm free." Ryder stood and stretched and winked at Leo. "We can play after, if you like."

"Yeah, I want to break in my bandolero."

"He sure broke in that saw today." Jim smiled at Ryder, gathered the empty paper plates, and pushed them into the steel UFO trash barrel near the door.

It was a good 007 movie, but with the concert still going on outside, the quiet scenes were hard to hear. Leo didn't mind too much because these were also the times James Bond French-kissed women while he unzipped or unsnapped or untied or cut off their clothes, and Leo's erection was constant, which felt as wrong as could be, sitting between his father and Ryder. All Leo could think about was Allie, about making up then making love. And wearing a rubber this time, which he would go out and buy first thing Monday.

When the movie let out the sun was gone and what little light was left in the sky was a pale cherry. The lights of the marquee were lit up, Beatrice's too. Leo and the men walked back for the car. On Thompson Green, the gazebo was empty. Leo saw two families still lounging on their blankets, though there was nothing to see anymore but a couple of men from the Am Vets band folding up chairs and stacking them into a blue pickup truck. The window booths inside the diner were full of people. The back kitchen door was propped open with a mop handle, and Leo could hear somebody scraping a pot with a spoon or a wire brush. The jukebox was playing. The air was warm and smelled like popcorn from the theater, fries from Beatrice's, but Leo felt fall coming, saw himself sitting in classrooms like Mr. Jewett's, GP off to world adventure, him and Allie back to loving each other; and as he sat in the back seat of his father's car while Ryder and Jim got in front, he closed his eyes a second and wished hard for everything just to hurry up and come.

33

It did. The envelope was propped on the handle of the screen door. It was the long kind bills came in. The outside light wasn't on so Jim had to walk inside and turn on the overhead kitchen light to read who it was for. Leo stood right there beside him. He saw his full name written in black ink in the middle of the envelope. Up in the left hand corner, crossed out with the same pen, was:

———

Donovan's Renovators
Spoon Hill
Heywood, Massachusetts

Jim handed it to his son. "I don't want anymore of this, you hear?"

Leo took the letter and almost ran down the hall to his room. Ryder called after him from the parlor to strap on his harps, but Leo closed his door, switched on the bedside lamp, sat on the mattress, and ripped open the envelope. He pulled out what looked like the last page of Chick's manifesto pamphlet. He turned it over and took his first full breath since the kitchen:

August 21, 1967

Leo,

Just who you think you are is beyond me. I never should have told you a thing. In fact, I never should have slept with you, period. You are a mere boy, Leo Suther. But don't think that excuses you for acting like the deceitful pig you are. I was right the whole time—you never wanted to keep the baby, you just didn't have the manhood to say it to my face. You'll tell my parents anything they want to hear. And if my mother didn't need that money so bad, I would burn it and send you the ashes. You're worse than other boys, Leo. At least the others don't pretend they're angels when all they really want to do is screw.

I NEVER WANT TO SEE YOU AGAIN. (Even if my family has to stay in this smelly town, don't even try to approach me at school. You'll regret it. *Believe me.*)

Sincerely *Not* Yours,
Allison Marie Donovan

The letter was shaking. Leo lay down on his bed and read it two more times, then he turned it over and stared at Chick's political words as if the real letter Allie wrote might be in there somewhere. He read the letter again, then he lay there awhile. He could hear Jim and Ryder tuning up together out in the parlor. His back still burned a little but he didn't move. He looked up at the ceiling. Jesus, how could she have misunderstood him so much?

"I see a harness on a bureau and my harp man on a bed." Ryder stood in the doorway. He glanced at the letter Leo held to his chest. "Bad news?"

Leo nodded. He wanted to say more, but he knew if he did he'd cry, so he shook his head and blinked. Ryder looked down and said to come on in when you're ready, then he left.

Ready. We never are, are we? Not really, Leo thought. Not for what happens to us. Or the ones we love. Or the ones who we think love us.

Jim began singing over his guitar picking out in the parlor. It wasn't a blues song, it sounded more country, something Ryder always had a hard time playing to and was quiet for now. Then Leo heard the chorus, his father's voice singing it high and fast and almost cheerful,

"Kate made me late
But I love her anyway—"

And Leo remembered his mother writing how much he had liked that song as a little boy, how one night she hugged him close on the couch as Jim played it for them and Leo had laughed against her. He reached over and turned out his lamp, and he listened to the music the two men made. If there had been a thousand men, women, and children camped out in the trees around Saunders Hill, Leo couldn't imagine feeling any more alone or by himself than he did right now. The air in his room smelled like pine pitch. The woods were quiet. The night did not have a moon.

Going to church was Leo's idea, but when he walked through Jim's bedroom doorway and suggested it, he found his father lying there wide awake, looking out the window at the morning sun on the trees, his hands resting on his chest. He nodded once at what his son said, his lips pursing slightly beneath his black mustache. Now Leo waited at the kitchen table. He wore the same pants, shirt, and jacket as yesterday, but a different tie this time, the maroon one with the stenciled half-moons. The water in the stove pan came to a boil and he got up and poured it a little at a time over the coffee grounds in the pot. He could hear his father tapping his razor against the side of the sink in the bathroom. Outside, the sun shone bright off the car windshield, though it was only 9:30 and half an hour till the start of the St. John's mass.

Last night it came to Leo there was no way he could stay in the same town as Allie Donovan, no way he could go back to the high school this fall to watch her move around so sweetly in her bell-bottoms and white T-shirts, giving so many boys a friendly time of day. And he knew where he was going, too: Springfield. To live and work. He was going to find himself a cheap one-room place some-where, he would get a job with a building crew, and nights he'd go to regular practice sessions with Anthony and the Holy Roaders. Now he was good enough to do it, to take Tony up on his offer.

Leo poured himself coffee. He added milk and three spoons of sugar and drank the hot sweet liquid that he'd grown to like this summer. There was a word for what he was feeling right now. He couldn't think of its name, but he did know how it felt: that last night, and today, and tomorrow—these were not just normal days, but days somehow full of diamond-clear water, the kind that had a current that you, and only you, were supposed to be stepping in, then floating out on, and if you missed it, or didn't even let yourself get wet, then you were finished for good; no more chances, no rivers in the desert. Tonight he was going to pack his clothes and tools and harp harness and that was that.

Jim walked to the fridge, took an ice tray from the freezer, and broke five cubes into a glass. He poured coffee over them, added milk and sugar, then sipped quietly. He wore black pants and shoes, a freshly ironed white short-sleeved shirt, and a black string tie from Texas. He leaned against the counter next to Leo, and they both looked out the window at the sun in the woods and on the car, drinking their coffees, and it came to Leo that before he went anywhere, he was going to have to go up to the Donovans' and get the other half of his six hundred back.

"Know that place where I got your Mexican guitar strap?"

"Sure do." Jim shook a Lucky Strike out of its pack and lit up.

"The owner has a band and he wants me to join up. They need a harp."

"Springfield?"

"Yeah, but they tour on gigs all the time. I'll probably even get paid."

Jim took a long drag of his cigarette, and blew smoke out his nose. "You got a year of school left."

Leo shrugged. "I think I'll learn more with a band, don't you?"

"What do they call themselves?"

Leo told him.

"Gospel?"

"R&B."

Jim glanced at the wall clock, then turned on the faucet and put out his cigarette. "Well, let's get going."

It was a twenty-minute ride to Holyoke. As Jim drove quiet along the sunlit river, both their windows open, Leo knew he was thinking it over, and he also knew because Jim had paused to ask what the band played, because he had not come right out with his usual no, that even if he did end up saying no, that wouldn't really step in Leo's way, at least not enough to make a difference. But Leo didn't feel he was winning anything extra; all he felt was free to do what had to be done, and the only true good that could come from it would be a quick rise to fame with Anthony and the Holy Roaders, Leo's name in the paper under a picture of him wearing a full harp harness, his arms around Tony and the rest, then Allie showing up at one of their gigs, alone and beautiful, coming backstage to apologize to the man who, it was so clear now, had never been fooling around in any area of his life.

Jim drove up the steep hill to the churchyard and parked the car in the shade of an oak tree. The wood clapboards of the St. John's Church were painted white, and the steeple rose above the trees to a black-shingled point that gave way to an eight-foot-high white wooden cross. Leo and Jim joined the other families going inside. Jim crossed himself with holy water. Leo did the same and followed his father a few feet to sit in the last pew on the right. He smelled perfume and wood. Most of the congregation was sitting in the middle of the church. Along each long wall were six tall stained-glass windows. More light came through the ones to Leo's left, on the cemetery side of the hill. He thought how someday he was going to bring a dozen roses to lay on Katie Faye's grave. How could she really care when it was Jim who she had made promise never to do that?

The priest, a small man with gray hair and thick glasses, walked onto the altar with two boys in white robes. Leo and Jim stood with everyone else, and as the mass got underway, they knelt when the others did, sat when they did, stood, even crossed themselves. Then it was time for the sermon, and the priest climbed up to the wooden lectern, switched on the microphone, and started to speak about there being no peace in the world and why not?

Leo looked around for Tom Burrell, or maybe his son Billy, but then remembered Tom was Lutheran or something, not Catholic. Leo liked sitting here in church with Jim. He liked how tall the ceiling was, how long and wide the floor. A man could think here, and Leo found himself thinking of Chick Donovan, thinking of how much he liked him—even though Chick never listened to what anybody said unless it had to do with him or what he thought. And Leo knew why, too: Chick wasn't trying to figure out the world anymore. That man Mr. Marx had done it for him. Now all Chick had to do was find a way to live out what the man had said. The funny thing is, Tom Burrell, in his own big gentle way, was sort of like that himself; if it didn't fit in with the Bible, it didn't fit, period. Christians and communists. Leo would write a song on them, a blues riff of some kind. He'd polish it up and play it for Tony as an audition. 'Course, he could always do "The Love Abode," though he didn't want to. He didn't really want to see or hear or play that song again.

Jim tapped Leo's knee and motioned with his head for them to go. The priest was still talking, reading from the Bible about the peacemakers being called the sons of God. Jim and Leo rose quietly, and on the way out they crossed themselves again with the holy water. From the steps Leo could see whole miles of the river valley. The water looked more blue today, less muddy. On the other side were wooded hills of juniper and spruce, and down near the bend to Heywood was a mile-long bank of poplar trees, their leaves silver in the sun. Leo followed Jim up the narrow flat-stone path to the cemetery. It was at the highest point of the hill, well behind the church. On the western ridge was a long row of huge white oak trees, two or three deep. The path moved along the hill in front of the tombstones, but Leo stepped off it and walked over grass-covered mounds between polished squares of granite to the far southwestern corner. He got there first and folded his hands in front of him. Her stone was short and made of rough-cut brown granite. Carved deep into its left half was Jim's full name, his birthday, and a dash. To the right of that was carved:

KATHERINE FAYE SUTHER
OCTOBER 9, 1929—APRIL 10, 1955

Leo heard his father walk up beside him, and he tightened the tie knot at his neck. The sun actually felt good on his back, on his new blue jacket. Jim stepped close and squatted next to the slight mound in front of the stone.

"She always said she'd never be here, but I feel her every time."

Leo heard the distant hum of a plane engine above them and he thought of what Katie Faye had written of that hot summer afternoon when the three of them drove to his grandmother's and great-grandmother's house in San Antonio to say good-bye, Katie Faye whispering to her mom about how Jim's mother will be gone soon and they'll be back in no time, how her own mother held herself like it was cold instead of ninety-seven degrees under a tree. "Thank you for letting me read her notebooks."

Jim took a white handkerchief from his back pocket and held it. The congregation was singing in the church now. Leo heard more women's voices than men's, and no organ or piano, just voices.

"I wasn't very good to her in the end. I never told you that, but I wasn't." Jim wiped both eyes quickly and stood up. "She just gave in so fast I couldn't watch it. I tried to push her into fighting it, but—Lord."

"What?"

"That pain was *enough.*" Jim blew his nose and stuck his handkerchief back in his pocket. "Some things we learn late, that's all."

Leo put his hand on his father's shoulder. "Guitar Jimmy." Leo smiled, and Jim rested his hand on Leo's.

"You can join the band if you want to. You should go farther than me. Heck, maybe I should've made records." He patted Leo's hand once, then turned and let it pull free as he started walking back down the path, the wide open valley dropping away in front of him. He stopped and smiled up at his son, his eyes looking dark and deep. "Let's go find some pancakes and eggs."

34

Tess Donovan sat in the first booth near the door in front of Beatrice's cash register. It was almost 9:00 on a Sunday evening and she felt thankful there weren't too many customers either at the counter, or in the other booths. The jukebox was quiet and she heard the faint static of a radio baseball game from the kitchen in the back. She ordered coffee from a young waitress Allie's age. The girl had blue eyes and black hair to her shoulders. She was slightly plump, and Tess told herself once more it was time she stared taking on people in her work. Perhaps she could begin with some figure drawings of her husband, who wasn't going anywhere for a while anyway, who at this moment thought she had driven to town to see if Beatrice or Sidney would sell her an emergency quart of milk for tomorrow morning.

She'd waited over an hour after Leo's phone call before pouring the last of the milk down the sink, grabbing her car keys and walking onto the knit rug where Allie sat next to Chick's bed reading aloud to him from *The Naked and the Dead.* Her daughter looked so lovely in the lamplight, her hair held back behind her ears, her long legs crossed at the knees, the book resting there. And it was a relief seeing her out of her room, where these last few days she'd barricaded herself, crying into her pillow, her mother knew. Allie kept reading but Chick smiled up at Tess and gently rubbed the back of her leg with his arm cast. She bent over and whispered about Christopher with no milk in the morning, maybe Beatrice has some, be right back.

Now Tess tasted her coffee and watched the boy through the window as he stepped into the light of the diner's neon sign and walked over the dirt lot for the stairs. His hair looked freshly combed, and he wore a short-sleeved button-down shirt tucked into blue jeans. On his feet were work boots. He could be Chick's son, or little brother, she thought. He glanced up at her as he approached the door, and she looked away as if he were a stranger she hadn't meant to engage.

Leo asked the girl behind the counter to please bring him a Coke, then he sat down across from Tess, who didn't want this to last any longer than necessary but would wait for the girl to bring Leo's drink before she took the money from her purse.

"So. Where is it you're moving to?"

"Springfield."

"Alone?"

"Yeah, I'm joining a band. They play all over the country."

The waitress set an iced glass of Coca-Cola and a straw down in front of Leo. She held a steaming pot of coffee and asked if Tess wanted a refill. Tess smiled and shook her head, resting her hand lightly over her cup. She saw Leo looking down at her fingers, at the engagement and wedding ring there. The girl walked back behind the counter, and Leo took a swallow of his soda and looked out the window. Tess had come to view this polite boy as a stray dog Allie should never have fed herself to, but now, for this moment anyway, she saw that he had no idea if what he was doing was right or not, that he hadn't yet lived long enough to know he was in the middle of something he would surely emerge from. She reached across the table and touched his hand with her fingers. "You're a good boy, Leo. We all know that."

The boy looked at her, and took a breath. "Why does she *hate* me?" His eyes were wet.

She patted his hand. "We can never hate someone we don't love first."

"She still loves me?"

Tess started to nod her head, then stopped herself. She tried to smile at him but he glanced away so quickly at the effort of it that she pulled her hand back and sipped her coffee. The boy stared down at his hands resting sideways on the table. They were big hands, Tess thought, though a little pink, with just a few calluses on the palms. "You'll have a family someday, Leo. And you'll be glad it turned out the way it did."

The boy shook his head. His lips were tight now, his eyes still wet. Tess took her wallet from her purse, pulled out the fifteen $20 bills, and laid them on the table in front of him. Then she took out another dollar and slid it beneath her cup and saucer. "The soda's on me." She pulled her purse strap up over her shoulder and scooted to the edge of the seat cushion.

The boy nodded, though he was looking straight ahead at where she'd just sat, his eyes dry and flat now. Outside, she realized she'd forgotten to buy milk, but when she turned to go back she saw the boy still in the booth staring in front of him as if there were more there than a blue vinyl seat back; as if he were seeing with absolute resignation something no one else could, something that had happened, or was happening, or was about to—and not simply to him alone—but to all of them.

Tess walked to her car, started it, then drove slowly out of the lot across well-lit Paper Boulevard and into the darkness of the covered bridge.

When Leo woke, rain was falling on the roof of the house and he smelled coffee and frying bacon. His room was still dark, but out his window the trees were framed in pale blue, and water ran down the top panes onto the screen where it spread out and stopped. Beneath the sheet, his erection pushed against his underwear. He reached down, lifted the elastic band, and let his penis roll straight, nudging his skin. He left his hand where it was and he immediately thought of Allie standing out behind her house Saturday afternoon, her long skinny legs looking so tanned and warm. Then he thought of her mother last night in the booth at Beatrice's, her hand on his while a sadness opened up in him that he hadn't seen coming. And he didn't know if he wanted Chick's wife to tell Allie about that, or not.

He could hear Jim walking down the hallway. He let go of himself and turned on the lamp as his father walked in holding a mug of coffee.

"Two eggs or three?"

"Two." Leo sat up and took the hot mug in both hands.

"You should bring your harpoons along just in case. He might want you to audition."

Leo nodded and drank. He tasted more coffee than milk and sugar. "Will I need a birth certificate to register?"

Jim said yes, probably will, he'll go get it. He stopped in the doorway and glanced at his watch. "Let's be on the road by twenty to seven."

Paper Boulevard ended two miles upriver where it forked. The left fork led away from the Connecticut towards Route 116 and the town line. Jim drove the Valiant down the right fork towards the water and open green iron gates of Heywood Paper Products, Inc. Two summers in a row Leo had worked in the mill yard cleaning the inside cabs of trucks, checking tire pressure, greasing the axles, sometimes even painting the bodies. He looked the trucks over now as his father pulled up to the entrance of the main building, where men dressed in coveralls and Dickie pants, some in cut-off shorts and steel-toed boots, walked through light rain to the open doorway big enough for eighteen-wheel trucks to drive through. Alongside the building were stacks of bundled papers and cardboard twelve to twenty feet tall. Fifty yards upriver were the three pulp pool tanks, swirling with white foam, and the air was heavy with that sour turned-inside-out smell that those summers Leo's nose and lungs had never been able to get used to.

Jim stopped the car and put the gearshift in neutral. "She's all yours. Ryder will give me a lift to the club. Don't forget, numbers night; there's leftover haddock and corn in the fridge."

Through the slow slap of the windshield wipers, Leo watched Ryder laughing with Lars and another man just inside the doorway.

Ryder had his hands in his pockets. He stuck out a leg and scuffed Lars's shin with his boot. Jim opened his door and started to get out.

"I'll probably have to move to Springfield, you know." Leo kept looking at Ryder and the men as he said it. Lars, still laughing, took off his plant cap and slapped Ryder on the shoulder.

"You in a hurry for the working life? You see how it goes today, first." Jim took his lunch bag, got out, and shut the door. He leaned towards the window as Leo scooted over behind the wheel.

"Don't forget Euterpe, son. Good luck."

The glass doors of the Springfield municipal building were locked and streaked with rain. Leo cupped his hands and peered inside. On the inside door was a black and gold sign listing the work hours as 9:00–5:00, Monday through Friday, and the wall clock in the lobby told him he had almost an hour to wait. The rain had eased up, but the sky was still spitting drizzle and he wished he'd left his harmonica harness in the car in front of Tony's Musical Suite that didn't open till 9:30. He waited for an approaching red Galaxy to drive by, then he held the harness with both hands and ran across the street to the coffee shop where he and Burrell had eaten lunch last week.

The same black-haired man was behind the counter, cooking breakfast this time. On the heated griddle in front of him were two pairs of frying eggs, one steaming pile of scrambled, a mound of home fries, and off to the side in a pool of bubbling grease were a dozen strips of bacon. Four men sat at the round table in front of the window. One wore white painter coveralls and Leo's heart skidded to a brief stop in his chest, but it wasn't Dewey or Olin. This man was older, and the three with him wore ties and short-sleeved button-down shirts. Leo asked the cook for a bottle of Coke, then he sat at the short counter against the wall, laid his harness on the stool next to him and sipped his soda, watching the cars go by wet on Main Street.

The men were talking about Tony C, about that fastball Hamilton had pitched into his head last Wednesday. One guy was saying Conigliaro's all through. The other three couldn't disagree more; he would be back better than ever. Leo unbuttoned his shirt just above his belt and pulled out his birth certificate. It was dry and unwrinkled. There wasn't much to one of these, really:

Leo James Suther . . . male . . . August 20, 1949 . . . 3:51 P.M. . . . Pedernales Military Hospital . . . San Antonio, Texas . . . Katherine Faye Suther . . . White . . . Age 20 . . . Birthplace Texas . . . James Francis Suther . . . White . . . Age 23 . . . Birthplace Massachusetts . . . 1st Sgt. . . . U.S. Army . . .

Leo buttoned it back into his shirt. On the opposite wall was a black and white poster of some Greek ruins overlooking the sea. Next to that hung a hardware store calendar with a big color photograph of a blue lake surrounded by fir trees. A man stood on a rock smiling and fishing, and at his side sat a red Irish setter. Leo thought of Lake Calaveras in Texas, of the boulder his mother and father kissed and hugged and fell in love on. Someday, when the Holy Roaders would be working the Southwest circuit, he'd talk Tony into taking the band bus on a detour to San Antonio and he would find that lake. He thought that even though Jim and Katie Faye didn't make love there, it was almost as if he was conceived on that rock. And you would think places where life was planted would stick out somehow so you'd recognize them later; they should glow a little bit or something. Leo smiled at his own dumb thinking. Nobody would be able to sleep at night with all those lit-up places in the world: a flat rock on some lake or stream, the front and back seats of rusted-out cars in junkyards, new cars in driveways, millions of bedrooms around the world, couches in living rooms, cots on porches, thousands of low spots in woods and forests, they would glow too; old canvas hammocks hung between palm trees on beaches, huts in Mexico, igloos up north, caves in mountain ravines, maybe even flattened places in the snow where a man and woman—or a boy and girl—lay down in a sleeping bag to make love, to spurt life trembling one into the other. And his bedroom back on Saunders Hill would glow for sure; he pictured some kind of soft amber light, like the sun shining through a bottle of root beer, or the colors a campfire gives off just before somebody lets it go out.

Leo got off his stool and asked the cook behind the counter if he could borrow a pencil and something to write on. The man was busy dishing out eggs, potatoes, and bacon on four plates in front of him, but he gave Leo a white paper plate and the pencil from behind his ear. Leo sat back down and started to write.

We made a light,
My baby and me,
We loved each other right,
My baby and me,
But some things she said at night,
Man, she didn't mean in the day,
Now I'm playing the blues
Every damn way.

She's a light taker,
She's a night-faker,
Lord, I ain't lying
About my baby
And me.

Leo wanted pull out his C harp and give it a whirl with a standard blues intro, but not here. Outside on the sidewalk a woman and a girl about twelve years old walked under the same umbrella. The girl had a dark strand of wet hair stuck to her cheek. She was pudgy but sweet-faced, just like Gerry's little sister. Leo folded up the paper plate and finished his Coke.

It was 9:05, but in the lobby of the municipal building there was already half a dozen people lined up at the Filing and Information desk. The ceiling was high as a church's, and both sides of the room were lined by the open frosted-glass doors of offices ready for business. On the right were the recruiters' rooms. Stenciled in black on a wooden sign jutting out above the first door was: "UNITED STATES ARMY/UNITED STATES AIR FORCE." In the next room were the marines and navy. And in a third office farther down were the Coast Guard and National Guard. Leo walked over the shiny tile floor to the office of the army. He rolled up his harp harness and buckled it together as tight as he could. He stood at the office doorway a second before knocking. Two big metal desks were pushed up facing each other, and a man in a green uniform with three yellow stripes on each upper arm sat at the one farthest from the door, his head bent down, writing something very deliberately with a ballpoint pen. He was chewing gum, and he wore a flattop hair cut like Tom Burrell. On the wall behind him was a color poster of a crew-cut guy in an ROTC sweater sitting on stone steps with a notebook in his hand, laughing with three blonde girls, who sat around him all dressed up in skirts, blouses, and cardigan sweaters. Their teeth were white and perfect. Sprinkled around their feet were fallen autumn leaves and beneath those was written: "Leadership has its rewards . . ." On the walls to the sides of the other desk were two posters of fighter jets flying in the kind of arrowhead formation Leo had seen in Canadian geese.

"Hey, come on in." The man stood and walked over and shook Leo's hand like he had been waiting for just him. He pulled a chair from against the wall, set it next to his desk, and sat back down. He was chewing gum pretty fast and his cheeks were shaved so close they were shining in the fluorescent light.

Leo sat down and rested his harp harness in his lap. The soldier, a sergeant Leo figured, was still smiling as he chewed, leaning back in his chair like they'd already been talking a long while.

"Is this where I register for my card?"

"What are those? Harmonicas?"

Leo said yes.

"You a musician?"

Leo nodded. A smile showed up on his lips that left him feeling apologetic, so he cleared his throat and glanced over at the jets on the wall. A Negro man walked in carrying two Styrofoam cups of coffee, a clear-wrapped packet of chocolate cupcakes hanging from his teeth. He wore a uniform with a lot of the same ribbons and buttons and stripes as the sergeant's, but his was beige instead of dark green. He set the coffee down on the empty desk and unwrapped the cupcakes.

"What's your name, partner?" the sergeant asked.

"Leo."

"Leo, I'm Bill. This is Earl, our air rep."

The Negro officer said hello to Leo, then handed the sergeant his coffee.

"Hey Earl, Leo's a musician. Show him your setup, Leo. Look at that, it holds all his harmonicas."

"One's not enough?"

"No," Leo turned in his chair. "They're all in different keys."

"Boy, *I* knew that." The sergeant held out his hand. "Can I see one?"

Leo pulled out his C harp and handed it over. The sergeant studied first one side, then the other. "Marine Band. I never heard a jarhead play one of these, have you Earl?"

Earl's mouth was full of cupcake. He shook his head, then raised his coffee cup to them both and left the room. The sergeant smiled and gave Leo back his harp. "We share the same office, but our appointments are private, you know?" He took a sugar packet from a drawer, then stirred his coffee with a metal letter-opener. Rain fell softly against the wire-meshed window behind him. "So why do you want to fill out a draft card, Leo?"

"I turned eighteen last Friday."

"What I mean is, why humiliate yourself? Why put your name in with the *no*-shows like that? Be a player, Leo. Why not show some leadership and enlist?"

Leo hadn't expected this. In fact, he hadn't thought about this meeting much at all. He shook his head and glanced down at his harp harness, but he didn't like this picture of himself so he sat up straight and looked at the sergeant's face, at two black hairs above the bridge of his nose. "I can't, I'm joining a band today."

"We can put you through the best damn music schools in the U.S. Have you thought about that?"

Leo shook his head. "They don't teach blues music, that's just something you have to teach yourself. Nobody ever studied it like that."

"Have you seen much of this world, Leo? You ever been to Japan or Germany? England? You can take those Marine Bands wherever you go, right?"

Leo looked down at his harness.

"Do you sing, too?"

"A little bit."

"Well heck, think of all the things you'll be able to sing about. Now me, I'm a big Elvis fan. Do you know he says his voice got *better* in the army? Best damn thing he ever did."

"How did it get better?"

The sergeant narrowed his eyes. His lips tightened in a straight line. "The life, buddy. Being back with the common man for the common good. I mean it, that old saying is true: you just can't build a strong house on a flabby foundation. Now, by rights, it's up to you to decide what kind of house you want; you're a musician, that's A-OK. That'll be your house."

Leo glanced over the neat stacks of papers on the sergeant's desk.

The sergeant cleared his throat. "You look in good condition. Are you?"

"I've been working construction."

"Excellent. Play any sports?"

"I used to wrestle."

"Even better."

Leo thought of Gerry's dad bragging about GP in the marines. Leo undid two shirt buttons and pulled out his birth certificate. "No offense, sir, but I just want to register like I'm supposed to, that's all." He dropped the certificate on the soldier's desk. The sergeant read it from where he sat, then he leaned back in his chair and rested his elbows on its arms. He touched his fingertips together. "Your father served in Korea, didn't he?"

Leo said yes, he did.

"Well listen up. I'll let you in on a little secret." He sat forward again. "Our enlistees get automatic PA status. Do you know what that means, Leo?"

"No, I don't."

"Preferred Assignment. In other words, you get a choice of where

264

you want to go. Nobody wants to jump into a combat zone, buddy. If you join of your own free will, well then you can ask to go right to Germany for your whole tour. How's that grab you? Fräuleins, beerfests, skiing. You ski?"

"No, sir." Leo stood up. "Look, sorry, but I'll be late for another appointment. I'll have to come back later." He picked up his birth certificate from the desk, turned, and walked out of the office. He heard the sergeant say, "Roger that," but by then Leo was back out in the lobby, and was heading for the main doors, when he saw across the floor a small corner office with a Selective Service Board sign screwed in the wall next to its open door. Inside a man in glasses sat at a desk. Leo walked right in and introduced himself. The man handed him a form sheet and a pen, and after Leo answered all the questions about his address and school and parents' names, he gave it back along with his birth certificate. The man looked at both, initialed next to where Leo had filled out his date of birth, handed back the certificate and said, "You'll receive your card in the mail, thank you."

On the way out, Leo saw the two recruiters standing near their office doorway talking and drinking coffee. The sergeant watched Leo go, his eyebrows arched as if Leo had just said something the officer didn't quite catch.

Leo stood under the awning of Delores the Florist and watched Tony park his van across the street. It was painted a whole jungle of bright colors and in the middle of it all, in big blue letters from the back bumper to the front, was: "Anthony and the Holy Roaders!" Tony waited in the light rain for the cars to go by. He held a Styrofoam cup of coffee. His hair was tied back in a ponytail, and he wore sneakers, a dark green T-shirt, and tight jeans that hugged his skinny legs. When a break came in the traffic, he ran across the street, unlocked the door of his building, and went inside. Leo waited a couple of minutes for him to get settled, then he uncoiled his new harp harness and draped it over his left shoulder. The leather was still stiff and he could smell the dye, but the harps hung there pretty well without slipping. He walked away from the florist's and into the shop.

Tony had already put on music, something classical with a lot of brass. The store's lights were still off, though. Leo looked at all the guitars hanging on the back wall. Most were electric, but there were some acoustic too, even a steel slide. On the floor in front of them were two full sets of drums, the cymbals wrapped in plastic.

"Ciao, man. Be right with you." Tony was squatting behind the lighted glass case, making room on a display shelf for three tuning forks and a small stack of guitar picks. His fingers were long and thin. The nails on his left hand were clipped short. The ones on his right were filed sharp. Beneath the tuning fork shelf were the harmonicas, still arranged on a dark blue cloth so they shined more silver than ever. In the center lay a chromatic harp, the big kind with a key switch-button at one end, a double row of reed holes from corner to corner. Ryder said bluesing on one of those was like playing a twelve-string, drunk; too many damn things to juggle. Still, it was a good place to get the talk rolling, so Leo cleared his throat and asked to take a look at it.

"Certainement, monsieur." Tony straightened up and set the chromatic on the glass top. "I dig your rig. You make that?"

"My uncle. He's a harp man, too."

"Cool." Tony took his coffee out back and flicked on the lights. Leo picked up the new harp, pressed the button, and watched the metal slide block off the holes of the top row while opening the holes at the bottom.

"You can give it a quick blow if you want, my reed tester's cracked."

"No thanks. I don't go for this kind of harp much. It's a cheater, you know? I like to use my tongue to block off the notes."

Tony smiled and put the chromatic back in the case. He said something down there, but Leo didn't quite catch it.

"I'm sorry, Tony, I didn't hear you."

Tony stood. "Nada. Just said the harp player in my band uses them a lot. We've met, right?"

"Yeah."

Tony was smiling but Leo couldn't keep looking at him, not after what he just heard, not after that. Leo turned to the guitar wall, to maybe ask a question about the Dobro, but as he opened his mouth, his harp harness slipped backwards off his shoulder and fell to the floor.

"You're the cat who was going to jam with us. I gave you my card, right?"

Leo squatted for the harness. One of his C harps came out of its sheath and he had to get down on his hands and knees to pull it from the dust under a music book display rack.

Tony tossed him a felt cloth from behind the counter. "You with a group?"

"Sort of." Leo put the harness on the counter, wiped off his harp, blew in the reeds, then wiped it some more.

"Four-man? Five-man?"

"A trio, really. Two harps and a guitar."

"Sounds cool. We got two guitars and a harp. Then the bass man, and the drums. I'm thinking of throwing in a horn of some kind, you know? Really bust out with it."

Leo pushed the C harp back into its sheath. "Who's your harp man?" His voice sounded fine for that one. He looked right into Tony's boyish smooth-shaved face.

"Michigan Joe. Heard of him? He plays some righteous riffs. Only black man in the band. I'm thinking of auditioning some black chick backup too, you know? Really knock out the walls."

"You mean Negro?"

Tony looked at Leo a second. "Sorry, man, I forgot your name."

Leo told him.

"Cool. Leo, they don't want to be called Negro anymore. Black is it. You wanna be hip, you gotta say black. What's the name of your band? We'll come hear you sometime."

Leo rolled his harness up and started to buckle it. He glanced up as far as Tony's smooth pale throat. "The Bandits. We call ourselves the Blues Bandits."

35

Leo started up the car and drove as purposefully as if he knew where he was going. The rain had stopped, but the sky was still gray. He rolled his window down and he could smell the wet asphalt outside. He drove as far as the Springfield city limits, then turned around and drove back. He steered down the main street past Tony's shop, taking a left up the hill to the house where he and Tom had worked. He pulled halfway into the drive. The new black shingles were even darker from being wet, and their newness made the old small house top-pretty, like a hobo wearing a store-bought hat.

He was tapping the steering wheel with his hand. It was a half-time backbeat he could tap his foot to and hang any number of tunes on, but playing by himself wasn't what he had in mind at all, and forget being part of the Wednesday Night Poker Show, bluesing with his father and Ryder for big bald men who called Leo "Einstein" just because he had published an essay on the blues; for dangerous simpletons like Dwight, who would come back around any day, for all the rest of them, drinking their Narragansetts, smoking their Garcia Vegas, acting like they've been places and seen things and there's nothing like Heywood, Mass., and Jimmy Suther's cabin down on the river.

And Allie had said Leo had vision; she saw it in his room, right up there in Big Bill Broonzy. Damn, she was so gentle.

Leo backed down the hill, parked at the corner, and ran across the street to the flower shop. The same woman as before was behind the counter. Her dyed red hair looked brighter, and the bit of mustache she had had was bleached away. She wore a sleeveless yellow blouse with white polka dots. The backs of her arms hung loose as she gave a businessman his change. Leo asked her for $100 worth of flowers.

"I'm sorry, hon, did you say one *hun*dred dollars' worth?"

"Yeah, please, and all kinds."

She shook her head smiling, said he would have to wait a few, then disappeared into the back greenhouse. Above the doorway was a white cardboard sign: "Back Our Boys Overseas!" A red, white, and blue bow was taped to each corner. Leo pulled out his $300, counted out five twenties, and waited.

It was close to noon. The rain had finished and the sky opened up blue in some places, the sun shining down on the wet tar of Paper Boulevard as Leo pulled Jim's Valiant into the lot of Beatrice's UFO Show, turned it around, and backed up alongside the white rail fence of Thompson Green. He took up his A harp and sucked out a hard wailing wah-wah that he hand-cupped for a swoony tremolo.

"She's a light-taker, she's a night-faker." He didn't sing it, he just said it, flat and loud. He kissed the harp and sistered the tune before sliding into another hand-cup that he really bluesed up.

"Man, I ain't lyin' about my baby and me!" This time he shouted it out the window. He stepped out of the car and played some more. Two men walked out of Beatrice's smiling at him. They got in a pickup truck and the driver tooted his horn as he pulled away. Leo launched into his best bent-chord combo, really smoking the reeds for the buildup to the refrain. He closed his eyes tight, breathed air through his nose, then blew it out in bass chords before sucking in a single long bead of a note he lip-pursed and throat-constricted to a point so sharp he just had to hold it, drawing in so steady and high he thought of a jet plane skidding without its wheels down a runway, sparking and smoking towards who-knows-what. When his lungs were full, Leo lowered his harp and let the air out his mouth, the sound gone just like that.

The sun was on his face. Sidney stood at the back door smoking a cigarette, watching him, his black hair wet with sweat. Leo turned to see Chick's flatbed drive over gravel, entering the other side of the lot. Allie's hair was tied up in a bobbing ponytail and the truck radio was playing. Leo opened the car's rear door and pulled out the four-foot-long, three-foot-high flower basket from the back seat. Every kind of flower he'd ever seen was in it: daisies, roses, irises, dahlias, lilies, daffodils, tulips, and all sorts of long green stems surrounded by tiny white baby's breath. The handle was wrapped in yellow and pink ribbon and a fat blue bow was stuck to each end of the basket. When he turned around, Allie was already inside the diner.

———

He walked fast, the basket knocking against his leg and jerking down on his arm. He swung open Beatrice's door just as Allie was tying on her UFO apron behind the cash register. In one of the booths sat a mother and father and two little boys. Two men in janitors' clothes drank coffee at the far end of the counter. Leo heaved the flower basket up onto it; the tulips and daffodils swayed, the baby's breath shimmied.

"I'm leaving. I joined a band and we're going on the road for a long time."

Allie stood perfectly still. She had one hand on top of the register. Her lips were parted, and she looked from him to the flowers, then back at him again. Her eyes were big and a little shiny.

"Oh, aren't they beautiful."

It was the woman in the booth with her family. She had short brown hair and large breasts. Her big husband glanced up from his eating. They looked like farmers.

"She thinks I don't love her but I do."

"Of course you do." The woman kept smiling.

Leo looked at the two young boys across from her. One of them was chewing on a french fry, watching him. "We lost our baby last week, but, you know—"

"Shut up!" Allie shoved the flower basket off the counter with both hands. It cleared the stools, hit the floor, and rolled over once, spilling dirt. One of the men at the counter said uh-oh. The mother in the booth stopped smiling.

"Stay *away* from me!" Allie cupped her hand to her mouth and ran out to the kitchen.

Leo knelt and pulled the basket right side up. The handle was wobbly, but only a few of the flowers were ruined. He looked up at the farmer lady, who was now shaking her head. "Just needs dirt," he said. "You can have 'em." Leo could hear Sidney coming, then he felt him, felt his big wet hands dig in beneath Leo's armpit to yank him up, but the hearing made all the difference. Leo leaned forward as Sidney pulled, and when he was on his feet, he stepped out of Sid's grip and swung around with a lunging right hook that cracked into Sid's ear. Sidney hopped sideways and dropped to one knee. Leo could see Allie through the food tray hole on the kitchen wall. She wasn't crying anymore but her cheeks were still wet, and she was blinking fast. When her eyes caught his she turned her back to him and folded her arms as if he'd just called her name.

One of the men at the counter stood and was talking about calling the cops. Sid held his ear with both hands and rocked back and forth on the floor.

The noon horn blew as Leo drove fast up the left fork, away from the mill and the Connecticut, for 116. When the road dipped back down towards the water Leo pressed the accelerator all the way, the engine shifting into higher gear, and he only let up when the road leveled out into a curve and the right tires rolled through dirt. The sun was gone again, covered by a huge steel-colored cloud. The river looked green, the trees along it brown, almost blue. He steered with one hand as he drove into Holyoke, then found the hill road leading to the St. John's Church and gunned the engine all the way up.

A yellow Volkswagen Beetle was parked near the steps. Leo got out of his car and strapped on his harp harness. The dark sky loomed huge, the river valley small beneath it. He walked up the slate path to the far corner of the cemetery, but when he got to Katie Faye's grave he walked past it, turned around, and sat down on the ground under one of the white oak trees at the ridge. His mother's stone seemed so small there ahead of him. And he cussed himself for not bringing *her* all those flowers. But it was Allie's face through the food tray hole he kept seeing, just before her eyes locked with his and she turned her back on him, on Sid, on the whole scene. Her lips were in an actual pout, and her eyes were blinking fast, like somebody was holding a flame to her fingers; boy, she looked like a little girl, like some small child and it was him, Leo, holding the fire. But he couldn't help what he'd said; that farmer woman looked more mother than anything else, and Leo just had to tell her.

His own mother would have been almost forty years old now, probably the same age as the lady in Beatrice's, the same age as Chick's wife, even Betty Poitras. Leo wondered if they'd all be her friends. Probably not Betty or the farmer, not close anyway, but for certain Katie Faye and Allie's mother would have hit it off. Katie Faye with her poems, Mrs. Donovan with her paintings; with their men and kids in common, too. They would probably be fast friends, Leo thought, maybe even tight enough to help out Allie and me. With those three words his face felt funny and he shook his head. A cool breeze blew over the stones and the oaks. The big cloud was moving fast now, and across the valley the trees were tinged with sunlight.

When Leo read about Jim and Katie Faye in his mother's note-books, his and Allie's love seemed small and young and too horny to be the real kind that started families. True, they *did* start a family, but starting only counts when you finish starting. And he remembered the wrestling awards dinner last year, when Betty Poitras insisted Jim and Leo sit with them—like the two Suthers weren't quite a family on their own, like the picture wasn't quite all there and was in need of some help. Last night, when Mrs. Donovan's warm hand had been resting on his, her dark brown eyes looking at him softer than they ever had, he'd felt it in his groin, and even though he was feeling true hurt about Allie, he knew he could easily kiss her mother, even saw himself making love with her somewhere. In her car or out in the woods, he would nudge and slide his erection into the hot opening Allie herself had come from. And man, how could Jim go twelve years without a woman? Leo didn't know. Maybe Jim was keeping two vows, the marriage one to Katie Faye, and the one he made in the parking lot of that dance hall down in Texas. Because he never broke that one either. Ryder too. They had never stopped playing. His father had called country music cardboard and the blues oak, and man, here he ended up in a *paper* town, Leo thought, where out on the green they don't even play country music, but ancient off-key military tunes.

Leo stood and walked down to Katie Faye's headstone. The breeze had died down again, and now the sun broke through on the hill.

It was she who never got to finish what she started, it was she who never went to France.

The late-afternoon sky was clear and blue but this side of Heywood was already in the shadows of the Berkshires when Leo drove the Valiant up behind the Elks club. On the white cinderblock rear wall someone had written: "TRUDY WAS HERE AND SHE HAD A FINE TIME." Leo could hear the glide and crack of the shuffleboard puck inside, a woman laughing, men talking. The gas tank was almost empty. He unlocked the trunk, dropped the harp harness there, and slammed the lid.

Jim and Ryder stood at the long bar with a dozen others playing their numbers. The place was heavy with cigar smoke and Leo could hear the wet hum of the air conditioner in the corner. He wanted to go tell them now, get it over with, but Lars was with them, Bill O'Donnell too. Leo walked over to the drinking tables against the back wall and sat at a small empty one beneath the framed photo of the 1955 Elks Softball Team. The shuffleboard lady laughed again. Two men from the mill stood with her. Her dirty-blond hair was pinned up to the side of her head and she wore jeans and a work shirt like a man. Her chest and shoulders looked wide and soft. She gripped the steel puck with the same hand her cigarette was in, standing up straight, smoking between two fingers. She licked her upper lip, pulled back the puck, then shoved it down the sawdust-covered runner right into the center pin for a strike. She shrieked and laughed again, turning around fast to pick her glass of beer up off the table.

The bartender called out numbers behind the bar, but there was no winner and he went to collecting all the cards for another round. Leo saw Ryder shake his head. His back looked so small there between Lars and Jim. To Jim's right was Bill O'Donnell, leaning one elbow on the bar, talking to the side of Jim's face.

No sense waiting. Leo walked over the empty dance floor. Bill O'Donnell's heavy-lidded eyes caught him, and Leo remembered the feel of big Sid falling away from that one punch. He stepped between Ryder and Jim, put his arms around their shoulders, and pulled them in close. Jim laughed and Ryder wriggled free. "It's the Leweyville Kid." Ryder faked an uppercut to Leo's chin, then he broke out in a laugh. "Hey rascal, come to play?"

"Nope."

"You got in, didn't you?" Jim was smiling. They both smelled like the mill.

"In what?" Ryder faked another punch.

"Bull*shit*," O'Donnell said to the air.

273

"Can we go outside a minute?" Leo said.

Ryder said sure and ordered a Miller High Life, though he had a full one in front of him. Jim kept his back to O'Donnell. Ryder slipped Leo the cold bottle and the three of them walked outside.

"Think Frankie'll up our dues for this?" Ryder held up his beer. Jim's bottle was almost empty but he wasn't paying it any attention. His eyes were on Leo. "Well?"

Leo took a long pull off his Miller. It was ice cold. He heard the call of a bird in the trees at the edge of the lot.

"Well?" Jim was smiling again.

"Aw, you two," Ryder said. "What's the damn secret?"

Leo's throat was thick and dry and he couldn't just come out and say it, so he handed Ryder his beer, unlocked the trunk, and pulled out his harp harness. It unrolled itself, the buckle clanging the rear bumper. "I'm taking these to Paris, France."

"Hot damn, I'm gettin' old." Ryder did a little jig in the dirt.

"Your band's going there?"

"I'm not in the band, Pop. They already have a harp."

Jim's smile was gone now. His mustache was thick as ever, his eyes deep-set and brown as a bull's.

"You hopping a train over there, Young Buddy?"

Leo hadn't pictured Jim like this, but now it made all the sense in the world. He looked up at his eyes, then his lips, which were red and parted beneath his mustache. "I'm going to Paris for Katie Faye, Dad."

Jim's eyes went shiny. "You bought a ticket?"

"I don't have enough money."

"You don't?"

Leo shook his head. "I joined the army."

"Oh, Lord," Ryder said.

"I volunteered, so they're gonna send me where I want to go. This sergeant in Springfield said I could take a train from Germany to France every weekend."

Jim looked at Ryder like he wanted to make sure Ryder was hearing the same thing he was. He looked right back at Leo. "There's a fucking *war* on, boy! You think those sons of bitches care whether or not you see Paris?"

"Don't call me boy; I'm not a boy." Leo took his beer from Ryder and raised the bottle to his lips, but Jim backhanded it twenty feet into the parking lot. "*Damn* you!"

The bird at the edge of the lot went quiet. Leo rolled up his harness and started to buckle it. His fingers were steady and he took his time. His father was breathing like he'd just walked up Saunders Hill Road from the river. Then Leo heard him turn and walk away. He looked up and watched him go, watched his short swinging arms and wide back, watched the empty beer bottle he let fall from his hand before he pulled open the door and disappeared back into the club.

"Did you really do it, Young Buddy?" Ryder's head was cocked to the side, and his mouth looked ready to smile. When Leo showed up again, the sergeant had smiled too, a real wide one that revealed a gold cap on one of his molars, and again he had gotten out of his chair to shake Leo's hand like he was right on time.

"Yeah, Ryder, I did."

36

It took Leo close to an hour to walk home. When he got to Saunders Hill Road he was thirsty and his stomach felt pinched with hunger. He took the casserole dish of leftover haddock and creamed corn from the fridge, sat down on the front step, and ate the food cold, sopping up the corn juice with a slice of Wonder Bread, swallowing it all with Coke. The sergeant had given him an easy written test with questions like who was the first president of the United States, and how much is twelve times twelve. After Leo wrote down all the answers, the sergeant asked if he'd ever been in trouble with the police. Leo said no, though right away he thought about Sid at noon, and wondered whether Sidney was the kind to call the cops. Then the sergeant asked if Leo had graduated from high school, and when Leo told him no he said that's no problem, we'll teach you plenty.

"Before we swear you in, you take a physical. Have you got transport? Wheels?"

"Just today."

"That's fine. Give me your address and I'll pick you up tomorrow morning at 0800. That's 8:00 your time."

Leo finished off the last bite of fish. He thought of Jim's words about the war and those sons of bitches not caring whether he got to Paris or not. But so what if they lie; part of Leo didn't care, he knew. He pictured Allie's face a summer or two from now when he would walk through town an ex-warrior, with maybe a limp like Ryder, a haircut like Floyd, muscles like GP's buddy Logan. Then Chick came into his head. Leo saw him sitting in his wheelchair on his porch, shirtless and talking too much. Man, he wouldn't go for any of this. And Jim had said damn you. *Damn* you. That was too much; that sounded like automatic bad luck.

But Jim didn't say anything more, not when he parked the Valiant in front of the house after dark, not when he walked into the parlor where Leo lay on the couch with his A harp to get the newspaper, not even after he washed up and went to his bedroom. Leo was in his own room by then. He stood in his doorway and said down the hall loud enough for Jim to hear, "I gotta go for a physical tomorrow. A sergeant's picking me up."

But Jim didn't answer. Leo heard the slight knock of his watch on the night table, then the bedsprings, and the light switch. Leo gave him another minute or two but the house was quiet, so was the river. It'd gone down the last couple of days. On the way back from Springfield, the second time, Leo saw the easy chair that had been stuck under the covered bridge. It had floated to the pebbled beach at the Springfield line, where it snagged itself upside-down between boulders, its four short legs sticking up in the air.

Leo knew he would pass the physical. He wondered if he would get sworn in right then and there.

When Leo got up at seven Jim was already gone and he hadn't left any breakfast, just his coffeepot, which was still warm when Leo touched it. But he didn't need coffee. He looked over the kitchen, even the parlor, half hoping to see a note or something, anything from Jim. But there was none. At two minutes to eight, the sergeant drove up to the house in a light blue Ford sedan. It had white U.S. Government license plates, and it was funny, but Leo had been expecting a jeep. He also thought they'd be driving to a fort of some kind, but the sergeant chuckled when Leo told him that. He was chewing gum again, driving with both hands on the wheel. He wore an ironed pale green shirt, a dark green tie held in place with an American flag tie tack, and dark green pants with shiny black shoes. Leo had put on his work boots, jeans, and a clean T-shirt, but he felt a little dirty, a little too informal sitting there in the front seat as they drove south along the river in the sunshine. The sergeant blew a bubble and popped it.

"Nope, MEPS is down the street from my office. Convenient as instant coffee."

"What's that, sir?"

"Military Entrance Processing Station. We'll do the whole meal right there. Your lucky day too, Doc Trudeau's on call. You probably know her, she's got an office in your town."

"I'll get sworn in after that?"

The sergeant blew another bubble and popped it. Leo could smell his aftershave.

"After the doc you'll do an SI and prints, then you'll see a CO and take the oath."

Leo nodded like he'd understood what he just heard. They passed the Springfield line, and he looked out the windshield at the sun on the river.

"You did well on the test. That's good, means you get your pick of jobs."

"I don't really mind what my job is; I just want to get to France. I mean, you know, Germany."

The sergeant spit his gum out the window as he turned onto Main Street and drove past the shops. Tony's Musical Suite wasn't open yet. "They'll know about my preferred assignment thing, right?"

"Roger that."

"I mean, there's no way I won't go to Europe, right?"

"Take it easy, with your scores you're off to Oktoberfest. Eight weeks at Fort Dix and you're gonzo."

Leo wondered what the test had to do with any of this, and he'd forgotten about basic training or boot camp or whatever they called it. He hadn't thought of an eight-week delay like that. He followed the sergeant to the second floor of the MEPS office building into a room full of fold-out chairs. Two other guys were waiting to see the doctor. They both looked Leo's age, and one of them was pudgy in the face. He was reading a book he'd brought along. The other had his lean arms folded in front of his chest and sat staring at the toes of his cowboy boots. The sergeant whispered, "These guys are draftees, you go to the front of the line." His gum smacked in Leo's ear.

Not long after the sergeant left, a red-haired nurse opened the opposite door, glanced at her clipboard, and called Leo in. The fat kid looked up from his book like he was about to say something, but he didn't. Leo followed the nurse into a small brightly lit room. On the walls were eye charts and a diagram of a man's body with no skin on it.

"I'm Dr. Trudeau, Leo, please take off your shirt."

The doctor, who wasn't a nurse after all, had thick hair put up in a bun. She had dark brown eyes, and across her nose was a light band of freckles. She seemed smart, kind too. She put the stethoscope plugs in her ears and told Leo to take a deep breath and let it out slowly. She put one hand on his shoulder as she pressed the cool metal to his chest, then his ribs, then his back. She took his pulse and blood pressure and wrote something down on a clipboard. She shined a flashlight in his ears, put headphones on his head, and asked him to tell her in which ear there was a sound, a high beep that showed up first in Leo's left ear, his right, then both. She smiled, pulled off the headphones, and wrote down more.

"Sit down, please."

Leo sat in a padded chair. Bolted into the wall behind it was a folding steel arm with a metal mask at its end which the doctor set up right in front of Leo's face. She leaned close to adjust the eyepiece so it was touching his nose. Everything he saw looked red in the left eye and green in the right. He could smell her shampoo. She stepped back, turned off the lights, and asked him to tell her where the colors were. Then she hit a lever on her goggles and everything went white and there was a letter chart in front of him. He could read every line but the last two, and they were smaller than any he'd ever seen. She flicked on the lights, pulled the mask away, and wrote more things on the clipboard. She kept her eyes on what she was writing and told Leo he could put on his shirt. Leo buttoned up and watched her write; her forehead had slight lines in it, her lips were pursed in concentration. "I'm a bluesman, actually. I'm joining so I can go play my harps in France. You know, on the weekends."

She stopped writing and looked at him as if she hadn't understood a word of what he'd just said. Then she smiled. "Well, have fun. You're certainly in good health."

Leo smiled back and was about to mention his mother never having got there herself, that she died young and all that, but the doctor turned and left the room. Leo followed her back to the waiting area where the sergeant sat. He stood, took the form sheet from the doctor, and secured it to a clipboard of his own. "Is he up to snuff?"

"Quite." Dr. Trudeau smiled at Leo once more, then tapped the pudgy one on the shoulder to follow her.

The sergeant wasn't chewing gum anymore, which was fine with Leo. They left the room and walked down the shiny-floored hallway.

"Security Interview's a cinch. An LT will ask you some questions and fingerprint you. Then you see the captain for the oath." The sergeant reached over and squeeed Leo's shoulder. Leo thought of Lars, the way he did that a lot.

The lieutenant was a young guy with a soft voice and dark skin like a Greek or Italian, but his last name was Martin. He stood across from Leo at a wooden table beneath what Leo figured was the Massachusetts state flag, and he started fingerprinting him right away. He held Leo's fingers and rolled them one at a time over an ink pad, then onto a white piece of paper with empty squares marking which finger was which. Leo could feel the sergeant standing somewhere behind him.

"How many felony convictions do you have?" The lieutenant's voice was calm, almost uninterested, like he was asking Leo how he took his coffee. He dropped Leo's left hand and started working on the right.

"None, sir. I've never been arrested before."

"How about the drugs? Smoke a lot of reefer, do you?"

"No, I never have."

"Sergeant Ryan tells me you're a musician."

"Yes sir, I play the blues harp."

"That a stringed instrument?"

Leo shook his head. The lieutenant's eyes were on what he was doing, though, and he didn't see him. "It's a harmonica."

The lieutenant nodded. He rolled Leo's middle finger into the ink pad, then onto the paper. "Why are you in such a hurry to go over-seas? The sergeant says you're not particular about any specific train-ing we have available. Why is that?" The lieutenant paused and looked up at Leo. He was probably twenty-six or -seven. Leo glanced down at his black fingertips, then up. "I'm just ready to get going, you know? That's all."

The lieutenant regarded him a second longer, then he finished up with Leo's pinky finger, twisting it a little too much as he rolled the print out onto the paper. He closed the ink pad case and handed Leo a white cloth.

"Have you got a sweetheart?"

"No."

The lieutenant smiled. He reminded Leo of Gerry, though he didn't look anything like him.

"Are you shy with girls?"

Leo shook his head. "I almost got married this summer, but it didn't work out."

"I see." The lieutenant glanced over across the room. "We're fin-ished here, Sergeant. Captain Bennett will see him."

Captain Bennett was not in his office. In front of three tall win-dows overlooking downtown Springfield was a dark walnut desk, big as a pool table. Loose papers were scattered all over it, and Sergeant Ryan placed a clipboard in the middle of it. "Have a sit-down, Leo. I'll wait in the hall."

Leo sat in a straight-backed chair in front of the desk. Outside the day was bright and he almost had to squint. Above the windows hung four green banners, each holding a different yellow word. From left to right, Leo read

COURAGE CANDOR COMMITMENT COMPETENCE

Candor was a strange word, and it made Leo think of the huge birds that swooped down on rabbits and snakes. The room smelled like floor wax. The middle window was half open and Leo could hear the cars going by, two women talking and laughing down on the sidewalk. In three weeks school would start. Long days at a desk. In the same building as Allie, the same room as Allie, the same air as Allie. He saw himself working weekends for Chick, making $2 an hour times fifteen or sixteen hours: that'd give him $30 a week; keep a twenty to blow, and that's still $100 dollars a month. He'd have $1,000 by graduation, plenty for a ticket. Plenty.

A side door opened and the captain walked in wiping his hands on a paper towel. He smiled at Leo right away. Leo stood, but the captain waved him back into his chair. He was tall and looked older than Jim or Ryder. He had short sandy-colored hair. Double silver bars were sewn into the shoulders of his short-sleeved shirt, and his brass tie tack was crooked. Above his left shirt pocket were rows of colored ribbons: red, green, white, and yellow. He reached over the desk and shook Leo's hand, then he sat down and picked up the clipboard, the smile still on his face. "Leo Suther. Do you like Heywood?"

"Sure thing, sir."

"We have a house up in Holyoke."

"My mother's buried there."

The smile left the captain's face. "Is this a recent passing?"

"No sir, I was a little boy then."

The captain nodded, keeping his eyes on Leo, then he flipped the page up over the clipboard and read some more. "Superior test scores, that's outstanding. We're quite fortunate. Tell me, do you like writing?"

"I like to write songs."

"Really." The captain lowered the clipboard. "A songwriter."

"Yes, sir."

"Have you heard of our *Stars and Stripes*?"

"The flag?"

The captain smiled. "It's our newspaper, Leo. And they are always on the prowl for new talent."

"Is there anything in my papers about Europe, sir?"

"Europe?"

"The sergeant told me I get preferred assignment status because I'm enlisting instead of getting drafted. See, sir, I didn't get a notice. I mean, I didn't have to join."

Captain Bennett's eyes got smaller and he sucked in his lower lip. "Why Europe, Leo?"

"It's a long story, sir."

The captain put down the clipboard. He tapped his fingertips on the desk.

"I will be going to Germany though, won't I, sir?"

"Do you consider yourself a moral young man, Leo?"

"I try to be."

"Do you expect the same from others?"

"I think so, sir."

"That's fine, that's fine. Now, if Sergeant Ryan said you will be stationed in Germany, then I am sure you will be stationed in Germany." The captain stood. His head and shoulders were silhouetted against the sun reflecting off windows across the street. "When an officer stands, you follow suit, Leo."

Leo stood.

"Are you familiar with the writings of Samuel Johnson?"

"No, sir."

"'The torch of truth shows much that we cannot, and all that we would not, see.' That's from *The Rambler*. Do you like it?"

"I don't think I understand it, sir."

"I like your candor. Definitions are found in experience, Leo. Raise your right hand and repeat after me, please."

Leo raised his right hand, but he was standing close to the desk and he knocked his fingers on the way up.

"I do solemnly swear that I will support and defend the Constitution of the United States."

Leo repeated the words.

"Against all enemies foreign and domestic."

"Against all enemies foreign and domestic."

"That I will bear true faith and allegiance to the same."

Leo's voice sounded funny to him; it came from deep inside his chest. He kept his eyes on the captain's shadowed face, the ears sticking out from the side of his head.

"That I take this obligation freely, without any mental reservation or purpose of evasion, and that I will well and faithfully discharge the duties of the office upon which I am about to enter."

Leo pronounced it as clearly as he could.

"So help me God."

"So help me God."

Leo lowered his hand and the captain shook it. "Congratulations, son. We're glad to have you."

37

Sergeant Ryan drove up in front of Leo's house just before noon. The air was probably ninety degrees and smelled like pine needles and the sun-dried tar shingles from the roof of the cabin. The whole way back, the sergeant had told stories of his own basic training at Fort Dix in New Jersey, of an officer there named Potovich who was so hard-charging gung-ho nobody made fun of his name even in private. But now, sitting there behind the wheel of his sedan, the engine still running, Sergeant Ryan spit his gum out the window, sat up straight, and spoke in a flat, even tone of voice, reminding Leo that 0500 meant 5:00 A.M. and that is exactly when he should expect his transport to arrive this coming Saturday morning. He handed Leo a small U.S. Army pamphlet, shook his hand, then drove up Saunders Hill Road and took a left back for Springfield.

———

Leo stood there a good minute or two. The sun was hot on his face and the top of his head. He heard two pine cones drop out in the woods, then the steel rattle of a mill truck going by up on Paper Boulevard. He went into the house and changed into shorts. In the parlor he stacked three albums on the record player and turned the volume up as loud as it would go. The first one was all Chicago city blues, Buddy Guy and Junior Wells, and they started out with "Messin' with the Kid." Leo grabbed the broom in the kitchen and started sweeping the floor, but then he stopped and began wiping down the counter and stove, the table, and the top of the refrigerator. He washed out Jim's coffee pot, dried it, and put it on the back burner. He sprinkled Comet on his sponge and scrubbed the sink, then he rinsed it and wiped it dry. Junior Wells began a song with a short harp solo, and Leo pictured himself playing a harmonica reveille down at this Fort Dix. He could get up before dawn with the trumpet guy and play a blues backup to it, bending the notes to get the day going honest. And maybe he'd get assigned a bunkmate like his father, not a harp man like Ryder, but some kid with a guitar, maybe a steel slide Dobro.

Leo finished sweeping the floor, then swept the hallway down to the bathroom. He ran back to the kitchen for the sponge and Comet and glass cleaner, then he scrubbed down the bathroom sink, the tub, and the outside of the toilet. He sprayed the mirror and wiped it clear. He swept the floor across the hall into his room, then did that floor too. Buddy Guy's electric guitar was really whining the blues now, holding on with a long single note right behind Junior's singing about the man mistreating him. Leo took a T-shirt from his bureau drawer to use as a dust cloth. He wiped down his bureau top, his bedside table, the window sills, even Big Bill Broonzy's face. He pulled up his window screen, then swept all the dust and floor grit onto his new Sonny Terry and Brownie McGhee album cover and dropped the dirt out onto the pine needles. He was sweating now and he thought after he cleaned the whole damn house he might do some push-ups and sit-ups, maybe even go run down the road.

He was on the roof sweeping pine needles and twigs out of the gutters when Jim drove up. He was early by about an hour and Leo figured he'd skipped going down to the club altogether. Leo waved and said hi, but Jim didn't say anything back. He barely looked up as he carried a grocery bag into the house. Leo hurried up and finished. He dropped the broom off the roof and climbed down the pine closest to the house. Inside, his father's coffee was brewing and Leo heard the shower water running in the bathroom. He wondered if Jim had noticed how clean everything was. He went into the parlor and did forty-six push-ups. Then he started doing sit-ups. He remembered GP telling Allie on the raft on Empire Lake how he could do 350 of these, but at thirty-five Leo's stomach muscles burned and his lower back hurt, so he stopped at forty-three. He changed into sneakers, then ran up Saunders Hill to Paper Boulevard. He jogged away from town and stayed on the shoulder, running against any traffic. During wrestling season they had to run three times a week but only for a couple of miles. Leo thought he could do that. He'd run a mile down and a mile back. There was a break in the trees at the first bend to Springfield, and he could see the river. The water was green again, blue near the banks, and he thought of Allie crying in Beatrice's yesterday, the way she put her hand to her mouth after she pushed the flowers off the counter, the way she turned her back on him.

His legs felt heavy and even though the sun was hanging close to the Berkshires, his back was tender and he wished he'd worn a T-shirt. On the way back he ran as fast as he could. He tried to hold the pace, and he imagined doing this with a rifle in his hand and a pack on his back, boots on his feet. Sweat burned his eyes and his ribs started to hurt. At his mailbox, he stopped and walked down Saunders Hill Road under the trees. He could see his father standing down at the bank. Leo took long deep breaths as he walked. He wiped his forehead with the back of his arm but both were wet.

Jim glanced back at his son, then flicked his cigarette out into the water. The river had gone down another foot overnight and was almost out of the hardwoods, back where it belonged. At the opposite bank was a line of yellow foam from the mill. Leo leaned over and rested both hands on his knees. He was a little behind Jim and to the side, and he heard the clink of ice as his father drank from his coffee. Leo swatted a mosquito at his neck. Jim lit another cigarette and Leo waited. Two more mosquitoes began working on his leg. He was breathing close to normal now. He killed both bugs and turned to go back up the hill.

"When do you leave?" Jim said it without turning around. You'd have thought he was talking to the river.

"Saturday morning." Leo crossed his arms. He felt the eyelash kiss of a mosquito on his spine, but he didn't move. Neither did Jim. Leo didn't like looking at his back, but if he went around to the other side of him he'd be standing in water. "A captain swore me in."

Smoke blew out in front of Jim. The back of his head looked so big and square, his hair still so black. Leo wondered who the hell he thought he was, keeping his back to him like that.

"He said if the sergeant said I'm going to Germany, then I'm going to Germany."

Jim nodded, his attention still on the river. Then he turned around. "I joined up in Texas. Did you know that?"

Leo shook his head.

"I was hitching a ride to a night picnic in Chicopee. This man in a LaSalle was going to Hartford, said he'd drop me right off, but when he slowed down at the line I asked him if he wouldn't mind taking me to Connecticut instead. He was happy for the company, bought me a dinner in the city." Jim finished his Lucky Strike and lit up another. He looked very tired, his nose a little wider than normal, his eyes deeper set, an ash-colored band beneath each one. "That was my last full meal till I got to Kentucky and found work on a horse farm for a month. I would've stayed if the owner hadn't sold two mares to a Texan from San Antonio."

Jim dumped the last of his coffee and ice into the river. "Texas isn't as pretty as Kentucky, son, but something about those Mexicans and their food got to me so I stayed. I starved for three weeks, then I enlisted." He took a deep drag off his cigarette, his eyes squinting in the smoke. "My dad was dead only two years, but I couldn't breathe in that damn house." He looked at Leo, then away just as fast. "You look more like Katie Faye than you ever have, but you're just like me, son. You're just like me."

* * *

Jim cooked kielbasa sausages on the grill, and Leo sat on the kitchen stoop with one of his C harps. He was working on the intro to "Messin' with the Kid," which was such a clean shot into the number, he didn't think he could do it without a band backup but he was getting close to sucking out the skeleton. He kept his eyes on Jim while he played, on his thick forearm and big hand that held the barbecue fork. He couldn't picture his father so young and hungry in Texas; three weeks without real food. He closed his eyes and tongue-blocked four different notes in a row, but it was the wrong combination, and when he opened his eyes, Ryder's Impala was driving down under the trees. He had a woman with him. Leo could see her pretty well through the windshield as Ryder parked behind the Valiant and waved. She had fluffy auburn hair kept high on top with a wide red headband. She got out and smiled at Leo over the roof of the car, her teeth big and straight and white. She was wearing too much rouge, and the blue-green smudges above her eyes didn't quite match her hair.

"Young Buddy, this is Helena. Her brother made your bandolero."

"Hello, Leo. Pleased to make your acquaintance."

Leo stood and waved.

"Hi, Jimmy." Helena smiled even more. She tilted her head and waved her hand real stiff, like a beauty queen in a convertible parade. She was wearing a light purple blouse with puffy sleeves, dark blue pants, and white sandals with heels, her toenails painted red to match her headband. Her earrings dangled almost to her shoulders, gold balls hanging off tiny gold chains. With her big hair and big teeth, Leo expected her to have big breasts, but she didn't; they were as compact as Allie's mother's.

Ryder walked up to the stoop with a case of Pabst cans and a quart of potato salad from B&G Grocery. "Come give your Uncle Ryder a hand with these."

As soon as the screen door closed behind them, Ryder put the case on the table, walked over, and gave Leo a short hug. He smelled like women's perfume. He stepped back and looked into Leo's face. "You're scarin' hell out of your old man and me, but we're damn proud of you." He squeezed Leo's shoulders, then turned and opened the fridge. Leo handed him two cans at a time.

"And you ain't going nowhere without a party, I can tell you that. You like Helena?"

"Sure thing." Leo looked out the window as he handed Ryder more cans. Helena stood near the barbecue with her back to the house, talking to Jim, who was smiling and nodding his head at what she was saying. Jim poked the sausages with the fork, but didn't roll them over any.

Ryder set up the poker table outside against the trees, Leo brought out the chairs, and everyone sat down and ate smoking kielbasa on Wonder Bread with mustard and ketchup. The potato salad was dry and cold, and Jim and Ryder were talking about the German food they used to eat in New Braunfels, Texas, before Leo was born, how they'd drive up there with Katie Faye on a weekend and the three of them would swim all afternoon, then end up at an outdoor restaurant with iced mugs of German beer and plates of hot sauer this and that.

Helena took small bites, keeping her lips closed while she chewed. When the men mentioned Katie Faye, Leo saw her look at him. Jim talked of Ryder having drunk so much one day he almost drowned in the Guadalupe River. Ryder was laughing with a full mouth he had to cover with his hand. Leo smiled with the others but he was thinking of Allie putting her fingers on his knee the first time he was at her house, when he told about his mother and Allie'd said she had no idea. Helena wasn't looking at him anymore, but still, he felt her there.

The last of the sunlight hung in gold breaks in the trees of the woods, and the mosquitoes started to hit. Helena insisted she clear away the paper plates so the men could haul the furniture back in. Inside Jim brewed a pot of coffee, and Ryder served Helena a cold can of Pabst wrapped in a napkin. Leo got a Coke and followed them both into the parlor. While Helena remarked how clean the house was and what a view they had, Leo squatted and put his new Sonny Terry and Brownie McGhee album on the record player. His thighs were starting to shake from the run and he couldn't stay in a squat for long. He sat down on the couch with his Coke just as Brownie's guitar started in, and Ryder whirled around from the window. "Hell Young Buddy, they'll upstage us. Give 'em the hook, we're gonna *play*."

"Oh goody, goody." Helena sat down on the couch. Jim came in with iced coffee. He set it down, then sat on his guitar stool and tuned up his Dobro. Leo got his harp harness from his room. When he came back into the parlor, Ryder already had his own strapped around his waist and was blowing Jim a C to tune to. Helena sat back in the corner of the couch with her napkin-wrapped beer, smiling up at the three of them. Leo buckled on his harness from his left shoulder to his right hip, then pulled on it until all of his harps hung against his chest. Ryder launched right in with a C lead of something low and funky but fast that Jim began picking to right away. It was a Joe Hill Louis number. Leo pulled a C from its sheath and began sucking out a low bass chord backup to Ryder's lead. He glanced at Helena on the couch, but she was looking at him, so he closed his eyes and listened to the music and the music only. Jim sang the intro loud and at near perfect pitch:

"Well she may be yours
But she comes to see me sometime,
Well she may be yours
But she comes to see me sometime,
When I go to love my baby
She's always in the street—"

Ryder took it flying from there and Leo followed as best he could. Ryder was really on a showoff of a roll though, so Leo dropped to a drum beat, sucking the chords out straight without a bend. Jim sang two more refrains with no variations and Leo kept steady while Ryder took it out in a harp-smacking flurry that he ended with a tremolo fade.

Helena put her Pabst on the table and clapped fast and hard, her ball and chain earrings swinging and jerking along her neck. "Oowee, you boys should be *famous.*"

Jim tapped his boot in time. He nodded at Ryder and Leo, then set off with "Sittin' on Top of the World." This time Ryder backed way down for the low chords in a G harp and winked at Leo to pick up the lead. Jim sang the intro, then Leo put the fine metal to his lips, closed his eyes, and blew out the exact sister tune of the song before he sucked in a few wah-wahs of his own, ending them on just the right note for Jim to take off singing from. Now Helena was sitting on the edge of the couch. She slapped the empty Pabst cans in time and a gold ring she wore made a metal tapping sound that fit in pretty well. They played six more tunes without a break, Jim cued them, and all the numbers were upbeat until the last one, "Natchez Burning" by Howlin' Wolf. On the album, Wolf had only a piano backup going to the guitar, no harps, so Leo wasn't sure how to proceed. Even Ryder was playing it safe, hitting wide bass chords while Jim sang high to his low thimble-sliding on the Dobro. He looked and sounded wonderful, really; his eyes were closed, his chin was tilted way up, and his voice couldn't have been truer to the words about the burning of Natchez Mississippi Town, his baby lying on the ground. Leo watched Helena watch Jim. She was sitting back on the couch now, and in the growing dark of the room, her eyes glittered. She was smiling but she seemed sad too; it was an expression Leo had never seen on a man. A man looked either up about something or else downhearted, but Helena seemed to open herself to the whole picture in front of her, and she was prettier in this light.

Jim was taking it out now, touching down on the last refrain, and Leo watched him do it, watched him keep his eyes closed while he sang out the last trembling notes. It came to Leo that when his father played in front of women—Allie that once, and now Helena—he sounded sweeter somehow, and even more in tune. He wasn't just Jim anymore; he was Guitar Jimmy, who was drawing out the last line now, really sliding the notes on the Dobro, and he sounded so fine, his music blowing right over the bridge into Truth City, that it was plain to Leo those very notes had had as much of a hand in getting him born as did Jim and Katie Faye. Helena stood and clapped. She stuck two fingers between her lips and whistled.

After, they all got into Ryder's Impala and drove to Beatrice's for ice cream. Leo sat in the back seat with his father, and when they turned off Paper Boulevard into the lot, Leo saw Chick's flatbed truck parked in the far corner. There were other cars too, the neon letters that spelled out "The UFO Show" shining down red and white on the hoods and the picnic tables in front of them. In the sky were wide streaks of bruised orange and green, the sun gone now. Leo walked behind Ryder and Helena for one of the outdoor tables. He looked up through the big lighted windows and saw Allie standing at a booth pouring two men coffee. She was smiling at something one of them was saying. The diner's door was hooked open and the juke-box inside played the Beatles' song "Help."

Ryder took orders and went in for the ice cream.

"You men amaze me." Helena smiled at Jim and Leo across the table. "Why don't you ever play down at the club, Jimmy?"

"We put on a show every Wednesday night."

"You do not."

"He means at our house," Leo said. "For Lars and the poker guys."

"Oh that man wouldn't know real music if it gave him back a head of hair. You need to perform in public. My Lord, your only competi-tion in this town is that silly Ladles' Auxiliary League."

Jim smiled and started talking about what it's like to play in honky-tonks, how a jukebox gets more respect. Leo looked back up through Beatrice's windows, but didn't see Allie. She was probably back behind the counter, but he wasn't going to stand up to find out. And he sure didn't need to give Sid a view of him either.

Ryder walked up carrying two ice cream cones in each hand. Helena took her chocolate. "I was just telling these handsome men that you boys should put on a show in that darn gazebo. I don't even think you need a permit this time of year. You just sign your name on the roster."

Ryder winked at Jim and Leo as he handed them their ice creams. He sat down and bit into his vanilla.

"I'm *serious.*"

"That's fine, my lovely, but Young Buddy here's shipping out Sat-urday morning."

Helena looked at Leo straight on again. The neon light made her cheeks seem smooth, younger than they were. The wide red head-band holding her hair so high appeared brown. "The military?"

Leo nodded yes.

"Drafted?"

"No," Jim said. "He volunteered."

Helena looked at Leo like he was some kind of zoo animal she'd seen once before but that was long ago. She raised her ice cream to her mouth, then lowered it. "All the more reason, you two."

"Not in this town, sweetie."

"Why not?"

They were quiet a moment.

Leo wiped his lips. "Because this isn't even a cardboard town, it's paper. Pretty soon I'll be playing in an oak town over in Europe."

"What did that boy just say?"

"He said it all, is what." Ryder shook his head and bit into his ice cream. Helena looked at Jim. Jim's hand was resting gently on the back of Leo's neck. He squeezed once and let go.

"She's right," Jim said.

"She'll be the only audience, too, Jimmy. Lest you forget, we don't play any Pat Boone."

"You're underestimating these people, honey."

"I doubt it."

Jim wiped ice cream off his mustache. He turned to Leo. "Be good for *you,* get you ready."

Leo looked past Helena and Ryder at the dim white of the gazebo through the trees on Thompson Green. He shrugged. "Okay with me."

"Aw *hell.*"

Helena pinched Ryder's cheek and gently shook it. "Don't be scared, skinny. I'll be along for the ride."

"Short ride. We only got three days."

"Friday night?" Jim said.

Leo nodded. He looked up again at Beatrice's windows and saw Allie carrying a tray of empty glasses past the booths. Ryder mentioned that the Am Vets boys had signs up two weeks in advance. Helena said she'd be happy to make up flyers to hang around town. "How shall I bill you?"

"I'll think something up."

"No, skinny. I mean what will you call yourselves? You need a name."

Leo swallowed the last of his cone. "The Blues Bandits."

———

292

Ryder laughed. "Everyone'll expect to get robbed."

"No they won't," Helena said.

"How 'bout the Heywood Trio, Young Buddy?"

"Nah."

"He's right," Jim said. "Sounds like folk."

"What, then?"

"I like Leo's." Helena gathered the wadded napkins off the table and went to throw them into the barrel near the door.

"Katie Faye's Band." Jim looked off toward the street and the Fremont Theater lights. "How's that?"

"They'll expect a lady singer, Jimmy."

"Good," Jim said. "They'll stick it out for the whole gig waiting for her to show up." He looked at Leo.

"Sure."

Helena sat back down and Ryder put his arm around her shoulders and pulled her in close. "Looks like we got our name."

38

Wednesday it rained, and Leo stayed in bed until almost noon, when Jim and Ryder walked into the house and Ryder said they were given the rest of the week off for good behavior so get the heck out of bed, we got rehearsing to do. Leo's legs, chest, and stomach muscles were sore, even his upper arms. While the two men made themselves tuna fish sandwiches in the kitchen, Leo put on cut-off shorts, sneakers, and a T-shirt and went running in the rain. He ran in the same direction as yesterday but now, instead of turning around at the bend in the river, he jogged on for another quarter mile, maybe half. When he started back he felt a cramp behind one of his right ribs and slowed his pace. The rain came down in a soft spray that felt good on his face and chest. An empty logging truck rattled past him, splashing his calves, and by the time he reached Saunders Hill Road his shirt and shorts were sticking wet against him.

Ryder and Jim sat at the kitchen table finishing their sandwiches, each with a section of the *Boston Globe* in front of him. Ryder looked up as Leo walked into the parlor. "What's your hurry? You'll be gettin' your fill of that soon enough."

Jim said something low that Leo couldn't hear. His push-ups hurt much more than yesterday, his sit-ups too, but he did five more of each. After his shower he drank a Coke, ate a slice of toast, then grabbed his harp harness and met Ryder and his father in the parlor for rehearsal. Jesus, he couldn't believe it, a *rehearsal.*

It was 4:00 on Thursday and Allie stood at the far end of the counter pouring half-full ketchup bottles into half-empty ones. Beatrice called this marrying. She wanted Allie to scrape the last of the ketchup from the empty bottles with a butter knife, but when Allie tried, the ketchup missed the hole and ran down the sides, so instead she would glance at Beatrice down near the register, make sure she wasn't looking, then drop the empty one into the trash. She was working on her fourth pair of bottles with three to go when one of Beatrice's girlfriends walked in from the sun shower outside. Yesterday had been awful, all clouds and rain, and today was only half better; the sky had cleared and the sun was out, but it still rained. A lot of people liked sun showers but those downpours always left Allie feeling so unfinished, in danger almost, like she was living on a planet that couldn't make up its mind.

Beatrice's friend was loud and pretty, but she looked cheap. She wore too much rouge, and one of those terrible wide headbands that held her beauty-parlor-dried hair a foot high on her head. She had a slim figure though, and she held a packet of orange papers. She gave one to Beatrice to read, but before Beatrice could adjust her glasses, the woman placed the rest of the papers in a neat pile next to the register. "Thanks a million, Bea! *Toodles.*"

An hour later Allie rang in a man's check for a hamburger and a glass of milk. She gave him his change, then picked up one of the flyers off the counter. In the middle of the page was a hand drawing of a guitar, and on either side of it was drawn an oversized harmonica with short straight lines shooting off it like magic rays.

KATIE FAYE'S BAND!!
REAL BLUES MUSIC AT THE THOMPSON GREEN GAZEBO
THIS FRIDAY NIGHT, 7:00
NO RAIN DATES

At the bottom right corner was a phone number to call for more information: Leo's.

Allie's hands shook as she folded the flyer into the front pocket of her UFO Show skirt and went to set up the booths for the dinner crowd. The diner slowly filled with people. The jukebox began playing nonstop. And gosh, who could the rest of his band *be?* Two more waitresses came on duty and the third showed up five minutes before the end of Allie's shift. At 8:00 Allie untied her apron and threw it in the canvas hamper out back. Sid stood at the smoking grill, sweating, working fast. Tuesday a doctor had told him his left ear drum was broken, and Allie had seen him take at least six aspirin today already. He didn't look up at her as she punched out. In fact, he hadn't talked to her once since he stepped in to help Monday afternoon.

She drove the flatbed down Paper Boulevard, through the covered bridge and onto the river road. The rain had stopped and the air blew by her open window cool as autumn. The sky was a glorious purple and yellow, and out over the mountains the sun had left a rim of light the color of blood. Allie thought again of Leo as she steered the flatbed up Spoon Hill and stepped on the gas. She kept seeing his face, the way it looked at Beatrice's Monday afternoon just after he hit Sid and just before he walked out; he was breathing hard, his curly hair had fallen down over his forehead, and his cheeks were spotted red in some places, pale in others. But it was his eyes that kept pulling her back: they were naked; everything was open from them to her. He had actually gone there with a ton of flowers to tell whoever was in the diner how she'd aborted their baby, but that face of his, so stunned and hurt and bewildered, it just didn't match what he'd done at all.

Her father was on the porch when she parked the truck. The darkening sky was gorgeous, sun shower day or not, and just before

295

she got to the porch a hundred starlings flew over the cabin and halfway down the hill, where they banked south and disappeared into the trees along the drive.

"*That's* what your mother should paint."

"What?"

"You in a *white* dress against *that* sunset with *those* birds."

Allie leaned down to kiss him. His forehead was wet with sweat, and in his lap was a dumbbell. "Does Mama know?"

"Took me two hours to talk her into getting the damn thing. How were tips?"

"Awful." Allie stepped over his leg cast and sat down beside him. She watched him push the small dumbbell over his head, lower it, then do it again nine more times. His glasses slid down his nose and he was breathing hard. She rested the orange flyer on his leg cast. Christopher had drawn long crayon lines from the hip of the cast to the foot, like a rainbow river. Chick unfolded the flyer. "Who is she?"

"Leo's mother. He named his band for her, I guess."

"His *band?*"

"And he's going on a tour with them."

Allie's mother stepped out onto the porch. "We saved you some watermelon."

"How do you feel about this, Allie?" her father said. "This tour thing, for how long?"

Allie shrugged, and as soon as she did, the skin of her chin trembled. She sat back and looked out over the hill and across the dark river at the national forest beyond Heywood. All the trees looked brown, purple, and maroon, the sky above them a shade of steel. In a few minutes her mother would turn on the porch light, which would attract flying bugs. Allie knew her father's eyes were on her and for the fiftieth time since he'd been home from the hospital she felt her belly and throat and face stiffen up with the words *pregnant— Boston—procedure—Leo.* Especially him. Oh, especially Leo.

"Is this woman's band supposed to be any good?" Allie's mother said.

"It's Leo's, hon. And tomorrow night you're gonna load me into your car and take me to it."

* * *

Thursday night, they'd called it a day an hour after midnight, and even though Leo didn't fall asleep for another hour after that, here he was at 6:00 Friday morning awake again, his lips feeling slightly numb. He could hear the birds down at the river and in the trees close to the house, and he thought of waking Ryder on the couch to ask about the lips, was it normal? But then he figured if a man played his harps for over almost two days straight, it probably was. He pulled on his shorts and sneakers, slipped on a T-shirt, and walked softly down the hall. Pink and tangerine light came through the parlor window. Ryder's cowboy boots were on the floor and Leo could hear his short sleeping breaths from the couch. The whole house smelled like Jim's Lucky Strikes.

Outside, Leo peed on the dew-wet pine needles near the house, then jogged up the road. This time at Paper Boulevard he went right towards downtown. He could see the red pumps of the Esso station up ahead, the raised wooden plank walks in front of the stores. The sun's light was just beginning to open from the east, spreading out over the town, and all along the road was a shifting layer of mist an inch or two high. Leo ran across the empty street for the Fremont and the Green. He glanced over at the gazebo, then ran faster into Beatrice's lot where he turned around and jogged back through town and past Saunders Hill. His right knee felt a little stiff, his back too. When he was a quarter-mile past the break in the trees he headed for home and sprinted the last hundred yards or so to his road. He pulled the rolled newspaper from the mailbox, bent over, and rested his hands and the paper on his knees. Part of one of the headlines was about twenty GIs getting killed. He straightened up and walked down the hill, still catching his wind. The mist had lifted and he could see the first of the sun on the river.

They spent the morning and the first part of the afternoon going over their show list, playing whatever numbers they were unsure of. Ryder wanted to give a two-hour performance but Jim talked him down to an hour-and-a-half performance with a ten-minute intermission halfway through. That would be roughly twenty-five songs, but they'd put thirty on the playsheet to be safe. Big Bill Broonzy was going to lead the list with his "Louise, Louise Blues." That was Jim's idea. It wasn't a real slow number, but not jumping fast either, and it could hold both harps so all of Katie Faye's Band could light right in at the start. From there they would swing into some Johnny Shines, Pinetop Perkins, and Champion Jack Dupree. Ryder suggested they bring it back down every three or four songs and Jim agreed. Leo said Jim should sing "Natchez Burning" the way he had the other night in front of Helena, that was something. So Jim started writing up a short list of downhearted tunes that they could fold into the show whenever it got too hot: some Homesick James, Honeyboy Edwards, Sleepy John Estes. He wrote down a lot of numbers Leo didn't know but Ryder said not to worry, backup on all of them was easy as spit.

At close to two, Helena called to say she'd talked Lars into signing out the bingo mikes and amplifiers from Frank down to the club. Baldy was going to meet everybody at the gazebo around 5:30, 6:00. A surge of heat swung through Leo's stomach and down his legs. He went into the kitchen and got a Coke from the fridge. Outside the screen door the day was sunlit, the sky above the pines blue. When he picked up the bottle opener his hand was shaking. The last time he felt close to this nervous was wrestling season last year, the day of semifinals against the Springfield Sprockets. The Woodies won the meet, and GP had taken his man down in seventeen seconds, but Leo ended up losing to a short weight lifter who smelled like mustard and milk. And it wasn't just the show; it was the army too, starting tomorrow, early.

In the parlor Jim and Ryder were talking about what to wear. Ryder said nothing fancy was his choice; work pants and a clean shirt. But Jim sat on his guitar stool shaking his head.

"This is new music for these people. We should look like gentlemen up there."

"Horseshit, Jimmy. Let the blues do the talking. What's Young Buddy want to wear?"

"Just my harps."

"That's it." Ryder laughed. "We'll wear our damn birthday suits."

"Were not celebrating a birthday," Jim said. "We're giving this one a sendoff, and I don't think a tie will kill you."

"Aw hell, *shame* me into it."

Jim looked at his watch and said they had a couple of hours till setup, did they want to do one more run-through of the show? Or else nap, shower, and get dressed?

"You forgot the third task, Jimmy." Ryder unbuckled his harp harness and set it on the floor. "Sittin' on johnny for the jitter poops."

Friday afternoons were always busy, but when the 6:00 girl punched in, Allie switched stations with her so she could keep working the corner booth with the window view of Thompson Green. Leo was out there under the gazebo with his father and thin harmonica teacher. A big bald man was walking backwards over the grass, uncoiling wire to a generator out behind the Fremont Theater. Beatrice's cheap-looking woman friend was taping blue crêpe paper and balloons on all six posts under the gazebo roof, and Leo and his father were pulling a huge speaker from the open trunk of a car parked up by the steps. Leo wore a white shirt, that striped tie from his suit, and dark pants. Allie was looking for the members of his band, but didn't see anyone else.

"Hello, Allison. May we sit?"

It was Nancy Titcomb, her face tanned, her lipstick red, her black hair sun-bleached to brown. Behind her stood AnnaMaria Slavitt and two tall blond boys, both tan. One of them wore a tank T-shirt, and spots of skin on his shoulders were peeled back to pink. AnnaMaria was chewing gum. She smiled and wrinkled her nose at Allie, who said hi back and stepped aside for them all to sit in the corner booth. She gave them each a menu and was about to turn and leave when Nancy smiled up at her. "Did you have a nice summer?"

"Of course."

"Oh, tell her who we saw yesterday." AnnaMaria had her arm around the peeling-backed boy.

"*Bobby Kennedy.* The entire summer in Hyannis we didn't see *one,* and then on our last day—*Bobby.*"

Allie left them for a few minutes. She rang in two checks at the register, then helped Beatrice stack clean plates from the kitchen. She was surprised Tittiecomb knew her name at all and she remembered Nancy's nauseatingly cheerful speech in the Woodies stadium in June. From behind the counter, Allie looked back out the window at the green. Leo's harmonica teacher stood under the gazebo adjusting three silver microphones on their stands. He also wore a tie, one of those bolo things cowboys wear, and she wanted to be out there too, helping Leo get ready. In the shade near the fence a couple of families had laid out a picnic on blankets. Allie went back to the corner booth. Titcomb and Slavitt would only order onion rings if the boys did, so the boys did and the one next to Nancy said to put his in his cheeseburger. AnnaMaria thought this was so amusing she had to take her gum out of her mouth to finish her laugh.

The big surprise was, people were showing up. Leo tried not to look out at them. He got on his hands and knees and helped Ryder tape the microphone wires to the gazebo floor, but he heard them, heard their lawn chairs unfolding, their blankets snapping in the air on their way to the grass, their kids running around between the trees laughing. Leo's tie hung to the floor in front of him and he had to keep swatting it out of the way so he could lay tape over the wire.

"Stay cool, Young Buddy."

"How can you stand it?"

"It all goes away once you get inside the music. Believe me, she'll protect you."

Helena and Jim were hanging a banner Helena had made out of half a sheet. In blue magic marker she'd written: KATIE FAYE'S BAND!!! Jim stood on the gazebo railing putting thumbtacks through the linen into the post. He hadn't put on his stringed tie yet, and the late afternoon sun shone through the banner in front of him. The taping was finished. Ryder set Jim's guitar stool in front of the center microphone, then Jim climbed down and told Helena to count into each mike once he and Ryder got to the rail fence at the edge of Beatrice's lot. Leo didn't think Helena looked a bit nervous. She wore blue jeans, those white sandals, and a pink sleeveless blouse. She cleared her throat into the first microphone and smiled at anyone watching. And that was quite a few people. There were a good dozen or so families spread out on the lawn between the trees, and now most all of their faces looked up from their picnic suppers to the gazebo and Helena's high counting voice. Leo felt like squatting to the floor behind the railing, pretend he was checking wires again or something, but instead he rested his hands on his hips and made himself stand straight and not move. He kept his attention on his father and Ryder, and when they started back for the gazebo, he looked over at Beatrice's windows. The last of the sun was on them though, and he couldn't see inside. He knew Allie was working. He wondered if she'd be able to hear them.

Then he saw Chick Donovan in the parking lot. His wife was pushing him in his wheelchair, headed for the entrance to Thompson Green, and little Christopher sat in his lap, his sneakers resting on Chick's leg cast. Mrs. Donovan wore a straw sun hat whose brim bobbed slightly as she pushed the chair onto the grass. Chick waved his good arm. Leo wanted to wave back but Jim and Ryder showed up at the base of the steps, so he looked away from Chick and down at them.

"You still want to introduce us, my lovely?"

Helena said of course she did. "I think I like show business, skinny."

Jim looked at his watch. "Give us till ten past. Let's go, son."

The three of them walked back to the car parked behind the Fremont Theater. The generator was humming at a steady pitch. Lars had set it up on a short two-by-eight over two cinderblocks. He was sitting in a lawn chair next to it sipping a Narragansett and on his bald head was a Heywood Paper Products cap, its cloth visor shading his eyes. Ryder faked a bootkick at Lars' knee, and Lars yelled something back, but Leo couldn't hear over the engine. He followed Jim to the Valiant.

"Will we have water?" Leo's tongue clicked dry against the roof of his mouth. He reached into the back seat for his harp harness and it was warm in his hands, the metal of the harmonicas probably even warmer. Jim squatted at the sideview mirror to knot his string tie. "You can have some iced coffee. Scared yet?"

"No more'n us, Jimmy." Ryder already had his harness on around his waist. Leo was glad his strapped on like a bandolero. It would feel better stepping out in front of the picnic crowd with his chest covered like that. Ryder blew air through all his harps one at a time, checking for any dead notes. Leo did the same. Jim slipped the Mexican guitar strap over his head and started retuning his Dobro. He buckled a capo around the second fret and did a Missouri pick, sliding his finger thimble up and down the neck. Leo couldn't hear his harps too well with Lars's generator going, so he walked away from the car and the men. He kept all of his C's in the bottom sheaths, then his B-flat, D, G, and A. The B-flat had a dull lisp in its mi note, and Leo tapped the harp on the palm of his hand, but the bad note was still there. He probably wouldn't use that key tonight anyway, but it left him feeling a little undressed, not quite ready.

The sun was an hour from the tops of the Berkshires, and the only shade was in the Green where all the people were. Leo figured they thought Helena was Katie Faye, the ones who didn't know Helena anyway. And there were probably two or three who knew Jim and had maybe even known Leo's mother. From behind the Fremont, Leo did recognize a lot of the grownup faces, and there was a small group of kids from the high school sitting under a tree close to the gazebo. One of them was Billy Burrell. He was usually quiet like his old man, but now he was laughing very loud with a kid wearing glasses and a light blue suit jacket. Trying to be like college boys already, Leo thought, and he hoped Burrell would come up to him later so he could tell him he wouldn't be back in Jewett's class this fall either, he was gone too, off to bigger things, off to Paris with the U.S. Army. Then somebody touched Leo's shoulder and he jumped back half a foot.

"Shit man, you scared me." Ryder was wearing the dirty white Stetson cowboy hat he only wore two or three times a year, winter mainly. "Your daddy wants a powwow 'fore we go on."

Jim was at the hood of the car pouring iced coffee from a red thermos into two paper cups. At the generator stood Officer Petrucci. He had his hands behind his back and smiled at something Lars was saying. He looked over at Leo and nodded.

Ryder popped open one of Lars's Narragansetts but he waited until Jim handed Leo his iced coffee.

"To a good show," Ryder said.

Jim looked at Leo, then down at his own hand. "And a quick tour of duty."

The three of them drank just as Helena's girlish flirting voice echoed "Hi, everyone" over the speakers and off the trees. Jim cleared his throat, swung his guitar around under his left arm, and started walking. Leo and Ryder followed right behind. Leo looked down at the back of his father's legs and shoes in front of him, but with his heart going so fast that left him a little dizzy, so he looked up at the treetops just as Helena's amplified voice said how proud she was to present, "the boys, of Katie Faye's Band!"

There was some clapping as the three of them stepped up into the gazebo and it had ended before Jim sat on his stool and adjusted the microphone. Leo stood to Jim's left, closest to the steps. His mike seemed a couple of inches low, but he didn't trust his fingers to stay still long enough to loosen the wingnut and pull the mike higher. Jim was tightening his E string and Ryder already had his C harp in his hand. He nodded at Leo to grab his own G and Leo did just as Jim tapped his shoe three times and started in slow and controlled with Broonzy's "Louise, Louise Blues." Ryder drew out a low and sweet backbeat to the intro, and when Jim started singing, Leo raised the G harp to his lips, cupped it tightly, shut his eyes, and began blowing a low sister echo to Ryder's harmonica. He heard his own sound leaving the speakers in front of him. His face was hot and he could feel all those people out there. He kept his eyes squeezed shut.

Jim's voice sounded a little high and dry-mouthed but he was really taking his time with the picking. And Ryder's harp never sounded more pure. Jim cut it all fairly short and launched right in without a break to "Sittin' on Top of the World." Leo had to open his eyes to put away his G harp for another, and when he did, he saw GP's father bent on one knee on his picnic blanket between Betty and Ruth; he had his box camera raised, ready to take a picture. Leo pulled his newest C from its sheath and joined in with Ryder, the two of them honing in on the same riff. He kept his eyes opened this time and he turned a little to the side so he could see Ryder's face under his hat. Jim finished singing the intro and pulled back for the harps. Ryder took the lead, flying off into the trees with some throat pops he butterflied into a wailing tremolo that sounded so good, so deep in Blues River, Leo let his own bass chord fan speed out of time, but he caught himself and slowed it back down just as Jim glanced over at him, winked, then picked up the singing again.

The third number came in on the tail of the second and it was an even faster Chicago blues tune. Halfway through it Jim let up for the harps, but Ryder kept playing the backbeat, standing there, eyeing Leo over his harmonica. Leo waited a half-count for the cue, emptied his lungs, then he sucked in his best single-note wail that he hung right in on top of Jim's chords. He closed his eyes and did it again, bringing the note to a sharp point he scattered all over with a cup-handed tremolo. Ryder cued him down for the backbeat and when Jim's singing voice came over the speakers, Leo heard clapping. He wiped sweat off his forehead and looked out over the gazebo railing; the crowd had grown. It was at least the size of the one for the Ladies Auxiliary League. In Beatrice's lot people were stopping to lean against their cars and listen, and some were walking over to join the others on the grass who had stopped chatting now and had their faces pointed up at the gazebo. Chick's wife had found a place for him close to the rail fence under an elm tree. She sat on the ground next to his wheelchair, and both of them were bobbing their heads in time.

Jim finished singing his last refrain and Leo raised his harp to his lips and gave Ryder a bass chord backup for the exit, but Jim and Ryder ended on the exact same note, which left Leo's a hole higher than he'd planned. Ryder winked over at him and smiled, but still, Leo's face felt hot all over again. Jim paused to pull the capo off his guitar neck, then he leaned forward and said into the mike, "Good evening."

Someone yelled out, "Hi, Jim!"

Leo watched his father so he wouldn't have to see the crowd. Jim looked so calm and relaxed on his stool, and he took his time as he retightened his E string.

"To my right, on lead harmonica, is Ryder Stillwell."

There was a fair amount of clapping. Leo heard someone whistle, Helena probably. His mouth was suddenly so dry he couldn't work up any spit. He squatted for his cup of iced coffee and drank it all down.

"And on backup, my boy, Leo Suther."

The applause was scattered and polite and it stopped as soon as Jim started talking again. "Leo's shipping out to Fort Dix tomorrow morning. This is kind of a send-off."

Now the clapping was loud and it came from all over the green. It kept up while Leo's father said, "I'm Jim," and it stopped as soon as he began playing the first sliding notes of "Natchez Burning." Leo didn't know what to do; this was Jim's solo number, no harps at all, and while Ryder was tapping the flat of his harmonica in time on the palm of his hand, Leo couldn't just stand there, not after his father flew the news about the army, not with—of all people—Chick Donovan sitting in the audience. But no way could he walk off the gazebo till the next number either, so he turned his attention to the music and the music only. He watched his father pick and sing, his mustache looking so thick, his head so big. Jim's eyes were closed, his face tilted up towards the trees, and if his voice had sounded true to the words earlier this week in front of Helena, it was three times that now; Jim was singing the part about his baby lying on the ground, and his voice was high with no gravel in it at all. His thick finger was thimble-sliding smoothly, there was sweat on his creased forehead, but his voice sounded as pure and naked to Leo as a child's.

At the finale, Jim let the end notes strum off his fingers like someone's last breath, and the audience started in clapping before the final note had finished ringing through the mike. Leo glanced out there and saw straight into Chick's face. Chick was pushing his glasses up the bridge of his nose with one finger, and of course, he wasn't able to clap at all.

305

39

At five minutes to eight, Allie untied her apron and punched out as fast as she could, leaving Titcomb and her friends to order from her relief. Outside, the lot was full of cars and pickups, a few motorcycles. The sky had a rosy light left in it and Beatrice had just switched on her neon sign. Two men at a picnic table said "Oh, man" and "Sweet thing" to Allie as she walked by in her white UFO dress, but she had her eyes on Leo and his band, who were returning to the gazebo from their intermission. They'd spent it back at the generator with the bald man, and she knew where she'd seen him before too; he was one of the poker men who had made everybody laugh, Leo most of all, on Leo's birthday night. His band. Gosh. She watched as Leo followed his father back up under the gazebo. His shirt was too baggy in the waist and his tacky striped tie got lost under that wide leather contraption he kept his harmonicas in. He pulled his microphone closer to his face, then Jim said a few words into his own mike about what a good audience everyone was and he began playing a fast song with no singing, just his instrument and Leo's and Ryder's too.

Allie walked up behind her family. Christopher was asleep on her dad's chest. She put her hands on her father's shoulders, leaned over, and kissed the top of his head. Her mother smiled up at her, and her hat started to slip off, but Allie caught it. Her father reached up with his good hand and squeezed Allie's at his shoulder. He held her fingers tightly in his and didn't let go until the song was over and Leo's dad started singing another one.

Allie sat on the blanket next to her mother and listened. They sounded wonderful, the three of them up there. Especially when Leo and Ryder played to each other over Jim's guitar. And his dad was so handsome. There weren't many mustaches in Heywood. His made the rest of him seem darker, like a Spaniard. And it was hard to hear him sing without moving a little in time. After a few more songs, Leo played a harmonica solo. He was going on for a good two or three minutes and it seemed he didn't make any mistakes. Allie's mother touched her knee: "Did you hear what Leo's father said about Leo?"

Allie shook her head.

"He's joined the army. He's leaving tomorrow."

Allie's father was looking at her now, from his chair, in his casts. Allie looked back at the gazebo, at Leo fanning his hand so fast against his harmonica, his eyes closed, his chin almost touching his chest, his legs bent slightly at the knees as he leaned back and hurled that sound out over the Green and onto them all like handfuls of fine gravel.

Leo's lips felt waxy just from the final number, Mance Lipscomb's in G, which they'd dragged out to twice its normal length. Ryder and Jim really gave it their all too, trading notes off each other like only on their best nights back home. Helena was the first to come up to them after the show. She walked right up to Ryder and gave him a hug and a kiss. Jim thanked everyone for coming, and the crowd clapped almost a full half-minute. They were all still out there, some of them standing to go, others lying back on their blankets talking again. Right away Leo squatted and started pulling tape off the mike wires; it wasn't the crowd he minded so much now—Ryder was right, once you got into the music everything was fine—it was the Donovans under that tree near the white rail fence. Chick was staring at him and Allie wasn't looking his way at all, was, in fact, walking back through Beatrice's parking lot holding her little brother's hand. During the harp solo, Leo had opened his eyes only once and they started to burn from the sweat coming off his forehead. His father and Ryder were giving him a complete chord backup and Leo knew he had the reeds honed in on a dime, but before he closed his eyes again he saw Allie watching him, sitting perfectly still on the ground in her white uniform dress next to her mother. Allie's hair was down and even though she was blonde she put Leo in mind of an Indian, and that's what he pictured as he closed his eyes and played out the rest of the riff: tipis and wild horses; prairies, woods, and rivers; shirtless braves and warrior girls like Allie; black-haired babies wrapped in buffalo and rabbit skins; Allie crying in the rain gulley behind Spoon Hill, a long strand of hair stuck to her wet cheeks, looking at him with the same eyes that watched him play to the whole damn town right now.

"Terrific job, fellas. Real different." Gerry's father came up to the gazebo steps, his box camera hanging around his neck. He wore baggy plaid shorts, black socks, and scuffed loafers. He shook Leo's hand, then Jim's and Ryder's as they walked by carrying their microphone stands back to the car. Leo ripped the last of the tape from the wires.

"Congratulations."

"Thanks, Mr. P. I only started playing this summer."

"Why sure, but I meant your enlistment. I'm going to dash off a memo to Stick tonight." He shook his head and smiled. "You and Ger on rival teams, boy he'll get a charge out of that. Well listen, good luck in basic. Come see us before you get stationed and we'll have you and your dad over for dinner."

Leo watched Mr. Poitras walk back to Betty and Ruth, who were standing waiting with their basket and folded blanket. Betty smiled hard at Leo and waved. Ruth looked like she was going to but she didn't. Her face had gotten longer this summer, her hair too.

Leo stepped off the gazebo and was feeding the wire coil back between two railing spindles when three motorcycles roared out of Beatrice's lot. He saw Billy Burrell near the fence talking to Chick and his wife. Chick was smiling and nodding his head, listening. Burrell's friend stood off to the side in his light blue jacket, his hands crossed in front of him. Chick offered Billy his good hand and Billy shook it.

The sky was purple and the lot was full of crisscrossing headlights as half a dozen cars pulled away and out onto Paper Boulevard. Chick's flatbed drove around behind Beatrice's and pulled up to Chick and Mrs. Donovan. Christopher poked his head out the passenger window laughing. He opened and shut his hand down at Chick who reached up and tried to touch it. Allie said something to her mother, then she put the truck in gear and drove off past the green for the bridge. Leo watched her go and he felt silly standing there in his harp harness.

"That was a solid show." Jim walked by and got his guitar stool from the gazebo. Leo looked away from the road. He began coiling the wire again, walking back toward the cars.

"Ryder's gal wants to celebrate back at the house, but I told her that's up to you; you're the one with the early reveille."

Leo said it was okay with him, and his father stopped to talk with a big man and woman, both in coveralls. The street lamps on Paper Boulevard were on, so were the lights of the Fremont Theater. Lars was loading the generator into the trunk of his car, and Ryder and Helena were kissing against the Valiant. Ryder was leaning back with his boots crossed, his hat low, his fingers interlocked together at Helena's waist. They were both giggling about something. Leo could smell popcorn, and the gas from the generator. He hadn't expected Chick and his wife to just go off like that. He thought for sure Chick would wheel up to him and say something about the show, or at least the army, even though Leo knew it wouldn't be good.

"Let's go, *Einstein.*"

"Don't call me that, Lars."

"Ooo, touchy." Lars widened his eyes at Ryder and Helena. "Must be all those autographs he had to sign. Right, Einstein?" Lars reached for the coil of wire but Leo jerked it out of his hand and whipped it down at his feet. Lars stood there a half-second, the wire uncoiling on the ground, then he charged at Leo but Ryder jumped in and wedged his shoulder up against Lars's chest.

"Ease it down, buddy. C'mon, ease it."

"That little *dog*shit."

Leo stood there, his hands in loose fists. Lars's eyes were pooled up from drinking and he wasn't taking them off Leo, but he wasn't pushing much against Ryder anymore either. Then his smooth face broke open into a drunk grin, and he stepped away and belched.

Ryder's hat was pushed way back on his head. He looked at Leo and rolled his eyes in the car's direction.

"I'll walk." Leo unbuckled his harp bandolero, rolled it up, and walked around to the front of the theater. Ahead of him was the long row of streetlights lit all the way down Paper Boulevard, not a single one broken, and after the stores and Esso station, the woods looked thick and dark on both sides of the road. A few cars rolled by, and Leo felt like he was seeing it for the first time, Paper Boulevard at night; it was so straight and dry and well lit, so safe from the wild on both sides of it, but even with a car or two going down it, it felt empty, only half used, if that, and it hit him that these same lights would probably still be on when somebody from the army came for him in the morning. He wished he could go there instead, just leave tonight and walk right down this street that's lit up way more than it has to be. He'd foot it all the way to Springfield and he wasn't sure if he would even have a harp with him; he felt like hiding all the ones he carried now. When a station wagon or truck passed by he didn't turn his face to it, and he held his harness tight under his left arm like it was nobody's business.

Tonight, he'd played everything he knew. He didn't have a note left in him; he'd emptied himself out in public and he almost felt ashamed, like he'd confessed things about himself nobody had asked to hear. Leo heard the tap of a car horn and he looked over and saw his father driving back towards Saunders Hill. Ryder and Helena probably had to bring Lars and his equipment to the club. Leo didn't feel right about having thrown the mike wire like he did; Lars never called anybody by their real name. Jim slowed the car and pointed his finger over the steering wheel towards home. Leo nodded and waved and watched the Valiant pull away.

40

Jim was in his bedroom changing clothes, the door open, when Leo walked into his own room and dropped the harp bandolero on the bed. He switched on the lamp on the night table and took off his tie. His room seemed small for some reason. Big Bill Broonzy too. He heard crickets outside the window.

"Your old boss just called." Jim stood in the doorway tucking his T-shirt into baggy work pants. He still had on his black dress socks though, and at first Leo thought he meant Tom Burrell, then he saw his father's face.

"He doesn't know what happened between you and Allison, does he?"

Leo shook his head. "What'd he want?"

"Invited us up for watermelon." Jim walked in. "It's okay by me if you want to go up there."

Leo sat down at the edge of the bed. Jim was looking at the window though Leo knew he couldn't see anything but dark glass. On the bureau a few inches from Jim's head was Katie Faye's box. Above that was Big Bill Broonzy's face.

"You sounded good tonight, Pop."

"You too."

"I screwed up a couple of times."

"But you caught yourself; that's what pros do." Jim was looking at the wall above Leo's pillow. Leo took off his too-tight shoes.

"What are you going to pack?"

Leo wasn't thinking about tomorrow; he was thinking of what to wear up to the Donovans' right now, and he wasn't sure if his father had just said he was going up there too, or not.

"You won't need more than one change of clothes." Jim took a pair of underwear and socks from the bureau, then he pulled out Leo's best pair of jeans. They were broken in at the hips and knees and the hems went all the way down Leo's ankles, even with his work boots on. "I'll pack the ones underneath those." Leo took the pants from his father, then went into the bathroom, undressed, and took a shower. He turned the water as hot as he could stand it, then cold. He towel-dried his hair and combed it straight back to dry that way. He hadn't heard them pull up but he could hear Helena laughing out in the kitchen, Ryder too.

In his room, on the floor beneath the window, was a white Heywood Paper Products bag, neatly folded and creased. Next to it was his father's worn black leather shaving kit. Leo tried on three button-down shirts from the closet and finally decided to wear a green- and white-striped short-sleeved one. He tied on his work boots, combed his wet hair once more, and walked out into the kitchen.

Helena was sitting on Ryder's lap in the chair by the door. She wore his Stetson tilted way back on her head. In her blouse and jeans, she looked about twenty years old. Then Leo saw another woman. She had straight black hair and sat at the other end of the table. She smiled up at him with her lips pressed together and he could see she had a little bit of an overbite. Helena hopped off Ryder's skinny legs, grabbed Leo's hand, and led him to the woman. "Leo Suther, I would like you to meet Mary Anne Walker. She's a superb seamstress. Mary Anne, this is Jim's son Leo, and you should hear him play that harmonica."

"Young Buddy's a bluesman." Ryder was at the fridge pulling out beaded cans of Pabst. Leo shook the woman's small hand and told her it was good to meet her. Her lipstick was pink with some white in it and she'd painted both her top and bottom eyelashes very black.

"Here you go, man." Ryder handed Leo a cold can of beer.

"I was just going out."

"By God, you'd better have one with me before you go."

Leo leaned back against the sink and drank from his beer while Ryder filled in Mary Anne on the fact that Young Buddy here's joined up so he can go to Europe on Uncle Sam.

"But gosh, skinny," Helena said. "What about that darn war?"

Lightnin' Hopkins started singing off the record player in the parlor and Jim walked in. Leo noticed he'd changed back into his dress pants, and he wore a dark blue short-sleeved shirt. The colors didn't quite go together and it reminded Leo of the Woodies' black and blue wrestling uniforms. Ryder handed Jim a Pabst.

"Well, fellas," Helena said. "To a great success."

"Damn straight."

Everybody drank, including Mary Anne, who sipped from her beer real slow, careful not to smudge any of that baby pink lipstick. Leo glanced at his father, who was looking down at the floor as if something very important was just said or was about to be. Leo rested his half empty can in the sink. "I won't be long."

"Better not," Ryder said. "'Cause I'm not leaving till I get a good-bye kiss."

Helena slapped Ryder with his hat and said he got enough kisses as it was. On his way out, Leo glanced at Mary Anne. She was smiling at Jim, still not showing any teeth.

Leo stopped the Valiant in front of the Hungry Pioneer Inn. He left the engine going and ran across the street to buy a package of Junior

———

Mints at the Fremont concession counter; he didn't want to smell like beer, but he didn't want to smell too much like mints either, so back in the car he drove up to the job site to give his mouth a few minutes to air out to halfway normal. He left the headlights on, aimed at the locked barn, and got out of the car. The air was warm and smelled like sunbaked grass. There was a quarter-moon, and the field down the slope stood out dim in the dark. He looked up at his roofing job. The shingles were too black to make out but he was sure Floyd was right, that his ridge line was way off. He wondered who would end up fixing it. He got back into the car and as he started it up he thought how this was the last place where he and Allie had made love; he remembered the way she swung her bare leg around him and pulled him into her like there was no time to lose. He backed out of the drive and drove down the hill past the poplar trees, the leaves looking so small and round in the peripheral path of the headlights, and he hoped Allie would be home, though he had no idea what he would say to her at all.

Mrs. Donovan's hair was pulled back in a braid and she smiled as soon as she opened the screen. She stepped to the side for him to come in and as he did, she said quietly how nice it was to see him and wasn't your father able to come?

"No, Mrs. Donovan. He has guests over."

"Her name's *Tess,* man. *Jesus.*"

"Please, hon. I just put Chris to bed."

Chick sat in his wheelchair at the end of the picnic table, his leg cast resting on the corner of a bench. Allie's door was open. Leo smelled fried fish and Crisco. He waved at Chick, walked over, and shook his outstretched hand. Chick's nose was sunburned, his glasses were pushed down the end of it, and his watery eyes looked straight up at Leo over the rim. Chick squeezed hard and held on a couple seconds, then he let go and pointed to the bench his foot was propped on. "Sit."

Leo sat down. On the table was a bottle of Old Crow next to an uncut watermelon. In front of Chick was an empty glass jigger. Mrs. Donovan walked into Allie's room and shut the door behind her.

"Thanks for coming to the show."

———

313

Chick poured whiskey into the shot glass and pushed it over the table to Leo.

"No thanks."

"Drink half."

Allie's door opened and Mrs. Donovan walked to the table, where she began slicing up the watermelon. Leo raised the glass and sipped off the top half of the Old Crow. It numbed his tongue and the back of his throat and he was relieved watermelon was coming. He could feel Allie's open doorway to his right. He tried not to look.

"You three sounded wonderful," Mrs. Donovan said.

"I especially liked your father's singing. I've never said this about a man before, but he has a sweet voice, doesn't he? That's what I told Tess."

Mrs. Donovan slid a slice of watermelon onto a plate and set it in front of Leo. She told him to help himself and he did. It was red-ripe and cold from the fridge. A rivulet of juice ran off his chin and onto his plate.

"Here's to your harmonica playing, Leo. I wish to hell I'd heard more of it this summer." Chick drank down the remaining half-shot. He set down the empty jigger and looked at it as intently as if it were singing him an old song. His hair had grown longer in the back and he was two days short of a shave. Leo ate his watermelon slowly. He watched Mrs. Donovan's knife work itself through the rind. Then Chick yelled Allie's name and Leo jerked on the bench.

Mrs. Donovan set Chick's plate down with both hands. "*You* can sing Chris back to sleep, *not* me." She walked behind Leo, past the hospital bed, and up the stairs. Allie came out of her room. She had changed into her tight bell-bottom blue jeans and a white T-shirt that had green and yellow crayon marks on one shoulder. Her hair hung loose and she had some kind of dark makeup on her upper eyelashes. She said hi in her waitress voice from Beatrice's, all business and forced smile, but she looked wonderful.

"Sit down, Allie Cat. Next to Leo."

Allie walked behind Leo, then sat beside him on the bench. He wanted to look at her, but he didn't want to turn his head, so he glanced as far as her crossed legs, not more than half a foot from his.

Chick told her to take a slice of melon but Allie said no thank you, she didn't want any. Her voice was still polite, even with her father, and it seemed to Leo she sounded almost scared. Chick hadn't touched his watermelon. Allie was bouncing the calf of her top leg against her knee under the table, and it made the bench rock a little. Leo wiped his face with the back of his arm.

"Some might say it's none of my business, Leo, but why in hell did you do it?"

Now Leo looked at Allie, but she was staring in the direction of the far kitchen wall, her foot going faster under the table. "I didn't want to do it. Allie really did what she wanted, I guess."

"Allie?" Chick looked at her, then back at Leo. "You're the one who enlisted."

Leo's face began what felt like a slow slide off his skull. Chick was looking at Allie now, who just took a slice of watermelon and started chewing.

"Sorry," Leo said. "Just kidding. I was trying to make a stupid joke. I'm pretty tired from the show, I guess."

"You sounded good," Allie said through her watermelon.

"Thanks."

Chick was quiet a second or two, and Leo couldn't look at him.

"I don't think it's anything to joke about, Leo. I don't. What does your father think about you going in?"

"I'm not sure."

"He's *for* this war?"

Leo swallowed. "I don't think so. Anyway, I'm not going to that war."

"Are you going into the U.S. Army tomorrow, Leo?"

"Yes."

"Then you are going to that goddamned war. Jesus." Chick started to pour more Old Crow into the jigger, then stopped. "Please answer my question."

A fly buzzed against the windowpane in the kitchen. The light was bright in there and the sink was full of dishes. Leo could hear the floorboards creaking upstairs. "It's personal, Chick. No offense."

Chick looked at him a second longer, then he poured. "So's death,

315

Leo. And for *whom?* For *what?*" He drank down the shot, then pulled his leg from the bench and wheeled towards the hospital bed on the knit rug. "I have to rest my damn back."

Allie got up and went to help him. She put her hand under the pit of his broken arm, the other across his back, then they both counted to three and Chick stood on his good leg and hopped two steps to the bed, where Allie helped him turn around and sit on the mattress. The heel of his long leg cast barely touched the floor. Chick's glasses had slid to the tip of his nose. He pushed them back up with his free hand. "It's not too late. You can take my truck and drive to Quebec tonight. Get him the keys, Allie."

"No. Thank you, Chick, but I'm going to Europe. They're sending me to Germany."

"You think so, do you?"

Leo wanted to say France, that it was France he was heading for, on the weekends, Paris actually, but Chick's lips were in a tight line and he was shaking his head; it was how he used to look talking with Floyd, and Leo didn't like having that face pointed at him. He stepped away from the bench and pushed it gently under the table. "Thank you for the watermelon."

"Wait." Chick scooted back. Allie held his cast at the calf and as he turned to face the fireplace, she swung his leg up onto the mattress. Chick looked at Allie, then at Leo. A bar of light reflected off his glasses from the kitchen. "You two go for a drive or something, Jesus. And take the keys, Leo. I'm serious. Give him the keys, Allie."

While Allie got them from the kitchen counter, Leo went to the bed and shook Chick's good hand. Chick pulled him down and half-hugged him with his arm cast, then he let go just as quick. He lay back on the pillows and pointed at the portrait of the bearded man above the mantel. "I have to explain myself to him now. Can't even keep you from signing on."

Leo wanted to say more, that he wasn't signing on, but he couldn't open his mouth to do it. Allie handed him the keys, then brushed by him to kiss her father.

"Get him pointed north, damn it."

"Say good-bye to Mrs. Donovan for me, Chick."

316

"Tess; when you write from Montreal I want to see 'Chick and Tess' on the envelope. You can send Allie's separately. Now hit the road."

Leo drove the flatbed slowly over the river road. One of the headlights was out of center and pointed up and off at the trees. Allie sat over on the passenger side. She had her elbow propped out the truck window, her cheek resting against her fingers, and she hadn't said a word since they stepped off the porch and both got into the truck as smooth and regular as if they were off to buy groceries. And then all she had said was, "You can drive." Her voice wasn't polite anymore; it sounded tired, let down, as if she'd just asked fifteen questions in a row and not one of them had been answered.

Leo drove by the fork of the job site and kept the flatbed going along the river. He could smell the mud by its bank and he thought again of the day he and Allie had made love all afternoon in his room. He felt the blood begin to fill his penis, and he wanted to reach over and touch Allie's blue-jeaned leg, but not to start anything really, not that.

"So I did what I wanted, huh?"

"Didn't you?"

"Don't you dare lecture me; I can't believe you're going to that war. That's some *band*, Leo. That's some *tour*. God."

Leo slowed the truck and guided it over the dry rain ruts in the gravel. The headlight path dipped and jerked as they went and he was gripping the steering wheel pretty hard; he didn't want the conversation to go this way. He would give her an inch or two more rope and that was it, but he didn't want to yell. These days he'd been feeling more hurt than mad, and if they were going to talk about anything, why not talk about that? He wanted to tell her about Paris and Katie Faye, that he had no intention of going down to Asia to fight anyone, but he couldn't open his mouth to speak because he also knew that if the army did fly him down to that war, he wouldn't run away from it either. And Allie was smart; she'd hear that part of him in his voice too, no matter what he said about his mother's plans.

"Thank you for not telling him, though." She was sitting up

straight now, looking at him, though he couldn't make out her face. He wanted to get to a good place to stop the truck, but the river road went on narrow like this for miles so he stepped on the brake, pulled the gearshift into neutral, and turned off the engine. He left the headlights on, and moths and mosquitoes flew in half-circles in the beams, ticking at the glass. They were both quiet. Leo took a breath and spoke up.

"I'm sorry about what I said at Beatrice's. It just came out, Allie. I didn't mean to hurt your feelings."

Now Allie took a breath. In the dim light of the cab, she looked like she might cry.

"Why did you do it, Leo? Boys like Gerry Poitras do what you're doing. You sounded *good* tonight, you should be out in California playing your harmonicas in the sunshine. I mean, God, this is the Summer of Love, Leo. *Free* love, not war." Allie sat still a moment, looking straight ahead. Then it seemed there wasn't enough air in the cab for her and she gently opened the door and got out of the truck.

Leo looked out the rearview mirror. He couldn't see anything but night. He stepped on the brake and there she was in the red glow of the taillights, standing bell-bottomed and barefoot, her arms crossed like she was cold. Her hair looked like marmalade, her T-shirt like blood. He opened his door, walked to the back, and leaned up against the flatbed. He could barely see her in the dark, just the white smudge of her shirt.

"Why are you so mad at me, Allie? I'm not mad at you."

He heard her step closer. A small rock rolled out from under one of her feet. She stopped. "I don't like being blamed."

Something small jumped in the water downriver from the bank and Leo wanted to say he didn't blame her, but he knew that wasn't all true and he didn't want her to catch the lie in his voice.

"You do blame me, don't you?"

"Allie—I miss you."

They were both quiet. She didn't move from where she stood, and Leo felt like he was in a bus or train with someone he hadn't met

---

and probably never would. He heard her walk fast back to the truck. She climbed in and pulled the door shut.

He got into the cab, started the engine, and asked her if she wanted to go home.

"You're not going to Canada, obviously." Allie let out a short breath. "No. I don't want to go home."

He had to do a nine-point turn to get them headed back for Spoon Hill. They were both quiet, and he drove even slower than before, so slow he had to use the brake in first gear. The air was warm and he could smell the heat of the engine. He wanted to tell her that he was going to Paris before he did anything else, that, honey, he *saw* it, saw himself on a train dressed in a soldier's uniform, his harmonicas rolled up in their harness in his lap, that Eiffel Tower coming into view out the window in a late Friday sundown. But the picture in his head wouldn't come out his mouth, almost as if telling it would risk killing it, killing it like everything else.

They rode into the clearing of Spoon Hill and Leo could see the lights of town across the river near the bridge. Allie had her legs crossed, bouncing the top leg against the bottom. He kept driving down the road, then through the covered bridge across the river. He didn't know where they were going or what they were going to do once they got there. A pack of cars was parked out in front of Beatrice's. The U of her neon sign looked like an L and he wanted to say something funny to Allie about it, but he knew his voice would come out as wrong as could be. He turned left and drove through Heywood past the stores and Esso station. It was a Friday night, not ten yet, but Paper Boulevard was an empty over-lit straightaway in front of them. "Want to drive to Texas?"

"Go down your hill, Leo."

"No, my father's got friends over."

"Just for a second. We won't go inside."

Leo slowed the flatbed, shut off the headlights, then turned down Saunders Hill Road. A little over halfway down she told him to stop, and she got out of the truck and went into the woods that were partly lit from the light of the house. He watched the back of her white

T-shirt until she squatted in the trees. He could hear Jim and Ryder playing something soft out in the parlor, a Broonzy number in half-time. He wondered what Allie would wipe herself with, and he kept his attention on the house through the branches. Helena walked into the kitchen and opened the fridge to get three cans of beer. Allie slid back into the truck and pulled the door shut. "Found it."

"What?"

"Let's go."

"Want to go down to the river?"

Allie didn't say anything so he put the truck in neutral and didn't start it up, just let it begin rolling down over dirt, past the house, and into the almost complete blackness of where the road met water. He could see the stars over the treetops. He flashed on the headlights and saw the muddy river water moving slow and indifferent six or eight feet in front of them. He pulled up the handbrake just as Allie dropped something into his lap.

"I suppose it can be a good-bye present now."

The light was dim in the cab from the headlights shining off ahead of them, but Leo knew what it was just by holding it. The wrapping paper had dry welts in it from having gotten wet, and when he tore it off and opened the harmonica case, a piece of tightly folded paper fell out. Allie picked it up off his leg.

"I want to read that."

"No, play something."

Leo raised the harp to his lips and sucked out a moaning riff from the middle keys. It was a D harp; D for Donovan, D for downhearted, D for decided already. He didn't want to blow another note.

"I was planning to give it to you on your birthday, but I didn't."

"But this was in the woods."

The music stopped up the hill. It sounded like they were all moving into the kitchen. Helena was laughing at something and Leo could hear his father and Ryder talking through it. He looked at Allie. He could make out just so much of her hair and face and T-shirt. "Please read me the note."

"Sorry."

"Why not."

"It doesn't apply anymore, Leo. No Irish Need Apply."

"What?"

"That's what NINA means, didn't you know that? It's carved in stone above all those factory doors where my father grew up."

"Well I'm not Irish." Leo reached for her hand but she pulled away, stuck both her arms out the window, and ripped the note up into tiny pieces she dropped to the road. She sat back in her seat, breathing harder than before.

Leo let his hand rest on her leg. It felt narrow and soft and she seemed to hold her breath. He started to slide towards her across the seat, and when he kissed her lips she kissed him back. She was crying, and Leo felt afraid.

"Please take me home. I just want to go home."

At the top of Spoon Hill, in front of the porch, he handed her the truck keys. He could see the side of Chick's face in the lamplight behind her, through the screen door. He had his glasses on and was looking straight ahead, wide awake, and Leo was sure he was listening, though there wasn't much to hear; they hadn't said another word on the short drive back, and now, facing each other in the shadowed light coming through the windows of the house, they both looked away at the same time, Allie at the ground, Leo out at the darkness of the river valley below, the black broken only by the lights of Beatrice's and the theater and street lamps.

She hugged him tightly but quickly, then she turned and walked up onto her porch and into the house. She tossed the truck keys onto her father's bed and kept walking. Leo heard her door close and he wanted to run around to the side of the cabin and climb through her open window; he'd grab her by the shoulders and whisper her his whole story which was so much his mother's story and his father's too, and he'd tell Allie's tired and pretty but listening face everything he knew about Katie Faye, about her never having gotten to Paris, about how he, Leo, looked just like her which meant, in a way, that she was still a kind of flesh of this world and he was taking it all to France. Don't you see? And I never meant to hurt your feelings with those flowers, I never did. And he was already stepping into the shadows of the house, seeing the quiet love he and Allie would then make, her palms pulling against his moving back, her breath on his face. Rubber or not, they would start again, and she'd be here when he got back and—

"Good-bye, Leo." Mrs. Donovan leaned out the half-open screen door. She was wearing her African afghan. Her hair was down, and in the overhead glare of the porch bulb the lines in her face looked unnaturally deep. "Take care of yourself."

Leo nodded. He waved. He walked back to the Valiant and drove home.

Ryder's Impala was gone, and even though the kitchen and parlor were still lit up, the house was quiet. Leo knew Ryder wouldn't have left without saying good-bye and so he figured all four of them had gotten hungry and gone down to the UFO Show or the club, he hoped not for long. He got out of the car as fast as if he were going someplace, and he thought about heading down the hill with a flash-light, picking up the scraps of Allie's note, and taping it together back in his room. But no, she probably wrote something fine, some-thing that after her too-fast good-bye just now would hurt to see in words, would leave him feeling even more like the wrong man on the wrong train speeding fast in the wrong direction.

Then he heard the toilet flush and he walked into the house as Jim came down the hall and stepped into the bright light of the kitchen. His mustache whiskers were wet just above the lip. "How'd it go?"

"Ryder gone?"

"He drove the girls to Helena's car. I told him to hurry. He knows how early we're getting up." Jim walked to the table and cleared it of three empty Pabst cans and an ashtray full of cigarette butts rimmed with lipstick. He smiled as he dumped the cans and butts all into the wastebasket under the sink, and Leo felt the skin of his face get hot; he didn't feel like smiling and he didn't think his father should be smiling either. "She's got buck teeth, Dad."

Jim paused in shutting the cabinet door and he looked at Leo, his head turned a little to the side. "Who?"

"That tailor lady, or whatever she is."

"Oh." Jim straightened up and walked past Leo to the hallway. "Have a seat, son. I got something for you."

Whatever it was, he was taking a while coming out with it. And Leo did not like how cheerful Jim seemed. Not tonight. Why tonight? Allie's new harmonica was pressing into Leo's hip bone through his front jeans pocket. He pulled it out and lay it on the table. He could hear Jim open and close a drawer back in his room. Leo looked down at the yellow linoleum of the kitchen floor, then at the sink counter and the stove, at his father's black-bottomed coffeepot sitting clean and dry on the back burner, and he wondered if the same man who recruited him would be picking him up. Then the picture of the smiling, gum-chewing sergeant came into Leo's head and he felt a hot shuddering cave open up in him because in the dark of that cave was Allie's last hug, so tight, and so full of love for him, that he had to stand and walk out to the stoop to breathe better, but the shine of the outside bulb was in his face and so were the bugs, one of them skimming across his cheek before it perched itself in his ear. He crushed it with his finger and stepped into the driveway just as the headlights of Ryder's Impala made a scanning arc through the trees on his way down Saunders Hill Road.

"Come on in, son."

The three of them sat at the table, Leo in the middle facing the window. Ryder had opened them all beers, even though Jim said no thank you, he didn't want one. He was keeping the surprise in his lap till he was ready, and he wasn't smiling but his eyes seemed to hold something warm, and right now it left Leo feeling a little better to see it.

"You and your damn ceremonies, Jimmy."

Jim's eyes didn't change. He pulled out a green hardcover book and slid it across the table in front of Leo. "'Member this one, Ride?"

In fancy gold letters on the cover was printed: *The Concise Dictionary of French*. Ryder reached for it and began to thumb through the pages. He looked tired, his small eyes moist from the beer, but now he sat up and read something on the inside cover.

———

"Show him."

Ryder flipped the book around for Leo to read. In Katie Faye's small handwriting was her full unmarried name in blue ink, but later she'd crossed out Hewson with green ink and written Suther over it. Then she wrote under her name Jim's and Ryder's. And an inch under Ryder's name, in black this time, was Jim's blocky handwriting: LEO J. SUTHER August 1967.

"Here." Jim lay down a folded map. Leo opened it. It was brand new and took up the whole table.

"Our old one didn't make it." Jim leaned closer. "Look at this."

"The Arch of Triumph, Young Buddy."

"We were going to play under that, this one too." Jim pointed to a tiny sketch of the Eiffel Tower on the other side of the river. He was shaking his head, smiling again, though now his eyes had lost something.

Leo cleared his throat. "What do you want me to play when I get there?"

"Every damn thing we taught you."

"Whatever you want, son." Jim stood up and got the bottle of Jim Beam from the top of the fridge. He took three water glasses from the cabinet and poured four capfuls into each. He set them on the table in front of Ryder and Leo and sat down. Ryder raised his glass, but Jim looked away as he pulled a small brown jewelry box from his pants pocket. Ryder put his glass back down, and Leo watched his fingertips rest on the case of Allie's harmonica.

"I know I don't have to tell you not to lose these on your way over."

"Plenty of pickpockets in the barracks, Jimmy. You ought to mail it on over after his training."

Jim shook his head, opened the box, and pushed it over to Leo. Inside, on folded white toilet paper, were two wooden pink star earrings. "I don't know if you'll get time away before you go over or not, but I'd like you to take these with you, son, and leave them there somewhere. In a park or something. But don't bury them. She wouldn't like that. Leave them where a woman might find them and take them home to wear all over town."

Ryder let out a short laugh. "I'm laughing, Young Buddy, 'cause your mama sure loved to tip a canoe. What's that saying, Jim?"

Leo's father shrugged, and his face looked pained, like he wasn't up to hearing Ryder talk.

"You know, 'Something old, something new—'"

"'Something borrowed, something blue,'" Leo said, though he had no idea how he knew those words or where he'd heard them before.

"*Right*, well, day before the wedding, Kate went on down to San Antone to get those earrings. From that Mexican on Texarkana, wasn't it Jimmy?"

Leo's father nodded, and he took one of the stars from the box.

"She wore her Mama's wedding dress—"

"A new pair of ladies' shoes," Jim said.

"And she borrowed some costume pearls from her gramaw. Thing is," Ryder picked up the other earring. "These were *blue* when she bought 'em."

Jim looked at Leo, his eyes warm again. "She went home and painted them pink."

"Why?"

Ryder laughed again. He put the star back in the box and Leo picked it up. It felt as light as the balsam wing of a model glider. Jim gave him the other, and lifted his glass. "To my son."

"And Uncle Sam's generosity." Ryder winked and Leo touched his glass to theirs. "And our band."

"Damn straight."

"To Katie Faye's Band."

They drank, and as soon as Ryder had put down his glass he stood up and pushed his chair back under the table. "Give me a hug, Young Buddy. Lightning good-byes are the only ones for me."

Ryder squeezed Leo pretty hard, then he picked him up off the floor an inch or two. He groaned as he let him back down. He held him off at arm's length and looked him in the face. "Do whatever your CO's tell you, but don't expect 'em to know their balls from their nose." Ryder let go, picked up his can of beer, and paused at the door. "Write me some songs. Adios." He walked off the lighted stoop to his Impala, started it up, and backed away without looking at the house.

———

"He's off to see Helena." Jim stuck the map in the French book. He placed the small jewelry box on top of it, then he left the table and filled his coffeepot at the sink. To Leo the kitchen felt no bigger than a harp box. He sipped his Pabst and heard Ryder's tires spin out once on the gravel as they turned onto Paper Boulevard. He knew Jim was right, Ryder would be screwing Helena later tonight. He felt Allie again.

"Dad?"

"Yeah, son." Jim was digging his spoon into the coffee can, not looking over at Leo. His blue shirt needed tucking in and his shoulders hung somehow more relaxed, his face so calm, so at peace. He blinked and yawned, then he looked at Leo, smiling, waiting.

"Nothing. Thanks for everything. I guess I'll go to bed."

Jim wiped his hands on the front of his pants. Leo turned to go but his father took a step, put his arm around Leo's back, and pulled him shoulder first to him. He squeezed once, held it, and let go. Leo smiled and glanced at him and walked down the hall to his room.

He stripped to his skivvies, shut off the bedside lamp, and lay down on top of the sheet. He heard Jim take care of the kitchen and parlor lights, then make his way down the hall. Jim stopped in the doorway but all Leo could see was the orange-tipped glow of his cigarette. "Will you want breakfast?"

"Coffee and toast, I guess."

The cigarette tip rose in an arc, then burned brighter. Jim blew out the smoke slow and long, as if he were very tired, the way he got after working a double shift, empty, but that's all right because everything's done and done right. Jim stood there in the dark another ten or fifteen seconds, not smoking, just standing, and Leo wanted to say something, though he didn't know what. Then his father said from the hallway, "I'll wake you at 0400." He closed his own door and Leo heard the faint engine rumble of a far-off plane. He'd also heard the pride in his father's voice, just now, when he'd used military time on him.

Leo pulled the sheet out and got under it. The air was warm and smelled like jack pine. On the far wall the shadow of a branch hung still against a triangle of moonlight, and Leo reminded himself to put his harp harness in the clothes bag his father had packed, that and the book and map, the earrings, though he knew he wouldn't forget. Down the hill the river was so quiet Leo knew it was back to being summer-low and lazy. He didn't feel scared now; he felt calm, and sadder than he could imagine. Tomorrow, as soon as he got a chance, he would write a long letter to Allie and explain everything. He might even call her on the phone. Then she would write him, and they would keep writing, no matter what, and by the time he got back they would know each other ten times better than they did now.

In five hours, before light could reach the ridge of Spoon Hill, he would be sitting in the front seat of an army car with some soldier, a sergeant probably, heading down street-lit Paper Boulevard for Springfield and a plane or bus to New Jersey, to Fort Dix, a place that sounded like its name was chopped off before it could finish itself. And he thought of his mother and father. He reached up behind him and felt for their photograph. He found the thumbtacks, pulled them from the walls, then set them and the picture on the bedstand. He wished he'd had a picture of him and Allie to pack too. He remembered how she said this was the summer of free love, but Leo didn't believe love was free. As far as he could tell, love cost people more than anything. But without it, no one would be here at all.

He took a long deep breath and let it out. There was a slight ringing in his ears, low and constant, and he realized it had been there all night. It was from the show, from those amplifiers so close to their mikes, his and Ryder's harmonicas cutting through the air like sound knives through butter, Jim singing like a king.

Leo was sweating and he pushed the sheet down to just above his penis. He caught the sour smell of the mill from outside, and he knew there was an electric fan in the hall closet but he didn't want to go get it because then he wouldn't be able to hear anything but that, and he wanted to keep this ringing in his ears, the quiet of the woods out his window. Soon the morning birds would start up

———

327

down at the river and he wanted to hear them too, hear them sing and whistle and fly from tree to tree. And he hoped they would wake him in time to swing his legs over the bedside in the near-dark, to be sitting straight and ready as Jim's alarm went off, and his bedsprings squeaked, and Leo heard his father, coming for him.